Dark

of the

Sun

By Chelsea Quinn Yarbro from Tom Doherty Associates

Ariosto
Better in the Dark
Blood Games
Blood Roses
A Candle for D'Artagnan
Come Twilight
Communion Blood
Crusader's Torch
Dark of the Sun
Darker Jewels
A Feast in Exile
A Flame in Byzantium
Hotel Transylvania
Mansions of Darkness
Out of the House of Life
The Palace
Path of the Eclipse
States of Grace
Writ in Blood

DARK
OF THE
SUN

A NOVEL OF SAINT-GERMAIN

Chelsea Quinn Yarbro

TOR®

A TOM DOHERTY ASSOCIATES BOOK
NEW YORK

This is a work of fiction. All the characters and events portrayed in this novel
are either fictitious or are used fictitiously.

DARK OF THE SUN: A NOVEL OF SAINT-GERMAIN

A Tor Book
Published by Tom Doherty Associates, LLC
175 Fifth Avenue
New York, NY 10010

www.tor.com

Tor® is a registered trademark of Tom Doherty Associates, LLC.

Library of Congress Cataloging-in-Publication Data

Yarbro, Chelsea Quinn.
    Dark of the sun : a novel of Saint-Germain / Chelsea Quinn Yarbro.
        p. cm.
    "A Tom Doherty Associates book."
    ISBN 0-765-31103-8
    EAN 978-0-765-31103-0
    1. Saint-Germain, comte de, d. 1784—Fiction. 2. Transylvania
(Romania)—Fiction. 3. Krakatoa (Indonesia)—Fiction. 4. Volcanic eruptions—Fiction. 5. Vampires—Fiction. I. Title.

PS3575.A7D37 2004
813'.54—dc22   2004049573

First Hardcover Edition: November 2004
First Trade Paperback Edition: September 2005

Printed in the United States of America

0 9 8 7 6 5 4 3 2 1

For

Lindig Harris

in spite of the temperatures

Author's Introduction

More than twenty-five years ago while researching the fourth Saint-Germain book, *Path of the Eclipse,* I ran across references to the Year of Yellow Snow, sometimes called the Year of the Dark Sun, in Western reckoning A.D. 535–36, which was characterized by catastrophic drops in temperature, crop failures, and famine throughout Asia and Europe, with disruption of trade and movements of populations resulting from these losses—just the sort of event to set the speculative juices flowing, but not the object of my research, nor the period with which I was dealing, promising though it appeared. Then, about ten years ago, other researchers did some serious scholarship on those disastrous events and tried to determine the cause of what turned out to be a worldwide famine and, after considering a number of different scenarios from meteor collisions to a mini-ice-age—which indeed occurred—at last identified the probable source of the trouble as an eruption of that all-time bad-boy volcano, Krakatoa; this eruption was more overwhelming than many of its others, for, according to records in Indonesia, this eruption broke Sumatra off from Java—Krakatoa is at the hinge position of those two islands—and opened the Sunda Strait to a deep-water sea passage instead of its remaining the complex of reefs and shoals that had allowed passage of only the shallowest-draft boats, which it had been for centuries. The eruption occurred in late February or early March of A.D. 535, and its explosion was heard all the way to Beijing. It had been heralded by many months of regional instability, earthquakes, and drastic variations in ocean temperatures in and around what was becoming the Sundra Strait, making the shipping lanes more treacherous than they had been in the past. Many ships' captains reported dangerous sailing in and around Indonesia, and over time, merchant ships avoided the region.

In April, following the eruption, the ash from the volcano had spread all around the world, and disaster followed after it, impacting global weather patterns and lowering the average temperatures sufficiently to keep crops from growing in most of Asia and Europe, as well as large portions of Africa and the Americas. Although every part of the world was affected, there were regions that bore more of the brunt of the tragedy than others. Many of the nomadic people of the Central Asian Steppes were driven out of their traditional grazing lands when their herds began to die because of lack of food as the grasslands became arid plains, and their struggle to find new pastureland was made much more difficult by the impact of the colder weather; the significant westward migration from Central Asia began as an attempt to find grass for their herds. In China and Tibet, the snow that continued to fall all the way into June and July was yellow due to the high levels of sulfur in the upper atmosphere. Closer to the eruption site, actual flakes of sulfur fell from the sky, burning people, animals, and fields alike and contaminating wells, springs, and rivers; the devastation of the Indonesian Islands was calamitous, with tens of thousands of people killed in tsunamis spawned by the eruption, by gaseous emanations, and by sulfur contamination, records of which still exist in the royal archives of the Srivijava Empire, which comprised most of modern Indonesia. For months afterward, the remains of humans, animals, trees, sea-life, and buildings washed up on the shores of what are now Indonesia, the Malay Peninsula, the Philippines, China, and India.

To add to the difficulties besetting China, this disaster occurred during the difficult period known as the Six Dynasties, when China was a cobbled-together collection of principalities, each with its own emperor and administration: the Northern (A.D. 386–581) and Southern (A.D. 420–581) Dynasties as well as the Eastern (A.D. 534–50) and Western (A.D. 535–56) Wei Dynasties. During the two years following the eruption, the level of relief required could not be adequately addressed by this loose and hostile federation of regional governments.

Whenever possible I have used the names of places as they were known at or about the period of this novel—Sunda Kalapa for modern Jakarta, Tumasik for modern Singapore, Thang Long for modern Hanoi, Kuang-Chou for modern Canton, Chang'an for modern Xian, the Southern Islands for the Phillippines, and so on, although the precise locations of these locales have shifted somewhat over the intervening centuries; other cities have vanished completely or relocated a significant distance from their sixth-century sites, such as Marakanda (Samarkand), Yang-Chau (Shanghai), and Sarai, which has changed location at least five times in the last two thousand years; those I have kept contemporary to this story as much as research can make possible. When there has been inadequate information, I have placed the missing towns and cities where it seems most likely they were and have used the most recognizable names for them. A few of the minor locations are fictional, but typical of the regions and era. The names of seas and oceans I have used in their modern forms, to make the descriptions accessible to those wishing to follow the mariners on maps, and the caravans along the branches of the Silk Road.

One of the most difficult aspects of researching the Silk Road at that period is that most of the various clans, tribes, and peoples were illiterate, and so records of their societies and behaviors come not from internal sources, but from observers such as Chinese, Persian, Byzantine, and European travelers, whose accounts are heavily flavored by their opinions and agenda. The occasional Christian churches in Asia kept written records of their districts out of religious duty; their accounts are often the only reliable information on the workings of trading centers that still remain; one of the reasons for Christianity's remarkable success in the region was its high rate of literacy among its clergy, and the emphasis on record-keeping. There would most likely have been more records before the rise of Jenghiz Khan, who had an almost superstitious dread of the written word and systematically destroyed all books and other records he encountered during his conquest of Asia. Thanks to such policies, and the exigencies of the passage of time, what remains is fragmentary and often inconclusive, requiring a kind of informational triangulation to create a sense of the various groups that lived along the various trade routes from Europe to Asia, especially in these very disruptive years.

For Europe, north of Naples, there was frost every month of the year 535, and the pattern continued into 536, the first break in the cold taking place around August of 536. There are reports from Greece to Norway referring to the sun having lost its power or been darkened by an invisible eclipse; in the New World, the temperatures shifted enough to force certain tribal groups to begin to wander, searching for a place where they could get enough food to survive. In part because of this period of cold weather, the military aggression of the Byzantines was put on hold for almost a year due to the dramatic changes in climate, which the Byzantines in particular called the Year of the Dark Sun, due to the failure of crops to thrive and the generally lowered temperatures; nautical trading in the Mediterranean was cut in half due to inclement weather and a lack of surplus goods and foodstuffs to sell. Shipping stalled and overland caravans had to be abandoned due to lack of food for the horses, ponies, asses, camels, and donkeys. In many areas where agriculture had been marginal, it had to be abandoned altogether because of the failure of what had been chancy crops at best, and subsequent famine. The results were far-reaching and endured for many years, even after the climate began to recover, and the sun once again penetrated the dust layer in the upper atmosphere.

General shortages of essential food and matériel brought about social unrest and collapse, as well as a declining birthrate and an increase in epidemic disease. From the western Pacific to the eastern Atlantic, outbreaks of many kinds of illness spread, in large part a result of the malnutrition that was pervasive everywhere, the effects of which were felt for many years after these events by those who survived them. The rate of miscarriages and stillbirths rose sharply, as did death among the very young, the aged—and by aged, it means anyone over thirty-five—and infirm. The resulting malaise affected every aspect of life and led in many cases to extremes of social behavior and religious exercises that attempted to deal with the calamity.

This crucial loss of food was far from the only impact the Year of Yellow Snow or the Dark Sun had on regional policies in the world. To a greater or lesser degree, every portion of the world was impacted by the prolonged eruption; no place was immune to the influence of this catastrophe. As far away as South America the weather was marked by unusual cold, as well as a sharp increase in storms; it was observed by the Maya in Central America that the sun had lost its power, shining without warmth, a development that left a lasting impression on the emerging city-state of Copán, among others, compelling a great deal of increased military adventurism in order to augment their failing food supply. From Chile to Canada, the peoples of the Americas were struck by this worldwide calamity almost as drastically as the peoples of Asia and Europe were.

Widespread refugeeism became increasingly prevalent, and it was not long before the various marginal clans and similar groups took to traveling in the hope of finding a haven, or at least enough to eat. Soon the population disruption became so vast that whole regions of Asia were changed from that time onward because of the migrations of whole tribes. The desperation among the peoples of the world expressed itself in many ways, from religious austerity to wholesale carnality, from willing slavery to reckless adventurism, from rigorous adherence to tradition to dramatic revolution, from passive withdrawal from the world to the most heinous aggression. Attempts to explain the reason for the loss of the strength on the part of the sun, as well as the dramatic shifts in weather patterns, varied from place to place; few of them made any association between the volcanic eruption—even if they were aware it had happened—and the resultant environmental chaos, although the royal archives of Indonesia proposed the connection for obvious reasons, since Indonesia was ground zero for the event, and the self-destruction of a large mountain accompanied by tsunamis was hard to miss.

By A.D. 500 Christianity had spread to India and China, but Islam had not yet arrived in the world; most of the Middle East was Zoroastrian or worshiped a large variety of local gods, usually connected to the weather. Judaism was not as splintered as it had been at the height of the Roman Empire, but it was not so cohesive as to be able to unite in the face of so comprehensive a disaster as this period provided. There were still pockets of classical Greek and Roman deities, and some traces of Mithraism, usually among the Greco-Byzantine military. The utter failure of most religions to address this dreadful environmental collapse did much to hasten the rise of Christianity, which attributed power and worth to suffering, as well as to create the social climate that made Islam possible.

Of the many aspects of daily life impacted by this catastrophe, trade probably suffered the hardest immediate blow and was the one that took the most time to recover from. Trading meant covering significant distances, and in this hard period, it required that all the necessities of life be carried by the travelers, for opportunities to resupply were either far between or nonexistent. Because of the scarcity of food and matériel, not only were foreigners—and most merchants were foreigners—regarded with dread, but the economies of almost every region engaging in trade collapsed, leaving traders stranded in hostile societies. Required by law to have names that could be written in Chinese but were obviously not Chinese, foreigner traders in China were easy targets for punitive taxes, customs tariffs, and other legally justified seizures of goods and monies that became increasingly prevalent as the crisis deepened and spread. Travel, which had been risky but fairly routine, became much rarer and therefore more dangerous. This change in safety and commensurate increases in costs and risks exposed the merchants to more hardships than those within any settled group faced, and it left an impact on trading that lasted for almost a century, resulting in policies that were designed to make trading a treacherous enterprise for the next seven centuries.

As always, there are many people to thank for their help in researching this novel: James Atterling, who provided his thesis on Romanesque European agricultural history; Roland Bai for his information on the history of foreign trade in China, with emphasis on its general collapse in the first third of the sixth century; Rhea Crovander for access to her books on early Christianity in Asia; Dorthy Daur for access to her thesis on the trade routes of Europe, Russia, and Siberia, 1–1000 C.E.; Patrick K. Doughle for his many insights into the worldwide impact of the eruption, particularly on the Americas; Michel V. Felipov for providing information on Jou'an-Jou'an (Avar), Hun, Turk, and Mongol names and naming customs; S. W. "Daisy" Gerunstein for the loan of her atlases of historical maps; Julian Hasp for his information on east-west caravan routes and trading centers of the Byzantine period; Wilma Jacobssen for showing me her collection of historical bits, horseshoes, and other equestrian equipment as well as her information on historical saddlery and the evolution of the stirrup; Marynelle Losely for providing variant place names used along the Silk Road in the sixth century; Jonas McChesney for his references on European climatology from A.D. 400–800; Ng Xiaoli (Lealand) for providing so much material on names and nomenclature in sixth-century China, particularly as pertained to resident foreigners; Edgar Pomeroy for discussing his theories about the Dark Ages in Eastern Europe, particularly the rise and fall of the Khazar Empire; Morgan Reyes for his information on sixth-century climatological shifts; Elihu Sayles for showing me the results of his research on the history of seaports in China; Alicia Slavin for her material on volcanoes and the environment; J.A.T. for allowing me to see his analysis of soil chemistry from sixth-century samples; Benjamin D. Vollsung for his information on Eastern Europe during this period; Conrad Wentz for his research on the east-west slave trade; and Hilary

Yout for her thesis material on the agricultural collapse in Central America in the sixth century. Any errors in accuracy or historicity are mine and made for exigencies of story, not as a result of the expertise of any of these very helpful people.

At the other end of the process there is another group deserving thanks: my agent, the redoubtable Irene Kraas; my attorney, Robin Dubner, who watches over Saint-Germain's legal interests; that Internet wizard Wiley Saichek, who gets the news out; Maureen, Alice, Stephanie, Sharon, Randy, Elizabeth, Charlie, and Peggy, just because; my readers for clarity, Eli Dunn, Paige Mitchell, and Leighanne Skuce; my readers for continuity, Libba Campbell, Gaye Raymond, and Michael Spinali; Melissa Singer, my editor at Tor; and Tom Doherty, who mans the Toric helm. Thanks are also due to the booksellers and book buyers who have faithfully kept Saint-Germain . . . um . . . alive all these years.

CHELSEA QUINN YARBRO
Berkeley, California
October 2003

SOUTHEAST ASIA
AND INDONESIA
AD 534

Kuang-Chou

Mekong River

Vijaya

South China Sea

MALAYA

Sulu Sea

Tumasik

Celebes Sea

SUMATRA

BORNEO

Makassar Strait

CELEBES

Indian Ocean

Sunda Passage

Sunda Kalapa

Krakatau

JAVA

Chelsea Quinn Yarbro '04

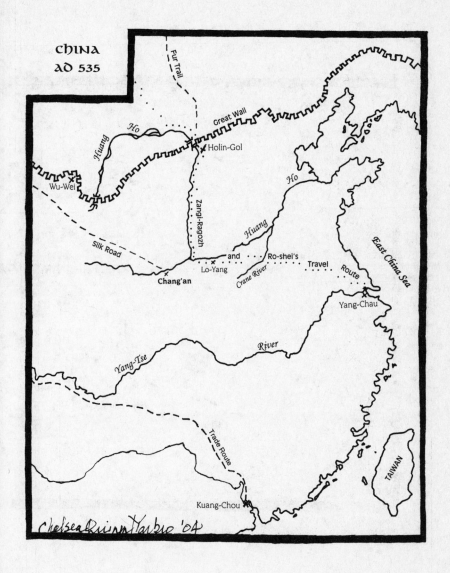

CHINA
AD 535

Fur Trail

Great Wall

Huang
Ho

Holin-Gol

Wu-Wei

Ho

Huang

Zangi-Ragozh

Silk Road

and
Lo-Yang
Ro-shei's
Chang'an
Crane River
Travel
Route

East China Sea

Yang-Chau

River

Yang-Tse

Trade Route

TAIWAN

Kuang-Chou

Chelsea Quinn Yarbro '04

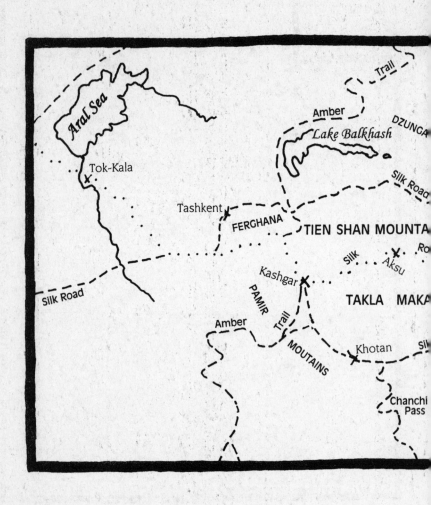

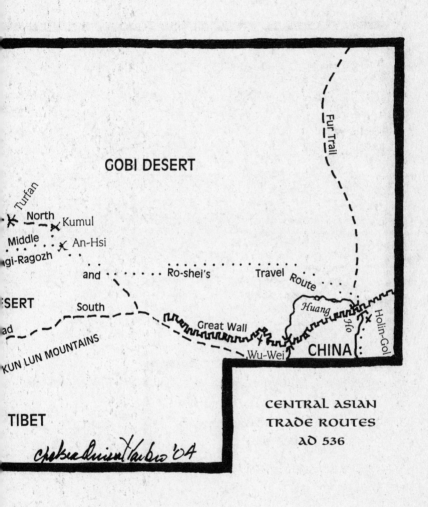

GOBI DESERT

Fur Trail

Turfan

North Kumul

Middle An-Hsi

gi-Ragozh

and Ro-shei's Travel Route

Huang

SERT South

ad

Ho

KUN LUN MOUNTAINS

Great Wall Holin-Gol

Wu-Wei CHINA

TIBET

CENTRAL ASIAN
TRADE ROUTES
AD 536

CARPATHIAN MOUNTAINS
TO THE ARAL SEA
AD 538

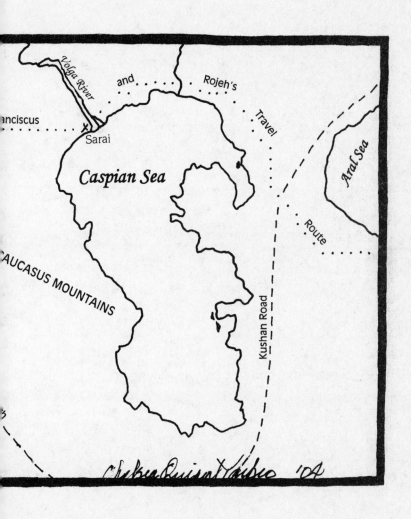

Volga River

anciscus

and • • • • • Rojeh's

Travel

Sarai

Caspian Sea

Aral Sea

CAUCASUS MOUNTAINS

Route

Kushan Road

Chelsea Quinn Yarbro '04

PART I

ZANGI-RAGOZH

*T*ext of a report from Captain Tieh Wei-Djieh of the merchant ship *Golden Moon*, sent from the southern port city of Kuang-Chou to his employer, the foreigner Zangi-Ragozh, at Yang-Chau on the Yellow Sea; sent two weeks before the Winter Solstice.

To the most honorable foreign trader Zangi-Ragozh, this report from Tieh Wei-Djieh, Captain of the trading ship Golden Moon, *now lying at the docks of Kuang-Chou in the south of the Illustrious Kingdom at the Center of the World, at the approach of the dark of the year after a long time at sea.*

First it is my duty to tell you that we have lost but one sailor since we left Yang-Chau fifteen months ago, and that death was to accident, not to fever or the ravages of any disease. For this we have burned incense to the Three Immortals and have given wine and money to Ho-Tai in thanks for his generous protection. May it continue throughout our voyage.

Next, I am pleased to inform you that the cargo from the ports on the Indian Ocean has arrived here safely, but not without hazard. Spices and dyes are all carefully stored and only one barrel has taken any damage from our passage. In Burma we did not make the trade in brasses we had anticipated, but we took on a small load of teak and rosewood. The merchants of Tumasik are eager for goods from India, for the recent storms have taken more than one merchant-ship to the Lord of the Ocean and kept many Captains from leaving port altogether, which has slowed many sales.

Although you had put Sunda Kalapa on our ports of call, I had heard of trouble in the waters near that city, for the great mountain that is the heart of the Sunda Passage has been spitting out rocks. Some have said that the sea has boiled around it. I have been warned by more than one mariner that the entire region is perturbed and no longer safe to enter, and I have decided that these rumors must have some basis in fact, for the stories are similar enough to make me believe that more than fancy is working here. Whatever the case, it did not seem worth the risk to me to venture into such uncertain waters, and that we would preserve our fortunes more readily if we made for Thang Long directly, which we did. Pirate activity made it advisable to come to Kuang-Chou instead, which we have done. Even though we have avoided the great volcano, we have encountered rough seas and severe storm conditions in and around the islands of Sumatra and Java, and have been told by many other seamen that there has been much trouble from small eruptions from the tremendous volcano that stands in the midst of the shallow channels and sandbars that mark the joining of the two islands. The Sunda Passage cannot be considered safe water for now, and perhaps will never be so again.

You cannot imagine what fear has possessed the sailors since we saw the sea roiling as if moved by gigantic serpents. The sailors shared my dread. A few have vowed not to go to this region again and have declared they will tell others they meet not to risk the treacherous waters of these southern islands. It is most appalling to see the waves thrown up to the height of substantial hills, and to know that the course of the winds can no longer be sure.

Also, it is said that there is an odor in the air in the vicinity of the mountain, that is the rotten smell of the burning yellow powder that men gather in the inner slopes of volcanoes when they are not spewing forth rocks and fire. Sailors say it is the bodies of all the dead who have died in the seas of the world, which the God of the Underworld has guarded, and who are now left to decay in the caves at the base of the mountain. No man of my crew will agree to go where that scent is on the air, for fear of taking contagion from it, nor would I ask it of them. You will not find anyone worthy of the trade of sailing who will agree to such an undertaking, not now. I most humbly apologize for failing to do your bidding in this, but for the sake of this ship, which you have entrusted to me, I cannot continue as I have done in the past.

I am handing this packet of accounts and my report to Shang Ko-Lim, who will carry it with him to Yang-Chau and will see it placed in your hands. His ship, a lighter and faster craft than the Golden Moon, *is leaving in the morning with the tide, carrying messages and small items such as jewels and spices to the north. This should mean that you will have this in your hands in three weeks, if there are no* storms strong enough to force him to seek a safe harbor until the sea is passable.

I have made a full copy for myself, and I will keep it aboard this ship, in case there should be any inquiry made regarding our voyage, our cargo, or our business, as you have instructed me from the first. Li Fan-Fan, my scribe, vouches for all I have told him to write and adds his assurances that there is no deliberate error in any of the material I am sending to you, nor any in the records I am keeping aboard this ship. I have receipts for taxes and duties paid, copies of which are part of this communication; the originals will be provided to you upon our arrival in home port, with copies made for your senior clerk, Hu Bi-Da.

We will remain here in port through the dark of the year and, with the first return of sunlight, set out to the north and the Yellow Sea. In the certainty that you will find all the accounts satisfactory, and the protection of your ship given highest priority, I commend myself to you and ask that you regard me as your most respectful ship's Captain,

> Tieh Wei-Djieh
> (his chop)

1

Rising out of the East China Sea beyond the mouth of the Yang-Tse River, the sun was brass over a world of bronze. Though it was midwinter, the port of Yang-Chau was bristling with all manner of ships, and the cold wind off the distant mountains served to drive the larger craft into groups, as if they were seeking warmth. Clustered around them were masses of small boats offering every conceivable service to the crews of the seagoing vessels; the noise of shouts, calls, and the groaning of battened sails shuddered on the air. Along the wharves men scurried and struggled, some off-loading cargo, others preparing to take to sea, and all with the underlying urgency that came with the shortened days, as if everyone was determined to make the most of the sunlight.

"How soon until rain comes?" Ro-shei asked his master in the language of Imperial Rome.

"Another day or so," said Zangi-Ragozh, the broad sleeve of his thick black-silk sen-hsien almost touching his sheet of paper on which he had just entered a column of figures drawn in Arabic numerals. "The *Black Pheasant* and the *Morning Star* are due back in port shortly. I hope the weather holds long enough for them to return." He sounded doubtful as he spoke, but not worried, either.

"The *Morning Star* hasn't been away very long," said Ro-shei as he removed the paper from danger, taking care to move it very gently until the ink was dry.

"You weren't here when she left, were you? Her task is a specific one. She has gone over to the northernmost port on the east coast of Korea to pick up furs from the peoples of the forests."

"But the Koreans charge high tariffs for their export," said Ro-shei.

"And they charge the men from the forests who bring the furs to store and market them," said Zangi-Ragozh. "All in all, a fine business for Korea." He smoothed the next sheet of paper and sketched his eclipse sigil on the upper right-hand corner with his brush, indicating this was a personal document, not an official record.

"So furs will be here in good time, and eventually dyes and spices. How many other ships are still unaccounted for?" Ro-shei inspected the pigeonholes over Zangi-Ragozh's writing table. "I make it seven."

"Yes." Zangi-Ragozh tapped the paper in front of him.

"I thought you had determined to purchase a tenth."

"That was before you left on the voyage to Saylan. I had hopes that there could be an arrangement made that would—" He stopped.

"And doubtless worth the two years I had to be away," said Ro-shei. "Still, it is good to be back in Yang-Chau."

"Yes; and I am relieved that you have returned. I thank you, old friend, for all you accomplished," said Zangi-Ragozh with quiet conviction.

"It was prudent to make such arrangements, and it was more sensible for me to do it than for you," said Ro-shei, dismissing the praise. "I hadn't realized you had decided against adding a tenth ship to your fleet."

"Hu—my clerk; you know him—warned me that my taxes would have doubled on all the rest if I purchased a tenth; you know that foreigners in Yang-Chau aren't encouraged to have large merchant fleets," said Zangi-Ragozh. "Hu was right: doubling taxes would delay actual profits for decades." He pressed his lips together a moment, then added, "I doubt we will be here a decade from now."

Ro-shei did not question this decision, but wanted to know, "Have you decided where we will go next? Saylan may be a good choice now you have a business established there."

This time Zangi-Ragozh hesitated a bit longer before he spoke. "No, I do not know, not yet. I will make up my mind shortly."

"So you still think we should leave," said Ro-shei.

"I think it would be wise. I've been here almost eight years, and I've been trading in the region for nearly thirty years. It's time to depart, or I may overstay my welcome." He began to make more notes to himself, summing up his plans for the year to come, as he had done every year since his arrival in Yang-Chau. "The *Golden Moon* should be back in port here by April—the Fortnight of the Flower Rains, perhaps— and the *Bounteous Fortune* has only been gone six months. According to the reports, the *Bird of the Waves* and the *Dragon's Breath* are only halfway through their voyages, so we will not see them for another ten months at least, and the *Black Pheasant* is laid up for repairs in the Indian islands; they are almost finished, according to the message brought to me last week, and the ship will come directly here. The *Phoenix* is somewhere in the Bay of Bengal, the *Joyous Winds* should be in the Southern Islands by now, and the *Shining Pearl* is on her way to Vijaya. The *Dragon's Breath* is due for a refitting when she returns. And every ship will need a full inspection."

"Small wonder, when you consider all they go through," said Ro-shei. "Besides, it doesn't pay to skimp on maintenance."

Zangi-Ragozh frowned as he stared at his schedule. "Do you know if Chiu Tso-Feng will be available to repair sails for us? If the storms have been as bad as we've heard, there will be much to mend and replace."

"I'll send word around to his warehouse, to find out," Ro-shei offered. "And I'll put a deposit on his labor for this company. He will have a great deal of work to do."

"And I would prefer not to be at the end of his list. I'll give you money for the deposit—it may need to be substantial." He looked down at his notes to himself; he had written them in Chinese characters so that no official suspicions would be raised about him. "I'll prepare a work order for him, as well, so that we needn't spend days squabbling."

"A good notion," said Ro-shei. "I'd prefer to spend my time at the house rather than this office."

"Yes. This place is too exposed," said Zangi-Ragozh. He shook his head. "Here, at least, the clerks know they can order every aspect of the business dealings. At the house, the servants fear there may be something too foreign about me, and that frightens them." He chose another sheet of paper and began to write out his instructions to the sailmaker, pausing thoughtfully over the amount of money he was prepared to advance to Chiu.

"But you've entertained almost all the important officials here in Yang-Chau. You have guests coming tonight, and they must not fear you if they accept your invitation, no matter how much trepidation they may harbor toward other foreigners."

"Personally of me, perhaps," Zangi-Ragozh allowed, "but the policy toward foreigners remains the same, and a pleasant social association will not change it. As much as Councillor Ko and Professor Tsa may like my company, it is not the kind of contact that will stand much testing, particularly with the current dynastic conflicts, for knowing strangers can appear sinister to those whose hold on the throne is shaky. As far as is prudent, the local officials have come to like me as well as tolerate me, but the liking is superficial: no friendship will supersede patriotic duty, not when the friendship is with a foreigner with whom there is no larger obligation than good manners." His face took on an ancient exhaustion that vanished almost as quickly as it appeared.

"I've spoken to Meng about dinner," Ro-shei said, aware that it would be unwise to pursue their discussion. "He assures me the kitchen will have everything ready on time. Nine courses, and rice wine throughout. By anyone's measure, a handsome offering."

"Thanks to Meng." Zangi-Ragozh smiled, and the reserve that had claimed him eased a little. "Splendid. That man is a treasure—a prince among cooks. I wish I still ate when I smell the dishes he has concocted."

"Even his treatment of raw meat is wonderful. On my return, he prepared a marinated loin of beef that was astonishing," said Ro-shei.

"So you said at the time." Zangi-Ragozh finished making notes to himself and remarked as he held up the paper to help the ink dry, "You know, I like this better than parchment and vellum. Or papyrus."

"It doesn't endure as well," Ro-shei said, reaching up to pinch out the oil-lamps that hung over the writing table. Now that the sun was a bit higher in the sky, the office had sufficient illumination to make the oil lamps unnecessary.

"No, perhaps not. But with reasonable care, it could hold up for some years, I would think." He laughed. "A few centuries, at least, provided it is kept dry. The surface does not crack. And the ink stays with it, soaked in."

"It does the same on silk and cotton," said Ro-shei, not to argue, but to point out the comparisons.

"Yes. I still prefer this," said Zangi-Ragozh. He reached out for the red inkpad and his chop to fix it on the sheets of paper he had used. "This will keep Magistrate Lin satisfied when he makes his semiannual review of my businesses."

"Do you think he will be inclined to adjust your taxes yet? You met the residency requirements three years ago. He has the option of adjusting the percentages you pay, doesn't he?" Ro-shei glanced at the stack of receipts that lay under a paperweight in the figure of a naked dancing dwarf. The little statue was Roman, and Zangi-Ragozh had had it for almost five hundred years, a gift from Titus Petronius Niger after he had fallen from Imperial favor.

"Ah, but since that would mean lowering what I pay, I doubt he will exercise that alternative scale of taxation." He printed his chop on the three sheets of paper that would be part of his official record of transactions, then added a dollop of sealing wax and stamped his sigil into it as well. "There." Zangi-Ragozh handed a small string of cash to Ro-shei; the coins clinked softly as Ro-shei slipped the string onto his wrist. "For Sailmaker Chiu. And here is my work order."

"Very good. I take it you're going back to the house now?" Ro-shei was already busy tidying the office, imposing a strict order on the room.

"Yes. With guests coming at midafternoon there are a few preparations I still need to attend to." Zangi-Ragozh started toward the door. "You'll make sure the dancing girls and musicians are prompt."

"Of course. I've arranged for Yei-Lan to remain for the night; with Dei-Na leaving, you need not deny yourself," Ro-shei said. "You'll like her. She's a very capable young woman—not jealous or too greedy." He rolled the work order and secured it with a narrow silk ribbon, then tucked it into his capacious sleeve. "Will you change clothes for the dinner?"

"I may," said Zangi-Ragozh. "It depends on how much I have yet to do."

"Are you still planning to present your guests with gems?" Ro-shei asked.

"I know you do not approve. Can you tell me why?"

"Well, such generosity can create more envy than you think it will," Ro-shei said cautiously. "You know how venal some of your guests are."

"This isn't Rome, and these men aren't Senators, and the Emperor is not a young, capricious degenerate, as was the case when we were last there. The Wen Emperor in the west may be new to the throne, and as much Turkish as Chinese, as are many men of rank in the north, but he has capable men around him, which counts for something," said Zangi-Ragozh with a touch of impatience. "In the two years you were gone, I have done much to improve my dealings with my fellow-merchants and the authorities, and I hope that will hold me in good stead now." He smiled briefly. "I will not rely on them, but I will not despair, either."

Ro-shei did not quite smile. "You said yourself that they are not staunch in their support."

"No, but they are not malicious, either. That would take too much time, and they have better uses of it." Zangi-Ragozh opened the door and stepped into his outer office where two junior clerks were busy calculating on abacuses. "What news?" he asked the nearest clerk.

"Four bales of rough silk arrived in the warehouse," came the answer. "Hu is there now, inventorying them."

"Has it been paid for yet?" Zangi-Ragozh took a step toward the long writing table.

"Yes; three months ago. Shipment was delayed because of hard rains," said the clerk. "It is scheduled to be shipped out for the Southern Islands."

"That won't be for several months," said Zangi-Ragozh.

"No, it won't," said the clerk as if expecting a rebuke.

"Then make sure it is properly stored in the warehouse. I would rather not lose the cloth to rats or rot or moths." He nodded toward the little oil-powered stove. "Have you enough tea?"

"Yes, thank you," said both clerks almost in unison.

"Very good." Zangi-Ragozh made a sign of approval as he crossed the rest of the outer office to the door that led down a flight of stairs to the street. He squinted at the sun's glare as he stepped into the light and was glad once again of his native earth lining the soles of his leather boots. Still, he kept to the shadows as much as possible as he made his way to where he could hire a sedan-chair to carry him to his house.

The bearers accepted the coins he offered and went off at a jog as soon as he had climbed into the covered chair. They made their way through the traffic of the waterfront and the markets to the broad roads that led to the city gates, over the great bridge spanning the river, turning along the north bank of the Yang-Tse toward the part of the city where prosperous merchants had their extensive homes.

Zangi-Ragozh's house was in an extensive park, set back from the road and surrounded by a high wall. At the gate he got out and tipped the bearers before entering the grounds of his compound, then paused to ask the gatekeeper if anyone had called.

"Yes. The foreign merchant Lampong-Chelai is waiting for you. He arrived a short while ago."

"Thank you, Sung," said Zangi-Ragozh. "I'll just go talk to him now."

"Do you expect anyone else?" Sung called after him.

"I had not expected Lampong-Chelai," said Zangi-Ragozh. "But no, I expect no one else until my guests arrive for dinner. Oh, Ro-shei will be back shortly, with musicians and dancers."

"I will see they are admitted," said Sung.

Zangi-Ragozh nodded and walked up the long, curving path that led to his house; around him, the gardens were murmuring in the cold wind, many of the trees with bare branches, and only a few, hardy shrubs showing much color. As he reached the front of his house, Zangi-Ragozh paused to survey the building, then trod up the broad, shallow steps to the door, where his steward, Jho Chieh-Jen, admitted him promptly.

"You have a visitor," he announced.

"So Sung informed me," said Zangi-Ragozh. "I suppose you have seen to his comfort?"

"He is in the main salon; I have sent in oil cakes and bitter mountain tea." Jho ducked his head respectfully. "If you would care to see him now?"

"I'll go," said Zangi-Ragozh, waving away Jho's offer of escort. He noticed that the Roman painted-plaster panel was askew on the wall again and reminded himself to reweight the frame so it would hang evenly. As he opened the door to his salon, he straightened the red-edged cuffs of his black-silk sen-hsien. "Good day to you, Foreigner Lampong-Chelai. I trust fortune smiles upon you."

"Good day to you, Foreigner Zangi-Ragozh," said his guest, rising from a rosewood chair near the window. He was a middle-aged man, round-faced and plump, also in a sen-hsien, as law required, but one of persimmon-colored silk decorated with embroidery in the style of Vijaya, his home: Lampong-Chelai was the Chinese version of his name, just as Zangi-Ragozh was of his.

"I am delighted to see you," Zangi-Ragozh went on, following the dictates of good manners, "and I wonder what I am to have the honor of doing for you?"

"I was hoping I might ask a favor of you," Lampong-Chelai admitted, getting down to business without the usual social persiflage expected of morning visitors. "As you must know, there have been reports of rough seas and other dangers in the vicinity of Krakatau, the large volcano in the middle of the Sunda Passage."

"I know the mountain you mean, and I have been one who has had reports concerning the troubles there," said Zangi-Ragozh, aware that his visitor was truly worried.

"Ah. That makes my visit a little easier." He sighed. "It seems that some traders are avoiding ports in the region, and that is causing many problems for the merchants in the area."

"I can well imagine," said Zangi-Ragozh.

Lampong-Chelai paced the length of the salon, then came back toward Zangi-Ragozh. "And no doubt you have seen how it can damage trade far beyond fears justified."

"I have; but I have also seen situations when the dangers exceeded fears, as well." He kept his tone completely neutral, not wanting to offend this fellow-foreigner.

"I believe this may be one such instance where the postulation of danger is far beyond any actual risk," said Lampong-Chelai. "You know how the stories of such things are exaggerated. You must have seen volcanoes from time to time and know what one can expect from them—not like the merchants who have only traveled the rivers and never venture more than two days upstream. Volcanoes can be unpleasant; mostly they smoke and bellow, but nothing much happens."

"True enough," said Zangi-Ragozh. "But occasionally, they do erupt."

"Yes, yes, they do. And for a while it is inconvenient," Lampong-Chelai declared. "Then it is over, and the world goes on." He came up to Zangi-Ragozh. "The same thing will happen now. In a year at most, the mountain will be still again."

"I hope that may be so," said Zangi-Ragozh.

"And those merchants who are not frightened out of our waters will be the ones to profit the most, taking advantage of the timorousness of others, who have not the foresight to seek out regions where trading has declined, and taking up the slack that exists," said Lampong-Chelai, finally reaching the point of his discourse. "You can be among those who make this temporary misfortune into a shining opportunity, for your perspicacity will be long-remembered by the merchants whom you aid now." He was becoming enthusiastic, using his hands for emphasis. "I can't approach any Chinese merchant about this without going against the foreigners' laws, but you may hear me out and benefit from the fortuity."

Zangi-Ragozh heard him out, standing still while Lampong-Chelai made his way around the salon again. "Of course, this would also benefit you and your business," he remarked while his visitor marshaled his next round of arguments.

"Yes, and it would spare a great many tradesmen a year of lean earnings. There may be some hazard at present, but those who do not let fear stop them will rejoice later, when times are better. We remember such gestures in Vijaya, as the merchants will in Sunda Kalapa, and we express our gratitude in real terms. All those ports are languishing now, because superstitious Captains avoid us in favor of more tranquil seas. If you would guarantee to keep your ships coming to the ports on the South China Sea, the Java Sea, and the Sulu Sea, we Champa may hope to prosper again when the danger is over." He came to a stop near the windows that looked out on a small formal garden.

"I have ships in those seas even now," said Zangi-Ragozh. "The Captains have the authority to decide which ports to visit, but they have an itinerary, and I expect them to keep to it except in an emergency."

"A prudent provision," said Lampong-Chelai. "But your Captains may panic and turn back northward if they hear too many ill reports."

"Some of my ships have gone to trade with India and Burma," said Zangi-Ragozh. "They will have to come through the South China Sea to reach this port, and they are not likely to turn away from ports where they have done good business before, not unless there is a concern that overrides their desire for profits. Their shares are decreased when they fail to—"

"I know, I know. It is the same with all traders," said Lampong-Chelai impatiently. He made fists of his hands and glowered at a place just over Zangi-Ragozh's left shoulder. "If your Captains panic, you may lose a great deal of money."

"So I might," said Zangi-Ragozh. "But I would rather lose money and save ships and the lives of sailors than risk too much in the name of gain."

"But you *won't*," Lampong-Chelai insisted energetically. "That's what I'm trying to tell you. You need not risk anything. There is profit to be made, especially now, when so many of the southern ports are seeking merchants to trade with, for they need to find markets and will show favor to those who help them in these trying times. The merchants who will not go to the ports of Sumatra and Java and others in the region are being superstitious fools. They are shying away from nothing—*nothing!* This volcano, Krakatau, is often spewing rocks and emitting odors and causing the sea to froth. Every year something happens that puts the timorous to flight. And every time it happens, sailors are frightened by it and stay away from many ports, even some distant ones, for fear of what might—and that *might* is a remote one—happen."

For a long moment, Zangi-Ragozh said nothing. Finally he gave a little nod. "Very well. I'll consider what you have told me, and if it is in accord with the opinions of my Captains, I will do what I can to encourage them to keep to their itineraries. Better than that I cannot promise, what with the time it takes to get messages to my ships."

Lampong-Chelai took a long breath. "I am most grateful to you, worthy foreigner. You have given me cause to hope for my business and my people. If you are willing to tell your friends among the Chinese merchants that tales will not deter you from attending to your voyages, they may follow your example. If enough of them continue to trade in our region—"

Zangi-Ragozh held up his hand. "No. I may choose to order my Captains to continue—at their discretion—but I will not attempt to influence the Chinese. First and foremost, they would not listen to me. Second, if any mishap occurred, I would be held responsible. That could lead to ruin and prison if their ships came to harm on what they deemed to be my account. As you are well-aware," he added with a stern look.

"They wouldn't hold you responsible," said Lampong-Chelai.

"Wouldn't they." Zangi-Ragozh shook his head, recalling an incident from his past when precisely that had occurred. "I am not prepared to gamble on that."

"Well, at least you can keep such cautions to yourself," Lampong-Chelai said, doing his utmost to recover himself; he had seen something in Zangi-Ragozh that had shocked him, an implacability he had not realized the foreigner possessed.

"I would be a fool to do that," said Zangi-Ragozh calmly; his eyes were intent.

"But you can help us—all merchants must be willing to stand with other merchants, or we will all be the tools of the tax collectors and the customs agents. You are one of the most successful of us foreigners, and we must act—" Taken aback at his lapse in conduct, he went to the table where the teapot stood, and he poured the last of the tea into his cup while struggling to restore his composure. "I thank you for hearing me out. You have been most gracious. I fully comprehend your reservations."

"I have not promised to continue to order my ships to visit the ports in question," Zangi-Ragozh pointed out, his dark eyes still unfathomably grim. "I have said only that I will recommend that my Captains do so unless in immediate peril. I will defer to their judgment in matters of safety. They are the ones braving the oceans, not I, and they will have to face the dangers when they arise." He looked away, his discomfort at the thought of so much water making him queasy.

"Yes. I understand. I still thank you. Not many will even do me the courtesy of listening to me." Lampong-Chelai drank the tea and smiled.

Zangi-Ragozh inclined his head. "Very well. So long as we understand each other."

"We do," said Lampong-Chelai, setting the cup down with care, and attempting to conceal the nervousness that had taken hold of him. "You have many beautiful things, foreigner. I have rarely seen so many."

"I have gathered them for many, many years," Zangi-Ragozh said, not mentioning that the many years were counted in centuries.

"Obviously you have the favor of the God of Fortune. May he continue to guide you." Lampong-Chelai fitted his hands together. "I won't trespass on your good nature any longer." With that, he started toward the door. "Your steward may see me out."

"He could. Nevertheless, I will have the pleasure of saying farewell to you at the front door," said Zangi-Ragozh, preparing to follow his visitor out into the hallway, and all the while wondering how dire things were in Sumatra and Java that a Champa merchant from Vijaya should come to plead for them.

Text of a writ of manumission from Zangi-Ragozh, presented to Dei-Na, and recorded in the office of the Magistrate's Archives of Yang-Chau:

Be it known throughout the city of Yang-Chau and all the Middle Kingdom, that the twenty-five-year-old concubine Dei-Na is herewith granted her freedom by the foreign merchant Zangi-Ragozh, who purchased her from her father, the wheelwright Ma Fan-Long, on the ninth day of the fortnight of the Frost Kings in Dei-Na's eighteenth year, for the sum of four gold bars and two unpolished emeralds, is now and perpetually a free woman, with no bonds or other considerations mitigating her freedom.

This Dei-Na has been a most devoted concubine, and her devotion deserves every emolument to which she may be entitled under the rule of the Magistrate and the will of the Emperor. Any attempt to lessen what I provide or to diminish her provision in times to come impugns the honor of the Middle Kingdom as well as my own, and for that reason I am moved to provide a fund to vindicate her liberty and to permit her to enjoy her possessions and privileges in peace, without arbitrary impositions of the demands of court, of Magistrate, or of relatives. She is to be entitled to the support of such counsel as she requires in order to preserve what she has been granted.

There are no limits or conditions attached to this release, which is total and without qualification or hindrance. Her status is that of any freeborn woman without obligation to her family or to anyone seeking to make a claim upon her. She is not being returned to her father or any member of her family, and they have no cause for pursuing any hold on her, for they accepted full payment for her from me seven years ago, and a document to that effect is recorded at the Tribunal. I, Zangi-Ragozh, who paid for her, guarantee her freedom and independence, and ensure that no one may vacate the unconditional terms of this writ, save the Emperor himself, in accordance with the law of the land.

In order that she may maintain herself, I, Zangi-Ragozh, give to her a house in Yang-Chau located on Waning Moon Street, which has been completely paid for and staffed with three servants, whose salaries are to be paid by my shipping company, and further provide her with the income from my merchant ship Golden Moon *so that she may continue to enjoy the freedom she has been granted and live in a manner appropriate to virtuous women. The sum of ten gold bars and fourteen jewels of various sorts, along with six fine pearls, have been given to Dei-Na so that she may not have to marry or sell herself in order to survive. If she wishes to marry, there are five gold bars on* deposit with the Magistrate of Yang-Chau to pay her bride-price so she will not have to ask anything of her father.

The furnishings of her house are hers, as are two horses and a carriage for her use. No one may make a claim against any of these gifts, and any such attempts are to be paid through my business, the Eclipse Trading Company.

In verification of this, I fix my name, my chop, and my sigil on this day, the tenth day after the Winter Solstice in the Magisterial Records Offices of Yang-Chau.

> Zangi-Ragozh
> (his sigil, the eclipse)
> (his chop)

> The Seal of the Magistrate's Secretary
> (his chop)

2

"Do you think you ought to leave just now? I realize there's some urgency, but we are in the full grip of winter. Wouldn't you prefer to travel in spring?" Ro-shei asked Zangi-Ragozh in Imperial Latin as they watched through the open salon doorway while half a dozen servants loaded up a wagon at the head of the drive. A second, smaller wagon stood waiting behind it. There was a light dusting of snow on the ground and a pale mist hung in the air.

"Would you rather not go with me?" Zangi-Ragozh asked, looking up from the book he held. He set this down in order to give Ro-shei his full attention.

He did not answer directly. "Matters in Chang'an are still very uncertain, and it will be cold and wet on the road."

"If it is any comfort to you, I think it probably is a trifle precipitous to go just now, but a nearly-royal summons is a nearly-royal summons. Under ordinary circumstances I would remain here for a month or so, preferably two, before setting out for the west," said Zangi-Ragozh in the same tongue. "But I have been sent for by Wen Emperor Yuan Buo-Ju, as he styles himself, to meet with him and a number of merchants in Chang'an; it would be foolish not to obey, as he is about to ascend the throne there, and he needs to show everyone his power."

"By summoning merchants at the end of January," said Ro-shei in annoyance.

Zangi-Ragozh waved his hand as if to express his will. "Better merchants than warlords. He wishes to make his authority recognized, and not just in the west but throughout the Middle of the World; the most efficient way to do this is through merchants and other travelers, for such endorsement means a quick concession from other rulers. Chang'an is a crucial crossroads for all traders, and you may be certain Wen Emperor Yuan intends to make the most of it—he would be a fool not to. I do not want to give him any reason to detain my caravans or tax them more ferociously than is already the case. If that means I must travel in winter, so be it." He had donned his heaviest black-silk sen-hsien and had a fur cloak sitting out, ready for him. "You do not have to come with me. I can manage this myself."

"I know," said Ro-shei. "But I feel it would be unwise to remain here alone. You have Professor Min Cho-Zhi arriving here tomorrow, to watch over your house, and that should be sufficient to reassure the Magistrate and the Councillors that you are going to return. This isn't Wen Emperor Yuan's territory, and your being gone could lead to trouble for me as another foreigner, should I remain."

"So it could," Zangi-Ragozh said thoughtfully. "And Professor Min might change his mind."

"That is a possibility, but there are others, and the problems they could create are closer to home. He will have access to your equipment, to the athanor and your other alchemical supplies," said Ro-shei, running one hand through his short-cropped, sandy hair.

"Not the athanor." Zangi-Ragozh lifted one brow as a kind of commentary on his decision. "I've taken that to the main warehouse and crated it as if it has been cargo, then stored it under a number of other crates and labeled it in Persian as an oven—which, technically, it is. It will not be seen, let alone used, in my absence. I've packed my stash of jewels in my travel chests except for a handful of diamonds, which I have put in the strongbox in my study. Jho has been told about it, but not Min."

"Professor Min has great curiosity, and I doubt he will leave such instruments or containers unexamined. He might decide to claim them as his own."

"He might," Zangi-Ragozh said. "But it would be a dangerous thing for him to do."

"When he came here yesterday morning, he asked a great many questions of me, not all of them ones I was comfortable answering." Ro-shei paced the room, his faded-blue eyes worried.

"Yes, he concerns me, as well. Is that why you are considering staying here?" Zangi-Ragozh asked, and before Ro-shei could answer, he went on, "Because if it is, you need not worry. I have made certain provisions that will protect all my possessions from Min or anyone else; I sent an accounting to the Magistrate last evening and assigned temporary legal power to Councillor Ko and Professor Tsa, which provides them with authority to preserve my holdings."

Ro-shei looked relieved. "I should have known you would take measures to guard yourself."

"You should," Zangi-Ragozh agreed with a sardonic smile. "I will be glad of your company, but I do not want to compel you to travel in winter if you would rather not. You have already spent two years roaming about on the ocean on my behalf. If you would prefer to stay—" Zangi-Ragozh put the tips of his fingers together and regarded his pleasant salon over them.

"I have benefited from the excursion, and I will not mind setting out again. I am only concerned with the conditions we may encounter," said Ro-shei, and went back to watching the progress of the loading. "At least you need not suffer, traveling overland."

Zangi-Ragozh nodded. "Truly. So long a journey over water, in a box in the hold of a ship, would be hard for me to endure." He coughed gently. "As I know from experience."

"There will be rivers to cross," Ro-shei reminded him.

"And that will be more than enough running water for me, I think," said Zangi-Ragozh. "As to my affairs here, I hope they are sufficiently organized to withstand my absence and anything Min, Tsa, and Ko can do. I can only hope this journey will be useful: that will depend on how the regions sort out their dynastic bickering."

"Which has been the case for decades, and no solution has come, as witness the new dynasty in Chang'an," said Ro-shei with a hint of disgust in his voice. "Whatever the result, you will find a way to accommodate it, or we will leave for the far west again."

"We should have to travel fairly soon, in any case," said Zangi-Ragozh. "I know I will be watched on this journey, and I do not want to give any ruler cause to be dissatisfied with me. Besides, I have not made enough gold for an extended trip, and I'll have to do that before we return to Europe. Even with the jewels, it would be safer to make more gold. It is accepted everywhere, by everyone," said Zangi-Ragozh. A sudden oath from one of the servants loading the wagons intruded, and Zangi-Ragozh went to the window to watch them work, remarking, "They're not usually so careless." When he was satisfied that all was well, he went on, "Tell me what you would rather do: travel or remain."

Ro-shei shrugged. "I assumed that was settled: I will do either, abiding by your decision, whatever it may be. I am prepared to travel in a little while, but I can also stay here, as suits you best."

"You humble me, and you may remind me of that on the road," said Zangi-Ragozh, his voice quietly sincere. "Well," he went on a short while later, "it is a relief to know Dei-Na has a home of her own to go to now. I would not have wanted to leave her here without some provision for her."

"She could have remained in this house," Ro-shei pointed out. "There is no reason to set her up away from here, is there?"

"This house—indeed this whole compound and my trading business—is subject to seizure by the Prefecture as the property of a foreigner; the edict was handed down from the Vermilion Brush itself, last year, and it is still in effect in spite of changes. That would be a poor gift to Dei-Na—to leave her with nothing if someone in power should decide to confiscate my holdings." Zangi-Ragozh shook his head. "No. Better that she has something entirely her own that cannot be taken from her."

"Do you miss her?" Ro-shei asked, fairly certain he knew the answer.

"Of course. She may not have wanted to know me as I am, but she never refused me her dreams, and for that I am deeply grateful," said Zangi-Ragozh, a certain distance in his eyes.

"You could have made her willing to have more," said Ro-shei quietly.

"Perhaps," said Zangi-Ragozh. "But then I remembered Nicoris, and I was acquiescent, accepting Dei-Na in the manner she preferred. I would not like to lose another of my blood, especially not by her own hand. Nicoris' True Death is enough to bear." He looked down at his handsome display of jade figures. "I may take the lions with me."

"Do you want me to find boxes for them?"

"No. I'll have Jho do it." He reached for a small Byzantine bell and rang it. "If you would like to do something for me before we depart, distribute New Year money to the staff for me. I do not want to provide any excuse for complaint." He shifted to the dialect of the region. "This way, the servants will not say I ignore their customs."

Ro-shei spoke in Chinese as well. "Do you have the envelopes prepared, or should I find red paper to make some?"

"They are ready to be handed out. In the second drawer of my writing table," Zangi-Ragozh said, pointing. "Thank you for doing this, old friend. You are always a great asset for—" A discreet tap on the inner door claimed his attention. "Come in."

Jho Chieh-Jen slid the door open. "The wagons will be ready shortly," he announced. "How much grain do you want the stable-hands to load?"

"Two medium barrels," said Zangi-Ragozh. "And a small barrel of oil, as well. Sheh will know which I want."

Ro-shei took up the red paper envelopes, each containing a small gold coin, and said, "I'll return shortly," before letting himself out of the salon.

The steward paid Ro-shei no heed, concentrating his attention on Zangi-Ragozh. "The chief groom has already filled a small barrel for you, as you instructed. I suppose it is the sort of oil you want. It smells of garlic." There was a suggestion of disapproval in Jho's tone which might have been the result of his long-standing rivalry with Sheh.

"That is the oil, which I add to the grain. It keeps the horses' coats from damage, and worms from their guts." He nodded toward the jade figurines. "Will you be good enough to find boxes for those two lions, and pack them to travel with me?"

"Certainly," said Jho, doing his best not to appear curious.

"It being winter, I would like to have a bit more protection with me—for luck. Those two lions should ward off danger," Zangi-Ragozh told him, knowing it would appeal to his sense of propriety.

"Everyone needs luck," said Jho, taking a liberty he would not dare had his employer been Chinese.

"Indeed. See them packed in boxes and stowed with my things in the second wagon. Have the gifts for Wen Yuan been loaded yet?"

"All but the ivory screen. That is being wrapped in quilts and bound with soft ropes," said Jho. "I have made an accounting of all the items you are taking to Chang'an. Will you endorse it with your chop?" He pulled a small rolled scroll from his sleeve.

"Bring it to me," said Zangi-Ragozh. "I trust you have made a copy for me to take with me, for the customs officials?" He went to his writing desk and opened it, removing his chop and inkpad.

"Of course," said Jho, handing over the scroll. "Both sheets are rolled together."

"I thought as much," said Zangi-Ragozh, a bit distantly as he reviewed the items on the list, pausing to add two notations to the information contained in the accounting. "This appears to be complete, and sufficient for the customs officials' specifications." He put the scrolls down and secured them open with small jade paperweights, then affixed his chop to the bottom of both of them.

Jho waited while the red ink dried. "Do you know when you'll return yet?"

"As soon as I may properly do so," said Zangi-Ragozh. He picked up his large square, red visiting card with instructions written on its back. "You should be able to reach me at these places. I'd like to have fortnightly reports from you, carried by official courier. The service has already been paid for."

"I will do as you ask, of course," said Jho, taking the visiting card and one of the scrolls; he tucked them into his sleeve and prepared to leave the room. "Is there anything more you require?"

"You have checked the stores? You have brought them all up to the levels I requested? The regular ones and the emergency ones?"

"They are all in order," said Jho. "Food for a year in the cellar of this house, all sacks and barrels labeled, all fruits dried. Blankets and bedding in the attic, along with cloth for new clothing. Food for a month in the kitchen. Food for horses for six months in the stables, and grazing areas at the west side of the inner wall. A clear well in the garden, an orchard and berry bushes within the compound. We may take

in ten people beyond those who already live here and still be able to last
a year inside the compound; this will allow four wives and their children to be given shelter. All the medicinal supplies are on the second
floor in your herb-room, next to your workroom. The herbalist Pao Yan-
Fen has the keys to the chests there. He is to be consulted if any illness
or injury should occur, and his recommendations followed." Jho recited
this by rote. "No fevered person is to be admitted if there is disease in
Yang-Chau, no soldiers are to be admitted if there is an insurrection.
Otherwise we are to cooperate with all authorities."

"Excellent," Zangi-Ragozh said. "See you observe these rules."

"Do you really expect a plague, or a war?" Jho asked, voicing a
question that had long puzzled him.

Zangi-Ragozh considered his answer. "If I have learned anything in
my long travels, it is that pestilence and war do not wait until it is convenient to visit cities. You cannot expect them, as you would spring or
the Dragon Boat Festival. So I do my best to be prepared for their appearance at any time."

Jho frowned in distress. "I did not mean—"

With a rueful chuckle Zangi-Ragozh laid his hand on Jho's shoulder. "You need not apologize. I'm not offended."

"May you have soft beds and good fires for the whole of your
journey," said Jho, taking refuge in correct conduct.

"Thank you," said Zangi-Ragozh, fitting one hand around the
other to show great respect to his steward.

"And may you return quickly." Jho said this last with heavy implication. "The Emperor here may not like you going to Chang'an for
the convenience of his competitor."

"No, he might not. But even he knows a foreigner like me cannot
refuse to obey an Imperial order, no matter which Vermilion Brush
signs it." Zangi-Ragozh went over to his writing table and indicated
one small drawer. "The original summons is in there. You may show
it to the Magistrate or any Imperial Censor to account for my absence. The language is formal, but it makes Wen Yuan's intent very
plain."

"I will make note of this," Jho assured him.

"Just make sure that none of your staff is alone in this salon."

Jho put his right hand around his left and nodded respectfully. "I will serve your interests in your absence, Illustrious Foreigner. I will give you no cause to complain of me, now, or in the future."

"Thank you for that," said Zangi-Ragozh. "I am sure you know your duty."

"That I do," Jho responded emphatically. "Your household will be kept in order, just as your clerks will tend to your business." He stepped back, turned, and went to the door, waiting there for Zangi-Ragozh to dismiss him.

"For which I am deeply appreciative." He waved Jho away. Once he was alone, he went back to the writing table and took out his ink-cake, water, and brush, then selected a sheet of paper and began to prepare the ink. When he was satisfied with its density, he dipped the brush into it and began to write a general letter to Professor Min, one that could be presented to any official. It indicated where he was going, by what route—away from any open fighting—and why, as well as approximately when he intended to return. He authorized the paying of taxes and other charges and gave permission for Min to dispense money to Jho to manage the household from certain established accounts. Then he outlined the planting he wanted done within the compound as soon as the ground was ready for seeds, prepared a schedule of maintenance on the house and other buildings, and stipulated what would be Min's and Jho's prerogatives to order in an emergency. This he signed and fixed with his chop and sigil, then placed in the center of the writing table.

"I will be ready to go in a short while," Ro-shei announced as he came through the door; he was dressed for winter riding, in a sen-gai of quilted wool over Byzantine leather leggings, not unlike the ones Zangi-Ragozh wore. "Sheh has saddled your favorite gelding and is providing two remounts for each of us, and replacement teams for both wagons. He will have them, and the drivers and the groom, ready directly."

Zangi-Ragozh shrugged on his cloak. "You'll want fur-lined gloves."

"That I will. And a fur hat." Ro-shei patted the large wallet hung on his belt. "I have all of them with me, in here. I will put them on directly." He gave Zangi-Ragozh a pointed look.

"And I have mine," said Zangi-Ragozh, picking up on his intent and duplicating Ro-shei's gesture. "Black Toba lamb."

"Of course," said Ro-shei, and took a last, red-paper-wrapped coin from his sleeve. "This is Jho's. I thought he would prefer to have it from you."

"Very astute of you," said Zangi-Ragozh, and took the New Year coin with the characters for *long life* and *prosperity* on one side, *many children* and *honorable conduct* on the other. He weighed it in his hand. "A goodly sum. Have we given all as much?"

"No. Most of the senior staff have three silver and two copper coins, the understaff one of each. Only Sheh and Jho have gold coins," said Ro-shei.

"A richer gift than usual," said Zangi-Ragozh.

"Since we will be gone when they celebrate, I thought they should have nothing to complain of. Dissatisfied servants can mean trouble—"

"As we saw the last time I was in Rome," Zangi-Ragozh finished for him.

"Truly." He reached the door and slid it open.

"Are Jong and Yao prepared? Is Gien?" Zangi-Ragozh asked as they went out into the cold morning. Jong and Yao were the cousins who would be driving the wagons, and Gien would be the groom for their journey, an odd fellow from the far northwest who had a way with horses.

"Sheh said they were just drinking their bitter tea," said Ro-shei. "It's supposed to help keep them warm."

"Then let them drink it, by all means," said Zangi-Ragozh as he went down the broad, shallow stairs and into the edge of the garden.

Half the household had come to see them off. They stood at a respectful distance, saying little above occasional whispers as Ro-shei went toward the stable while Zangi-Ragozh checked the various ropes securing the barrels lashed to the outsides of the vehicles. He tugged at one line that seemed loose, and when it slipped, he retied the knot that held the barrel, making sure it was firm. Satisfied, he inspected the harness of the two teams—one of four horses, the other of two—and the lead-lines to which the remounts and second teams would be tied. All the braided-leather leads were new, without wear or weakness, and the harness was shiny with recent applications of oil and beeswax. "This is all to my liking," he announced as he approached the stable where his gray gelding was being saddled. "You have done well, Sheh."

Sheh Tai-Jia nodded his appreciation as he finished tightening the second girth on the gray's Mongolian saddle. "I replaced the billets, as you asked, and put new reins on the bridle."

"Very good," said Zangi-Ragozh. "It won't do for any of us to present a shabby appearance."

There was general laughter, for Zangi-Ragozh was known for the high quality of his possessions and his elegance of person. Sheh brought the gelding up. "Would you like a mounting-block?"

"It's hardly necessary," said Zangi-Ragozh as he vaulted up into the saddle and fitted his boots into the long leather foot-loops. "This is very good," he said, settling into the saddle.

"It is strange to pad your saddle with earth," said Sheh's young assistant.

"Foreigners have their ways," Sheh said sharply, stopping any further inquiry. "I think you will find the reins sufficiently oiled."

Zangi-Ragozh flexed the leather as he gathered them up. "Yes. Well done." He glanced over his shoulder. "Where are Jong and Yao?" he asked as he guided his horse out of the stable, Sheh walking beside him.

"They are coming," said Sheh. "If you will give them a moment more—"

"Of course. And where is Ro-shei's mount?"

"Hou is saddling her in the stall." Sheh saw Zangi-Ragozh nod his approval and looked up as Gien came out of the stable leading four sturdy horses, which he hitched to the rear of the first wagon. "He'll have the second team out shortly, and your remounts."

"That is most acceptable," said Zangi-Ragozh. "I'm going to ride down to the orchard and back, to keep Flying Cloud from standing too long." Saying this, he nudged the gelding with his heel and started down the path toward the orchard. Exercise for his horse was only part of the reason he was doing this; he wanted to look at the orchard again, for even bare in winter, it reminded him of the coming spring. Patting Flying Cloud's glossy neck, he reluctantly turned back toward the stable.

Ro-shei had mounted up and the two drivers were in place on their boxes as Zangi-Ragozh came up. Gien was tying the last of the remounts to the lead-line, testing the knots before he clambered onto the box of the first wagon beside Yao. "We are ready, my master," he said as Zangi-Ragozh rode to the front of the group.

"As am I," said Zangi-Ragozh. "Warder," he called out in a voice that carried all through the front of the compound, "open the gate."

In answer to his command the large, iron bolt was drawn back and the warder operated the pulley that swung the gate open, the large hinges creaking. As much of the household as could find an excuse to be there gathered to see Zangi-Ragozh and the others depart. Some shouted good wishes for luck and safety while some were content just to watch as the two horsemen and the two wagons with their reserve horses went out the gate and onto the broad, rutted road that led into Yang-Chau and away from the city along the river toward the west-by-north. The little party turned away from the city, joining a stream of carts, wagons, men on horseback and on foot, moving into or out of Yang-Chau, and were soon out of sight of the compound.

They made their first stop shortly after midday at a tavern that catered to travelers. Yao, Jong, and Gien all got down and went to have hot rice-wine, oil-cakes, grilled onions, and broiled goat while Zangi-Ragozh and Ro-shei watered and changed teams on the wagons and shifted mounts. When the drivers and the groom emerged from the tavern, they brought gourds filled with hot tea, which they wrapped in heavy cloth to keep in the warmth as long as possible. Visibly refreshed, they took their places in the wagons and set off once more, all huddled down into their fur-lined cloaks against the biting chill of the wind.

Through the afternoon the weather closed in, the mists turning to sleet and coming at them in a sharp, slanted angle as if determined to cut them to the bone; the number of travelers on the road grew fewer. Finally, as the sun sank behind a bank of thick clouds, Zangi-Ragozh gave the order to look for a place to spend the night, for he had given up any hope of reaching the town of Kai-Mung before dark.

"There is a village about half a li ahead," said Jong. "There are places for us to stay there—taverns and inns."

"Is it on this road?" Zangi-Ragozh asked, moving his horse close to the wagon to hear what Jong had to say.

"Yes. It borders a little stream that runs into the Yang-Tse, and they keep the bridge," Jong said.

"Guan-Tse?" Zangi-Ragozh asked, remembering it from other journeys.

Jong was pleasantly surprised. "Yes. My cousin keeps an inn there—the Silver Cockerel—just off the market-square."

"Then lead us to it," said Zangi-Ragozh, and rode forward to the larger wagon. "Yao," he called out over the weather, "let Jong take the lead. He is taking us to his cousin's inn at Guan-Tse."

"So we stop before we reach Kai-Mung?" Ro-shei guessed aloud.

"At Jong's cousin's inn," Zangi-Ragozh said with a half-smile.

"So Jong has a cousin who keeps an inn," Ro-shei remarked. "And one on this road. How convenient."

"We are not keeping to our original plan, and so Jong has had no opportunity to make any arrangements with his cousin," said Zangi-Ragozh. "No, I reckon the worst we will face is that a portion of the price we will be charged will go into Jong's pocket, just as his cousin will raise the amount we pay above his usual rates. I have sufficient gold for even the most exorbitant costs."

"That's hardly unusual," said Ro-shei.

"My point exactly," Zangi-Ragozh said, and fell in beside Jong's wagon as it took the lead.

Text of a letter from Marakam on the east coast of Borneo, from the Burmese scholar Ymer ai Pagan to Captain Pao Sho-Feng of the merchant-ship *Joyous Winds,* delivered seven weeks after the Winter Solstice.

To the most perspicacious Captain, Pao Sho-Feng of the Joyous Winds, *a merchant-ship out of Yang-Chau, and much-traveled in the Southern Islands and other ports of the south, the scholar Ymer ai Pagan sends his most enthusiastic greetings and gives the Captain his assurances that what he says in this letter is complete and correct as far as he is able to make it so, with the promise that should he fail in any point of accuracy, he will answer for it with a beating. It is this facility that the scholar offers to Captain Pao.*

Your note informed this scholar that the Captain and his crew are lately arrived from the Southern Islands, and are bound for Madura on Java and Samudra on Sumatra, with intentions then to turn north in the Andaman Sea, and seek information on the waters hereabout, and reports on new conditions. To the most pressing development: the mountain in the middle of the Sunda Passage often spits rocks and noxious gases, and once in a while, there is a brief flow of lava from its summit cone, and the people of the islands pay little attention. But recently those have become troubled in ways they have not been in the past. The Sunda mountain, Krakatau, is smoking and trembling more constantly than is its habit, perturbing the waters and land around it, causing many of the people living near it to move away from the proximity of the mountain until such time as it quiets once more. If those who live near the mountain are willing to sacrifice their homes in order to be assured of safety, then it would be sensible for you, as a commercial seafarer, to keep away from those waters, at least until such time as the natives of the region return to their houses.

You may confirm anything this scholar reports with others who have recently traversed the waters in question. Among the number of such voyagers, there are two ships recently arrived from Sunda Kalapa, neither of them merchant-ships, but filled with those who have decided to remain in the lea of Borneo until they are certain that all jeopardy from their mountain is over. Those persons have a far better understanding of the situation than this scholar can, for they know their islands and are cognizant of their behavior in a way that you or this scholar cannot be, lacking the familiarity of long residence.

To assist in such an endeavor, this scholar offers his skills as a translator. As stated before, this scholar knows the language of Java and Sumatra, and his Chinese, as you see, is adequate to any task you may impose. In addition, this scholar can speak the main tongue of Saylan, and three of the dialects of India, so he may be useful with many other travelers and all manner of merchants. In addition, this scholar will be willing to keep records for you and to make copies of all discussions you have with those with whom you wish to speak, so that you may present this record to your employer upon your return to Yang-Chau. The charges for such services will not be beyond what is reasonable, and this scholar warrants his work will stand proof to all scrutiny. Submitted with profound respect to Captain Pao Sho-Feng,

Ymer ai Pagan

3

At Jun-Chau, at the edge of the foothills of the well-worn range of pic-
turesque mountains, the travelers were warned of fighting to the immediate west; Zangi-Ragozh spent a day in the market-place, doing his
best to ignore the blustery rain, asking as many questions as he could of
merchants who had arrived in the city by various routes; he was glad
now that he had taken the time that morning to put an extra layer of his
native earth in the soles of his boots. In the evening he returned to the
Inn of the Immortal Peach, which catered to wealthy and influential
travelers, where he informed the rest of his party that they would turn
north. "We'll see what the reports tell us in a day or two," he said to the
others.

"It delays our arrival," said Yao. "We've already been on the road
nine days—two days longer than we would have been in summer. The
weather will slow us still more."

"Better a few days' delay than getting caught in a battle," Zangi-
Ragozh pointed out.

"Are you certain there is a battle, then?" Jong asked, looking up
from his cup of hot rice-wine.

"No, I am not," said Zangi-Ragozh. "The rumors are very consistent, however, and that gives me pause."

"Then we go north, and that adds at least a week to our time on
the road," said Yao, spitting into the fire at the center of the dining
room of the Inn of the Immortal Peach. He had been sullen for the
last two days, inclined to brood and to give abrupt answers to anyone
foolish enough to talk to him.

"What is the matter with you, Yao?" Jong demanded, completely
exasperated. "Are you ill?"

Yao hitched up his shoulders. "I know I'm out of sorts. I don't
know why. My grandmother was like this, too, always irritated before
a blizzard."

"A blizzard!" Jong exclaimed. "Not here in the lowlands, certainly."

"No, in the mountains. It would probably bring sleet here." Yao put his hands together.

"A blizzard would be inconvenient," Jong declared.

"No doubt it would," said Zangi-Ragozh. "And yet, I would rather have some warning than be caught in the open when it strikes."

"Far better to be safe indoors," Ro-shei agreed with a knowing nod. "For all of us."

Jong rounded on Zangi-Ragozh. "Do you believe this nonsense?"

Zangi-Ragozh considered his answer. "Blizzards are not uncommon at this part of the season, at least not in the mountains, and although Jun-Chau is a bit southerly for one, his saying such a storm is coming is not so astonishing as hearing something of the sort in high summer would be. I propose to put up here for another day, to see if the weather gets better or worse. Rain makes the road a muddy morass, and snow would render it impassable." He pulled off his gloves and held his small hands out toward the fire.

"A waste of time," Jong grumbled. "I think this is an absurd—"

"Absurd it may be," Zangi-Ragozh interrupted him, "but it is my decision to make, and I have made it." He took two steps back from the fire and went to pay for the men's supper.

"Will you want your own meal served in your room?" the landlord asked with an obsequious smile; he recognized all the trappings of a wealthy merchant, foreign or Chinese, and knew such rich patrons were rare in winter; a little extra attention now could pay off handsomely in the future, so he laced his plump fingers together and strove to appear as helpful as possible.

"I think not. I would rather be told where I might find a dancing girl—very accomplished, at a first-class establishment," said Zangi-Ragozh.

The landlord considered, weighing various possibilities in his thoughts. "There is La-Che at The Silver Fan," he said at last. "Very desirable, very temperamental, fiery, but accomplished in every amorous art; there's some barbarian blood in her, and you know how they can be. She's considered expensive but a real prize."

Zangi-Ragozh shook his head. "That was not the accomplishment I meant," he said smoothly. "I would like to see a truly skilled dancer, and, if she is willing, I would like to spend the evening in her company."

"Ah, a connoisseur; a different matter entirely," said the landlord, revising his opinion of his foreign guest a little. "How remarkable, that a foreigner should seek such a dancer."

"If concern for art is so remarkable," said Zangi-Ragozh.

The landlord heard an implacable note in his voice and decided not to make the jest that had sprung to mind. "Artistry. Yes. Then you would be best-pleased with Jo-Hsu at the Heavenly Flute. I could send a messenger to bespeak her for you for the evening."

Ordinarily Zangi-Ragozh would have turned down this offered service, but he suspected it would not be a good notion in this instance, so he drew a string of copper cash from his sleeve and took four coins off the cord. "Two for you, two for your messenger," he said, handing over the money. "I will visit the Heavenly Flute in a short while." His slight smile was polite enough, and his respectful manner gained him another notch of approval in the landlord's estimate.

"It will be done at once," the landlord assured Zangi-Ragozh, and clapped his hand for one of his servants, his round features set in a professional, meaningless smile. "My lad will go on the instant."

"I thank you. And where is this establishment?" He rested his hand on the high counter as he waited for an answer.

"It is three streets away from here. You cross the market-square and bear left at the first street beyond the square. The mouth of the street faces the Temple of the War Gods, and it runs south for four blocks. The Heavenly Flute is in the second block on the right. You will see the sign."

"Very clear and concise. You are an asset to your profession," said Zangi-Ragozh, and returned to the fire to draw Ro-shei aside for a few private words.

"You're going out," said Ro-shei in Byzantine Greek. "For the evening, or all night?"

"I hardly know yet, not having seen what is out there," said Zangi-Ragozh in the same language. "That will depend upon what I find, will it not?"

Ro-shei shook his head. "I hope you will not abandon your search too readily or assume you cannot obtain what you require. We have a long way to go yet."

"We do," Zangi-Ragozh admitted. He looked directly at Ro-shei, continuing purposefully, "If the dancing girl is unwilling, then I will try to find a widow to visit in her sleep."

"So long as you have nourishment," said Ro-shei with feeling. "Ever since you freed Dei-Na, I have noticed that you deny yourself what you most truly need, and this causes me concern."

"I am in no danger," said Zangi-Ragozh.

"It is going to be a demanding journey; you said so yourself. You need to maintain your strength. Days are beginning to lengthen, and the increasing sunlight will make greater exactions upon you, and that, too, will deplete your stamina. If you do not feed your hunger, how are you to maintain the discretion you have been so determined to preserve?" Ro-shei glanced over his shoulder and lowered his voice. "This is not Yang-Chau. You are not known here; anything you do will be noted and considered. Your true nature would not be welcomed by anyone in this town."

"Do you suppose Jong or Yao or Gien is likely to take advantage of me if they knew?" Zangi-Ragozh asked.

"Probably not. But highwaymen often have agents at inns such as this and are not above setting ambushes."

"I know," said Zangi-Ragozh. He went on in Chinese, "I have arranged for the men's supper. Do you want me to send a request to the kitchen, or do you want to fend for yourself?"

"I have a duck I bought in the market-place. It will more than suffice," said Ro-shei, also in Chinese.

"Then I wish you a pleasant evening," he said, fitting one hand into the other.

"And I wish a pleasant evening to you, my master," said Ro-shei, moving aside so that Zangi-Ragozh could draw on his oiled-leather cloak and leave the inn.

The evening was turning raw, the wind more penetrating, the rain colder. Zangi-Ragozh drew up the hood of his cloak and lifted his shoulder to the wind as he made his way along the side of the nearly empty market-square toward the Temple of the War Gods. He stopped for a moment to look into the elaborate interior of the building and heard the drums sounding to summon the gods to receive their worship, which asked for protection from the dangers of battle. The odor of incense was strong, and the shine of lamps and tapers made the tall windows of the temple glow. When the chanting began,

Zangi-Ragozh moved away, knowing that as a foreigner he would not be welcome at the celebration. He made his way down to the Heavenly Flute, which had the look of an exclusive dining establishment. Ducking in through the hanging over the door, Zangi-Ragozh approached a tall desk and identified himself, presenting a business card and saying, "The landlord of the Inn of the Immortal Peach sent a messenger a little while ago, bespeaking the talents of Jo-Hsu."

"Indeed he did. Are you the man who asked for her?" The landlord looked Zangi-Ragozh over carefully; he was as tall and angular as the landlord of the Inn of the Immortal Peach was rotund. "I was told you are a foreign merchant. Beng's boy described you."

"Yes, I am a foreign merchant," Zangi-Ragozh agreed at once. "And I am presently here on my way to Chang'an."

"A foolhardy thing to do, but still, I suppose, someone must begin, or the disputes will spread farther." The landlord waved his hand toward the central corridor of his establishment. "Take the door on the left, the one standing open. Two bars of silver buys Jo-Hsu and a musician for the night. Food is extra."

Zangi-Ragozh handed over the two silver bars from the wallet on his belt. "There will be a third bar in the morning if we are undisturbed. In the meantime, send in whichever tea Jo-Hsu most prefers."

Scowling, the landlord put the money away. "If Jo-Hsu calls for help, I will send my men in to protect her, silver or no silver."

"Of course, of course," Zangi-Ragozh said. "A wise precaution, especially with someone unknown to you." He removed his hat, pulled off his cloak, and draped it over his arm before proceeding down the corridor as the landlord had indicated, entering a good-sized room with two broad couches, three chairs, a table, a small folding screen, and a slightly raised platform on which Jo-Hsu would dance. A fire had been laid and only recently kindled, so there was a little smoke in the room, and a persistent odor of charring sap. He draped his cloak over the back of the longer couch and closed the door through which he had entered.

A maid came in from the far end of the room bearing the tea-tray. She set this down and withdrew in silence with no acknowledgment of Zangi-Ragozh's presence.

Zangi-Ragozh walked around the handsome chamber, seeming to be looking at its decoration, in actuality trying to locate the peepholes he was certain were hidden in various parts of the walls. He had counted three of them when a middle-aged woman in a nondescript gray sen-mo and carrying a two-stringed instrument came into the room, nodded to Zangi-Ragozh, and sat down on a small stool, where she began to tune up.

A wooden gong sounded, and the side door was opened to admit a slender young woman in a long-sleeved sen-lai of jade-green silk embroidered with golden peonies. She turned to Zangi-Ragozh and fitted her hands together. "This person is Jo-Hsu," she said.

"I am Zangi-Ragozh," he replied as he acknowledged her greeting.

"You have requested me to dance for you," she said a bit doubtfully.

"Yes. I have heard you are a true artist," he said, and made himself comfortable on his chair.

"Shall I start now with a dance of my choosing or is there something you would rather begin with?" Jo-Hsu asked, and as Zangi-Ragozh nodded his permission to start, she took her place on the raised floor, shook out her sleeves, and signaled to the musician. Apparently they had agreed upon what to perform, for the music began without any discussion. The first few notes were jarring, but then the melody became plain, and the dancer began to move, following the traditional movements of the *Spring Dawn* dance with precision and elegance. She had the gift of seeming to float, so that every step and gesture appeared to be suspended, ethereal; even the rapid passages were unhurried, graceful, and effortless. When she was done, she bowed to Zangi-Ragozh.

"Truly excellent," he said, and put a gold coin on the tray with the tea things.

"Would you like to see another?" Jo-Hsu asked, still panting a little.

"Yes, I would," Zangi-Ragozh told her. "But take a little while to recover your breath."

She ducked her head. "Thank you." Straightening up, she looked about her. "What would you like me to dance next?"

"You know your preferences better than I," said Zangi-Ragozh. "Choose whichever you would like most to do."

"Would *The Last Petal* please you?" she suggested.

"I have never seen it," Zangi-Ragozh told her. "It would enlarge my understanding if you would dance it for me."

Jo-Hsu nodded. "Then I will do it. Some people think it's too sad, but I like it." She took a position in the center of her stage and said, "Play, Weh-Bin."

The musician complied at once, striking up the plaintive tune with more sensitivity than she had shown in the previous dance; the melody twined around three central notes, and the dance used this device, for it consisted of turns and twirls that recalled petals dropping on the wind. When the dance was finished, Jo-Hsu was on her knees, bent forward, hands extended.

"Lovely," said Zangi-Ragozh, looking over at the musician. "Perhaps Weh-Bin would like to retire for a short while, to reinvigorate herself, and you, Jo-Hsu, have some tea for refreshment."

Rising easily, Jo-Hsu spoke softly to Weh-Bin, saying to Zangi-Ragozh, "She will return directly."

"Very well," he said, and indicated the couch near his chair. "Please. Be comfortable." He poured out a cup of tea for Jo-Hsu and held it out to her. "Drink this, if you would."

She took the cup as she sat and tasted the tea. "My favorite. Thank you."

"You dance very well," Zangi-Ragozh told her. "Your reputation is richly deserved."

"You are good to say so." She drank more of the tea and lay back on the couch, watching him covertly.

"How long have you studied?"

The question surprised her, and so she answered more truthfully and directly than she usually did when patrons asked her about herself. "Since I was a little child. My mother was a dancer, very famous, with many rich patrons, and she taught me all she knew." She drank the last of the tea in her cup. "She died when I was twelve. I began to dance professionally two years later."

"So young," Zangi-Ragozh said as he rose to refill her cup.

"Many dancers begin their careers younger than I was," she said a bit brusquely.

"That was not what I meant," Zangi-Ragozh responded; he poured the tea.

Jo-Hsu was taken aback by his courtesy. "You need not . . . I will tend to the tea myself."

"There is no reason that you should," said Zangi-Ragozh, sitting down again. "It is the least I can do for you."

She stared at him, her face revealing the many emotions that welled in her, from gratitude to affronted indignation. Finally she said, "You are not my servant."

"No, I am not," he responded, his dark eyes on hers. "But you deserve my service."

"Because I dance well?" She was startled at the notion. "Surely—"

"Because you dance well," he confirmed.

"And is that all?"

He studied her for a long moment. "If it is all you want, then yes. If it is not, then no."

Into the potent silence looming between them, Weh-Bin returned. Taking in Jo-Hsu and Zangi-Ragozh in a single glance, she swiftly withdrew again and informed the servants that Jo-Hsu should be left alone until she sent for help.

Jo-Hsu's eyes flickered as she heard the side-door snick closed. She gave a long, languorous sigh and made herself more comfortable on the couch. "It is always pleasant to have a man demonstrate his admiration."

Zangi-Ragozh watched her performance, a bit saddened that she had decided to treat him as she would any patron; it was the life she knew, he reminded himself as he said, "If it is truly what you desire, then what am I but flattered."

"It is how these things are done. You've paid for my time, and you've liked my dancing." She drank her tea and held out her arm to him. "Come. You will be happier at my side."

He got to his feet and walked the three steps to the couch. "I am not what you expect," he said as he took her hand and bent to kiss it. "You have nothing to fear from me; believe this."

Jo-Hsu stared at him. "What did you do?"

"It is a custom among my people," he said, sitting beside her.

"Foreigners are so strange," she said, shaking her head.

"Yes. We are." He touched her cheek, his fingers so light that she gasped in astonishment. "Some more than others."

"How do you come to—" He leaned forward and touched her lips with his, so softly that she was only startled, not afraid. As he drew back, she did her best to laugh and only partially succeeded, for she was becoming breathless. "Another foreign custom."

"The same custom," said Zangi-Ragozh. "It expresses a different regard when done to the mouth instead of the hand."

"It is like you tasted me." She looked up into his face. "Are you hungry for me?"

"Yes, Jo-Hsu, I am," he said with utter sincerity as he moved his hands over her sen-lai, so gently that he hardly disturbed the sheer fabric.

She grabbed his wrist and regarded him somberly. "Shan will make you pay more if you—you know. Pregnancy isn't good for dancers."

"I won't do anything that would endanger you in that way," Zangi-Ragozh said. He did not add that he was certain they were being watched through at least one of the peepholes in the wall.

Jo-Hsu had heard that before. "If you do, if you forget your intentions, Shan will demand you pay for the loss of my time, and my dancing."

Zangi-Ragozh fixed his dark eyes on hers, this time with such attention that she was taken aback. "I gave you my Word, Jo-Hsu," he told her quietly.

She felt her pulse grow strong in her neck, and she took another deep breath to restore her self-possession. "All right. But I'll have to tell him what happened, in the morning."

"You will have nothing to tell him," said Zangi-Ragozh, straightening up. "I will leave something for you on the tea-tray and pay the balance of the evening to your landlord before I leave."

"Oh, no," Jo-Hsu protested, taking hold of his sleeve. "I don't want you to leave me. Not yet. Not until midnight, at least."

"I would rather remain," Zangi-Ragozh admitted.

"Then do so. I don't want it said that I would refuse a patron simply because he was foreign." She gave him her best smile.

What else had he expected? Zangi-Ragozh asked himself. He had sought out an available woman, a woman with something more than a functioning body to attract him, and he had found precisely that. She would not question how he took his pleasure so long as it did not include any risk to her of pregnancy or damage to her face. No matter how much he wanted more from her, given the reality of his circumstances, this arrangement was ultimately satisfactory, or so he attempted to convince himself as he bent over Jo-Hsu again. "Does my foreignness bother you, Jo-Hsu?"

"Not so much. You are not like many men, foreign and Chinese, for many of them are over-eager. You do not rush upon me. Or you have not done so yet." She studied his face; apparently she approved of what she saw, for she moved a little to give him more room on the couch and held up her hand. "You may taste me again, if you like."

Obediently he kissed her hand, continuing to hold it as he lowered it from his lips. "I thank you, Jo-Hsu."

Her laughter was softer and less forced than before. "You say such strange things, foreigner." She touched the standing collar of his sen-hsien. "Not that I mind them."

Zangi-Ragozh slipped his arms around her and gathered her close to him. "Then I hope you will not mind the other foreign things about me."

She returned his embrace with practiced ease, pressing her body to his through the many layers of silk that separated them. "You have been most gratifying thus far."

He took the compliment with a nod that led into another kiss. This time their lips met less gently and remained together longer, drawing more than titillation from Jo-Hsu; Zangi-Ragozh felt a change in her flesh as the first quiver of authentic passion ignited deep within her. He nuzzled her neck and worked open her sen-lai, exposing the slight rise of her breasts. "What gives you most pleasure?" he whispered.

"Your touch is very nice," she answered, her pulse becoming a little faster.

"Then let me offer you more of it," he murmured as he unfastened the last of the closings on the sen-lai.

The soft jade silk slithered off her, spilling onto the couch like a waterfall. "Oh. I will be cold soon."

"I will keep you warm," Zangi-Ragozh promised her, turning her a little so that the warmth from the hearth could enhance what his hands did.

"That's . . . wonderful." Jo-Hsu sighed once more, and opened her body to his eyes and hands with the practiced ease of her profession. She had done this many times before, but now there was a new sensation in her limbs that made her feel heavy and light at once. When he bent and touched his lips to her nipple, she gave a sharp little cry that turned to a quiet moan as he cupped her small breast in his hand and kissed her other nipple. She closed her eyes and gave herself over to her arousal.

"What would you like me to do next?" he asked, his voice low.

"I don't know," she said, not quite truthfully, but as she had been trained to respond. "Whatever seems best to you."

"It is what *you* want that suits me best," said Zangi-Ragozh.

She considered this for a long moment. "Then do as you like; I will tell you if I am not pleased."

"It will be as you wish." With a patience that was nearly reverence, Zangi-Ragozh sought out all the rapture her body contained. Hands and lips paid unhurried homage to her breasts, her flanks, her long, lithe torso, to her hips, to her legs, to the deep, warm recesses in the folds at the apex of her thighs. His touch was gentle and exciting at once, his nearness protecting her as well as fueling her ardor. With enchanting leisureliness, he ventured along the curves and hollows of her flesh, discovering the many ways in which she could be inspired with passion. So intent was he on learning the whole extent of her elation that he even devoted his attention to her feet and the backs of her knees. Every apolaustic response she possessed was awakened, so that as he continued his exploration, he brought her transports she had not realized she could attain, until every fiber in her was shivering with ecstasy. Only when she reached the culmination of her fervor did he fold her close to him, his mouth pressed to her throat while she trembled her fulfillment.

Gradually, as the wondrous riot in her flesh softened to a thrill, she opened her eyes and stared up at him. "How do you know such things?"

"My foreign nature," he said, and gently kissed the corner of her mouth.

She reached up and fingered a dark strand of his wavy hair. "Like so much of you." Her face seemed suffused with light. "I didn't notice until now—your eyes are dark as mine, but they're blue. Are you a Celestial Turk?"

"No," he said. "My people come from far to the west, in mountains called the Carpathians. My father ruled there until his enemies overcame him." It was true as far as it went; he did not add that those events had taken place more than two and a half millennia ago.

"Like what is happening in China," she said a bit sadly. "So you are reduced to being a merchant."

"Among other things," he agreed, moving back to allow her to sit up and gather her jade-green sen-lai around her shoulders.

"It is always hard when one ruler is cast out in favor of another," she said. "I have entertained men from Chang'an who told me that they had lost all now that there will be a Wen Emperor in their city."

"Have you encountered many of them, these unfortunate men from Chang'an?" Zangi-Ragozh asked, wondering what else they had imparted.

"Five," she said. "One was very bitter, the others were more angry." She winced at the memory. "Shan had to send two of his boys in to stop them."

Zangi-Ragozh was silent, then said, "I am sorry to hear that you had to suffer on their account."

She shrugged. "It is the way of men."

"It may be, but it does not excuse them," he said.

She put her hand on his. "You aren't like most men. You told me, and it is true."

Zangi-Ragozh looked down at her hand and knew that the gesture was more revealing than she had intended. "You have been most kind to me, Jo-Hsu."

"If I am, it is because of you," she said, as if something in his words had struck an injury; she withdrew her hand.

"I doubt that," said Zangi-Ragozh as he touched her cheek. "If you had no kindness within you, not I, nor anyone else, could find it."

She tugged her sen-lai closed and stared into the middle distance. "If it satisfies you to think so, then I will not stop you."

He moved away from her, thinking that if there was any tea left, it would be cold. "Ah, Jo-Hsu, do not despair."

"It's not that," she said bluntly. "You imagine too much, foreigner."

Rather than argue the point, he asked, "Shall I send for more tea? Or would you like rice cakes and plum wine?"

She scowled in the direction of the hearth. "I would like another log or two on the fire."

He rose at once to attend to her request, saying as he did, "Would you like me to summon Weh-Bin?"

"Why are you being so polite? You have what you wanted. You

need not linger." She pressed her lips together as if to stop saying worse things.

"If you would rather I leave, I will," he said, straightening up from tending to the fire. "But—"

"—you have paid for the night. So you are entitled to remain. You may ask me to dance again, if you like." She stood and adjusted her sen-lai, three fingers brushing the little nicks on her neck. She frowned slightly but said nothing.

Zangi-Ragozh had seen reactions like Jo-Hsu's before, and so he answered her calmly, "I want to make no demands upon you, Jo-Hsu. If you want to dance, then I will enjoy watching you. If you would like to eat, by all means send for food. If you want to sleep, then go ahead. But I tell you now that you will not incite me to anger."

"Nothing passed between us," she said, her hand going to her neck as if to defend herself. "You have no hold on me."

He took another two gold coins from the string of gold cash in his sleeve. "This is yours; do with it as you wish."

"So generous," she said spitefully.

He studied her. "Jo-Hsu," he said at last. "Tell me what I have done to offend you?"

The question took her aback, and she answered without thinking, "You make me want things I know I cannot have again."

Zangi-Ragozh met her gaze steadily. "If that is so, I apologize most sincerely."

Her face crumpled as she fought back tears. "Don't." She flung the word at him as an accusation, then turned away from him. "And you pay me better than anyone."

This time there was a trace of ironic amusement in his response. "I hope I will not further offend you by not apologizing for that?"

"I'd like sweet rice-buns and some plum wine," she said by way of an answer.

"Certainly," said Zangi-Ragozh, clapping his hands to summon a servant.

"How courteous you are," Jo-Hsu said with all the spite of her nineteen years.

By the time he left the Heavenly Flute it was nearer sunrise than midnight; he had presented the landlord with two silver bars, with the assurance that one would be set aside for Jo-Hsu's future use, to the ill-concealed amusement of Shan and his assistant. The blizzard Yao had sensed was beginning in the mountains, and here, at the edge of the foothills, sleet fell relentlessly on the angling wind as Zangi-Ragozh hunched into his cloak and drew his hat down over his forehead to make his way back to the Inn of the Immortal Peach.

Text of a letter written in Imperial Latin from Atta Olivia Clemens at Lago Comus in northern Italy to Ragoczy Sanct' Germain Franciscus in Yang-Chau; carried by caravan for two years, never delivered.

To the distinguished foreigner and my ancient, most honored friend, the greetings of Atta Olivia Clemens on this, the 20th day of June in the Year of the City 1286, or the 533rd Year of Salvation, according to the Pope, whoever the new one may be. Boniface II has been reported near death, so I must suppose he has departed this world for the next by now, and his successor, if one has been elected, is not known here at Lago Comus, nor is likely to be for a while yet, since news in these days travels very slowly.

You see, I have taken your advice at last and got out of Rome again. The distressing inclination of various barbarians to sack and loot the city is becoming inconvenient—not to say revolting in every sense of the word—and so I have come to your lovely villa here at Lago Comus to avoid the rape and pillage that has beome all too frequent in the city of my birth. I cannot tell you how much devastation has been visited on Rome, nor the appalling failure to protect its walls and buildings that has been the most consistent nature of its defense. If only I could be indifferent to Rome, I would be off to travel the world, as you do, but since I have not yet learned how to journey so far from my native Roman earth, Lago Comus must suffice.

Niklos Aulirios is with me, of course, and I have begun assembling a household from the various villages in the area. I have also begun work expanding your stables here: I trust you will not object, or, if you do, you will come here to voice your disapproval in person, which would make any chiding a most welcome experience. He has proven to be the most capable of bondsmen, and I thank you from the very marrow of my bones for providing him to me.

I have brought forty-three horses with me from my estate, and I'll look for good stock in this region to breed with. I have only eight stallions—*the rest are mares, and in good health. I might as well make the most of this opportunity and improve my stock while I avoid the continuing assaults on Rome. Next year I should have sixty to seventy in my herd, and that will be a satisfactory number. As you have remarked before, the barbarians may come down from the north to sack Rome, but they do not often attack such remote places as this one, having a number of towns and cities to attract their attention. The mountains here also provide a kind of protection, as well as providing a setting of impressive beauty. Not even Rome's seven hills are as beautiful as these mountains, though as a Roman, it galls me to say it.*

Another reason for my coming to this place is that there has been a change in the laws again in Rome, and now, without a Papal dispensation allowing it, women are no longer allowed to inherit or possess property. What the Pope can do about it is limited, for, of course, the power of the Church is growing, but it is hardly sufficient to dictate to the rulers, but through their superstition. Not that such fancies cannot be useful, but they are far from reliable, and it is my understanding that what may work in one's favor on one occasion may be contrary the next time. Certainly the Church gained prestige when Pope Leo bought off Attila, not quite a century ago, for the Pope accomplished what no General could, at least as the event is being reported in these times. However, as one who witnessed the occasion, I must declare it was not only Papal gold but pestilence and famine that turned the Hun back at Rome. There was a great deal of bad air in Rome that year, and although it has largely been overlooked, I believe the mal aria, and not invisible Saints and Angels, kept the Huns at bay, and the Pope's gold provided a good reason to withdraw. They are calling Leo a Saint now for what he accomplished. I will grant that he was very clever to use his office in so political a way, for it created leverage for the Church that it had not had before.

Pardon me for railing at you—I rail when I am frightened, and I am frightened now, for I fear I will lose all that I have sought for myself and have no means to maintain my autonomy. There is almost nothing I can do about this, and my fear increases as I become lessened in the world. So I howl at the stars and complain to you, and hope that I fear in vain.

I left your villa in good heart, the fields bountiful and the orchards producing in abundance, and with a caretaker and staff who have been reliable before; they currently number twenty-nine, counting the day-laborers, and they are all under the caretaker's administration, who has your present location and has been instructed to send you annual reports until such time as you return to Rome or I appoint his successor. I have permitted him to reduce the size of your stable from ninety horses to thirty-five. There is less likelihood of them being seized at this smaller number than the larger, so you will still have a few horses left when you return, rather than none at all. Romulus Ursinus will keep you informed on the numbers and genders of the herd.

I realize one of the reasons you have gone so far away is to rid yourself of all the reminders of Nicoris, which I understand, having occasionally done something of the sort myself. But, my most enduring friend, you are not to blame for her decision to accept the True Death. As you told me, almost five hundred years ago now, not everyone can live as those of our blood must. That she discovered she was unable to seek out the living for the sustenance of intimacy is hardly your fault, for you showed her how those of our blood must live, and you were more than generous with her as she wakened to your life. I am unliving proof that you are the very soul of all that is honorable, for you took me from my tomb when I had no hope of restoration, and you have extended your protection and guidance in all kindness. That Nicoris found others lacking where you had not been is hardly a lack in you, but a failure for others, as well I know. Pardon yourself for your caring and return to Europe once again. It has little to recommend it at present, but I would be glad of your company.

As I have already intimated, Rome is no longer thriving, and it is not for military reasons alone that it is so fallen from its former glory, which is now most apparent in the ruins that are the most noticeable features of the old districts of Rome. It is truly unsafe to live there, and that saddens me as much as seeing the peacocks in Constantine's City proclaiming themselves to the new Rome, and more magnificent than the old. They have the pomp but not the law, the wealth but not the roads, the Church instead of the gods. Magna Mater! They have abolished the rights of slaves to purchase their freedom! Women are forbidden to inherit property without a man to serve as guardian for her legacy. What kind of Rome is that?

It has been a very wet winter here in the mountains, or perhaps it is more usual than I know. The summer has been marked with

68   *Chelsea Quinn Yarbro*

thunderstorms and strong winds. While this location is generally protected, it is also inclined to be flooded when there is a great deal of rain. A fortnight ago the streams were over their banks as the water from the peaks came down the mountains. This time not much damage was done, but I have ordered that the walls of the streams be set with stones to help contain the water. Such measures helped preserve my fields in Clusium on the Via Cassia and may do so here, as well. That holding is long-gone, but I have not forgot the lessons I learned there. The work will be done in a month or so, when the water is at its lowest. We will dam the stream for a month and do the lining at a time when the water behind the dam may be used to water livestock and provide a chance for fishing. That has made the more recalcitrant peasants willing at least to try this approach. Some of the farmers in the region have said that if this succeeds here, they may do the same with their streams. It is most apparent that they do not expect these measures to work, but they are not set against trying such methods, either.

The last letter I had from you—and it took almost four years to reach me, and I count myself fortunate to have received it at all—was eight years ago. You had just arrived in Yang-Chau and had begun your business. I suppose you have sent other letters that have not arrived and may never arrive. I wonder what I should ask you, since I have little or no information upon which to draw. Still, I am curious to know how you are, wherever you are, and however you have fared since you left Europe. Very well then: are you still in Yang-Chau? What manner of city is Yang-Chau? Is Rogerian with you? This should be inquiry enough to ensure an answer from you, my oldest, most exasperating friend.

I am giving this letter into the hands of a Longobard merchant bound for the Dalmatian Coast, who will pass it on to a merchant sailing for the Black Sea, who, the Longobard assures me, can be trusted, especially since I am providing gold to ensure his help. From there, it will have to go overland, I suppose, on the Silk Road, and be carried into China by other merchants. I find it difficult to be optimistic about this reaching you at all. It is something like shouting into the void of the night, and hoping to hear an echo from the stars. As uncertain as this journey may be, I will assume that you will read this one day in two or three years. Remember when you see it that I would

be glad to see you again, and that you will always be welcome at my
house, wherever I am.

Before I can become maudlin with missing you, I will sign and seal
this, and start it on its way to you. It is my plan to remain here for at
least ten years, so by the time you read this, you should be able to get
one reply to me before I move on. I assure you I will be discreet, for
it would not do for the people here to discover my true nature, any
more than they would be pleased to know of yours. It is my intention to
look for my sustenance elsewhere, and to pursue my desires with those
who sleep, at least for now. And, my cherished one, I will dream of you.

Olivia

4

It was midmorning on a cold, clear day that was crisped by a whipping
north wind. Zangi-Ragozh and his men, wagons, and horses waited on
the wooden pier for the ferry to take them across the Crane River, one
of several southern forks of the Huang Ho; immediately ahead of
them was a farmer with four goats. Behind them, a Mongol merchant
with a train of ponies carrying casks and bales of goods was bound
northward for his homeland. After the Mongol came an enclosed carriage of splendid design, heavily curtained and ornamented, drawn by
four handsome Celestial horses and guarded by five armed out-riders:
the equipage and escort of a noblewoman. Finally, there were three
scruffy men with a heavy wagon drawn by a hitch of six asses.

"At least the rain and snow have stopped, now we're out of the
mountains. This wind is bad enough. Look how choppy the water is,"
said Yao as he watched the progress of the ferry coming toward them
from the opposite bank.

Zangi-Ragozh was already feeling a bit queasy, and he turned
away from the river, saying, "At least the ferry is large enough for
most of us." He patted the neck of his gray, hoping the mare would
not pick up his nervousness. He brushed the hilt of the sword that
hung on his saddle, hoping he would have no cause to use it.

"The crossing will be tedious," said Yao. "But once it is done, it's done. This is the end of winter, and the weather will change soon."

"Yes; spring is coming," said Zangi-Ragozh. "Our return trip should be much easier than this has been." He swung around in his saddle and studied the approaching ferry, making note of the degree of splash and bounce its present passengers endured.

"Unless there is more fighting," said Ro-shei. He was mounted on a broad-backed chestnut with three white feet.

"The new Wen Emperor Yuan is pledged to stop all fighting," said Zangi-Ragozh with a nice mix of respect and doubt.

"So we will all hope," said Yao, fiddling with the end of his whip. "Battle and bad weather are always hard on the horses."

"And on us," said Jong, who was suffering from a head-cold.

"We will be able to turn south again soon, into milder climes than this," said Zangi-Ragozh. "You will not have to freeze every night."

"Just so I do not inflame my lungs," said Jong, his sniff turning to a cough.

"I have something that might ease your illness; it is in my chest of medicaments," said Zangi-Ragozh. "I think it would help you to recover."

"Ro-shei has said you have made a sovereign remedy," said Jong. "Is that what you mean?"

"Yes," said Zangi-Ragozh. "The herbs you have taken have helped, and I would recommend them myself, were it not that you are developing inner heat. When that occurs, the sovereign remedy may be necessary if you are to avoid dangerous fevers." He recognized the worry in the startled look Jong gave him, and he went on, "I can see it in your face; your color is high."

Jong turned away from him. "I have herbs for it."

"And certainly the herbs will help you ease your discomforts," said Zangi-Ragozh, knowing his remedy would not be readily trusted, particularly since it was made from moldy bread. "Still, this remedy I offer can reduce the incidence of fever and the weakness it brings."

Jong was about to speak, but his words were drowned in a loud peal of what sounded like distant thunder. As the goats bleated, all the horses skittered, the laden ponies fretted, and the asses at the rear of the line brayed and rolled their eyes in alarm. The unearthly noise rolled on eerily, a counterpoint to the sudden cacophony, then was gone; the animals remained edgy, showing the whites of their eyes and straining at their leads and harnesses.

"And not a cloud in the sky," said Gien when the ominous, deep-throated grumble was over; he looked up and blinked in awe. Then, as an afterthought, he made a gesture toward the empty heavens.

"There must be a distant storm," said Ro-shei.

"Or a battle," said Yao. "In the mountains."

The travelers looked about uneasily, and finally the merchant leading the ponies forced out a laugh. "Whatever it is, it has nothing to do with us."

Jong tried his best to chuckle. "The Thunder God is parading with his drums, and it is well for us to be wary; it could mean rain in the mountains, and floods here. A big storm, no matter how far away, may raise the river by nightfall." He put his hand to his mouth as he coughed.

"Then all the more reason to cross as soon as we may," said Yao, keeping his attention on the approaching ferry. "If you must pay more to cross, Zangi-Ragozh, then I ask you to do it." He fidgeted nervously, holding the reins of his wagon-team so unsteadily that two of the horses began to toss their heads in protest. Yao forced himself to be steady. "The noblewoman behind us undoubtedly will commandeer a favorable place for herself, and this crossing is not a short one; the men accompanying her will insist that she have the ferry to herself, but today that would be folly, as well the ferrymen know. I don't want to be trapped on this bank if there is a flood coming."

"Your point is well-taken," said Zangi-Ragozh, reaching into his sleeve for a string of silver cash. "I'll be ready to pass this along as soon as the ferryman is ready to load us on." The amount was fairly lavish, and one that most travelers would not be willing to pay for something so simple as a place on a ferry.

"There looks to be a good number of travelers and their stock for the ferry, perhaps too much for a safe crossing if all get aboard," said Gien, frowning at the prospect of more delay. "The noblewoman is only one concern."

"Then let us offer the ferrymen our help in preparing their craft for the crossing," said Ro-shei at once. "That should incline them to give us a good place for the next crossing no matter how foreign my master and I may be."

"That should serve our purpose very well, possibly as much as the money," said Zangi-Ragozh; he was not looking forward to the ride to the opposite bank, for running water always left him feeling ill and disoriented.

"Then we will do it," said Yao. "I don't want to lose another day standing here waiting for the ferry to cross. We are going to arrive later than we are expected, in any case."

Zangi-Ragozh looked about him, relieved to see that his men were willing to extend themselves in this way. "Very good. You, Yao, if you would speak with the ferryman, we may manage better than if either I or Ro-shei should make the offer."

Yao nodded. "Foreigners aren't always as well-received as Chinese, especially in times like these, with dynasties changing and borders shifting. It is fortunate that the language here is comprehensible for us, for it makes us less strange. In some parts of the Middle Kingdom, I would seem as foreign as you." He saw the others nod and did his best to take on an air of authority.

"I will reward your service," said Zangi-Ragozh, and glanced at the Mongol merchant with the pony-string behind him.

The man muttered something in lower-class Chinese about generations of turtles all the while pointedly ignoring the foreigner in the black leather cloak. He had thrown back the wolf-fur hood of his long jacket, and his rough-cut hair whipped about his face.

"Here," said Yao sharply to the Mongol, "let's have no insolence."

The Mongol spoke again, in his own tongue, spat, and turned away.

Zangi-Ragozh knew enough of the language to be able to say, "I intended no slight to you, worthy traveler. My company and I are under orders from Chang'an to make haste there, and our journey has been longer than anyone expected it to be, so we are trying to make good time now."

The Mongol stared at Zangi-Ragozh, dumbfounded to hear Mongolian come from a Western foreigner. "Where did you learn to speak?"

"Your language?" Zangi-Ragozh considered his response, selecting the most basic answer. "I studied it for a time at Cambaluc and Kumul."

The Mongol regarded him thoughtfully. "Your ancestors have not lived for four hundred generations with turtles."

Jong sputtered an oath. "Is *that* what you said?"

The Mongol shrugged. "I admit I was wrong. He is no kin of turtles." He cocked his chin toward the river. "The ferry is almost here."

Zangi-Ragozh knew that an accusation of living with turtles was one of the most profound insults any Chinese could be given, so he said in Mongolian, "Since I am a foreigner, I am not offended."

The Mongol looked at Jong and Yao. "I was mistaken in my—"

The sound of a tuneless horn announced the arrival of the ferry, and all the slights were forgotten as the waiting line of travelers jostled for position to get onto the ferry, all the while leaving space for those crossing from the northern bank to disembark. One of the asses became vexed and lashed out with hooves and teeth, only to be called to order with a series of blows from a drover's whip.

As the front of the ferry was let down to make a ramp for the passengers, four of the six ferrymen jumped ashore and began to collect the fares from those waiting. Zangi-Ragozh held out the string of silver cash, saying, "This is to ensure passage for my wagons, my men, and our horses."

The ferryman stared at the money. "This is much more than the usual cost."

Yao intervened. "We are on an urgent mission, and it is worth paying a little more not to have to wait any longer than necessary."

"Yes," said Zangi-Ragozh. "If you have to require any of those here to wait for the next crossing, we would prefer it not be our company."

"We will assist in loading the ferry," Yao said. "And if you need any assistance during the crossing, we will provide it." He glanced at Zangi-Ragozh. "It is your order, is it not?"

"Yes, if the ferrymen or the waterman require any aid," he answered.

"That may speed matters along." Yao lowered his voice. "If more money is needed, let us know at once."

"I'll tell the master waterman," said the ferryman, slipping the string of cash onto his wrist before going to speak to the Mongol.

"What do you think?" Ro-shei asked as the ferrymen went on about their work, one guiding travelers off the ferry, the other two tending to those about to board.

"I think he is satisfied," said Yao. "We will be taken across this trip."

Zangi-Ragozh's gray began to sidle and he tightened his hands on the reins. "I had best dismount, so I can lead her onto the ferry," he said, and disengaged his right foot from the foot-loop, swung his leg over the mare's rump, kicked his left foot out of the foot-loop, and took hold of the saddle to lower himself to the ground. The mare minced in place, huffing her displeasure. "Be calm, Shooting Star," he said, going to the gray's head and stroking her cheek until she lowered her head, her nose touching his shoulder. "Are the leads for the spare horses well-tied?" he asked Ro-shei. "We do not want any trouble loading them onto the ferry."

"I'll check," he offered, and prepared to do as he said.

"No. Gien should attend to it." Zangi-Ragozh spoke more loudly than before.

"If that is what you want," said Gien, and he scrambled to follow these orders.

"It is not what I want, it is what will calm the horses. They're restive," said Zangi-Ragozh.

"Because of the thunder," said Jong, and coughed.

"If that is what it was," said Zangi-Ragozh.

"What else could it be?" asked Yao.

"I do not know," Zangi-Ragozh said, and prepared to follow the farmer and his goats onto the ferry, taking care not to rush the animals ahead of him. Reaching the ramp onto the deck of the ferry, he guided his horse carefully, steeling himself against the discomfort of the river's current. In spite of his native earth lining the soles of his boots, he felt sapped of strength, and he took hold of the railing at the side of the ferry to steady himself, keeping his mare's reins tightly in his grasp. He heard the rest of his company begin to move, and he took satisfaction in realizing that by midday he would once again be on solid ground.

Ro-shei came up beside him, leading his chestnut. "Do you need anything?" he asked in Byzantine Greek.

"Dry land and a willing partner," said Zangi-Ragozh with a faint, wry smile.

"You will have the dry land soon enough. The willing partner is up to you." Ro-shei looked over his shoulder at their wagons being crowded forward, their spare horses lined up behind the wagons. "Jong is not well."

"Yes, I know," said Zangi-Ragozh, leaning on the railing but keeping his gaze fixed on the far bank. He held his mare's reins securely so that she had to stand quietly.

"The fever has reached his lungs."

"It has," Zangi-Ragozh agreed. "His herbs have kept the fever in check, but he is too worn-down, and now he is in real danger."

"Will you order him to take your sovereign remedy?" Ro-shei asked.

There was a flurry of scuffles among the animals as the noble-woman's escort came aboard behind the Mongol and his ponies, taking care to surround her carriage so that no one would catch so much as a glimpse of her. This was followed by a hurried discussion among the ferrymen and the master waterman, and then the oldest of the ferrymen pronounced the craft fully laden and blew his horn, signaling that the ferry was about to cast off.

The scruffy men with the ass-drawn wagon shouted their exasperation at being left behind as the ramp was drawn up and secured; one of them went so far as to threaten to shoot the master waterman if they were not taken aboard.

"If the ferry is over-loaded, it will sink," shouted the oldest of the ferrymen as they pulled away from the shore.

"You could make room for us!" bellowed one of the men on the shore.

"Next crossing!" the ferryman promised him, and turned his back on the shore, giving his attention to the chain a short distance below the water that marked the line of passage to the other side.

The master waterman hung on the tiller, his massive shoulders hunched with holding the ferry on course to the opposite shore. All but two of the ferrymen worked their long poles, digging them into the bed of the river and trudging the length of the barge to propel it forward; the fifth stood in the flat prow of the boat, prepared to reach down into the river to snag the chain if they should start to drift off-course. Water splashed onto the deck of the ferry and was swept off by the youngest of the ferrymen, using a stiff broom and a shallow pail to accomplish his work.

"It's choppy," said Yao, addressing Zangi-Ragozh from the driving-box of his wagon.

"That it is," said Zangi-Ragozh, not wanting to dwell on the state of the river.

"I've been in much worse crossings," Yao boasted. "This is only bouncing a bit. I have seen it when the boats bucked like wild horses."

"No doubt," said Zangi-Ragozh, swallowing hard.

"The waterman knows his trade," Yao went on approvingly. "See how he holds the course."

"He does his work very well," Zangi-Ragozh said, sagging against the railing.

"Shall I take your reins?" Ro-shei offered, switching the reins of his chestnut to his left hand and holding out his right for the mare's.

"If you would. I will only make her more uneasy if I continue to hold them." He gave the reins to Ro-shei and wobbled as the ferry lurched over a rough patch of water.

"Are you all right, my master?" Ro-shei asked, attempting to hold the two horses and assist Zangi-Ragozh at the same time.

"I will be," he answered.

Yao watched this with ill-disguised dismay. "Is something wrong?"

Zangi-Ragozh managed a wave of dismissal. "Nothing dangerous. Those of my blood are inclined to sickness on the water."

"A strange affliction," said Yao.

"Certainly an inconvenient one, but not dangerous," said Zangi-Ragozh.

"All sickness can be dangerous," said Yao, adding the reproof, "You may cause harm to us, if you are ill."

"You will see how quickly I recover when we arrive on the far bank," Zangi-Ragozh assured him.

Yao was not yet satisfied. "You have crossed streams and rivers before and I saw no sign of this weakness."

"Those crossings were short, or the water was not flowing as strongly as this river," Zangi-Ragozh said, and clenched his jaw. He wanted to lie down out of the sun, on his bed that lay atop a chest of his native earth, but he knew this would create suspicions he did not want to address, so he remained where he was and did his best to resist the vertigo that pulled at him.

"Still, it is a strange affliction for one who travels as much as you do," Yao observed.

"I fear I must agree," said Zangi-Ragozh, and fell silent while the ferry continued on across the river. By the time the ramp was let down, he was dizzy and did not trust himself to mount his mare until his company was some little distance from the river. Walking the half-li restored him somewhat, so that he was able to vault into the saddle with the appearance of his habitual ease.

Ro-shei, who had been walking beside him, also got onto his chestnut, remarking as he did, "I believe we can reach Tai-Sho by nightfall, if the weather remains clear."

"Tai-Sho is a reasonable distance," Zangi-Ragozh agreed. "Just over four li, as I understand."

"That is about right," said Gien.

"Then if we keep up a good pace, we should arrive shortly before sundown." Zangi-Ragozh had raised his voice so that Yao and Jong could hear him clearly.

"Yes," said Yao. "If the road is clear and there are no other delays." He paused. "They say there are robbers in the woods hereabouts."

"Then we will have to be careful going through them," said Zangi-Ragozh, and patted the curved Persian sword that hung from the pommel of his saddle. "Get the weapons out of the wagon and make sure you all have a sword and a dagger."

"I'll tend to that," Ro-shei offered.

"Thank you, old friend," said Zangi-Ragozh as he took his place ahead of the two wagons and the spare horses. He made a point of sitting very straight and being as alert as he possibly could, for it would not be provident to appear truly weakened by the river crossing. He shaded his eyes with his hand and put his mare into a jog-trot.

"The swords and daggers are distributed," said Ro-shei a bit later as he rode up next to Zangi-Ragozh.

"Excellent," Zangi-Ragozh approved, and settled into the routine of travel, keeping a wary eye out for marauders and other possible outlaws as he led the company through an arm of the forest. "How broad are these woods?" he called back to his companions.

"Almost a li," said Gien. "We should pass through them while the sun is still high."

"Prudent," said Zangi-Ragozh.

When they forded a stream, a while later, they paused to water the horses and to change teams and mounts.

"Does this water bother you?" Yao asked Zangi-Ragozh as he tightened the girth.

"Yes, it does. Not as much as the river did, or the ocean would do, but it makes me uncomfortable," Zangi-Ragozh admitted, patting Flying Cloud before he vaulted into the saddle; he had already secured Shooting Star's lead to the rear of the larger wagon, and so was impatient to be off.

Jong was still buckling on the harness of his second team, his face mottled and his breathing strained. He started to apologize, but broke off in a rattle of tight coughing. He clung to the neck of the nearest horse and tried to bring his spasm under control.

Zangi-Ragozh swung off his gelding and thrust the reins at Gien. "Tie him to the wagon with a lead," he ordered as he went to assist Jong to get into the wagon. "You should lie down and keep warm."

"I will be all right," Jong insisted even as Zangi-Ragozh lifted him with amazing ease onto the narrow cot behind the driving-box.

"As soon as you have had a chance to recover, no doubt you are right," said Zangi-Ragozh as he took Jong's place on the box. "Gien, make sure the harness is properly buckled. Ro-shei, if you will lead us?" He waited until Gien gave him a nod, then he signaled the team to set off.

"You should not be driving a wagon," Yao protested.

"Do you fear I cannot do it?" Zangi-Ragozh inquired. "For I assure you, I can."

Yao looked confused. "Nothing like that. It is just that a man of your position should not drive a wagon. Have Ro-shei do it."

"I think not," said Zangi-Ragozh. "If Jong should become worse, I want to be able to attend to him without delay, which I can do if I am able to watch him. Driving allows me to do this."

Ro-shei brought his horse alongside Zangi-Ragozh's wagon. "I will trade places with you, my master."

"Thank you, but there is no need," said Zangi-Ragozh, his punctilious response so firm that there could be no doubt as to his determination.

The gates of Tai-Sho stood open when Zangi-Ragozh's company arrived and paid the travelers' tax to enter. Directed to the center of the town, they chose the largest of the inns for the night and went about stalling their horses and storing the wagons, then carried Jong to a small room at the rear of the inn that was used for quarantine.

"I will send for a physician," the innkeeper declared as he saw Jong laid on the bed in his isolated room; the man was middle-aged and showed signs of prosperity in his dress that was belied by his pinched mouth.

"There is no need," said Zangi-Ragozh. "I have some knowledge of medicaments, and I am willing to tend him."

"Foreign medicaments!" the innkeeper scoffed. "I will send a servant to Kuo and tell him that he must come promptly." He glowered at Zangi-Ragozh. "This man is Chinese. He must have Chinese medicines."

"If he must, he must," said Zangi-Ragozh. "But I will attend him until the physician arrives."

"That will not excuse you paying for his care," the innkeeper warned.

"He is my servant," said Zangi-Ragozh. "I will be responsible for any charges his care incurs."

"If Kuo agrees, then it is all right with me," said the innkeeper, and summoned one of his slaves to carry a message to Physician Kuo, telling him to assert that the need was urgent and required the physician himself and not one of his apprentices.

The man who arrived with the slave was a blocky individual with thick fingers and a crusty manner and the look of one used to being obeyed. Kuo Li-Dan contemplated Jong as he took his pulse, saying when he had done, "This man is very ill, perhaps beyond saving."

"His lungs are inflamed," said Zangi-Ragozh, "and they are congested."

Kuo looked a bit surprised. "Yes. Fire and wind have invaded him." He tugged on his long mustache. "An astute observation, foreigner. Have you had some training in treating the sick?"

Zangi-Ragozh ducked his head. "I have." He did not mention that he had spent more than eight centuries at the Temple of Imhotep, rising from slave to High Priest in that time.

The innkeeper, who had lingered in the doorway, regarded Zangi-Ragozh narrowly. "A merchant who is a physician?"

"Merchants are often wholly on their own, and if any injury or illness occurs, they must deal with it," Zangi-Ragozh said smoothly. "Knowledge of medicaments has proved extremely useful to me."

"You must be a good pupil, and your teachers more able than many foreigners are," said Kuo. "It has seemed to me that foreigners are not skilled in such matters. They rely upon the power of the Immortals or their powerless gods; they depend upon amulets for magic and not teas for the body." He laid his hand on Jong's chest and put all his attention on what he felt. "I will leave a tea that he is to drink as frequently as he can be roused to drink it. It will balance the heat and cold in his body, which should help him to fight the inflamation."

"While I am sure you are most diligent in your treatment, is there nothing more to be done?" Zangi-Ragozh asked, and went on before Kuo could answer. "For I have a remedy that may be of some help."

"Foreign potions!" Kuo glowered. "What sort of preposterous-ness are you—"

"It has been helpful before, where there is fever," said Zangi-Ragozh. "As this man is in my employ, I believe I am obliged to do all I can to help him recover from his illness."

Kuo was wary. "You learned of this where you were trained to treat the sick?"

"I did," said Zangi-Ragozh, and did not elaborate. "I have used it on many different injuries and illnesses."

"Has it been beneficial?" Kuo pursued.

"Yes, it has, or I would not recommend trying it," Zangi-Ragozh replied, doing his utmost to remain respectful, but growing impatient with Kuo.

The physician bent over Jong and smelled his breath. "If you can administer your remedy so that it will not keep this man from drinking the tea I will prepare for him, then I will not oppose your using it. I will call tomorrow to see what progress has occurred." He straightened up. "If there is no improvement, it will not be on the account of my tea."

"Certainly not," said Zangi-Ragozh, realizing that Kuo did not ex-pect Jong to survive and was seeking the chance to lay the reason for his demise at Zangi-Ragozh's door.

"So long as you tend to him yourself, I will not send any of my ap-prentices to treat this man," Kuo announced as much for the benefit of the innkeeper as Zangi-Ragozh. "By midday tomorrow, I will call here again, to see how he is responding. If he takes a turn for the worse, have one of the servants here inform me of it."

"I will be most grateful to you," said Zangi-Ragozh, and took a string of silver cash from his sleeve, removing six of the coins and handing them to Kuo. "This should cover the cost of the tea." It was half again as much as such teas usually cost, and both knew it.

Kuo slipped the money into his wallet and almost smiled. "I will need a large pot," he informed the innkeeper. "And it must be filled with fresh-drawn water."

The innkeeper hastily retreated to the kitchen to follow Kuo's instructions.

"He has been ailing for four days that I know of," Zangi-Ragozh told Kuo.

"When did he begin to cough?" Kuo asked.

"I first noticed it in the evening, three days ago. He may have had trouble during the day, but it was not sufficiently severe to alarm me." Zangi-Ragozh was chagrined by this admission. "With the weather so harsh, coughs are not so uncommon."

"And not all indicate heat in the lungs," Kuo agreed. "Do you have others with you?"

"Three other men," Zangi-Ragozh said.

"Do any of them show signs of the illness?" Kuo had started toward the door. "Should you like me to see any of them while I am here?"

Zangi-Ragozh fitted one hand into the other. "I would be most appreciative," he said, thinking of the extra fees Kuo would earn for this effort. "My men are in the dining room still, lingering over their suppers. You can find them there, all but my manservant, who is a foreigner like me; he is in the stable seeing to our horses and the wagons."

"He sounds to be in good health if he is doing such work," said Kuo, almost out the door.

"I would venture to say that he has less need of your skills than the others," said Zangi-Ragozh, laying his hand on Jong's forehead. "I'll remain here while you prepare your tea."

"That will suit me very well," said Kuo, and left Zangi-Ragozh alone with the suffering Jong. Only when the physician returned with his tea did Zangi-Ragozh slip away to fetch a vial of his sovereign remedy, an opalescent liquid that seemed clear when held up to the light. Kuo was just finishing tipping some of the hot tea down Jong's throat. "Let me look at that," he ordered, holding out his hand for the glass vial.

Zangi-Ragozh held it out. "The stopper has to be unscrewed."

"A good precaution," said Kuo, twisting the stopper and sniffing the liquid. "Nothing noxious, but still, an unusual odor."

"That it has," Zangi-Ragozh agreed, and waited while Kuo made up his mind.

"I can find no harm in it," the physician announced. "But administer it only after the tea is taken."

"Certainly," said Zangi-Ragozh. "I'll keep a record of when anything is given to Jong."

Kuo nodded. "A wise precaution." He made a polite gesture of farewell and went to the door. "I will look in on your other men. If I find nothing to alarm me, I will depart. If either of the two is sick, then I will come to consult you."

"Thank you." He lifted the oil-lamp. "This should burn most of the night."

"Very good," said Kuo, and left Zangi-Ragozh to minister to Jong.

Text of a letter from Captain Tieh Wei-Djieh of the merchant ship *Golden Moon* at Kuang-Chou to the foreign merchant Zangi-Ragozh at Yang-Chau; never delivered.

To the most illustrious foreigner Zangi-Ragozh, the greetings of his Captain, Tieh Wei-Djieh of the Golden Moon, *still at port in Kuang-Chou, at the end of the Fortnight of the Prosperity Lanterns.*

I am pleased to inform you that the Golden Moon *is once again ready to put to sea, and under other circumstances I would leave port within three days of entrusting this to Zhi Fung-Ho of the courier ship* Frigate-bird, *but I am disinclined to begin a voyage in such seas and under such skies as those that have marked this place for more than eight days, and I cannot but think that you would concur with my determination were you here to see for yourself what has occurred here. It is a most difficult time, with terrible tides and flocks of dead birds blown on the high winds until they fall into the ocean for sharks to dine on. The sharks themselves are hardly safe in these times.*

The tumultuous seas have increased dangerously following a deafening and prolonged explosion that came from the southwest nine days ago. No thunder was ever half so loud as that. It was approaching midday, and the sound was more dreadful than anything I have heard before. The first report was hideous, but there was an ongoing roar that has not entirely ceased yet. As if in answer to this horrendous blast, by evening the seas had risen and done damage to the docks here, making all the sailors I know stupefied with fear. The docks a short distance from the one where we are tied up were reduced to splinters, and the warehouses are hardly more than bits of wood clinging to their pilings. Some people have been washed out to sea, and it is believed that they are dead. The Golden Moon *sustained no significant damage, but many other ships were not so fortunate, and dozens of them were broken apart during the first onslaught of the waves. The seas are still running dangerously high, and so nothing much can be done to save or repair the ships, or the docks.*

Since that day, the skies have grown dark and remained so, as if storm clouds are gathering. Lightning accompanies them, and they are regarded as the most distressing of all omens. The odor of sulfur is everywhere, and no one can say why, but everyone knows it is a bad sign. Already fish are dying, their decaying bodies washing in on the tide. Some claim that this is the end of the world, and some say it is the gods making war on earth.

I should report that there has been trouble inland here, as well. These dark and lowering clouds have dropped yellow rain that has burned the fields, scalded livestock, and made wells all but undrinkable. Everyone who has gone out of the city says that the farmers are terrified at the thought of what is coming, for they cannot plant their spring crops in fields that are blighted by the yellow rain. I have no information to give about any of your other ships that may have been caught up in this appalling storm. No ships have come into port since the storm began, and no ships have left until the courier decided to depart today. I only hope that I may find some reliable news, which I shall then pass on to you as soon as I have verification as well as rumors to pass on.

In the meantime, I ask the God of Sailors to protect us all, and the Lord of the Sea to quiet the waters so that we may safely return home with our cargo and our men safe.

Tieh Wei-Djieh
Captain, the Golden Moon
(his chop)

5

One of the caravans had come farther than the rest; the leader of the procession of donkeys and camels was Persian, and two of his men came from the region on the west side of the Black Sea. This caravan was most carefully watched by the officers of the Tribunal of Dong-Lin, for it was rare that such merchants penetrated China as deeply as they had, or had brought so much red amber from the wild peoples of the far northwest. Three customs officials crowded around the Bactrian camels and demanded of the merchants to be told what the animals were carrying, beyond the two casks of amber.

"They carry furs for writing brushes, and dyes, among other things," said the leader in poor Chinese. "We have some trinkets, too. We cannot carry bulky merchandise, or we risk losing it to the bandits along the road, and we cannot transport anything very heavy, for the sake of our animals."

"Is that all? What else do you bring to sell? Answer, you dog's head!" the Tribunal Guard ordered as he slapped his leather trousers with a short whip, grinning at the threat he was making.

"I have an account of it all with me," said the Persian, reaching into his fox-fur, long vest and pulling out a folded cotton cloth on which he had written his lists. "Here. If you have anyone who knows Persian, you will know all."

The most august of the customs officials came up to the Persian. "You would do well to speak respectfully, foreigner."

With a shrug the Persian gestured his greeting in the Chinese fashion although he spoke in his native language. "I ask your pardon. It has been a long journey, and, what with the winter going on longer than ususal, I, my men, and my animals are tired."

The Guard reached out and grabbed the Persian by the shoulders. "You will speak in a civilized tongue, foreigner!"

"My Chinese is poor," he said in Chinese.

"You're right—it is poor." The senior customs official looked to his comrades. "Is there someone in Dong-Lin who could interpret this man's statements for us? Someone who speaks Chinese better than he does?"

"Among the foreign merchants?" The Guard looked about without any real hope of finding one.

"Of course, or one of the innkeepers," said another of the customs officers. "Whomelse would we call upon?"

The Persian shrugged again. "I have only just arrived, and this place is new to me. I have no . . . no idea of what merchants are here, and who among them knows Persian." He was reaching the limits of his ability to speak.

The senior customs official cut the Persian off with a motion of his moon fan that was marked with his chop. "A sensible solution, it seems to me." He gestured to the Guard. "Go about the area and find out if any of the merchants speaks this man's tongue—"

"Persian," he interjected.

"Persian," said the customs officer. He nodded to his comrades. "Let us inspect what we can and make a record of what we find."

"That is most reasonable," said the more eager of his two colleagues. "Shall I summon a scribe?"

"Not quite yet, I think. I think it would be best to wait until we can have somewhat clearer discourse with the Persian." He indicated a protected arcade. "Sit there, foreigner, until we tell you otherwise."

The Persian sighed. "And my men? They are tired and hungry."

"Send them to the Inn of the Two Camels." He pointed to the hostelry. "They cater to foreigners there, and we will know where to find your men."

"That I will," said the Persian, calling out instructions to his men in Persian, and, for the sake of the customs officials, ending in Chinese, "Go to the inn. I will join you when I am through here."

The man from Odessus on the Black Sea answered in his outlandish tongue for all the men, "As you order; you will find us there, refreshing ourselves," and signaled the rest of the men to hand over their animals to the grooms of the customs officials. There was a ruffle of activity as the men did as they had been told, most of them speaking languages the officials could not identify.

When his men had departed, the Persian bowed in the manner of his people. "I am at your service," he said in Chinese.

"As you should be," said the senior customs official, and signaled his assistants to look over the casks, chests, and bales on the pack animals, putting identifying marks on them, and numbers.

For a short while everyone remained silent, then the Guard returned from the second foreigners' inn, a black-clad stranger at his heels. "I have found a man who says he knows Persian."

The newcomer put his left hand into his right and spoke to the senior official. "This humble merchant is Zangi-Ragozh, whose business is in Yang-Chau and is here in Dong-Lin for a day, going from Yang-Chau to Chang'an. What may this respectful foreigner have the honor of doing for you?"

The senior customs official looked Zangi-Ragozh up and down. "Do you speak Persian?"

"Among other languages, yes, I do," said Zangi-Ragozh.

He glanced over at the Persian. "Then explain matters with this man, starting with registering a name."

"It will be my honor," said Zangi-Ragozh, and turned to the Persian, saying in his language, "I am here to serve as translator and interpreter. I am a merchant and a foreigner, like yourself, although my homeland is farther west than yours. I will help you deal with these men." He saw the Persian nod. "To begin, there are a few things the officials must settle before they can assess your merchandise. What is your name?"

"Ahmi Buthatani," he answered, glad to hear someone address him in fluent Persian, and now feeling more assured that he would be treated fairly.

Zangi-Ragozh frowned. "Ahmi is no problem, but Buthatani is."

"Why would it be?"

"You have not come far into China before, have you?" he asked, and not waiting for an answer went on, "In China, away from the borders, foreigners are required to register a name that can be written in Chinese but is plainly not Chinese. Ahmi can easily be written. Your family name is a problem; too long and not easily expressed in Chinese characters. Tsani would be acceptable, I think, if you would not mind using it."

Buthatani looked baffled. "Why should they need this?"

"So that foreigners may be readily identified, and so that everyone may be able to address them properly, which is of great importance in this country," said Zangi-Ragozh. "Would Ahmi-Tsani be acceptable to you?"

"If it is necessary, then do it, just so they are satisfied," said Buthatani, shaking his head in disbelief. "They are very strange here."

"No stranger than we are to them," said Zangi-Ragozh. "Which is saying a great deal."

For the first time Buthatani smiled. "Truly, foreigner."

Zangi-Ragozh turned to the customs official. "This foreigner from Persia will be recorded as Ahmi-Tsani. It is acceptable to him."

"It is acceptable to us," said the senior official. "Bring the scribe," he said to one of his assistants. "We have work to do."

"Is this usual?" Ahmi-Tsani asked Zangi-Ragozh. "I have been to Wu-Wei twice and never had to answer so many questions, nor accommodate the Chinese to this extent."

"Yes, it is usual. Even in Holin-Gol there are stricter rules than in Wu-Wei. I know that along the western border there is less attention given to these requirements, but you are a long way from the Great Wall, and the forms of commerce are very proscribed here." He indicated one of two inns facing the market square. "I and my companions are at the Caravan Bell."

"The customs officials already recommended I send my men to the Inn of the Two Camels," Ahmi-Tsani said.

"Probably because of your beasts; there are better barns and pens at the Inn of the Two Camels than at most inns," said Zangi-Ragozh.

"Find out what he is doing here," the customs official requested.

Zangi-Ragozh complied at once. "What has brought you so far south?"

Ahmi-Tsani tugged at his short beard. "Dreadful weather; this year has been harder than any I can remember. Surely you have heard about it? There is snow falling in the north, far too much for this time of year, and with no letup coming that I can see. The snow is not as it has been in previous years. It is unnatural, yellow in color, and it gives off an unpleasant odor."

"What is he saying?" the senior customs official asked sharply.

Zangi-Ragozh replied at once, "That he has come down from the north because of unseasonable snow that is of a yellow hue."

The officials laughed to show their disbelief. "Snow at this time of year, and yellow," said the senior official. "No one else had made such a report. What nonsense is this?"

"How many merchants have recently arrived from the north ahead of this man?" Zangi-Ragozh asked. "If this Persian is the first, his account is the more important, for it heralds more to come."

"Why do you think so, foreigner?" the customs official asked haughtily.

Understanding just enough of what the official said to be af-fronted, Ahmi-Tsani demanded of Zangi-Ragozh, "Does he doubt me? Why would I lie? What good would it do me?"

"Do not fret," Zangi-Ragozh advised. "Let me try to explain this to them."

"Very well," said Ahmi-Tsani, mastering his temper with an effort. "But I will not be called a liar, not for anything. You make sure you tell him that."

"I will do my best," Zangi-Ragozh assured the Persian.

"What is he telling you now?" the customs official asked sharply. "More inventions, no doubt. Yellow snow indeed."

"Official Lang," said Zangi-Ragozh, addressing the senior man with an elaborate display of respect, "this Persian has no reason to report falsely, and you have an obligation to keep records of possible hazards to travelers. I believe you would be well-advised to listen to what he has to say and to verify it with others, for if he is telling you the truth, there will be others coming here from the north. You know that spring has been very slow in starting everywhere and that the clouds are more persistent than in most years, and the rain they have brought has made travel slower than usual."

"Thank you; I know my duty," said Lang with great formality.

"And surely you know the importance of serving the orders of the government in these difficult times. So long as regional officials—honorable men like you—attend to their appointed tasks, the country will continue to hold together, no matter what changes may befall the Vermilion Brush." Zangi-Ragozh ducked his head respectfully.

Lang Bao-Jai glared at Zangi-Ragozh but nodded. "What you say is so."

"Is there a difficulty?" Ahmi-Tsani asked uneasily. He had been able to follow some of what was said; it was sufficient to make him anxious.

"Not for you," said Zangi-Ragozh. "I am only reminding Lang of his responsibilities, and of the honor in which his family is held." He looked over at Lang and went on in his most courteous manner, "Danger to travelers is always an intrusion to trade, but it is better that such dangers are known than that they are overlooked, for any laxness can only damage the trade that is the very heart of the Middle Kingdom."

"True enough," said Lang stiffly. He was still somewhat surprised that Zangi-Ragozh was so knowledgeable, but he did his utmost to take this in stride. "Tell the foreigner Ahmi-Tsani that I will hear his report and submit his information to the Magistrate."

Zangi-Ragozh did as he was told and added, "It will be best if you tell all you know as concisely as you can. If you have rumors to pass on, make sure you say they are rumors. You do not want to give Lang any reason to doubt you."

"That is apparent," said Ahmi-Tsani, his sarcasm poorly concealed. He looked over at Lang and said in the best Chinese he could summon up, "I will deem it a sign of esteem to answer all questions put to me."

"Well done," Zangi-Ragozh approved, adding for Lang's benefit, "I know you will make every effort to convey accurate information."

"That I will," said Ahmi-Tsani. "In the meantime, I would be grateful for a moment with my men, to have something to eat and to ease my aching back." He stretched conspicuously to show that he needed a period of recuperation.

Lang nodded, having understood the gist of what Ahmi-Tsani had said. "I will come to the Inn of the Two Camels after the evening rice. We will need to reserve a parlor. You, foreigner," he said to Zangi-Ragozh. "You attend to securing the room, and present yourself for our interview."

"Of course," said Zangi-Ragozh, and said to Ahmi-Tsani in Persian, "You would do well to have a bath and change clothes before Lang comes this evening. Better to be too gracious and accommodating than not gracious and accommodating enough."

"I have every intention of washing the mud from me, and putting on clean garments, for my own comfort. These itch like little demons." He copied Zangi-Ragozh's salutation to Lang and his two underlings, then cocked his head in the direction of the travelers' inns. "Would you care to join me? I would be delighted to have you as my guest."

"Thank you, but no. I have companions of my own who are waiting for me. One of them is convalescing from a bad fever, and he may need attention." Zangi-Ragozh paused, then said, "I appreciate your invitation, and I will come with you long enough to arrange for the parlor Lang wants. Then I must return to my comrades."

"Just so," said Ahmi-Tsani, and lengthened his stride.

Once the arrangements had been made and paid for with the landlord of the Inn of the Two Camels, Zangi-Ragozh went back to the Caravan Bell, where he found Ro-shei doing his best to calm Jong and Yao, who were uneasy about the attention Zangi-Ragozh had received from the customs officials. Gien was in the stables, tending to the horses, tack, and harness.

"What did that tiresome official want?" Yao asked as soon as Zangi-Ragozh entered the main room of the two he had paid for; it was small but it had a little stove for heat and to prepare tea, and there were two benches along with a pair of beds, as well as a long, low table. In the adjoining room were four beds; Jong, Yao, and Gien occupied three of them, and the fourth held three large chests. Oiled paper covered the windows, and there were shutters that could be closed and locked at night. The room was warm enough that Yao had taken off his cloak, but Jong still wore his.

"He needed the help of someone who speaks Persian as well as Chinese," said Zangi-Ragozh.

"Do you think that notice will benefit you?" Yao scoffed. "You don't want the officials looking into your business; no one does, especially on the road, for it always means more delays. Besides, they're sure to find a new tax or duty to impose upon you if you catch their notice."

"Ah, but if I do them a service, their attention may be more favorable," said Zangi-Ragozh, and went on more briskly, "Have you asked for supper yet?"

"I will carry down the order as soon as Jong and Yao have chosen," said Ro-shei.

Jong thought about his answer; since he had begun to recover from his heat-congested lungs, he had regarded Zangi-Ragozh as something of a magician and constantly tried to show his utmost respect. "If you would tell us what you would prefer we eat, then we—"

"Oh, God of Longevity, give me patience!" Yao exclaimed. "Jong, what is this? Our employer has used his foreign tricks on you, and nothing more."

"On that, Yao, you and I are agreed," said Zangi-Ragozh.

"It wasn't trickery," said Jong. "You did not have the Lord of the Dead singing your name, Yao. I did. And what Zangi-Ragozh did brought me back to health."

"Not magically," said Zangi-Ragozh, aware how suspicious Chinese officials could be about foreigners who practiced unknown arts. "I am an alchemist, and that gives me some knowledge of medicaments, that is all."

"Don't alchemists make weapons?" Yao was suddenly curious.

"Some do," said Zangi-Ragozh.

"No wonder the Wen Emperor wishes to see you," Yao exclaimed. "This explains everything. And here I thought you were just pottering among your potions and powders!"

"You're disrespectful," Jong reprimanded him.

Zangi-Ragozh wanted to change the subject. "If you want to serve me a good turn, Jong, say nothing of your treatment or any of my private skills to the customs officials, or any other authority in the town."

"Why should I not?" Jong looked shocked at this suggestion.

"Because the less the officials know of me beyond what goods I carry, the better it will be for all of us," said Zangi-Ragozh.

"Is there anything wrong with what you do?" asked Jong.

"No; but the officials might not see it that way. Why do you ask?" Zangi-Ragozh looked over at Jong. "To whom have you talked?"

Jong shrugged and pressed his hands together. "I told the landlord that you had given me a remedy that ended my illness."

"Praise may be misunderstood," said Zangi-Ragozh, who had seen more than his share of such misunderstandings over the centuries. He dismissed this with a wave of his hand that he hoped showed none of the dismay he felt. "I should bathe, and then I must go to the Inn of the Two Camels to assist Official Lang in questioning Ahmi-Tsani. Ro-shei, when you order the meal for the men, will you reserve the bath-house for me? Take silver to pay for it all."

"That I will," said Ro-shei, holding out his hand for the short string of silver cash Zangi-Ragozh handed to him. He glanced at the two men, his concern routine but unfeigned. "Would braised lamb and onions do for a start? Rice bowls? And a variety of dumplings?"

Yao nodded. "You know what would suit us. Pork of some kind, and the lamb would be nice, and a good, sustaining soup. Nothing fancy, but more than bean-paste in water. Something with a little fire in it, to keep out the cold. The dumplings can be spicy, as well. They make peppery ones in this part of the Middle Kingdom, and they whet the appetite." He laughed at Jong, who regarded him in disgust. "We must eat, Brother Jong. You know that as well as anyone." He nodded to Zangi-Ragozh. "So long as we don't starve, you may keep your customs and dine in private."

"Rice wine and mountain tea," added Jong, as close to an apology as he could manage. "If you have no objection, Worthy Foreigner?"

"Why should I have one now, when I have not had any before?" Zangi-Ragozh asked wryly. "By all means, order what pleases you."

"Then, if there is any minced beef, I'd like that as well," Jong dared to suggest, and saw Zangi-Ragozh signal his consent.

"I'll have it sent up, and the bath-house reserved. I'll let Gien know that supper is coming." Ro-shei nodded once and let himself out of the room.

"These are very good rooms," said Yao as soon as Ro-shei was gone.

"Gracious of you to say so," said Zangi-Ragozh as he went to take out a clean sen-hsien, this one embellished with silver embroidery on the black silk, showing his eclipse as a decorative border at hem and cuffs. "I will wear this after I bathe," he announced.

"It should impress the customs official," said Yao as he hunched over and crossed his arms so that he could rub his shoulders. "Weather like this! It wears on me."

"On all of us," said Jong. He rose and stretched. "I hope to sleep well tonight."

"I hope we all do," said Zangi-Ragozh with an irony that was lost on Jong and Yao. Then he gathered up a small case and left the men alone while he went down to the bath-house.

When he returned, he was carefully groomed, his hair damp and combed into neat waves, his face newly shaved. As Ro-shei helped him dress and shielded him from the curious eyes of Yao, Jong, and Gien, who sat over their rice-bowls eating their supper, he said, "I will probably not be back until late. If you will see to everything in my absence."

"Of course," said Ro-shei.

"I need not have asked." Zangi-Ragozh hesitated, then removed a seal-ring from his wallet and slipped it onto his hand. "As bona fides," he added in Imperial Latin.

"You are uneasy," Ro-shei observed, smoothing the hang of the silk, and speaking the same language.

"Yes. This weather troubles me, and now the report of yellow snow—" He broke off, shaking his head.

"Do you believe the account?" Ro-shei asked, his own skepticism revealed in the tone of his voice.

"Yes," he answered slowly. "I do. It is so unlikely that I cannot think how the Persian would come to invent such a tale."

"Have you ever seen such a thing before?" Ro-shei asked.

"Not yellow snow, but something like it, and so have you," he added. "Do you recall when we were at Lago Comus, when Vesuvius erupted?"

"I recall," said Ro-shei, his mouth set in a severe line.

"There was ash falling from heavy clouds," said Zangi-Ragozh.

"Not yellow snow," said Ro-shei.

"No, not yellow snow," Zangi-Ragozh agreed. "But that was high summer—August—and still, the ash blighted some of the crops."

"And there were unseasonable storms," said Ro-shei. "I take your meaning. But what would be the source? And what would turn the snow yellow? There is no volcano in this region, nor have there been any accounts of one, and no peasants fleeing ruined land. There are no rumors of such an event."

"What are you talking about?" Yao inquired, downing most of a cup of wine.

"Hazards of travel," said Zangi-Ragozh in Chinese. "I hope the Persian can tell me more this evening." He looked over Ro-shei's shoulder. "They're restless," he added, once again in Latin.

"It could be a problem."

"It could," Zangi-Ragozh agreed, and held up his hand. "If I did not feel the lack of sustenance, I would wait, but such opportunities may not come again for several days, and I would prefer not to rely completely upon the horses."

"Then you will try to—"

"—to acquire nourishment," said Zangi-Ragozh quickly. "When I have finished with Official Lang, I will take a turn about the town. Official Lang may have one of his assistants watching me, and I would rather he find out as little as possible about me, so I will avoid women's establishments. I have already drawn too much attention to myself, and Jong's obliging boasts on my behalf will only make things worse if there is an inquiry."

"Do you think there will be?" Ro-shei asked, speaking Chinese again as a knock sounded at the door.

"I trust not, but I would be foolish not to be prepared," Zangi-Ragozh said, also in Chinese, then raised his voice. "Who is it?"

"I bring two more jars of wine," called a voice from outside.

Yao spoke up. "I asked the waiter for them when he brought our food."

Ro-shei went to let the man in. "Put them down and tell me what to pay."

"The price paid for the meal more than covers it," said the waiter. "Your master must be a very prosperous merchant, to be as open-handed as he is."

"He is more than openhanded," Jong said, preparing to launch into a recitation; had he not caught the warning glance from Zangi-Ragozh, he would have said more, but stopped himself in time and pointed to the empty platters and bowls. "Just look how well he feeds us!"

"Shall I remove those?" the waiter asked, cocking his head toward the aftermath of supper.

"As they like," said Zangi-Ragozh, going past the waiter and out of the room. He made his way down two flights of stairs to the main hall-way, and along it out into the street, where the business of the day was coming to an end under a cloudy sunset. The Inn of the Two Camels was at the corner, and he walked quickly through the gathering dusk and into the hostelry, going directly to the parlor he had requested earlier that afternoon, noticing the strong odor of sandalwood in the main corridor as he went.

Ahmi-Tsani was there before him, in a sen-gai of curly shearling wool over a clean cotton robe of pale blue with a number of little brass buttons; clearly he intended to make a favorable impression on Official Lang. He rose from his low stool and offered Zangi-Ragozh a greeting in the Persian style, which Zangi-Ragozh returned. "You are good to come, and I thank you most heartily."

"I am glad to be able to assist you," said Zangi-Ragozh, "but it would be wiser to speak Chinese until Lang comes. You do not want it to be reported that those listening could not understand you."

"Oh? You think someone is listening?" Ahmi-Tsani asked.

"I think it very likely," said Zangi-Ragozh.

"But I don't speak Chinese well," Ahmi-Tsani reminded him.

"You speak it well enough for mild pleasantries, and that is all that are needed at present."

"If you think it best," said Ahmi-Tsani, shaking his head slowly. He motioned to one of two chairs drawn up near the fire. "Sit down."

"That I will," said Zangi-Ragozh, and settled back against the cushions. "This is very comfortable."

"Good," said Ahmi-Tsani, and went back to his stool. "When did you arrive here?"

"Shortly before midday."

"Today, then." For a short time, the Persian said nothing more, then asked, "Have you found travel hard?"

"Not precisely hard, but more trying than usual, what with the situation around Chang'an. Not all the fighting is over," said Zangi-Ragozh, considering his answer conscientiously. "And, as you know from your own experience, the weather has been a problem."

Ahmi-Tsani laughed aloud. "One may say that!"

"When did it turn, do you remember?" Zangi-Ragozh asked.

"Oh, over a fortnight ago, certainly. Perhaps three weeks." He folded his hands and looked steadily at Zangi-Ragozh. "You know something."

"I suspect something," Zangi-Ragozh corrected him with a self-deprecating turn of his hands, "and it is strange enough that I doubt my own assumptions, which I have no means to prove, in any case." He thought back to his journey from Yang-Chau and felt a quick, odd tweak of alarm.

"Do you say there was a change in the weather during your travels?" Ahmi-Tsani persisted. "Just as we experienced?"

"About three weeks ago? Yes. It seems that was about the time the clouds came. Shortly after we crossed the Crane River, spring faded."

Ahmi-Tsani frowned. "Three weeks, you say?"

"A few days less, but about that. I recall that after we crossed the river, there was a bad storm, and nothing improved after that." He thought a long moment, then gave a single, small shake of his head. "Well, it is not a thing any of us can change, whatever it is, and whatever its cause." Sitting forward in his seat, he put his mind to the immediate situation. "Let us consider how you are to win the good opinion of Official Lang."

Text of a letter from Professor Min Cho-Zhi at Yang-Chau to Zangi-Ragozh at Chang'an; delivered sixteen months after given to a merchant for delivery and never received.

To the most highly regarded foreign merchant Zangi-Ragozh, Professor Min Cho-Zhi sends his greeting and this report on the state of his property in Yang-Chau, with the assurance that the household continues as the merchant Zangi-Ragozh stipulated it should, and in accordance with the instructions he provided.

Jho Chieh-Jen, the steward, has informed me that the household has used more wood for fires and cooking than was anticipated would be needed. This is due to the lateness of the spring, but it is not cause for alarm, as the supply left was ample and could be used as steadily as it has been for another ten fortnights without impinging on the wood for winter. He also tells me that because of the cold, the trees in the orchard are late coming into bloom. There has been more rain than usual, and it has been less wholesome than in some years, which has caused concern among the men maintaining the orchard and gardens, for they tell Jho that some of the plants are dying, and the trees may not bear much fruit this year.

Sheh Tai-Jia reports that the first foal of the season has been born, but is not doing well, showing little inclination to be active, and preferring to remain at her dam's side; she does not thrive, and although she suckles, she shows little sign of flourishing. Now that two other mares are about to deliver their foals, Sheh is deeply troubled, because he is worried that the new foals may be as afflicted as this first one is. He wishes you to know that he will use all his skill to bring about better health in the foals, but that he fears this year may be a poor year in the stable.

Food in the markets is still quite expensive, for the farmers complain that their spring crops are slow in taking root, and that has meant dragging out the winter vegetables and the pickles for longer than Meng would like. He has drawn his own supply of rice and preserved fruits to improve the meals he serves, and the household remains properly fed, but without the variety of dishes usually available in the spring. Meng has taken to sending two of his assistants directly to the local farmers, to purchase food from them before they take it to market.

In other domestic concerns: I have taken the liberty of ordering repairs on the outer wall, for some of the stockade logs are rotting, their wood becoming porous and weak. If repairs are not undertaken quickly, the trouble will spread, and so I have ordered the work done, in the full conviction that it is what you would do if you were here. I am going to order regular inspections of the wall, just in case a beetle or other pest has got into the wood. If I have the wood inspected regularly, it may be possible to stop the damage before the stable or the house is damaged. If it seems necessary, I will expand the inspections to include the house and stable. Sheh and Jho both agree with this decision and have offered to help in the inspections.

I have received little news of your ships, although I am sent weekly reports by your senior clerk, Hu Bi-Da, providing a log of his activities and the developments at the warehouses and docks. He informs me that the Morning Star *is still in port, and that Captain I Mo-Ching is unwilling to put to sea while there are so many reports of storms. Hu reports that nine ships have been confirmed lost in these frightful storms—fortunately none of them yours—and there are rumors of many more, but there is as yet no way to obtain certain news.*

This completes the information I wish to convey. May the Gods of Good Fortune watch over you in your travels and bring you safely back to Yang-Chau, and may you prosper in Chang'an. Be certain that in your absence your affairs and property are being looked after honorably. I will report again in three or four fortnights, unless there is good reason to send you word before then.

> *Min Cho-Zhi, Professor*
> *(his chop)*

6

"We may still reach Lo-Yang by nightfall, don't you think?" said Jong, huddled on the driver's box of his wagon; although all his fever was gone, he still tired more quickly than the rest, and he was getting thinner. He glanced at the heavy clouds above, and the company of soldiers marching ahead of them on the road, and shook his head.

"We may," said Zangi-Ragozh from the back of Flying Cloud. He felt the cold less keenly than the rest, but he was glad of his leather sen-gai and curly lamb hat that shielded him against the stinging wind and persistent rain.

"Isn't this supposed to be spring?" Yao complained loudly from his place behind Jong's wagon, expecting no answer and getting none. "Where's the sun? Where are the blossoms?"

Zangi-Ragozh said nothing, making an effort to keep on the road without letting his horse get mired in the deep ruts. He glanced back to be sure Ro-shei was still in his position at the rear, behind Yao's wagon. He was growing uneasy, and what had been worry was turning to anxiety as the days passed and the weather grew steadily worse. "Lo-Yang is only two more li, and we have a few more hours of light."

"If the clouds part," said Jong with a kind of gloomy satisfaction. "The wind is growing worse, and the rain is increasing."

"So it is," said Zangi-Ragozh, aware that Gien had his hands full looking after the spare horses they were leading, for the approaching storm made the animals restless.

"Do you think you will be able to reach Chang'an before summer?" Jong went on.

"If the weather does not improve, there is not going to be a summer," said Zangi-Ragozh severely.

Jong shrugged fatalistically. "It might as well be the Fortnight of New Snows."

"True enough," said Zangi-Ragozh, not speaking the rest of his thoughts—that a year without a spring was also a year without a harvest, and that would mean famine.

"The army doesn't help, tearing up the roads and pillaging the farms," Jong continued as if taking satisfaction in this grim outlook.

"The army must eat, as must we all," said Zangi-Ragozh, feeling a pang of hunger; it had been six days since he had visited a woman in her sleep, and that encounter, sweetly poignant as it had been, no longer nourished him.

"At the cost of the rest of us. The army has the might to claim whatever it wants." Jong paused, then asked what had been on his mind. "Must we stay in Lo-Yang? With so many soldiers inside the walls, there could be troubles." He grew more forceful as he went on. "You know what soldiers are like."

"You're worried that we could become targets of . . . shall we say, excessive spirits?" Zangi-Ragozh suggested.

"It could be," said Jong. "Who in Lo-Yang would be willing to stop army men if they chose to rob us?"

This made some sense to Zangi-Ragozh. "It is a danger, but so is remaining in the countryside, for soldiers may well seek out small villages to seize food and livestock." He did not add *and women*.

"Or commit other outrages," said Jong primly.

"My point exactly," said Zangi-Ragozh. "At least in the city there are officials who have a duty to protect the place."

"If they will," said Jong. "Most of them will cower in their houses and wait until the army is gone and the danger is past." He swore by a god whose name Zangi-Ragozh did not recognize. "What a time! If only you could heal the earth as you healed me. Then spring would come and Merciful Kuan-Yin could rejoice in her festival." He scowled at the troops ahead and nodded his conviction. "I doubt this year many of us will observe it."

"It is in this fortnight, is it not?" Zangi-Ragozh asked.

"Yes. In four days' time," said Jong. "I usually offer her plum-blossoms, only this year there aren't any."

"She should understand," said Zangi-Ragozh. "She is compassionate."

Jong looked aghast. "Her goodness is nothing to laugh about, particularly not now, when her mercy is so much needed."

"No, mercy is not a thing to laugh about," Zangi-Ragozh agreed, and nodded toward a lane coming into the main road not far up ahead. "Do we take this road, or do we keep on?"

"Do you ask me?" Jong asked in surprise.

"You are tired—it is apparent in how you hold the reins. Since you need rest most immediately of all of us, which would you rather do? Stay on to Lo-Yang or hope for a village not too far away?"

A small detachment of soldiers broke from the line and started down the narrow track Zangi-Ragozh had spotted. Two mounted officers rode with them.

"Too late," said Jong. "Probably just as well. Who is to say what would have happened had we gone that way."

"Then Lo-Yang it is," said Zangi-Ragozh, and pulled up the hood of his cloak.

"Lo-Yang," Jong repeated dismally.

They went on in silence for some time, until the line of travelers began to slow at the approach to the city gates. By that time the sky was paved with clouds and the rain was slanting on the wind, and threatening to become ice once the last of the faint sunlight had faded. Torches were burning in huge iron sconces on either side of the gate, sending tatters of flame to do battle with the stormy evening. The soldiers had been marched off to another entrance to Lo-Yang, and so the crowd waiting to enter was composed of merchants, farmers, and other travelers; all of them were fretful, and most were worn-out from a day on the road in the rain.

By the time Zangi-Ragozh dismounted to address the Guard, it was full dark and the rain had grown heavier, running in the road and making Zangi-Ragozh shudder from its presence. He stepped into the lee of the gateway, holding out his travel orders for the Captain to read, and putting his right hand around his left in greeting. "I am Zangi-Ragozh, a foreign merchant from Yang-Chau traveling to Chang'an by invitation of the Emperor there. Will you be good enough to tell me—where do I go to get my customs assessment?"

"We will deal with such matters here. My scribe is a customs clerk and will see to it that all forms are properly recorded and filed," said the Captain.

"Will that be enough?" Zangi-Ragozh asked. "Do you not need the chop of an official to make his judgment binding?"

"That will be taken care of, Foreigner Zangi-Ragozh," the Captain declared. "Make a note of his name and those with him," he added to the scribe.

Zangi-Ragozh pulled a string of silver cash from his inner sleeve, lifting his sen-gai to hold it out to the Captain. "I trust this will suffice to pay anything we may owe, and any other taxes that might be imposed because of the army being here." He let the scribe take the money, continuing to the Captain, "My men and I need a place to spend the night. If you would be good enough to recommend one?"

"I see you have two wagons, four men, and spare horses," said the Captain, motioning to the scribe with him to make note of this. "Three of your men are Chinese and one is a foreigner, like you."

"Yes, a foreigner, and no, not like me," said Zangi-Ragozh. "Roshei comes from a city far to the west called Ga-Des. I come from ancient mountains; you would call them Carpa-Ti. But you are right: the other three men are Chinese."

"Barbaric names you foreigners give your places," said the Captain, but sounding so tired that there was no condemnation in his remark. He pointed to the bottom of the sheet of paper the scribe had filled out. "If you have a chop, fix it there."

"I have a chop and a sigil," said Zangi-Ragozh.

"Sigil! Another barbaric thing," said the Captain with an exhausted sigh. "Well, fix them both, if it pleases you. Then have your men come up to be identified."

Zangi-Ragozh did as he was told, watching carefully as the Guards looked in his wagons and inspected his horses. When all was done, he once again asked, "I asked you before for your advice, and I hope you will give it to me: is there an inn that caters to such travelers as we are?"

"That may be more costly than the usual places," the Captain warned him. "Such accommodations are at a premium just now."

"I am able to pay," said Zangi-Ragozh, doing his best not to sound resigned.

"Of course," said the Captain. "Go along to the North Market and turn east on the second street, the one with the lanterns strung over the entrance. You will find the Inn of the Graceful Birches. There is a stand of trees behind it that gives it its name. As far as I know, there is room still to be had there."

"Very good," said Zangi-Ragozh, swinging up into the saddle again. "May you bring honor to your ancestors."

"And you, foreigner," said the Captain, his polite response marred by the suggestion of a yawn.

Zangi-Ragozh waited on his restive horse while Ro-shei answered a few questions, and then Yao, Jong, and Gien endorsed the information on the scribe's page. The men got back onto the driver's boxes and at last they entered Lo-Yang.

"Do you know where you're going?" Yao asked testily.

"The Captain recommended an inn," said Zangi-Ragozh. "If you will keep to this main street, I suppose it will take us to the North Market."

Yao rubbed his flat belly. "I'm hungry and I'm cold."

"If it is any comfort to you, so am I," said Zangi-Ragozh, making his way up the broad avenue toward a good-sized walled compound that marked the heart of the city.

Yao sighed noisily. "The North Market it is." He clicked his tongue. "Probably on the other side of the Magisterial Palace."

"It seems likely," said Zangi-Ragozh drily.

Three blocks farther on they halted as a large group of soldiers came roistering by. Some of them were muzzily singing, but most of them were too busy drinking from wine-jugs to bother with melodies. As they reeled away toward a well-lit tavern, one of them raised a short sword menacingly at Yao's wagon, then was dragged away by his unsteady, laughing comrades.

"There'll be trouble by morning," said Yao.

"Very likely," Zangi-Ragozh said as he moved on. As they passed the walls of the Magisterial Palace, they saw banners that informed the city that Magistrate Wo Hai-Jian was in residence. "That should help keep order. No one wants to gain the disapproval of the Magistrate, not even soldiers."

"Perhaps so," said Yao, weighing his opinions before adding, "It depends on how drunk the soldiers get, and what kind of man Magistrate Wo is."

The North Market was largely deserted, but on the far side a number of heavily laden wagons were drawn up in front of the customs house, most with a few men keeping jealous watch over them. Guards in their city uniforms patrolled the large square, holding impressive halberds for weapons.

"We should find our lodging shortly," said Zangi-Ragozh, and turned right along the second street.

The Inn of the Graceful Birches was a short distance from the square, a large, well-made building with a busy forecourt where hostlers took charge of the horses and wagons, and two large stables off to the side; amid the general bustle of the place slaves brought cups of hot wine out to the new arrivals.

"Thank you," Zangi-Ragozh said as a good-sized cup was proffered, "but I do not drink wine."

"I do," said Yao, seizing one of the cups and drinking down the clear, hot liquid. "Another! And quickly!" He got off his box and climbed out of the wagon, his face set even as he strove to smile. "We're cold, wet, and hungry! Let us have heat and a dry place to eat!"

Jong descended more slowly from the wagon, and he frowned as he took the cup of hot wine offered. "It is miserable weather," he remarked as he took the cup from the slave.

"I would like to sleep in the stable with my horses and wagons; we have had a hard day on the road, and I am concerned about two of my horses," Zangi-Ragozh was saying to the landlord as Gien took the riding horses in hand. "I will pay for a room, but I want to be sure that everything is in order and my horses are all sound in the morning."

"You might as well send one of your drivers to tend to your animals; you have a groom with you, have you not?" the landlord suggested.

"These creatures and the wagons, with their contents, are mine, and therefore my responsibility, not that of the men working for me, though they are diligent and loyal," said Zangi-Ragozh in a tone that was at once firm and conciliating.

"Are you afraid that no one can guard your goods but you, yourself?" the landlord demanded.

"No, but I do say that with the army in town, many things become temptations that were not before, and your household staff cannot be everywhere; the demands of soldiers are not easily refused," Zangi-Ragozh assured him. "In times like these, no innkeeper—no matter how honorable—is proof against trouble."

The landlord relented at once. "You speak true, Worthy Foreigner." He indicated the door to his establishment. "I have food waiting, and a table near the hearth that would warm your men."

"And you have rooms for them? a suitable chamber with proper beds and a hearth or a stove to keep them warm?" Zangi-Ragozh asked as he gave a string of silver cash to the landlord; he had three more strings in his sleeve and two silver bars in his wallet.

"Yes. Two of my best are unoccupied. I will assign them to your men." He started toward his door. "Come in out of the rain, Worthy Foreigner, and let us conclude our arrangements."

"Thank you," said Zangi-Ragozh, and gestured to Gien, Jong, and Yao to hurry along ahead of him. As Ro-shei came up to him, he pulled his manservant aside, saying, "I am planning to sleep in the stable tonight."

"I will do it, if you prefer," Ro-shei said at once.

"No," said Zangi-Ragozh. "I want to sleep on my bed in the second wagon. I need the succor of my native earth. This rain is sapping my endurance, and I doubt visiting a dancing-girl would be possible tonight, with the army here."

Ro-shei nodded. "Let me make up a bed for you, then, so no one will think your decision a reflection on this city or this inn."

Zangi-Ragozh shrugged. "As you wish."

"If you will give me your boots, I will change the earth in their soles, as well," Ro-shei offered.

"Thank you," said Zangi-Ragozh, "but I can attend to that myself, later tonight."

Ro-shei nodded. "I'll tell the men of your decision. They will praise you for doing a task that should, rightfully, be theirs."

"I cannot blame them for preferring a comfortable bed to a stable on such a frosty night," said Zangi-Ragozh.

"It still is their place to protect the horses and wagons, not yours," Ro-shei said.

"No doubt. But I need a night on my native earth if I am to continue at our present pace."

"So it's not a woman you worry about, it's those around her," said Ro-shei, understanding Zangi-Ragozh's reticence at last. "You're thinking of Ignatia's mother."

"Egidia Adicia Cortelle, Domina Laelius was hardly the only woman who wanted to profit from revealing too much to those in authority," said Zangi-Ragozh, and went toward the table where the landlord waited.

"You had best remain until the men have eaten," Ro-shei recommended. "The landlord may not give full value for the payment if you are in the stable."

Zangi-Ragozh reached to draw up a chair. "See that my men have what they want."

The meal had just been served when three military officers came into the dining room, their heavy, quilted shai-fas still wet from the worsening rain. The leader held a company standard on a pole, indicating the visit was official; he came up to Zangi-Ragozh and put his hands together in greeting. He was a fairly young man but with the bearing of one used to authority. "Zangi-Ragozh: Captain Tan said we would find you here, Worthy Foreigner."

Zangi-Ragozh looked up at the officers, then rose to give them a formal greeting before saying, "I'm sorry, I do not have the honor of knowing Captain Tan."

"He admitted you at the gate," said the leader. "He recommended this inn."

"So his name is Tan," said Zangi-Ragozh, concealing the sudden chill that took hold of him as he realized he had played into the hands of the army and the Magistrate.

"Tan Jia-Ni," said the officer.

"And whom do I have the pleasure of addressing?" Zangi-Ragozh asked with meticulous good manners. "For I fear you have the advantage of me."

"I am Wo Mi-Dja," said the leader.

Zangi-Ragozh regarded the officer a moment. "I noticed the Magistrate's name is Wo."

"My uncle," said Wo Mi-Dja. "He has brought much honor to our family."

Yao, who had been watching this exchange attentively, spoke to Zangi-Ragozh. "You've paid your fees already. They can't claim any more." He pointed to Gien, who was drinking the last of his hot wine. "You saw, and so did you, Jong."

"This is not a matter of fees," said Officer Wo.

There was a short, uneasy silence, and then Zangi-Ragozh asked, carefully civil in demeanor and address, "May I know what you want with me, Officer Wo?"

"It is not actually with you, Foreigner Zangi-Ragozh," said Officer Wo with a studied superiority. "It is with the three Chinese men who are in your company."

"What about them? I have legitimately employed them; there are records of that in Yang-Chau." Zangi-Ragozh nodded toward the men at the table. "They have worked for me three years at least."

"And my uncle will arrange for you to receive compensation," said Officer Wo.

"Compensation for what?" Zangi-Ragozh asked, anticipating what was coming.

"Their services, and the commandeering of the larger of your wagons and all but four of your horses," said Officer Wo, a hint of fixedness in his manner.

Zangi-Ragozh had been apprehensive about the officers' purpose, supposing that some of his spare horses would be taken, but this was more than he had anticipated. "On what authority do you take my property and my paid employees, Officer Wo?"

"The army has need of them, and the Emperor has given us permission to seize what we need to defend his cause," said Officer Wo, adding with a bit of a smirk, "If this seems unfair, you may always take the case to the Magistrate."

"Your uncle," said Zangi-Ragozh.

"Yes. My uncle."

"I am not leaving Worthy Foreigner Zangi-Ragozh," Jong announced staunchly. "He saved my life and I am indebted to him for all he has done for me."

"He paid us the main part of our salaries before we left, so we could provide for our families, which will be the same as stealing if we cannot finish the work we are expected to do," Yao added. "I have a wife and a daughter in Yang-Chau. If I cannot continue to work for the Worthy Foreigner, how are they to live?"

Zangi-Ragozh was surprised to hear Yao mention his family, for it was a serious lapse in conduct to do so, and as such, eloquent testimony to his understanding of the seriousness of the situation. He saw Officer Wo stiffen and tried to minimize the breach. "I thank you for your good conduct, Yao, and I regret that you have had to embarrass yourself on my account."

"I have a mother whom I support," Jong put in, a stubborn set to his jaw. "She depends upon me."

"No doubt all men have such tales," said Officer Wo, trying not to be offended by the introduction of such private information into their arrangements. "And you"—he addressed Gien—"I suppose you have someone depending on your work for this man for a living?"

"No," said Gien. "But Zangi-Ragozh paid my family handsomely for me, and he is entitled for the labor he expected to have from me."

"All men have excuses," said Officer Wo.

"Hardly excuses," said Jong. "We know where our obligations lie."

"To the Emperor," said Officer Wo, settling the matter. "If you will come to the stable with me, Foreigner Zangi-Ragozh, we will settle the matter of the horses and the wagon at once." He signaled to his men. "Kan, you stay here; Dai, come with me."

Ro-shei cocked his head. "What do you wish me to do, my master?"

"I hope you will remain here. I can tend to matters in the stable, if Gien will come with me to show me where our animals and our wagons are; I will shift our chests and crates for the officer's convenience," said Zangi-Ragozh, and started out of the dining room toward the side corridor that led to the stable.

Gien jumped to his feet. "I'm coming," he said after a swift, skittish look at the Officer and his men. He followed after them at a respectful distance.

As Zangi-Ragozh made his way toward the stable, he asked, "It appears that you are commandeering men and matériel fairly routinely: how many seizures have you made today, Officer Wo?"

"Yours will be the fourth," said Officer Wo.

"All from this inn?" Zangi-Ragozh inquired, noticing the landlord staring at him.

"No. We try to make only one confiscation per day from each merchants' inn, in as fair a division of loss as can be arranged," said Officer Wo with a degree of pride.

"And the Gods of Fortune said I would be chosen for the Inn of the Graceful Birches today," Zangi-Ragozh marveled.

"You are traveling on the Emperor's business," Officer Wo reminded him. "This is also the Emperor's business. Captain Tan noted your orders from the Vermilion Brush, and he informed us of them."

They crossed the side-court to the stable where Zangi-Ragozh signaled to Gien to point out their horses. "I suppose they're tie-stalled."

"Yes. Over here," said Gien nervously as he picked up one of the stable lanterns and made his way down the broad aisle, the light uplifted to provide the most illumination. "There. Those are the horses. All sixteen of them are in a line, by that long manger. We lost two along the way." He pointed with his free hand. "From the two fine grays to the horse with the large brown spots."

Officer Wo made his way along the horses. "Very good stock, and well-kept. They look to be in good condition, properly fed and their hooves trimmed."

"They are," said Zangi-Ragozh, knowing that the army would not be able to care for them as he and Gien had, which saddened him.

"And you have two wagons?" Officer Wo went on.

"Yes. A larger one and a smaller one," said Zangi-Ragozh, anticipating what was coming. "One is drawn by two horses, the other by four."

"We'll need the larger one. You may take off your cargo, for we'll need the space for supplies. You may take the smaller one and . . . shall we say four horses? That way you have a team and a spare, or you can ride one, lead one, and harness two."

Zangi-Ragozh held back his protestations, knowing any complaint would likely lose him more. "May I choose which horses I keep?"

Officer Wo shrugged. "That seems a reasonable request, given the circumstances. I'll have my scribe draw up a writ of transfer and an authorization of compensation. You may present it to the Emperor's treasurers when you arrive in Chang'an."

Zangi-Ragozh's smile was ironic. "How kind of you, Officer Wo," he said.

"It is not the intention of the army to deprive you of property without recompense," Officer Wo said stiffly before abruptly shifting the subject. "I like that light bay. He has a fine neck."

"That he does," said Zangi-Ragozh. "He's a strengthy horse."

Officer Wo tried not to see how shocked Gien was. "And the one with the black spots? What about her?"

"Eight years old, steady and sensible," said Zangi-Ragozh, knowing that Ro-shei was fond of the spotted mare and sorry she had caught the officer's attention.

"Eight. So there are some good years left in her yet," said Officer Wo. "Army life is hard on everyone—men, dogs, horses—the lot. More so when the weather is so unseasonably bad." He coughed and lowered his voice as if to impart a secret. "The mud and the continuing cold have claimed almost as many soldiers, horses, and wagons as the enemy has."

"Which is why you have the task of acquiring more of everything needed," said Zangi-Ragozh.

Hearing the note of despair in the foreigner's voice, Officer Wo softened. "We will not waste anything we confiscate from you."

"You console me," said Zangi-Ragozh sardonically.

"You're a merchant. All merchants hate war," said Officer Wo, "unless they're selling to the army."

Zangi-Ragozh quelled his unease. "As you say—war is bad for trade."

"And this weather is worse, from what I've heard," said Officer Wo. "Well, I tell you what: you can keep that spotted mare. We'll leave you one of your choice, the sorrel with the white socks—my Captain says four white legs is unlucky—and the cinder-brown. Which one would you like to have?"

"One of the grays," said Zangi-Ragozh promptly, but unable to choose between Flying Cloud and Shooting Star.

"Keep the gelding. We'll take the mare," said Officer Wo. "Now, since we're taking the larger wagon, you had better start unloading it. If you need my men to help you?"

"No, thank you. I will manage," said Zangi-Ragozh. "Everything will be ready in the morning."

Officer Wo gestured approval. "I'll send men for them at first light." He gave a predatory smile. "Do not try to deprive us of what we need—it will only go hard for you if you do."

"I understand," said Zangi-Ragozh. "What about my three men?" He already knew he and Ro-shei would turn north in the morning, away from Chang'an; they had no reason to continue on, not with the men and horses gone.

"They'll come with us now," said Officer Wo. "I can't give them time to slip away to wait for you at some remote place in order to avoid their duty to us." Officer Wo clapped Zangi-Ragozh on the shoulder. "You have a good grasp of how things must be."

"For a foreigner," Zangi-Ragozh finished for him even as he prepared to return to the inn to explain how matters had changed for them all.

*   *   *

Text of one of three identical letters from Zangi-Ragozh to Senior Clerk Hu Bi-Da, Professor Min Cho-Zhi, and Councillor Ko She-Hsieh, all at Yang-Chau; entrusted to a Chinese merchant and delivered eleven months later.

To the most reliable clerk, Hu Bi-Da/ the most faithful deputy, Professor Min Cho-Zhi/ the illustrious Councillor Ko She-Hsieh, the greetings of the foreign merchant Zangi-Ragozh, who is profoundly grateful to you for your honorable service.

This is to inform you that I will be unable to reach Chang'an this year, for as much as I have attempted to avoid the fighting and make as much haste as the roads will permit, I find I am met with many obstacles. The army not only blocks the roads leading there, but it has taken twelve of my horses, my larger wagon, and demanded the services of Yao, Jong, and Gien in their current campaign, leaving me no correct way in which to complete the Wen Emperor Yuan Buo-Ju's commission to me. I ask that you will inform the families of the men, and my employees, of these events, so that they will not be distressed by our prolonged absence. I authorize continuing salaries to be paid as they have been from the revenues of Eclipse Trading Company and from my stored resources, the location of which are known to my steward, Jho Chieh-Jen, and may be used as need arises.

Since I am unable to continue on to Chang'an, I have decided to go to Holin-Gol, north on the Huang Ho, where Mongolian merchants have easy access at the gate in the Great Wall. Should the roads prove unpassable as many have done, Ro-shei and I will travel to Holin-Gol by barge, for although the river is high, shipping continues to move along it. If trade is thriving anywhere, it is thriving there at Holin-Gol, where I will strive to recoup some of the losses the military expropriation of my men and animals and property has brought about, and to do it in a place where such imposition is less likely than it is on the road to Chang'an. I cannot estimate how long this journey will take, or if it will lead me beyond the Great Wall, but I pledge now that I will endeavor to inform you of my travels as they progress.

I hope that the Gods of Prosperity will guide you, and that Kuan-Yin will be merciful to you all, and, until I can speak my greeting in person, this must suffice to assure you of my good-will and high regard.

Zangi-Ragozh
(his chop)
(his sigil, the eclipse)

7

Zangi-Ragozh emerged from the hold of the barge pale and shaken. He shivered in the predawn mist, his sen-gai hardly enough to keep out the gnawing cold that hunger had engendered in him during his long stupor aboard the barge. There was stubble on his chin from his lengthy isolation, and his hair had grown, not as much as that of living men, but enough to be untidy, the dark waves hanging in short curls around his head. Beside him, Ro-shei waited patiently while the bargemen, lanterns in hand, guided their four horses and small wagon along the broad, heavy plank to the shore.

"There was snow last night," said Ro-shei to Zangi-Ragozh as if this were nothing remarkable. "Not much, but still . . ."

"We've been a month on this river," Zangi-Ragozh said, shuddering in spite of himself. "With only three layovers, none of them more than two days." His Chinese sounded more foreign than usual. Zangi-Ragozh nodded slowly. "It must be mid-May in Europe at least, and here it looks like February."

"The Fortnight of Those Born in the South is ending. The Festival of Yo-Wang is over," said Ro-shei.

"The God of Medicine," said Zangi-Ragozh. "I hope Jong celebrated it." He looked out over the fog-wrapped river. "I hope he is alive to celebrate it."

"May all of them live—the men and the horses." Ro-shei adjusted the hat he wore. "Come. They're signaling from the dock."

"I seem a bit flimsy," Zangi-Ragozh said, taking an uncertain step.

"A month on running water almost constantly, small wonder," said

Ro-shei, offering an arm for Zangi-Ragozh to lean upon. "You'll be better for a bath and a shave and a trimming."

"I must get off the barge and into the town, or an inn at least, before I can avail myself of any of those," he said a bit sardonically.

"For that I can assist you," Ro-shei pointed out.

"Thank you, old friend, but I had better walk on my own. I'll recover sooner if I do." He steadied himself and stepped onto the broad plank that gave access to the dock. Behind the barge on which they had been traveling, the river junk that had been shoving the barge upriver lay still, oars banked and battened sails reefed, looking as insubstantial as a dream in the tarnished, misty light; four men on deck watched while Zangi-Ragozh and Ro-shei went ashore.

"We leave at this hour tomorrow," said the barge-master. "If you change your mind about going on, be here by sunset and we'll take you aboard again. The river turns westward in a day's journey, and that will lead you to Wu-Wei."

"In another month or so, if all goes well," said Zangi-Ragozh, moving a bit more securely.

"Holin-Gol is only two li ahead," said Ro-shei, handing the barge-master a silver bar as thanks for his service. "My master and I would prefer to spend a little time on dry land before arriving there."

The barge-master snorted a laugh. "Not much of a riverman, is he, your employer? Strange, for a merchant not to like travel by water."

"But so it is," said Ro-shei.

"Then be careful. There's a small canal up ahead, and the towpath is a drop from the road." The barge-master chuckled. "If your master can stand to go over the canal."

"I believe he can endure it," said Ro-shei.

"Sleeping in your wagon as if dead, and for days on end," said the barge-master. "Foreigners!"

"We're most perplexing," said Ro-shei agreeably as Zangi-Ragozh checked the harness that secured the cinder-brown gelding and the white-legged sorrel mare to the wagon; Flying Cloud and Ro-shei's spotted mare were saddled and ready to ride.

"I'll drive the wagon," Zangi-Ragozh decided aloud. "Tie Flying Cloud's reins to the rear of the wagon. I'd rather lead him than the wagon."

"As you wish, my master," said Ro-shei, and moved to do it.

The barge-master went back aboard his craft and drew up the loading plank, then signaled to the men on the junk. "We're secure. If you want to go ashore, you may do so now. Just remember to be here by sundown, for I want to be under way at first light and we must secure the barge."

"We will remember, but we will not be here," said Zangi-Ragozh as he climbed up onto the driving-box of the wagon; his gloved hands shook as he picked up the reins.

The barge-master chuckled and waved, showing his disbelief in the casualness of his gesture.

Zangi-Ragozh swung his pair away from the river, the wheels of the wagon rumbling like thunder along the dock. He lifted his head and sniffed the morning. "Something is not right."

"That smell from the snow," said Ro-shei, speaking Imperial Latin as Zangi-Ragozh had done. "The yellow makes it stink."

Zangi-Ragozh looked about as they approached the riverfront road that ran just above the path used by the dray-oxen of short-haul barges. "Not much travel, judging by the state of the road. At this time of year, there should be signs of active trade, but there are only these old ruts."

"True enough," said Ro-shei, bringing his spotted mare up just ahead of the wagon.

"Now travel is inconvenient. Later it may be much worse." Zangi-Ragozh adjusted the reins as he steered the pair onto the road, going northward beside the river; the fog brightened, creating a dim glare as sunrise grew near. "The canal is not far ahead, I must assume."

"And the towpath is a drop. I have no idea how much of one," said Ro-shei.

"The river is running very high; I must suppose the canal is, as well," said Zangi-Ragozh.

"Do you think there will be flooding?" Ro-shei wondered.

"In such a year as this, who can tell?" Zangi-Ragozh said. "It is as if the whole world is afflicted." He said nothing more, as if such an admission was more than he had wanted to concede.

"There have been more dead birds in the river," Ro-shei reported after they had covered a short distance. "The most recent was yesterday afternoon. A wind came up, and hundreds of small, white-breasted brown birds dropped from the sky." He took a deep breath. "There was also a hawk among them."

"Was this the only time birds fell?" Zangi-Ragozh asked.

"No; there were four others that I know of; the boatmen said there have been more flocks of dead birds floating on the river."

"In large quantities, or fairly small?" Zangi-Ragozh asked, a frown settling between his fine brows.

"Quite large ones. Most of the ones I have seen looked to have died on the wing." Ro-shei considered this a long moment, then added, "Some had feathers with yellow dust on them."

"Poor creatures," said Zangi-Ragozh with feeling. "And you say these deaths are increasing." He looked down as the wheels crunched on ice standing in the slicks on the road. "The canal is just ahead."

"Is there a bridge, do you think, or must we ferry across?" Ro-shei sounded exasperated.

"There is a bridge," said Zangi-Ragozh as he peered into the mists, his dark-seeing eyes making out the shape of it. "Two wagons wide, and raised in the middle."

"And the drop to the towpath?" Ro-shei's mare was sidling, reluctant to step onto the towpath.

"Not too much, I think," said Zangi-Ragozh as he did his best to judge the angle of the dip in the road ahead. "Our wheels should be safe."

"And the axle?" Ro-shei asked. "Do you want me to get down and guide us over?"

"I doubt that will be necessary," said Zangi-Ragozh as he pulled his team to a slow walk and carefully took them over the bridge. As he crossed the canal, he noticed the bodies of five dead cranes caught against the bridge supports. "You say the birds are continuing to die?"

"They seem to be" was Ro-shei's careful answer, his attention on completing their crossing.

"Ah," Zangi-Ragozh responded, to show he had heard.

A short distance along the road they came upon a track leading in from the narrow fields; there was a make-shift gibbet erected there, and a four-day-old corpse dangled from a butcher's iron hook. A crudely lettered sign around the dead man's neck identified him as a stealer of food; only the chill kept the body from reeking. The horses minced past the grisly thing, sweating in spite of the cold.

"There will be more of this," said Zangi-Ragozh. "And for less."

Ro-shei looked at the corpse. "Should we cut him down, do you think?"

"No. It would not benefit him, and it could cause trouble." Zangi-Ragozh shook his head. "Poor man. You can see how thin he was before this happened."

"So you think he must have been starving."

"He certainly looks it," said Zangi-Ragozh. "Being within a short distance of the town, and with so many loading docks along the bank here, someone must have reported this." Zangi-Ragozh squinted at where the eastern horizon should be. "The fog is thickening. We do not want to be surprised by anyone."

"No, we do not," Ro-shei agreed, and stopped talking as they continued on toward the walls of the town, hidden in the deepening mists ahead.

There were a few birdcalls and splashes, and the sound of a heavy cart in the distance, and then a faint jingle of tack, which brought the two up short. "How many?" Zangi-Ragozh asked, reaching into the well of the driver's box for the sword that lay there.

"It could be three," said Ro-shei cautiously in Latin.

"Three is acceptable," said Zangi-Ragozh in the same language, and rose, still holding the reins of the team, but ready to take on any attackers; by now the mists were shiny with new sunlight, almost blinding in their limmerence, and Zangi-Ragozh squinted into them, his whole attention on the faint squeak of leather and *ching* of brass.

Ro-shei pulled his sword from its sheath, getting ready to fend off the approaching horsemen. "Do I assume they've heard us by now?"

"It would be folly to think otherwise, since we have heard them," said Zangi-Ragozh, bracing himself on the wagon-frame, ready to fend off any attempt to take the wagon.

Ro-shei was about to speak when there was a loud cry to their immediate right and two men on horseback loomed out of the fog, both brandishing swords and apparently determined to frighten the foreigners into immediate submission. Ro-shei tugged his mare around to face the assault and swung his sword over his head, showing his readiness to fight, while Zangi-Ragozh held the wagon horses as steady as he could, for they were plunging with nervousness and took a short while to bring under control. "What do you dog's heads want?" Ro-shei roared in Chinese, showing no sign of fright.

A third horseman came in from behind, planning to steal Flying Cloud from the back of the wagon. He was brought up short as the wagon was pulled around to angle across the road and the driver swung out from the box and snicked his upper arm. With a fierce oath, the man stabbed futilely in the direction of the wagon, howling with determination and pain. He spurred his horse closer to the wagon and made a second attempt: this time the flat of the driver's sword struck him on the side of the head and he tumbled out of the saddle.

Ro-shei held his mare skillfully, making sure she did not begin to back up, for that might put them both in the river. He kept her nose close to her chest, then let her mince forward a few steps before signaling her to rear. As she did, he struck out with his sword and felt it strike bamboo armor.

"Give us your things and your horses and we won't kill you!" shouted one of the attackers in a local dialect that was almost incomprehensible.

"Why should we believe you?" Ro-shei demanded, his mare back on all four feet and ready to stand her ground. He swung up his sword and made ready to fend off a second assault. The mare faltered and dropped onto her knees as her front legs buckled. Ro-shei kicked himself out of the saddle and looked to see what had happened: there were two thin lances buried in her side.

The nearer of the two lawbreakers suddenly reeled and collapsed back onto his horse's rump, sending the animal into an uneven, panicky canter. Zangi-Ragozh lowered his small crossbow so he could fit it with another quarrel.

Cursing loudly, the third highwayman bolted, his horse pounding away from the river in pursuit of his comrade. The sound of their retreat faded quickly.

Ro-shei began to unbuckle the saddle, saying in Latin as he did, "I hate this kind of slaughter. The mare meant him no harm." He paused to move aside. "This should be a clear shot."

"Yes," said Zangi-Ragozh, and sent a merciful quarrel into the center of her forehead.

Tugging the bridle headstall over the mare's ears as she gave a last kick, Ro-shei said to the horse, "Thank you for all you did for me." He patted her neck as he lifted the saddle and got to his feet.

"Would you like to saddle Flying Cloud?" Zangi-Ragozh offered.

"No. For now, I think it best to ride on the box with you." He used the heavy spoke of the front wheel as a step up into the wagon; he lay the saddle on its front end and draped the girth and the bridle over the cantle, then settled beside Zangi-Ragozh on the box. "Not a very auspicious beginning."

"No," Zangi-Ragozh agreed as he signaled the horses to jog.

"Do you think the other man will be back?" Ro-shei asked in order to put his mind on something other than his dead mare.

"I doubt it. I think the three of them constitute the entire company, and with Holin-Gol so near, he would be a fool to attempt another attack alone. If we were in the forest or in the dry wastes where one man could create an ambush, then there might be trouble." He pointed. "The town is less than half a li ahead of us, and we will be within the gates shortly."

"I suppose we would do well to report the incident," Ro-shei said.

"We have no reason not to do so." Zangi-Ragozh squinted into the bright smudge of sunlight in the thinning mists. "The sun lacks power."

"With so much fog, it is hardly surprising," said Ro-shei, not fully paying attention.

"No, that is not what I mean: even without the fog, the sun is not as potent as I would expect it to be in late spring. It is vitiated, as if its light gave no heat. It might as well be hidden behind heavy clouds for all the vigor it provides the land." Zangi-Ragozh stared thoughtfully at the dark mass of the walled town that loomed ahead in the mist, then turned his head to count the docks and wharves that lined the riverbank with increasing frequency. "I wonder if there have been robberies here, or thefts from the boats and barges?"

"Do you suppose the local Magistrate would let it be known if there were?" Ro-shei laughed harshly.

"He might, if the problem were severe enough," said Zangi-Ragozh, and slowed the horses to a walk.

Ro-shei clapped his hands together. "That would mean the region would be almost in open rebellion."

"That may yet come," said Zangi-Ragozh.

"Most of the barbarous tribes go westward, not to the south," said Ro-shei.

"Because the Great Wall keeps them out," said Zangi-Ragozh. "But here in Holin-Gol there is a break in the wall, as there is at Wu-Wei. Such places could become centers for rebellion if the northern horsemen ever got through the Great Wall."

"Holin-Gol and Wu-Wei are both on the southern side of the Great Wall, and the gates they possess are fortified," Ro-shei reminded him. "There are garrisons of soldiers in both towns, and their commanders have a great deal of autonomy in meeting threats."

"One day that could work to the Emperor's disadvantage," said Zangi-Ragozh, switching back to Chinese.

"Which Emperor?" Ro-shei asked in Latin.

"My point exactly," said Zangi-Ragozh, and prepared to face the customs agents and Guard waiting just inside the double gates of Holin-Gol.

The duties demanded to enter the town were high—more than they were for two wagons at Lo-Yang—and taken peremptorily. With a studied lack of respect, they were directed to the Travelers' Quarter of the town and given the names of four inns from which to choose lodging, then curtly advised to move on.

"There is one thing I think we should mention: we were attacked by three highwaymen as we approached the town, just at dawn," said Zangi-Ragozh as he handed over a silver bar and two strings of copper cash; if the slighting demeanor of the Guard and customs agent offended him, he hid it well enough.

The Guard officer sighed. "This morning, you mean?"

"Yes. This morning, on the main road beside the river. We left the barge on which we had traveled at the dock, and as we made for your gates, the three attempted to steal our horses and the wagon," Zangi-Ragozh said very patiently.

"What did they do?" The Guard seemed disinterested in the answer.

"They rode up on horseback, armed with swords and cudgels, and probably knives as well, but I did not specifically see any," said Zangi-Ragozh.

"How did you escape them?" The Guard signaled to a customs scribe, his curiosity belatedly awakened. "Take this down."

The scribe bustled over, his brush at the ready, his paper spread on a portable table, his stance obsequious. "As you wish, Captain Ruo."

Zangi-Ragozh recounted the morning incident, ending, "I cannot tell you if the two highwaymen were killed or only injured. I did not think it wise to linger."

"Wise enough," said Captain Ruo. "I will send out a party of soldiers to look for them later this morning. Pass on!"

"The markets are half-empty," Ro-shei observed as they approached the best of the four inns the Guard had recommended.

"This town should be busy at this time of year," Zangi-Ragozh added as he turned into the innyard of the Shifting Sands, noticing as he did that the stables were far from full.

"More bad weather come up from the south," Ro-shei suggested as Zangi-Ragozh drew his pair to a halt; he climbed down to take the leads of the team. "I'd expect a groom to be available to—" Before he could say anything more, a short, middle-aged man came out of the inn; he was shaped like a ginger-jar, with a powerful upper body tapering to small, out-turned feet. His features were set and broad, showing as much Mongol as Chinese lineage. "The landlord," Ro-shei guessed aloud.

"Innkeeper; my father-in-law is landlord," the man corrected. "Kittu is my family name. I welcome you to the Shifting Sands."

"I am Zangi-Ragozh, a foreign merchant, coming from Yang-Chau," he said as he got off his box.

"You have come a very long way," Kittu said, clapping his hands. "Hagai, Jinje, come here!" Then he bowed to Zangi-Ragozh. "I am sorry. Those laggards have been shirking their duties to gamble. Jinge! Come at once! Hagai!"

There was a flurry of activity on the far side of the stable, and then a pair of youths came rushing out into the innyard, one of them shoving a fistful of copper cash into his pocket. "Sorry, Kittu," said this lad. "Business has been so slow that—"

"All the more reason you should be ready to attend to our guests," Kittu exclaimed, and glared at the two.

"Hagai said that you wouldn't mind," Jinje complained.

"It sounds too slim an excuse to me, and one that is more wishful thinking than fact, as you will learn before you have your supper," said Kittu. "Get to work for these good merchants." He clapped his hands again and turned back to Zangi-Ragozh and Ro-shei. "I will offer you my best rooms—two on the main floor across from the dining room, each with a bed and a table, no sharing with other travelers. They cost a bit more, but—"

"That will be satisfactory," said Zangi-Ragozh, preparing to pull a string of silver cash from his sleeve.

"Is there anything else I might provide?" Kittu asked. "As an innkeeper, I wish my guests to be well-satisfied with their stay here." He augmented this last with a broad wink.

"A bath would be welcome," said Zangi-Ragozh as if wholly unaware of the larger implications of Kittu's offer. "I trust you have a bath-house? And someone who can wash some clothing?" He saw the innkeeper nodding in response to each question and smiled. "My traveling companion would like to find a market to buy a duck or a chicken for his meal. And if there is an establishment where you recommend the women . . ." He left the last unsaid.

"We have a bath-house which can be heated for your use. As to the fowl, there is a market two streets away where the farmers bring their wares for sale. If there are ducks or chickens to be had just now, you may find them there. If you will bring the bird to the kitchen, the cook will prepare it in any manner you like." Kittu rubbed his hands together as if eager to tend to the meal himself.

"I regret that the practice among my people requires us to take our meals in private," said Ro-shei, interrupting Kittu with a deferential nod. "We have certain rites that must be—"

Kittu held up his hands. "Say no more. All foreigners have their ways."

"Very true," Ro-shei said.

"Well, provided you don't get blood all over the floor, then do as your customs demand of you." Kittu started back for his inn, motioning to Zangi-Ragozh and Ro-shei to follow him. "Don't worry about your things: those two scamps will be far more careful now than if they hadn't been caught neglecting their duties. They won't steal, either. They know I'd have both their right hands if they should take so much as a buckle from you." He stepped into the reception area, nodding toward the dining room. "Food is served four times a day. We don't do the midnight meals they do in the southlands."

"Given where you are, there are probably regulations against it," said Zangi-Ragozh. "When I was last through here, all businesses had to be shut by nightfall."

"We innkeepers have a little leeway, as do restaurants, entertainers, and licensed brothels, but yes, you will find that we often curtail our work as soon as the Great Gates are shut. The Guard patrols the streets and the army mans the Great North Gate. No barges can tie up within the town walls, as you know." He indicated a broad corridor. "The rooms I mentioned are down there. I have nine other guests just now, and only one of them is in, so you have the inn almost completely to yourselves."

"I'm sorry your business is down," said Zangi-Ragozh.

"It will improve again, in time. It is not as if my circumstances are unusual." He pointed toward the north wall. "The bath-house is just there, on the far side of the inn from the latrines. The water is wholesome and the tubs are scrubbed with every new moon. You may reach it through the door between the dining room and the kitchens."

"If you will have the bath-house heated?" Zangi-Ragozh offered a handful of coins.

"Certainly." Kittu held out his hand. "That will be four silver cash. The price is high because of the unusual cold—we must burn more wood to heat it, and to keep it warm."

"I grasp the problem," said Zangi-Ragozh.

"Without arguments?" Kittu marveled. "Then you are a most remarkable merchant."

"Would the prices be any less elsewhere?" Zangi-Ragozh asked.

"Probably not," said Kittu.

"Then what would be the point in disputing?" Zangi-Ragozh gestured the issue away. "I have three large chests in the wagon, set in the center of the bed. If one of them could be brought to whichever room you assign me, I would be grateful." He slipped a small string of silver cash off his wrist and handed it to Kittu. "This should pay for the bath and the extra service we may require."

Kittu took it at once. "You are a generous man, Worthy Foreigner."

Zangi-Ragozh shook his head. "I have been about the world a little, and I know how demanding hardship can be."

Kittu looked a bit startled. "Hardship?"

"This cold spring is a hardship, and one that will not be quickly settled. I saw frost on the ground this morning, and it will probably still be here in the Fortnight of the Thunder God, which is almost upon us; it may last into the Fortnight of the Descent of Kuan-Te." Zangi-Ragozh shook his head.

"Ordinarily we call that the Fortnight of the Desert's Breath," said Kittu. "Not this year. As you say."

"What do you hear from other travelers?" Zangi-Ragozh asked.

"I have seen so few travelers! They say some of the passes are still blocked with snow, as if it were late winter, and others have reported landslides on the road near Miran." Kittu shrugged. "The merchants coming on the northern branch of the Silk Road have not yet arrived, so who can tell what they may have encountered." He nodded. "I will tell my slaves to heat the bath, and I'll have Hagai and Jinje bring that chest to whichever of the two rooms you choose."

"Very good," said Zangi-Ragozh. "And my traveling companion will go in search of his dinner."

Ro-shei dropped his voice and said in Byzantine Greek, "When you're done bathing and I'm finished eating, you may look to your own nourishment."

"So I will," said Zangi-Ragozh.

"What did he say?" Kittu challenged, holding up his thick hand to show how serious he was. "I won't have any barbarian nonsense in my inn."

Zangi-Ragozh offered a brief, charming smile. "He was only reminding me to choose my woman carefully."

"Oh, very good advice," Kittu approved, and wondered why Zangi-Ragozh had smiled as he led the two foreigners to their rooms.

Text of a letter from the clerk Hu Bi-Da, in Yang-Chau, to his employer, the foreign merchant, in Chang'an; carried by courier but never delivered.

To the most excellent employer and Worthy Foreigner, Zangi-Ragozh, currently in Chang'an, his clerk, Hu Bi-Da, sends his most respectful greetings and the condolences in regard to the matters upon which I write to inform you.

It is my sad duty to tell you that your merchant ship The Shining

Pearl, *which had been reported missing, has been sunk. No man aboard her and no scrap of cargo was saved. This has been confirmed by two separate sources, neither of which may easily be impeached for accuracy or honesty. I have taken full accounts from the two Captains who have made this claim, and I am satisfied that their accounts are alike enough to show that they have not mistaken their information, nor have they done anything in the way of collusion together, to deceive or defraud you. The loss of the ship is a great one, and I must tell you that the settlement you have authorized for the family of the Captain will mean that none of the children need be sold, which must be a very welcome thing to his two wives. Yet I fear this may only be the first of many losses to come.*

I have ordered a new ship built, in accordance with your instructions, and I will seek out a proper Captain for her when she is complete and it is once again safe to launch a ship upon the waves. The plans are already in the hands of the shipwrights, and they have promised all due speed in the building. Gold is much in demand just now, with trade gone off so badly. As soon as the ship is ready, I will send you word so that you may instruct me where it is to sail. The Shining Pearl had traveled a long way, but she was by no means so ancient that she was in need of dismantling.

The Magistrate has issued orders for new taxes so that the damaged wharves and warehouses may be repaired. Our taxes will be higher than some, as you are a foreigner, and you will have to bear the full price of repairs to your property, but for once, I understand the need for such taxation, and I will not be adverse to paying it. Councillor Ko has told me that there will be additional taxes to provide some support to those businesses damaged by the storms, and those compromised by the lingering cold weather we are all experiencing. There are more than adequate funds to pay for such taxes, and once trade is properly resumed, you may be confident that I will not depend upon the generous deposits you have provided to fund the regular operations of your trading.

Your former concubine, Dei-Na, has informed me that she is planning to marry. The man is a widower, respectable, with a small but successful jade-carving shop. His work is held in high regard, and he has enough money of his own not to need hers. I have reminded her that she does not need your permission to marry, but that I was relieved that she had chosen such a worthy man to wed. She has asked me to notify you of this, and now I have done.

The Gods of Fortune show you favor, Worthy Foreigner; they have used us all most harshly here in Yang-Chau. In Chang'an, I hope things will be better, for if we cannot prosper trading by sea, then we must do so by land, and Chang'an is the key to such prosperity. Given how inclement the weather has been, and how feeble the sun's rays when they do shine, I must hope that your sigil, as you call it, reflects the Will of Heaven at this time, and for that, you will thrive when others are less fortunate. If you are visited with similar misfortunes as other merchants have suffered, then I will throw myself on the mercy of the Gods of Fortune for all of our sakes. Should you have an offering to make, this may be an auspicious time, for all the adversity we see, as it is known that when the depths are reached, change will come and end the tribulation.

Hu Bi-Da
Senior clerk, Eclipse Trading Company
(his chop)

PART II

DUKKAI

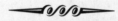

*T*ext of a letter from Atta Olivia Clemens at Lago Comus in northern Italy to Ragoczy Sanct' Germain Franciscus at Yang-Chau, written in Imperial Latin, carried by caravan and delivered to Eclipse Trading Company offices in Yang-Chau four years after it was sent; filed as unreadable.

To my most dear, most absent friend, Ragoczy Sanct' Germain Franciscus in the farthest reaches of Cathay, the worried greetings of Atta Olivia Clemens on this the Summer Solstice of the 1288th Year of the City, the Pope's Year 535, although it seems like the end of winter here, with the promise of spring very far off.

It has been an age since I wrote to you, although I suppose it is more like two years. I have hoped to have some word from you, but I have received nothing, and this is beginning to bother me, especially with the world in such chaos as I see around me. My thoughts turn to such horrors as must cause me sleepless nights, if I needed sleep. I comfort myself with the abiding trust that this terrible cold has not touched you in your distant lands, given how far away you are. We in the old Roman world have had to contend with frost well into June, and no end of it in sight, with July coming shortly, when heat should have wrapped us in its embrace, yet so far has done nothing of the sort. The farmers here at Lago Comus are in dismay, for they have not been able to plant new crops, the fields are not producing grass for their flocks and herds, and the orchards have not flowered and so will not fruit. Wolves have come down from the mountains, and bear, and the hunters vie with them for skinny deer and underfed boars. The flocks and herds of the farmers do not fare much better, although I have authorized the opening of the storehouse to provide fodder for sheep, horses, goats, cattle, poultry, and hogs, in the hope that this will stave off the worst losses of starvation. I have grain, oil, salt-beef, and dried fruit sufficient to last for two years, just as you suggested, and I will do all that I can to provide for the people of and around this estate, but I fear what may come once the full impact of the famine is upon us.

The people in this region are much troubled by the very red sunsets and dawns we have been having almost daily for the last four months or so. Many find this an omen, and it frightens them, for they say that blood in the sky means war in Heaven, or so the Christians preach, claiming that in their prophetic texts are allusions to such events, and that they bode ill for humanity. Even the moon is not herself, showing a ruddiness that is unlike her usual pristine face, making her a peach rather than a mirror. There is a demented priest in the village who, combining the distress of the times with the prophecies of his faith, is preaching the final battle of the world, and he points to signs, including red moons and bloody sunsets, as proof that the angels are engaging in war with the demons of Hell. I admit to all the Christians in his flock that it is true the sunsets have been brilliant and unusual, but I doubt this heralds anything more than the cold has done. The priest praises a kind of passionate passivity in the face of tribulation, and many are glad to acquiesce in his repeated assurances that their god is testing their faith in his mercy. I do not comprehend how such catastrophic events can be twisted into a sign of special affection, but then, I was married to Justus, and you and I know that his claims of devotion came with similar conditions, so it may be that my faith failed me then, not to return. Let the priest rail at me for apostasy; I believe it is more important to minimize famine than to preserve their god's dignity.

The one benefit this dreadful cold has brought to Rome is that for once the summer has no bad air. The fevers of mal aria are absent, and the Pope—and we have one at last, John II, who is reported to be in failing condition—has claimed this one good development to his own credit, insisting that his personal suffering has spared the people of Rome the burden of disease during this perverse time of cold, so you see, the Church has elevated suffering to an estimable goal, one that has merit, and is deserving of recognition and respect. In fact, it is seen as a means to emulate the suffering of Jesus, and therefore a pious state to achieve: to my view, any deity and any priests that demand more wretchedness from their followers than is given to them by nature are not worthy of worship, and I will say that in spite of what the Popes have done to preserve Rome.

My steward in Gaul, Briacus of Alesia, has sent me word that conditions are worse in his region than they are here. He speaks of an invisible shadow on the sun, and an earth that will not bring forth anything but loam. I have given him leave to use as much of my stored supplies as may be needed, but not in profligate amounts, for if this cold should continue into a second year, it is highly unlikely that there are sufficient foodstuffs in storage to prevent serious hunger for many of the peasants who are tenants of my estates. If the time comes that Briacus must choose prudence or his family, I do not believe he would hesitate an instant to care for his family first and his duties to the estate second. For that reason, I have contacted the Abbot of Santus Spiritu, the monastery a short way beyond the western border of my estate, to ask him to watch over the estate, and in exchange for his service to me, I have arranged to ship him six barrels of wine, two of oil, and nine of grain, for the use of his monks, who live in the manner approved by John Cassian and practice asceticism based upon the Egyptian hermits. Santus Spiritu has forty-six monks in residence, and the capacity to hold another dozen, should their numbers increase.

In the last four months, I have received letters from many landowners in Gaul and Germania, and I am much troubled by what they say, for they, too, have been unable to plant, and some have had losses among their stock, not just from wolves and foxes—and poachers—but from miscarriages and stillbirths, which I take as an especially sinister development, for it is one thing to see the danger of famine in this cold, it is far more troublesome to see the animals unable to sustain their young, for that implies that there is worse to come. Some of those who follow the old religions of this region have been offering pregnant ewes and cows to very old gods. I have come across stone altars in the forest and at the side of the lake, with gnawed bones that reveal the sacrifice. The poor animals may not help the deities to whom they're offered, but they do help the wolves and cats and foxes and other creatures roaming the woods, as hungry as the rest of us, and as cold. And because of the cold, I have ordered more trees to be cut down, not only to provide more wood for fires, but to allow the farmers to repair and strengthen their houses, for many complain of being unable to maintain what warmth they can create and must act to preserve themselves from the cold. So long as the men cannot plant, they can stay busy with saws and axes. I have sent to Rome for more saws, and I have ordered the local smiths to make ax-heads, using the iron I have laid up for times of trouble.

Sanct' Germain, my best, my oldest friend, I wish you were here to bear me company, to advise me, to help those unfortunates around me, to reassure me—when it is late and I am lonely and hungry—that this will end and we will thrive again, along with our living companions. Wherever you are in this broad world, I hope you are warmer and better-fed than I am just now, that you have spring and blossoms to brighten your daylight hours, and willing attendants to liven the night. You have been gone too long, or so it seems to me now, on this frosty Solstice night. The sun will rise shortly, and ordinarily I would begin to feel its might at this hour, but since early last March, it has been as if the sun is hiding behind a veil, and it does not leach my strength as has been its wont. In your many centuries, you have probably seen such fluctuations of the sun and could tell me something of its nature, were you here.

Pothinus the Gaul is setting out for Byzantium tomorrow, going into a blood-colored sunrise, and I will entrust this letter to him. He has a regular contact who travels the Silk Road, a Persian, who has carried messages and purchasing orders for Pothinus in the past, to their mutual satisfaction. For a small fee, he is willing to put this letter into the Persian's hands and instruct him where it is to go. This is entirely satisfactory to me, and I have said that I will also give a fee to the Persian and hope that Pothinus delivers it rather than adds it to the fee I pay him. The risk is acceptable to me, although it is hard not to want to leave here and go with Pothinus to Byzantium and beyond, no matter what risk there may be of rape and slavery. But once beyond this veiled sun, the dry expanses of the Silk Road could prove as unpleasant in their way as this cold is in its, and so I will remain here, and wish for your swift return.

Know that this comes with my very nearly eternal love,

Olivia

1

Behind them the ramparts of the Great Wall had fallen below the horizon, lost among the rise of hills and supplanted by the spread of the sands; aside from a hint of mountains to the very distant north and south, the Takla Makan desert stretched around them, like a tongue sticking out from the Gobi in the east. It was a high, oblong, arid declivity of rock, sand, and a cluster of lakes that many of the region's nomadic people considered sacred. Usually it was scorching in what ought to have been savage high summer, but now the sun did little to relieve the lingering nighttime chill, though it was midmorning.

"We will be in An-Hsi tomorrow," Zangi-Ragozh said in Byzantine Greek as he squinted into the glare ahead of them; a stiff, cold wind was blowing, flinging a cutting spray of sand at them and their ponies and two horses. "We can rest for a day at least; let the animals recover a little before we continue on."

"We'd best find camels instead of horses while we're there," said Ro-shei from his place in the wagon. His Greek accent was slightly different from Zangi-Ragozh's, more Roman than his master's. "These ponies do very well, but I have no confidence in the horses' ability to hold up through this hard weather, and with food so scarce, we should look for easier keepers than our horses."

"Yes. They are flagging," said Zangi-Ragozh sadly. "The sand is bad for their hooves, and nothing I can treat them with has been sufficient to keep them wholly sound."

"You do not want to give them up, do you?" Ro-shei observed.

"No, I do not," said Zangi-Ragozh.

"Why?" Ro-shei indicated the gray Zangi-Ragozh rode. "You have had countless other horses over the years. Surely Flying Cloud is not so remarkable a horse that you do not want to part with him. Celestial horse or not, he is not so very remarkable, is he?"

"Yes, I have had many horses, and no, Flying Cloud is not the epitome of them all," said Zangi-Ragozh with a sad, wry smile. "But I know how the peoples of this region live, and I know they will not value a Celestial horse—particularly a gelding—very highly. Were Flying Cloud a stallion, he might be worth something as a sire. As it is, he is likely to go into the stew pot before very long. So will many others if there is much more cold."

"And that offends you," said Ro-shei.

"And saddens me," said Zangi-Ragozh.

"You cannot save any of them, even if you purchase every last one," said Ro-shei with an air of resignation that spoke of long experience.

"No, I cannot; that is what troubles me the most." Zangi-Ragozh shaded his eyes as he looked up toward the sun. "I should not be able to do this."

"Do you think it is the end of the world?" Ro-shei asked with little emotion.

"I have no idea, if you mean the whole of the world," said Zangi-Ragozh. He sighed. "Things are dwindling—warmth, sunlight, food— and there seems to be no end to it. I wondered at first if I had sufficient gold for the journey—I should have made more, I fear—now, I am beginning to wonder if I have enough food, for reprovisioning is going to be difficult, and perhaps impossible. The ponies eat little, but they do eat, and they must be fed or they will be worse than useless."

"If you had the chance, could you make more gold? Or jewels?"

"That is one reason I wanted to go to Kumul. The teaching center there ought to have an athanor, and for a price they should permit me to use it for a few days, which is all I require. If we had a handful of diamonds and a handful of emeralds, we should have enough to pay for anything we may need between here and Byzantium, and they would not weigh as much as gold, nor take up space we need. We can put them in the bottom of the grain-barrels, for safety." He pointed off to the east where a thin billow of dust shone in the hazy morning light, marking the progress of other travelers. "We are not wholly alone, after all."

"Which may or may not be a good thing," Ro-shei warned, eyeing the dust with suspicion. "There are bandits in this region."

"They are moving no faster than we are, and we are small pickings," Zangi-Ragozh said.

"The better to take as slaves."

"They will not take slaves, not now," said Zangi-Ragozh with remorseless conviction. "If you want slaves to have any worth, you must feed them, and no one can spare food."

They continued on, west by northwest, throughout the morning and into the early afternoon, finally coming to a stop by a thin stream that welled out of a cluster of rock and ran for a short distance before disappearing into the sand; it was fringed with low-growing green plants, none of which were flourishing.

"Do you think it is safe?" Ro-shei asked, remembering the streams they had crossed that had stunk of sulfur, and from which the ponies had refused to drink.

"It is a spring and should be wholesome," said Zangi-Ragozh, dismounting and leading Flying Cloud to the spring. He watched as the gray lowered his nose and took a long draft. "I think this is assurance enough."

Ro-shei got down from the box and led the four harness ponies toward the little spring, the wagon clattering along behind them, then went around to the rear of it to go get the two additional ponies and his horse from their tethers. "Shall I prepare nosebags?"

"Yes. And we'll let them rest a bit. I want us to keep going until we reach An-Hsi tonight, no matter how late. The ponies will be able to make the journey, and if the horses flag, they can be led." Zangi-Ragozh pointed to the distant expanse of dust. "They're no nearer, but no farther, so unless they are bound for An-Hsi as well, they are pacing us, and that troubles me."

"They could be making for An-Hsi, as you said."

"Yes, they could," Zangi-Ragozh agreed so genially that Ro-shei knew he was worried.

"What about them troubles you?" he asked.

Zangi-Ragozh shook his head. "I wish I could tell you. I have a sensation not unlike ants crawling on me, and that, rare as it is, often announces trouble."

In his nearly five hundred years with Zangi-Ragozh, Ro-shei had known Zangi-Ragozh to make such an admission less then a dozen times, and in all instances it had presaged difficulties. "I wonder if you would want to change our direction slightly. Perhaps, if they do the same, that would reveal their intention."

"Go west, then directly north?" Zangi-Ragozh suggested; he

nodded to the wagon. "I will rest awhile and give you my decision when I rise."

"The sun does not seem to bother you as much as when we came here years ago," Ro-shei remarked as he watched Zangi-Ragozh climb into the wagon.

"You are right—it has weakened." He rubbed his face to get rid of the sand clinging to his skin. "That is the most worrisome of all." Before he let down the flap to close himself inside, he said, "Wake me if there is any change."

"You mean the other travelers?"

"I mean any change," said Zangi-Ragozh, and dropped the flap.

Ro-shei busied himself preparing nosebags for the ponies and horses, mixing grain, oil, bits of dried pears, and chopped hay for each animal, then fitted the nosebags over their bridles. Once the animals were eating, he undertook a little desultory grooming, brushing their coats free of the worst of the chafing sand. That done, he was about to climb back onto the driving-box for a moment's rest when he noticed a half-dozen large birds hidden in the verdure and decided to trap one for a meal. It took him a while to rig his snare and to bait it with a little pile of the horses' grain, but he was rewarded with a quick capture, and fresh, raw flesh for a meal. When he was finished, he buried the bones and feathers, then went to wake Zangi-Ragozh.

"Nothing untoward occurred?" Zangi-Ragozh asked as he came out of the back of the wagon.

"I managed to snare a bird to eat," said Ro-shei. "It was stringy and tough. The birds are not doing well."

"Better than dying and falling out of the sky, as so many have," said Zangi-Ragozh.

"The bird was still eaten," said Ro-shei.

"True enough," said Zangi-Ragozh, shrugging. "The travelers?"

"Still bearing west by northwest," said Ro-shei, pointing to the dust.

"Then we will change direction. It may delay us a bit, but we should still arrive at An-Hsi tonight." Zangi-Ragozh considered the sun. "We have a great deal of light left, but it is past its greatest strength—such as it is."

"An-Hsi by tonight," Ro-shei repeated as he led the spare ponies and his horse to the rear of the wagon to secure their leads. "You are determined on this."

"Yes. An-Hsi by tonight, and the road to Kumul in two days, three at the most, assuming we can buy camels for our horses," said Zangi-Ragozh as he tightened Flying Cloud's girth.

Ro-shei nodded. "Camels and ponies. We are joining all the other Silk Road merchants, if we acquire such animals."

"So much the better," said Zangi-Ragozh. "We will attract no notice, but for the smallness of our caravan."

"Would you want to travel with any others? Merchant trains, or others bound westward?" Ro-shei asked.

"Perhaps I might," said Zangi-Ragozh after a brief consideration. "It would depend upon the group and where they were bound."

"What about joining a caravan for part of the way?" Ro-shei recommended.

"That is a possibility," said Zangi-Ragozh. "I gather you believe that we would be safer in the company of others."

"It seems likely," said Ro-shei as he climbed back onto the driving-box and took the reins in his hands and gave the ponies the office to move, following Zangi-Ragozh westward, where the sun gleamed in the afternoon sky.

Less than a li later they found a jumble of nomad huts, most pulled over and torn apart, revealing the interiors of the structures, and the bodies of the inhabitants. A few carrion birds circled overhead, but not in the numbers that might have been expected a year ago. On the ground no herds of goats or ponies remained, only a few angry dogs that were circling a starving kid bleating for its mother. Zangi-Ragozh ran the dogs off and pulled in his horse, dismounting carefully, for Flying Cloud was sweating and tossing his head at the strong scent of blood and decay that hung over the place. "They wanted food; they killed everyone, even strong youngsters, and the women were not raped; they were hungry and in a hurry," he said as he made his way through the ruin of the camp. "The goats and ponies were for cooking."

"Anything else gone?" Ro-shei asked as he pulled the wagon in.

"I hardly know. I can find no barrels of grain or salt-meat, or butter, if they had any." He walked toward the largest hut, the only one that showed signs of burning. "They intended to do this, to raid quickly and slaughter anyone who stood against them. They singled this group out. They knew what they wanted and that they would find it here." He turned over a woven mat and found two beheaded children. "These people here were helpless, whoever they were."

"Do you know what group they belonged to? Is there a clan sign? I haven't seen one." Ro-shei stared about the destruction and pointed out a torn bit of cloth. "That flag is from the Land of Snows."

"So it is. And so is this embroidery, though these people were not, judging by their clothing and their faces. They must have traded with the people of the Land of Snows," Zangi-Ragozh said, holding up a cap of shearling wool. "They may have come from Chanchi-lah Pass."

"Not this year."

"No, probably not, which may mean they traveled between the Land of Snows and the Silk Road regularly or had contact with those who did. I am not familiar with all the clans between here and Kashgar, though someone must know them: we'll ask in An-Hsi," Zangi-Ragozh conceded as he continued to look for some sign of who had attacked. "I do not recognize this arrow," he said at last, lifting one from amid a tumble of kitchen pots. He went to give it to Ro-shei.

"Nor do I," said Ro-shei when he had examined it. "No, it's not familiar."

"Is there a new band of thieves or a warlord coming into the region? Or is this something else?" He took the arrow back, tapping it on his hand meditatively. "They say the Turks are becoming restive again."

"The arrow is not Turkish," said Ro-shei.

"I know; but if the Turks are moving, they will drive others ahead of them." He looked around again. "They are desperate, whoever they are."

"I surmise their numbers are small," said Ro-shei, "or they would have taken much more."

"I agree. They took what they could carry, and what they needed most." Zangi-Ragozh clenched his jaw. "The waste of it!"

"Do you want to feed on the kid?" Ro-shei asked. "If he is not to be wasted, as well?"

"I know it would be prudent to do so, and perhaps I can convince myself that such feeding is a kindness," Zangi-Ragozh answered in a tone of self-condemnation. "I can make myself believe—almost— that it would do no good to spare the creature to live another day;

those dogs or some other wild animals will return to devour it when we leave."

"Then I will catch it; he's not far from us," said Ro-shei, securing the reins of the wagon and climbing down from the box. "His life will do some good."

"That is hardly consolation," said Zangi-Ragozh, approaching the center of the tumbled shelters, making a sweeping gesture at the devastation around them. "Most were felled where they stood. I doubt these people fought back, which may mean they were ill or starving or both. They certainly were not ready to defend themselves." He considered what he saw around him more critically. "We have not time enough to bury them, and I would not like to burn this wreckage." Slowly he paced away from Ro-shei, then came back again. "Well, have a last look, get the kid, and let us leave."

Accepting this decision, Ro-shei picked up a good-sized empty brass cauldron. "This is useful."

"So it is," Zangi-Ragozh agreed, glad to have something else to hold his attention in place of slaughtered people.

"Would you protest if I were to take it with us?" Ro-shei kept his question level.

"Do we have need of it?" Zangi-Ragozh asked in some surprise. "We have no reason to cook."

"Who knows?" Ro-shei replied. "It may be useful. Occasionally you need hot water, and in time we may want to trade it."

Zangi-Ragozh considered. "Is there room in the wagon for it?"

"I can make room," said Ro-shei confidently, grabbing the arched handle of the cauldron and hefting it onto his shoulder to bear it up into the wagon. "I'll get the kid shortly."

"He will not go far," said Zangi-Ragozh.

As if to confirm this, the kid bleated and came trotting from around the broken poles of one of the dwellings.

"It would seem he is willing," said Ro-shei, watching the baby goat approaching.

"It would seem he is lonely," said Zangi-Ragozh. "But you are right. There is no kindness in leaving him here to be eaten by dogs or desert cats."

"And he would be," said Ro-shei. "Tonight, tomorrow, but no later than that."

"Yes. He would," Zangi-Ragozh said, holding his hand out and clicking his tongue to encourage the kid, petting the small head as the animal came up to him.

"Have you got him?" Ro-shei asked over his shoulder.

"Yes. I'll be quick," said Zangi-Ragozh, and picked up the young animal, calming it with a gentle pat and an expert touch.

"It was a wise thing to do," Ro-shei said as they pulled out of the ruined encampment, headed northwest. He had stored a haunch of the kid in a cloth sack under the driving-box; the horses and ponies had been watered and were willing to keep up a good, steady trot. "You needed the blood, and I the flesh."

"I know," said Zangi-Ragozh distantly as he rode slightly ahead of the wagon. He shaded his eyes and looked eastward. "The travelers have not changed direction."

"Then the slaughter we found may have been what has been troubling you," Ro-shei said.

"Perhaps." Zangi-Ragozh was unconvinced. "At An-Hsi, we will get what news we can." He said nothing for a short while, then spoke in a calm voice. "We are going to find as bad, and worse, before this is over."

"Whatever *this* may be," said Ro-shei.

"Yes. Whatever it is that has taken place." Zangi-Ragozh forced enthusiasm into his next words. "At least we will find warmth and plenty again in the West."

"So you hope," said Ro-shei with unusual bleakness.

"Do you doubt it?" Zangi-Ragozh asked.

Ro-shei hitched up his shoulders. "I hope you may be right, my master, but—" He broke off, then went on, "In Holin-Gol, the men in the market called it the dark of the sun, and I am afraid that they had the right of it. The sun is in the sky, but it has no warmth, no strength, and the land suffers."

"Yes," said Zangi-Ragozh.

"You have lived much longer than I have, and you say you have not seen anything to equal this," Ro-shei continued.

"That is true," Zangi-Ragozh admitted.

"Then it may be that the world is ending," said Ro-shei.

"It may be," Zangi-Ragozh said quietly.

"You say nothing more than that?" Ro-shei challenged.

"What more can I say?" Zangi-Ragozh asked. "I hope we may find that this dark of the sun ends as we go west, but if it does not, then . . ." He faltered, unable to continue. "The Egyptians called the West the abode of death."

"Can you starve to death? To the True Death?" Ro-shei asked bluntly. "Can I?"

"By all the forgotten gods, I hope so," said Zangi-Ragozh with quiet conviction.

This sobering remark silenced Ro-shei until after a brilliant sunset, when they turned northward; he pointed to the evening star. "It is bluer than I remember it."

"All the sky has changed colors," said Zangi-Ragozh. "Dawn and sunset and the midheaven at noon. Nothing is as it was."

"Do you think it is the same in the West?" Ro-shei asked uneasily.

"It is the same sky," said Zangi-Ragozh. "If this is some manner of invisible cloud, then it may dissipate—we must hope that it will—between this place and my native earth."

"Is that where we are going?" Ro-shei was startled.

"It lies between us and the farthest shores of Gaul, or Hispania," said Zangi-Ragozh. "It may serve our purposes to go there."

"To die?"

"If nothing else," said Zangi-Ragozh quietly. "There may be other advantages to going there if this cloud remains in the sky: I hope that the cloud is gone long before we reach those mountains, but if it is not gone, I will be glad that we have a place to go." Zangi-Ragozh peered into the deepening night. "The other travelers have made camp for the night. You can see their fires." He pointed eastward.

"So I can," said Ro-shei, and did not say anything more about their destination as they continued on toward An-Hsi.

It was nearing midnight by the time they saw the torches in the watchtowers of An-Hsi, and a short while later they could make out the fires of the travelers camped outside the brick walls of the town. The wind had come up, cold and cutting as knives, and the flames from the torches and campfires leaped and quivered under its invisible lash. As Zangi-Ragozh and Ro-shei drew nearer, they noticed that a mounted guard patrolled the limits of the camps, ready to fight off any attack that might come, so they made a point of making the kind of noise that meant little trouble as they approached, keeping to the center of the packed-earth roadway.

In a response to their arrival, a guard in a blue-dyed shuba and heavy, Hunnic leggings rode up on a feisty pony to halt them with his short lance. "Who are you? Where are you coming from? Where are you going? What is your business? What do you carry?" He spoke in Chinese and repeated himself in the strange dialect of An-Hsi, then in badly pronounced Persian.

"I am Zangi-Ragozh, a foreign merchant from Yang-Chau. I am bound for the Black Sea to trade in spices and dyes; at present I carry very little beyond dyes and feed for my ponies," he answered in Chinese as he got off his horse. "We have come from an encampment, half a day from here, which had been attacked and sacked by unknown men about a day before we got there."

"A sacked encampment, you say?" The guard was distrustful. "You will have to make a report to the Merchants' Council."

"I will. Others may be in danger from those who raided and killed," said Zangi-Ragozh.

"Small groups are always in such danger," said the guard with fatality. "Those who travel in the region know the risks they take. It is for them to prepare."

"And it is for you to warn them to be prepared," said Zangi-Ragozh levelly.

"So you may tell the Council," the guard told him.

"I certainly will. In the morning, if it is all the same to you, for I doubt the Council is sitting at this hour. Just now, my traveling companion and I are in need of sleep." Zangi-Ragozh made a sign of respect to the guard. "Post one of your men to watch us tonight, if you think that necessary."

The guard frowned, scrutinizing the two newcomers. "I will post a watch on you."

"Good," said Zangi-Ragozh.

"How does it serve your purpose?" The guard was unused to such cooperation and found such acquiescence made him uneasy.

"So our movements may be accurately reported to the Council," said Zangi-Ragozh, tugging at Flying Cloud's reins to lead him to the wagon.

"Is there reason to do so?" the guard demanded. "Draw your wagon over there, to the base of the third watchtower. I will send two men to keep you secure for the night. In the morning, you will go to the Merchants' Council to make your report and to be assessed a duty for entering An-Hsi."

"I am most grateful," said Zangi-Ragozh.

The guard snorted in disbelief, but pulled his pony back so that Ro-shei could guide the wagon to the place he had indicated. "My men will be with you shortly," he said, and rode off at a good clip.

"Grateful?" Ro-shei echoed.

"Yes," said Zangi-Ragozh, leading his horse up behind the wagon. "I hope the Council is willing to trust what I tell them, and it is more likely they will if we're guarded and prove safe."

Ro-shei drew in the wagon and secured the reins. "What do you want from the Council?"

"I want as much of a safe passage as we may be given," said Zangi-Ragozh, going toward the front of the wagon.

"Do you think we will need safe passage?" Ro-shei asked as he got down from the driving-box.

"Oh, yes." Zangi-Ragozh secured Flying Cloud to the rear of the wagon and turned to loosen his girth. "So do you," he added cannily.

Text of a safe-conduct granted by the Merchants' Council of An-Hsi to the foreign merchant Zangi-Ragozh, along with an inventory of all duty paid on goods being carried and a record of all animals held and purchased by Zangi-Ragozh.

The Merchants' Council of An-Hsi presents this safe-conduct to the foreign merchant Zangi-Ragozh of Yang-Chau, ensuring him safe passage from An-Hsi to Kumul, also known as Ha-Mi, without the pain of additional duties imposed upon the goods he carries in a single wagon and on three camels, which were purchased in the market here for six silver bars and the exchange of two Celestial horses. Any escort sought by Zangi-Ragozh, upon acceptance of terms of employment, is to be provided and honored.

On the sixth day of the Fortnight of the Young Camels, at the Merchants' Council House in An-Hsi.

The Seal of the Council

The Inventory of Articles carried by Zangi-Ragozh upon which duty has been paid:

> *six ponies*
> *three camels*
> *necessary tack and saddlery for all animals*
> *ten leather nosebags, and ten of heavy cloth*
> *brushes, combs, picks, and grooming cloths*
> *nippers, rasps, an anvil, a dozen iron ingots, mallets, and hammers*
> *a single wagon, with three replacement wheels*
> *four crates, three containing earth, one containing fabric, clothing, bedding, and bolts of silk*
> *clothing needed for the trek to the West, including shubas, shaidans, boots, Persian robes, sen-gais and sen-hsiens, cloaks, and hats*
> *four bolts of uncut silk, and six lengths of woven wool*
> *nine felt saddle-pads, and two sets of felt harness-pads*
> *four barrels of mixed feed for the ponies, and four for the camels*
> *six sacks of chopped hay*
> *two sacks of dried fruit*
> *a sack of crimped oats*
> *three sacks of buckwheat*
> *two barrels of oil*
> *five barrels of water, and a small tub for washing and catching water*
> *three cooking pots*
> *four rice-bowls*
> *a tea service*
> *four alabaster cups*
> *three brass trays*
> *cooking and eating utensils, including a cleaver and a ladle*
> *two caravan tents*
> *a large crate of spices and dyes*
> *a crate containing twenty-four jade figures, and nineteen small statues in precious woods*
> *a large box of paper, with inkpad and brushes*
> *a locked safe-box containing fifty-eight strings of copper cash, forty-six of silver, and twenty bars each of silver and gold*
> *a box-chest of medicaments, bandages, salves, balsams, unguents, and healing instruments*

two mattresses

six blankets

three oiled canvas roof-covers for the wagon

a small chest of bracelets, brooches, and pectorals, designated for trade

two crossbows and one standard bow, with fifty quarrels and thirty arrows

three axes, an awl, a mallet, a hammer, forty nails, and a wrench

wood for torches and fires, and a sack of kindling

flint-and-steel

strips of bridle-leather and a dozen leather patches

two dozen canvas patches, three dozen of cotton, and two dozen of silk

four lengths of hempen rope, three spools of silken twine, and a spool of cotton string

five needles and nine lengths of light thread, fifteen of heavy

This is the sum of the foreign merchant Zangi-Ragozh's provisions.

Authenticated by
Noshun-Ya Jailan
Clerk of the Merchants' Council of An-Hsi
(his chop)

2

Passage to Kumul was uneventful beyond the deepening cold as the sun moved southward in the sky and the days shortened. In slightly less than three fortnights, they went from An-Hsi to the easternmost rising of the Tien Shan range. During the first fortnight, Zangi-Ragozh elected to travel most of the night and into the morning, resting through the brightest part of the day, and then moving off again in late afternoon; it helped him stave off the worst of his hunger, for there were few opportunities for nourishment beyond the occasional blood of a goat or a wild ass, and that was barely sufficient to his needs. They encountered few other travelers on the road through that desolate waste, and those they did see were more small groups of horsemen, clans bound in search of flourishing pastures, not well-laden caravans from the West. The foothills of the Tien Shan range proved difficult to approach, for there had been a number of rock slides, and from time to time, Zangi-Ragozh had to dismount from his pony and clear the way for the wagon and the camels.

The stone walls of Kumul were a welcome sight when at last they came around a massive outcropping of rock and caught their first glimpse of the five watchtowers on the flank of the mountain's swell. On the floor of the narrow valley just at the town's foot where there was usually a sea of caravan tents, this morning there were no more than twenty, less than a quarter of the usual number.

"Not what I was expecting," said Zangi-Ragozh as he drew in his cinder-brown pony and stared at Kumul in the first, sizzling light of glaring dawn.

"No," said Ro-shei, on the driving-box. "Do you think there is trouble?"

"Beyond the cold and the first touch of famine? I do not know," said Zangi-Ragozh harshly.

"Does this surprise you?" Ro-shei asked, mildly startled. "With all we have seen—"

"I know; I know," said Zangi-Ragozh, and admitted, "I had hoped that there would be a lessening of difficulties by now, that the sun would be stronger, and that the peaks would not have yellow snow upon them, that there would be warmth, or new grass, or—I had hoped some sign of improvement would be evident."

"There are Jou'an-Jou'an tents down there; do you see? They have been forced off their usual lands, and the cold may be the least of it, for the clan markings say that this group is one of the more isolated ones," said Ro-shei, doing his best to find some less dire outlook than the one Zangi-Ragozh foresaw. "Because Kumul is out of their usual region of travel, they may be trying to find better conditions for their herds, and perhaps they may be willing to tell us what they have seen on their way here. Any information they impart could help us." He squinted at the sharp peaks to the west, with their crown of golden snow. "Wherever they have been, it could be helpful to know what they have encountered."

Zangi-Ragozh tapped the pony with his heels and felt the instant of resistance he had come to expect from the tough little animal. "The gates should be open soon. We will go directly into the town, and to the Holy Trinity compound. I hope Seraphim is still Apostle there."

"It is more than a decade since you have been here," Ro-shei cautioned him. "And Seraphim was not a young man then."

"No, he was not. But he had children of his three wives, and that might mean he has a successor, if he has died. In any case, Holy Trinity compound will not have been abandoned, not with the school and the library," said Zangi-Ragozh with determined optimism. As they passed through the clusters of tents on their approach to the town gates, he noticed that most of the men he saw showed signs of hunger, and that their animals were thin. The one woman he saw was gaunt.

The guard at the gate was in a leather shai-fa topped with a scale-armor tunic, as if he expected trouble. To reinforce this impression, he was more heavily armed than any town-guard they had seen since leaving Yang-Chau; his Chinese was in the western dialect of Chiu-Ch'uan. He was accompanied by three other soldiers, equally heavily armed, all lined up to block the entrance to the town. "Who are you and why are you here?"

Zangi-Ragozh identified himself and presented his safe-conduct to the guard. "I am going westward, if the weather permits. I have come to Kumul in order to visit Holy Trinity compound."

"To pray for good fortune, no doubt," said the guard caustically. "There is a duty to enter, whether or not you are here to buy and sell. You must pay it in full before you can be admitted."

"Of course," said Zangi-Ragozh as affably as he could. "I have strings of cash, gold, and silver, as you see on the inventory. What is the duty for my one wagon, my ponies and camels, to enter?"

The guard scowled at the documents in his hand, then glared at his three companions. "A string of silver cash for each of us, and two bars of silver to enter."

The amount was shockingly high, well beyond what a town like Kumul could usually demand, but Zangi-Ragozh took only a moment to consider. "These are hard times and travelers are few, and your town suffers the same privations as the rest of the world. You do what you must to make up the shortfall." He reached into the capacious sleeve of his shai-dan to retrieve the money he had put there; he was careful not to reveal how much more his sleeves held. "Is there a chit to show we have paid our duty?"

The guard looked annoyed, but he lowered his head reluctantly and produced a small, thin strip of wood. "Take this. If anyone should question you, show them this and say you had it from Tsomak at the main gate. I will vouch for you, Worthy Foreigner."

"I am deeply appreciative, Honorable Guard," said Zangi-Ragozh without a trace of irony as he put his pony to the walk to lead Ro-shei and his wagon and animals into the walled town.

They found the streets subdued, with few people abroad; those who were regarded Zangi-Ragozh and his little caravan uneasily. Although they kept to the major streets and went directly toward the Holy Trinity compound, they were aware of feeling out of place, in unfamiliar surroundings, among townspeople who distrusted them.

At Holy Trinity compound, the gate was closed and barred, and a tug on the bellpull did not bring a response for some little while. Finally a man of advanced years opened the grille in the center of the gate and peered out, summing up what he saw with a jerky nod; from his place in the saddle Zangi-Ragozh made the gesture of greeting, his left hand fitted into his right, and waited.

"God be with you," the man said in the local dialect, then in Persian, and finally in Chinese.

"And with you," said Zangi-Ragozh as he dismounted. Approaching the gate, he went on in Chinese, "I am the foreign merchant Zangi-Ragozh, come to pay my respects to Apostle Seraphim, and to seek the comfort of his school for a short while, if it is acceptable to him that I should do so."

The old man blinked. "The Apostle Seraphim died two years ago. The Apostle Lazarus, his son, is in charge here now."

"I am grieved to hear of the death of the Apostle Seraphim, who received me with great kindness more than a decade ago. I ask to see his son, the Apostle Lazarus, to express my condolences and to make his acquaintance," Zangi-Ragozh said, holding out a visiting card imprinted with his eclipse device on one side, and his chop on the other.

The old man took the visiting card and studied it. "I will show him. If you will wait?"

"Of course," said Zangi-Ragozh, anticipating a delay. He turned to

Ro-shei. "I remember Lazarus as a young man of fifteen or sixteen." Zangi-Ragozh shaded his forehead with his hands to see what lay inside more clearly. He blinked in surprise. "There are two Jou'an-Jou'an saddles on the rack in front of the stable."

"Are you sure?" Ro-shei wondered skeptically.

"The clan marks match those on the tents outside the town," said Zangi-Ragozh. "And they have those metal foot-loops the Jou'an-Jou'an have started using on their saddles."

"Are there Christians among the Jou'an-Jou'an?" Ro-shei inquired, much astonished.

"They may be seeking help. Apostle Seraphim was always devoted to charity, and the gathering of information about the middle and northern routes of the Silk Road," said Zangi-Ragozh, leading his pony to the rear of the wagon and fixing an empty lead to his bridle.

"Apostle Seraphim would certainly do so," said Ro-shei.

"Then we'll hope the present Apostle will share what he knows with us," said Zangi-Ragozh, glancing down the narrow street toward an open convergence of several ways; there was a well in the center of the space that was not large enough to be a square, but too wide to be only a part of the road. "I seem to recall that there were inns by that well."

"Do you think we should command rooms there?" Ro-shei asked.

"I think it would make it easier for me to find sustenance tonight if we are at an inn than if we are inside the compound," said Zangi-Ragozh rather drily. "Apostle Seraphim would have extended his hospitality, I know, but then food was not in short supply, and the town was flourishing. That sort of hospitality was easily provided, eleven years ago. His son might not be so willing to have us as guests." He made up his mind. "Yes, let us choose an inn; I will inform the Apostle that we are making our own arrangements for shelter and food. We should also make sure we let it be known that we have our own provisions."

"Would you like me to go to command accommodations?" Ro-shei could sense Zangi-Ragozh's indecision in the silence that met his question.

"Not just yet," Zangi-Ragozh said at last. "When I am admitted, then if you will, go secure a place for us."

"Very well," said Ro-shei.

"You may think this is an unnecessary precaution," said Zangi-Ragozh, reading the distress in Ro-shei's faded-blue eyes. "And it may be."

"But given the state of the town, you are concerned?" Ro-shei ventured. "If you were to give the Apostle some of our supplies, he would undoubtedly welcome us with thanksgiving."

Zangi-Ragozh shook his head. "We cannot spare the supplies," he said.

"I am aware of that," said Ro-shei.

"If he will permit me to use the athanor, then perhaps I can repay him in gold." Zangi-Ragozh was about to say more when a thunderous rolling of drums came from beyond the compound walls, and then gongs were added to the cacophony. "Their morning prayers are beginning."

Ro-shei held the alarmed ponies on short reins to keep them from bolting, and the camels moaned. "It may be a while until the gates are opened."

"So it might. Go on—find an inn and get our animals stalled and watered. Give them a little to eat. We'll make them proper nosebags later, when we can supervise their feeding."

"Do you think the nosebags might get taken?" Ro-shei asked, preparing to swing the wagon around in the narrow street.

"I think it is possible," said Zangi-Ragozh, raising his voice in order to be heard over the din.

Ro-shei nodded to show he had heard and continued to work the reins, finally facing the downward slope toward the well. "I will return here when I have made arrangements."

"Excellent; thank you, old friend," said Zangi-Ragozh, stepping aside to allow the wagon and the camels to pass.

The noise went on for some little while, then the compound grew quiet, and for another short while no sound came from within. Then there was a flurry of drums and gongs, and the babble of voices came from beyond the gate, and there was a loud report as the bolt inside was drawn back and the gate swung open, revealing a great number of men and women going purposefully toward their morning labors. The old man who had spoken to Zangi-Ragozh through the grille was waiting just inside, his seamed face creased into a smile.

"Enter, stranger, in the name of the Savior," he said formally.

"Thank you," said Zangi-Ragozh. "My traveling companion has gone to find us an inn. He will return when he has made arrangements."

"He will be welcome when he comes," said the old man with undisguised relief. "The Apostle Lazarus has asked me to bring you to him. He is with a magician of the Jou'an-Jou'an," he went on as he started across the courtyard toward a two-story building with a cross over the main door. "He says he recalls your visit some years ago and is anxious to speak to you again."

Zangi-Ragozh said, "It is a great honor to me that the Apostle should recall those distant days."

"The Apostle is mindful of his duties," said the old man.

"Will it be a problem for him to receive me if he is with this Jou'an-Jou'an magician?" Zangi-Ragozh was careful to ask without giving any implication of his opinion.

"It should not be," said the old man, going up the broad, shallow steps with sufficient effort to reveal painful knees.

"I have a medicament among my belongings that may ease your discomfort if you would allow me to present you with a vial of it," said Zangi-Ragozh.

"I thank you, but I offer what God has given me to Him," said the old man.

Zangi-Ragozh shrugged. "If you change your mind, you have only to let me know."

"I will not change my mind; this pain is mine to bear. It would slight Christ's suffering for our sins to refuse what I must endure," said the old man affably as he paused to bow to the altar at the end of the room, then indicated a well-lit corridor off to the left that connected to a single-story building next to the church. "If you will come this way? The Apostle is in his study."

"I will gladly follow you," said Zangi-Ragozh, doing so. The corridor made another turn, and Zangi-Ragozh found himself facing a shrine that showed Jesus dancing before the brilliant golden disk on which God's Throne was hammered. "This is new," he remarked.

"It was made shortly before Apostle Seraphim died, as a sign of his readiness for Paradise. He commissioned it as his last official act." The old man gestured, urging Zangi-Ragozh to hasten, and took the right branch of the corridor. "The door at the end there is the Apostle's study. Knock once and enter."

"I will. Thank you—" He paused, waiting for a name.

"My name in Christ is Ephraem," said the old man.

"For the poet from Niblisi?" Zangi-Ragozh asked.

"A most pious man," said Ephraem. "His life is a great example to all of us."

Zangi-Ragozh nodded and continued down the corridor, leaving Ephraem to go about his other duties. As he reached the door, he knocked as he had been instructed and waited for a response.

"The foreigner, Zangi-Ragozh, is that you?" called a deep, beautiful voice from beyond the door in excellent Chinese.

"It is," he answered.

"Then enter," said the voice.

Zangi-Ragozh opened the door and stepped into the study of the Apostle of Kumul. It was much as he remembered it—pale walls with ten recessed windows with iconographic pictures of the life of Christ hung between them. The room was not austere, but it was also far from lavish: its most prominent feature was almost a dozen manuscript crates of lacquered leather on shelves against the north wall. There was a small altar on the east wall, and a writing table against the south wall, facing into the room, where four chairs were set around a table. Just now two of the chairs were occupied, one by the Apostle—a handsome man in his midtwenties in a long robe and shuba; he wore a short beard and his hair was clubbed at the back of his neck—and the other by the Jou'an-Jou'an magician. This proved to be a woman, probably about the same age as the Apostle, for her angular Hunnic face was relatively unlined and she had all her teeth; she was dressed in the heavy, embroidered shai-dan of her clan and people. Her eyes were light-blue, nearly the color of ice, and her hair, cut as short as a man's, was almost entirely white.

The Apostle inclined his head in Zangi-Ragozh's direction. "In the Name of the Savior, I bid you welcome to Holy Trinity at Kumul," he said in Chiu-Ch'uan dialect.

"You are most gracious," said Zangi-Ragozh in the same vernacular, closing the door and coming into the room.

"I am Lazarus, son of Seraphim, Apostle of Holy Trinity," he went on.

"I remember you, but as a very young man, with only the beginning of a beard. You were busy with your studies when I was here the last time, and your father saw great promise in you," he said, and fitted his hands together in polite greeting, looking from the Apostle Lazarus to his other guest.

"This is Dukkai, of the Jou'an-Jou'an, the clan of the Desert Cats," the Apostle continued. "She is their magician."

"It is an honor to meet you, Dukkai of the Desert Cats," said Zangi-Ragozh with the same respectful gesture.

She regarded him in silence for a short while, then said, in fairly good Chinese, "It is interesting to meet someone from so far away." She, too, spoke the Chiu-Ch'uan dialect with ease.

"Surely you and your people often encounter travelers from great distances," said Zangi-Ragozh. "Do not the Jou'an-Jou'an follow the Silk Road in their course from pasture to pasture?"

"From time to time we encounter travelers, but they are not often like you," she said, and volunteered nothing more. "What do you call this town? Kumul? Ha-mi?"

"Kumul," said Zangi-Ragozh, "as most of those who live here do."

Apostle Lazarus indicated one of the empty chairs. "Come. Sit. Talk with us. Your presence is most truly pleasing to us, here in Kumul."

"Thank you," said Zangi-Ragozh, and chose the chair that faced the door.

"I must ask you how long you have been traveling, and from where you departed to come here," the Apostle went on as if resuming a conversation with Zangi-Ragozh rather than beginning one.

Knowing his candor was required, Zangi-Ragozh did his utmost to answer fully and without any appearance of deception or omission. "I left Yang-Chau about three fortnights after the Winter Solstice, on the order of the new Wen Emperor in the West, who summoned me to wait upon him in his new court at Chang'an; as a merchant I had good reason to want cordial arrangements with his court, for many of my caravans traveled through his territory. Since I am a foreigner, I must be punctilious in all my business negotiations, particularly where the good opinion of the court could improve my situation." He paused to give Apostle Lazarus a chance to change the tenor of his question. When nothing more was ventured, he went on, "I was, in response to the Wen Emperor's order, bound for that capital, but the weather changed for the worse, some of my men and goods were confiscated, and there was more fighting on the road; it became necessary to abandon those plans, for I could not reach the new Emperor, and there was as much trouble on the road back to Yang-Chau, or so the reports said, so I decided to begin a journey to my homeland. It has been a hard trek."

"Because of the cold," said Dukkai.

"And the lack of good food," said Zangi-Ragozh.

"They say that the south has food in plenty," said the Apostle.

"Not that I saw," Zangi-Ragozh said. "Everywhere I passed there were fears of famine, all well-founded. Perhaps much farther to the south there is plenty, but I would doubt it."

"Why is that?" Dukkai asked.

"Because I saw no travelers from the south bringing food to sell, only a few families who were looking for better farms to work. Given the lack of food in the north, I would expect southerners, if they had any, to make the most of their bounty." He waited again. "There are more robbers and bandits—that usually means want."

"You got here safely," said the Apostle.

"My traveling companion and I have but one wagon and six ponies and three camels." Zangi-Ragozh shrugged. "We are not worth the risk of stopping."

"Hardly a caravan," said Dukkai, and fixed him with her pale eyes. "Or is it better on the other side of the Great Wall, and you are telling us this to protect what they have?"

"Anyone who claims so has not been there recently," said Zangi-Ragozh, choosing his words carefully. "The market at Holin-Gol was half-empty when I was there."

"Then you say they lie?" Apostle Lazarus sounded troubled.

"I say they have not been there since last winter. The yellow snow has fallen in many places, and the veil over the sun has been present from near Lo-Yang to this place. It may extend farther, but I have not seen it for myself," Zangi-Ragozh told them.

"The yellow snow," said Dukkai, making the words a condemnation. "It has fallen steadily into the summer, not only in the Tien Shan, but on the wastes of the desert, and it still falls." She fingered her broad, embroidered leather sash. "It is not wholesome."

"No. It burns the fields and sickens many animals. I have seen whole flocks of birds fall dead from the skies," said Zangi-Ragozh.

"That has happened here, as well," said Apostle Lazarus. "It is God's Hand, laid upon us for our unrepentant behavior."

"It is the gods contending over the earth," said Dukkai in a tone of voice that suggested they often debated such things.

"Whatever it is, it is deadly," said Zangi-Ragozh.

"And many are suffering because of it," said the Apostle, going on with increasing emotion. "To have so much taken from us at one time can only mean that God wills it."

"If that is so," Dukkai countered with the ease of long custom, "why would your God demand so much misery of his worshipers?"

"God gave His Son to be the Light of the World. He allowed His Son to suffer on the Cross, for the sins of all men." Apostle Lazarus spoke as if to a recalcitrant child.

"If the son paid for the sins of men, why does your God visit more wretchedness on everyone? Was not that son's expiation sufficient?" Dukkai leaned forward in genuine curiosity as she waited for his answer.

"This is one of the many things that only Christians understand," said Apostle Lazarus. "I am sure that you must know there is only one Son of God, and He reigns in Paradise with His Father."

"So you tell me," said Dukkai, shaking her head slowly. "But that does not explain the travail of the world, not if the son's sacrifice was acceptable to your God, and of true worth. If it truly did redeem men, then no Christian should have to endure want or pain or loss, yet we see they do."

"There is the Fallen Angel, who brought Original Sin," said the Apostle.

"And that should have been discharged by the sacrifice. Are you saying that your God has rivals who are as powerful as he, and who prey upon his people? Why has he not killed them all? Or is it that his power is not without limits, and Fate has sway over him as well as everything else?" Dukkai broke off to take a cup of buttered tea from the table in front of her. She drank half the liquid and put the cup back. "I forgot to tell you this when I arrived last night: I have some tea bricks for you, Apostle Lazarus. Not as many as last year, but not too paltry a gift."

"You need hardly purchase your reception here," said Apostle Lazarus. "You are welcome if all you have is the breath in your body."

"You do credit to your faith to say so, but my gods would not favor me if I neglected the rules of hospitality," said Dukkai. "My escort will present the bricks to your kitchen-master, and that will please me, and Baru Ksoka, who leads the Desert Cats, will not be dishonored in accepting your hospitality."

"That is his understanding, not mine," said Apostle Lazarus with a warm smile. "It is an opportunity to serve God, having you and your escort here at Holy Trinity, and it is fitting that you should permit me to extend my welcome to your people."

"I believe you, but Baru Ksoka is the Kaigan, and I am obliged to respect his wishes," said Dukkai.

"After all these years? What is it?—seven years you have been coming here? Surely your Kaigan is aware that I expect no gifts other than your presence?" Apostle Lazarus shook his head again. "Your Kaigan is a stubborn man."

"And you are not?" Dukkai countered.

"It is fitting that I tell you that I need nothing from your Kaigan, that my hospitality does not depend on his gifts to me, although I will accept them as donations of our faith, for God will render what gifts I may need in this life, and bring me to glory in the next." He refilled her cup from a large, earthenware pot that sat on a warming plate atop a small butter-stove. "Let us assume that we have had our usual wrangle. I will thank your Kaigan for the bricks of tea and you will not have to insist upon it."

She laughed, sounding lighthearted. "I will tell him of your high regard for him and your gratitude for his gift, as I always do."

Zangi-Ragozh felt like an interloper, intruding on old friends, and it made him awkward. "You have had this discussion before, I take it?"

"It is a ritual, almost," said Dukkai. "I would be disappointed if we could not dispute the Kaigan's gift." She drank a little more buttered tea. "Baru Ksoka would not understand our amusement, and he would be troubled by what we say to each other."

"He will hear nothing from me," Zangi-Ragozh assured her, understanding her intent. "Why should he? We may never meet."

"I think you will," she said. "If you are to remain here for more than a few days, he will come to the compound and will want to know all strangers here."

"Is that part of his leadership?" Zangi-Ragozh asked.

"He is afraid that being in this place, dangerous teaching may leach away my magic," said Dukkai.

"You do not seem worried about that," Zangi-Ragozh observed.

"Magic cannot be taken in that manner. This place is a magical one for Christians, but that does not damage other magic. Few places are so pernicious as to do that." Dukkai drank down the rest of her tea. "I am expected to maintain the secrets of all the gods, to keep them apart from disbelievers, and to preserve their rites for the clan alone."

Apostle Lazarus stared at her in amazement. "So stringent a burden for you to carry. I am surprised that you speak to me at all."

"We share many things in our work," she said. "You and I have rituals to uphold, and many responsibilities to our people, who are afraid the gods may fail them. Yet you trust in the strength of your God as I trust in the strength of all of mine. It is not something the others understand. You probably do not understand it, Zangi-Ragozh."

"When I was a very young man, I was initiated into the priesthood of my people," he said quietly, and not quite comfortably, as it was a part of his past that he usually kept to himself. "It was a long time ago, and my people are disbursed over the earth, but I recall what I was taught in my youth." That had been two and a half millennia ago, but he had not forgotten that night in the sacred grove, when the god had made him one of his blood.

"Then perhaps you *do* understand," she said. "I would like to hear what your priests taught you. It makes a change from what Apostle Lazarus and I usually discuss."

Apostle Lazarus leaned back in his chair. "Yes, Zangi-Ragozh. I am most curious. My father told me about your skills as an alchemist but nothing of your having been a priest."

"From priest to alchemist to merchant," said Dukkai. "It must be a most fascinating journey."

"That is not a word I would have chosen," said Zangi-Ragozh, meeting Dukkai's ice-blue eyes with his blue-black ones.

"No; those living a life do not usually see the remarkableness of it," said Dukkai. "They leave that to magicians, and story-tellers."

"How can you say such things?" Apostle Lazarus exclaimed. "The lives and writings of holy men are examples, not tales to entertain." He grinned, ready for lively conversation.

"It may be so," said Dukkai, "but the tales of the gods are often as much adventure as instruction, so that people may understand the nature of the gods' powers."

"Of your gods, perhaps," the Apostle countered.

"Of all gods," said Dukkai firmly. "As well they should be, so that people will want to remember them."

The Apostle made a humorous groan. "This is going to be a long day," he said merrily.

"At least until Baru Ksoka arrives," said Dukkai. "Then there will be things we must do."

"I will keep that in mind," said Apostle Lazarus.

Zangi-Ragozh sat back and listened to the Apostle and Dukkai match wits while the shadows on the walls grew dim as heavy clouds covered the wan sun.

Text of a letter from Eclipse Trading Company senior clerk Hu Bi-Da to Councillor Ko She-Hsieh, both at Yang-Chau.

To the most excellent Councillor Ko She-Hsieh, the senior clerk of the Eclipse Trading Company, Hu Bi-Da, sends this requested report and provides the justly deserving Councillor with the information he has asked be included, on this, the first day of the Fortnight of the White Dew.

This person regrets to inform the Councillor that there has as yet been no further word from Zangi-Ragozh, the illustrious foreigner who is the owner of the Eclipse Trading Company, and who has been gone from Yang-Chau for fifteen fortnights. As the Councillor is aware, the company is well-funded and the instructions left by the illustrious foreigner Zangi-Ragozh provided for the continuing trading of the company, as well as guaranteeing the paying of duties and taxes. Should word come at any time, this person will immediately inform the Councillor of that fact and apprize him of as much information as is to be had. The messenger from Dong-Lin provided proof that Zangi-Ragozh passed through the town, paid the required duties, and went on, which at present is the sum this person knows of his employer's activities.

I Mo-Ching, Captain of the Morning Star, *has at last returned to port. His ship is somewhat damaged but not beyond repair. He has*

*brought a cargo that is generally satisfactory, and the goods will be
released for sale as soon as the customs officials decide on what duty
to charge. I Mo-Ching himself is preparing a report for the Council
regarding what he has observed on his voyage, the kind of damage
he has seen, the aftermath of such damage, and his assessment on
the impact of this on trade. This person urges you to give his account the utmost attention, for he will not lead you astray nor expect
you to embrace tales of fanciful events.*

*This person has provided a copy of the accounts of Eclipse Trad-
ing Company for the last twelve fortnights for your review. This person vouches for the accuracy of the records kept and, on pain of legal
action, declares they are complete and veracious in all details and
particulars. This person adds that the loss of the* Bird of the Waves
and The Shining Pearl *are listed separately for the value of the cargoes of these lost ships can only be estimated, and so this person has
based his assessment on previous cargoes of these ships. In addition
to the two lost ships, word has arrived that the* Phoenix *has been
badly damaged and must be extensively repaired before it may safely
sail to Yang-Chau. This person has arranged for funds to be trans-
ferred to cover such repairs and, further, has been advised that the
Captain is dead of fever and will have to be replaced. Should the Council authorize it, this person will hire a new Captain to carry the money
for repairs to the* Phoenix *and assume command of her reconstruction as well as her voyage home. However, this person will not ask any
Captain to take to sea after the Fortnight of the Frost Kings, when
darkness and bad weather make navigation hazardous in good times.
Given what has happened in the last twelve fortnights, this person
cannot in good conscience send any ship to sea, for great waves might
still strike out of nowhere, and ferocious winds drive all ahead of
them, sending ships to destruction. If this person is erring in these decisions, he asks that the Councillor remember that Zangi-Ragozh entrusted his business to my care, and this person is bound to use
caution in difficult circumstances, which these surely are. If, upon his
return, Zangi-Ragozh should choose to chastise or penalize this person for his decisions, then this person will accept what is meted out to
him as the right of his employer. Otherwise this person will continue
to uphold his position in the Eclipse Trading Company in as prudent
a manner possible.*

Submitted with the inclusions already mentioned, with the abiding respect and regard of

Hu Bi-Da
Senior Clerk, Eclipse Trading
Company
(his chop)

3

"What do they call you in the West?—certainly not Zangi-Ragozh," said Dukkai as she stood in the alchemical chamber a week after the foreigner had arrived in Kumul. "That must be what the Chinese call you."

"It is," said Zangi-Ragozh, looking up from the crock of moldy bread that stood on one end of the long table. He had donned his black silk sen-hsien and put his black shearling shuba over it, for the day was cold and the fire in the distant stove made little headway against the chill.

"What was the name you were given?" She cocked her head. "If you may tell me without offending your gods."

"My gods are long-forgotten by everyone but me," said Zangi-Ragozh with a wry, sad smile.

"Then why do you hesitate? I know you are hesitating." Dukkai moved out of the glare of brassy early-morning sunlight so that she could see Zangi-Ragozh more clearly.

"Yes, I am," he admitted, fiddling with the lid of the crock.

"Why? Is it because I am not of your clan?" She obviously regarded that as a good reason to keep such information private.

"No, that is not the reason," he told her. "I am not accustomed to revealing so much."

"Ah." She nodded. "But we will leave shortly, and then you will, as well, and even if we share the road for a fortnight or a year, once we part we may never meet again, so where would be the harm? Whom would I tell that could hurt you, or would even know who you are?" She paced down the center of the room and came back to him.

"Why does it matter to you so much?" Zangi-Ragozh asked her, puzzled by her persistence.

"It is a matter of trust and respect," she said after a reflective pause.

"That it is," he agreed.

"You have imparted much information to me, and to the Apostle, willingly and graciously, but you withhold this most intrinsic part of yourself, as if you seek to remain a stranger," she said. "I am glad for the knowledge you are willing to share, but I know it has little importance to you. So I ask for a token of your respect, something that you esteem, to seal our friendship."

"I have given you an emerald," said Zangi-Ragozh; it had been among the first batch he had made four days ago. "You said it was a pledge of mutual friendship."

"It is a beautiful stone, and a great treasure, but it is from you, not of you," she said.

"I grant you that," said Zangi-Ragozh, beginning to chafe; the first cordiality between them was already changing to something more profound, and more complex.

"You have been about the world a great deal—far more than I or anyone I know has been or ever will be. You have seen places whose names I have never heard, and you have walked roads leading beyond everything I have dreamed of," she said. "Your homeland is far away, you tell me, and your people no longer live there. For their sake, let me know who you were to them so they will not be completely gone."

"They are gone," he said flatly. "Many, many years ago."

"So you have told me," she said. "It must make you very lonely, to be the last."

"Upon occasion," he said, resisting the rare pang of isolation that gripped him suddenly.

"Because I am a magician," she said. "I have ways to ease the bonds that all carry."

"For your people. I am a foreigner, and your magic may not be mine, or accessible to one of my blood, no matter how generous your offer." He studied her broad, angular features, hoping to see an answer there that was as much a part of her answer as anything she might say.

"All the more reason to tell me," she persisted. "It strengthens my magic without upsetting my clan."

"How does it do this?" He fixed the lid on the crock.

"It gives me access to the heart of your being, and that provides illumination of an unearthly kind. I would cherish your name as I will treasure your emerald." She held out her hands to him.

Zangi-Ragozh relented. "My father was called Ragosh, so I am Ragosh-ski, my . . . I suppose you would call it clan, or territory, name is Franzic, for the area where my father's kingdom lay; my personal name is Holy Jermen," he said, slurring the *j* a little. He was a bit surprised at himself for telling her so much.

"How complicated," she said. "Are all men of the West so encumbered with names?"

"Some are more complicated, most are less so," he said, glancing at the door.

"Why are you called Holy? Is that your name or a title? Are you an Apostle, too?" She took his hands in hers, drawing him closer to her.

"No. I was called Holy because I was given to my gods."

"Your forgotten gods?" Her fingers tightened before she released his hands.

"Yes. Those sons of the King born at the dark of the year, as I was, were given to the gods, to become one of their blood, and for that blood were called Holy." He felt some of his despondency lift as he said this, and it surprised him. "Is Dukkai all your name?"

"As a name goes, it is Dukkai of the Desert Cats Clan, daughter of Gobor the One-Eyed, and niece of the magician Tejamksa, who served the clan and taught me."

"Why is he called Gobor the One-Eyed?" Zangi-Ragozh asked, considering what he had heard.

"He is called that because he is dead and there are many Gobors who have died. When I am dead, I will be Dukkai the Magician." She watched him inquisitively. "Do not your people distinguish the dead?"

"Not in that way," he said, and continued, "Baru Ksoka has two names: is it because he is your leader?"

"No. It is because he is his father's oldest son to have a child of his own. All those who are oldest sons who have a first child have second names. If the son with the name dies before he has a first grandson who is the first in the family, the second name passes to his widow." She saw his continuing interest. "Because I am the clan's magician, I have a number of titles, but they are not names, and they are only used on sacred occasions." She took one of the chairs, slid it away from the wall, and dropped into it, shifting about on the wooden seat to make herself more comfortable.

He moved the crock toward a large urn, one that would go into the athanor, the beehive-shaped alchemical oven standing at the far end of the chamber. "This will be a sovereign remedy when it is done. I will prepare other things tomorrow."

"More jewels?" She folded her hands in her lap.

"Gold and silver," said Zangi-Ragozh.

"Can you make food instead?"

"Sadly, no, I cannot make food." It was a troubling confession, and he gazed at the athanor to avoid her pale eyes.

"That is a pity," she said, preparing to rise, but sinking down once more as Zangi-Ragozh gave her his full attention. "I have already informed Baru Ksoka that we will have difficulty in reaching Cambaluc this autumn, although we often travel there. All the signs are bad." She watched him, curious and wary.

"That is a goodly distance out of the usual Jou'an-Jou'an territory, I would have thought," he said, remembering the village that was more of a permanent caravan encampment on the northern branch of the Silk Road.

"For many clans it is, but ours is a small group, much smaller than most, and we have to travel more and farther in order to keep from battles for pasture with the larger clans. Especially now, when the Turks are restless and pasturage is scarce." She let him consider what she had said.

Zangi-Ragozh contemplated her face. "What area do you travel, then?"

"We keep to the region between the rest of the Jou'an-Jou'an and the Uighurs, following the Tarim River."

"Are you expecting more trouble?" He knew it was a foolish question.

"I am, as you would, were you in my place." She studied him, saying suddenly, "I am pregnant with Baru Ksoka's child. I will give birth in the spring, if there is a spring."

"You are sure you are pregnant?" He chose his words meticulously. "Sometimes, when there are great hardships, a woman may not have her monthly courses. Could this be happening to you?"

"It could, but it is not," she said with great conviction. "Only the Kaigan is allowed to rut with me, and he has done so for more than a year. It is time that I bear him a child."

He turned and regarded her somberly. "Does he know, then?"

"Certainly he knows," she said. "He is the leader of the clan. He must be told such things."

"This is a hard time to have children," he said circumspectly.

"There is never an easy time to have children, not even for animals," she said bluntly. "Yet it must be done."

"While I do not disagree," he said, "I suppose that this coming year is going to be much harder than the last, and that the risks of pregnancy will increase as time goes by."

"Because there will be famine. I have contemplated what is to come, and it fills me with apprehension," she said, and caught her lower lip in her teeth.

"As it would any sensible woman," he said as a rush of compassion came over him. "You are afraid you will not carry the child to term."

"And if I do, that it will fail to grow and flourish. Weak infants are exposed, and if my child is not hearty, it will be left for the wild creatures to live upon. Baru Ksoka would declare as Kaigan that weak infants are not likely to live long and thus not only strengthen the clan but are spared suffering through their quick deaths, and I know this is the right way, so that the child remains part of the clan, just as the foals we offer to the gods and the cats become the spirit of our clan, and a source of power for the living." This last was spoken as if it meant nothing to her.

"With this year being so difficult, do you suppose there will be more offerings to your gods and your cats?" Zangi-Ragozh felt an abiding sympathy for her, but held his expression in check, for he sensed she had no wish to give in to her anxiety.

"There have been more foals and kids offered. Soon it must be infants, because horses and goats have proved insufficient." She made a mess of a chuckle. "Perhaps Apostle Lazarus could appeal to his God for another son to come to help us; after so long a time, a new sacrifice may be needed."

"He might well consider such a suggestion blasphemy," said Zangi-Ragozh.

"Most certainly," she agreed. "But in our many discussions, I have said much the same, and worse, and he does not chide me for it."

"Circumstances may change his mind," Zangi-Ragozh warned her.

"It may do more than that; already some of our clan pray to Apostle Lazarus' God."

"Why have you told me this?" Zangi-Ragozh asked her, coming toward her as she huddled in the chair. "What do you want of me?"

"I do not know what it is I seek," she said, continuing more tentatively. "I think perhaps I was hoping you might consider traveling with the clan until I deliver. We should have gone a long way westward by that time, and you are bound in that direction. My magic cannot protect me from the rigors of childbirth, or from anything else, for it has no impact upon me, only on others. But you might have skills that will be able to provide defenses for me."

"Are you having any difficulties?" Zangi-Ragozh put his hand on her forehead, concentrating on what he felt. "No sign of fever; that's something."

"No, no difficulties in particular. This is my first child, and I am worried because I am so old. Most Jou'an-Jou'an women have their first babies by their sixteenth year, and I am nine years older than that, which makes things harder for me than many." She looked up at him. "How will I—"

"Have you been ill at all? Is your appetite good?"

"I have been tired," she said. "I am always hungry. But all of us must have less just now."

"That could be hard on your child," said Zangi-Ragozh as gently as he could as he lowered his hand and scrutinized her face.

"Would the child starve, do you think?" Her face was impassive but her eyes burned.

"It is possible. I have seen it happen," he said, thinking back to the nine severe famines he had seen in his centuries in the Temple of Imhotep in Egypt.

"Is it likely?"

"That is hard to tell, at least at this point." He considered her in silence for a short while.

"If you and your companion were to travel with us, would you treat me? I am troubled by what I have experienced with this infant—so different than what I have seen other women endure. Apostle Lazarus says you have helped pregnant women before. Would you try to preserve my child?" She was so forlorn that Zangi-Ragozh was almost overwhelmed by her distress.

"What would your Kaigan say?" He waited while she framed her reply.

"I am the magician of the clan. He will do as I say, particularly for the sake of his child." She folded her arms and stared at him. "Travel with us, foreigner, and help us."

Zangi-Ragozh shook his head. "Your clan will have a hard time in any case: might not some of your people resent two strangers in your midst?"

Dukkai spoke with real purpose. "I am to see Baru Ksoka later today. I want to tell him that you will be part of our group when we depart."

"I would like to have a little time to consider my answer," he told her. "May I have until midday? I must speak with Ro-shei. It is not for me to make such a decision without consulting him."

"Is he of your blood, then?" Dukkai demanded, a touch of anger in her tone.

"No; he is an old, old companion, one who has been with me through many hardships and over many li. I have traveled with him for more years than I care to remember." Zangi-Ragozh took her hand in his. "I am grateful for your invitation; I would imagine that you may have to persuade Baru Ksoka to acquiesce in it."

"I am the magician of the clan; the Kaigan cannot challenge my position."

"You would not be wise to put that to the test just now, and not because you are pregnant," said Zangi-Ragozh. "I have seen families and clans rent apart by far less than what is happening now. You would do the Desert Cats no service by forcing more uncertainty upon them."

"Having you and your companion with us would be more help than hindrance," she said firmly. "Remember, it will be midwinter by the time we reach Aksu."

"If you are fortunate," said Zangi-Ragozh. "In such hard weather, travel will not be rapid."

She nodded. "All the more reason to have one of your skills with us."

He lifted her hand to his lips. "I thank you for the honor you have given me, Dukkai, and I will strive to reach a decision that will benefit all of us—my companion and me, and you and your clan."

"By midday," she reminded him, staring at her hand where he had kissed it. "Is this a custom among your people?"

"And among many in the West," he explained.

"A strange thing to do," she said, looking at the back of her hand as if she expected to see a mark upon it.

"No one in the West would think so," said Zangi-Ragozh.

"Do you miss the West?" She blurted out the question and then put her hand to her mouth.

"It is where my native earth lies," he said.

"Then you must want to return to it," she said.

"In times such as these, yes, I must," he said, thinking of the dwindling supply of native earth in his chests. Even now, with the sun lacking in power, he could not entirely escape the enervation daylight brought him. "However I travel, and with whom, I know I must go to the Carpa-Ti Mountains to be restored." Or to die, he added to himself.

She nodded. "I do not like going beyond the territory we usually travel."

He considered what she said. "I would hope that by the time you reach Aksu the weather improves and this region of yellow snow will be far behind you."

"And I, but it may not be." She rose and stood directly in front of him. "And you have thought of this, too; I can see it in your eyes. You are harried by assumptions of various mishaps and calamities that may lie ahead of us."

"I have never encountered such a year as this," he said somberly.

"No; and the stories my grandmother told had nothing of this sort in them, though they were filled with accounts of wars and famines and other misfortunes." She moved toward the door. "For your sake and for mine, I hope you will come with us. Your and your companion would provide—" She stopped suddenly.

"Between the dark and the cold, you will have hard-going; all of us will." He went with her to the door. "I will let you know when you return what I have decided: my Word on it."

"Good. I am going to speak with Baru Ksoka, to discover what he is willing to accept."

"I thank you for such a concession," he said with a quick, ironic smile.

"You may think I am being foolish," she said, "but I know what I know, and I see you have power beyond any that Apostle Lazarus recognizes."

"How can you be sure," he said, covering the disquiet he felt at this remark with a genial half-bow in the Western style.

"Tejamksa died in childbirth," she said. "There are those who think that I must do the same." With that, she slipped out the door and closed it softly before hurrying down the corridor to the stairs.

Zangi-Ragozh stood alone for some little while, his thoughts deliberately blank. At last he went to the athanor and opened its central chamber, placing the crock in the declivity in the center, then adjusting the lid one last time before closing the stone door and stoking the furnace, using small bellows to heat the fire to an intensity that was usually reserved for bronze- and iron-smiths at their forges. For as long as it took him to recite the *Death of Achilles* he kept steadily at his labor, then left the athanor to burn out and cool down.

It was approaching midday when Ro-shei came into the alchemical chamber, an empty cask in his hands. "You asked for this."

"Thank you, yes, I did," said Zangi-Ragozh, taking it and setting it on the trestle table. "It should not be long now."

"Why have you made such a great portion of your sovereign remedy?" Ro-shei asked.

"I fear we will have need of it before our travels are done, and I may not have many opportunities to make more." He took a clean cloth and wiped out the cask, checking it carefully for leaks. "The lid? Does it have a wire stay?"

"Yes; you can see the grooves for the wire." Ro-shei pointed them out.

"Very good. This is going to have to serve us for some time, I fear," said Zangi-Ragozh. "If anyone doubts that there is going to be a very arduous winter ahead, it is because he is living in a place where the sun is not darkened, and the land is warm—either that, or he is mad with optimism."

Ro-shei considered Zangi-Ragozh, measuring his demeanor with the knowledge of five centuries. "You are anticipating much worse to come."

"I wish I were not," said Zangi-Ragozh.

"Is that why you are still uncertain about when we might resume traveling?"

Zangi-Ragozh's answer was measured. "I see that there could be advantages to wintering here: we are known to the Apostle and he would extend his hospitality to you and me if I asked for it; I have no doubt of it. But I would find it difficult—or impossible—to have a lover, and it would not be prudent to go to the dancing girls, not if they are reduced to beggary, as I suspect many of them will be. Such contacts are . . . shall we say, unwise."

"So you intend to leave?" Ro-shei gave no indication of his opinion of this possibility.

"Dukkai has asked that we travel with her clan when they move on, which they will do shortly." He stared at the fire in the open stove. "The clan is small, and that will limit my chance for nourishment more severely than remaining here in Kumul will."

Ro-shei took a turn about the narrow room. "Have you broached the matter of your requirements?"

"No, I have not." He moved a little closer to the fire. "She wants my answer by midday."

"That will come soon," said Ro-shei.

"I know," said Zangi-Ragozh. "What do you think?"

"I think whether we stay or go, there will be difficulties. There is nowhere we have heard of that is salubrious now." Ro-shei went to put another length of wood on the fire. "But I think there is a better chance of finding a wholesome place if we travel than if we wait here for news to arrive, for that may be long in coming. Who knows when the next caravan from the West will come, or if one will come at all." At this last, he stared at Zangi-Ragozh as if to command his full attention. "Whatever this invisible darkness is, it may come from the West as well as the East."

"Or the North or the South," said Zangi-Ragozh distantly as he gave himself over to thought.

"But we know it has force here, and it might not be as bad else-where," said Ro-shei, then added before Zangi-Ragozh could speak, "And it may be worse. That is the risk, isn't it?"

"Yes; that is the risk." Zangi-Ragozh looked over at the athanor. "In a short while I can put the remedy in the cask and seal it."

"Would you like my help doing that?" Ro-shei offered, knowing Zangi-Ragozh would not discuss his ruminations until he had decided what to do.

"It is unnecessary, but your company is very welcome," said Zangi-Ragozh; he touched the bricks of the athanor and said, "Not quite yet."

Ro-shei could not keep from asking, "Do you think the money and jewels you've made will be enough to get us to the Black Sea?"

"I hope they will," said Zangi-Ragozh. "Either that, or they will take us back to Yang-Chau."

"If we go there, we would do well to go by way of Chang'an." Ro-shei's warning was given lightly enough, but with firm purpose.

"If the Wen Emperor has held on to his throne, I suppose it would be best." Zangi-Ragozh stared toward the window and the pale morning light. "There are storms coming. That high, veiled light promises severe weather, and soon."

"Better to remain here, do you think?" Ro-shei said.

"Or better to suggest to Dukkai that her clan stay here a while longer and depart once the storm is over," said Zangi-Ragozh.

"It would seem you have made up your mind," said Ro-shei with a short sigh.

"Oh, yes, I think so," said Zangi-Ragozh in the same remote voice. "If you have no objection."

"And if the clan will not wait to leave? What then?"

"Then I suppose we must go with them," said Zangi-Ragozh, and opened the athanor to remove the container of his sovereign remedy.

Text of a letter from Captain I Mo-Ching of the *Morning Star* from Tai-Wan to Councillor Ko She-Hsieh, both in Yang-Chau.

To the most illustrious Councillor Ko She-Hsieh, the most respectful greetings of I Mo-Ching, Captain of the Morning Star, *a merchant*

ship of the Eclipse Trading Company, now presently in her home port,
Yang-Chau, on this the beginning of the Burning Clothes Festival:

Not that we will burn many clothes this year, for the climate has
been too severe to spare any but the paper representations of clothes
for the fires. Still, the festival must be observed, and with especial care
to the traditions, or more calamities may be visited upon us, which is
something all would wish to avoid.

I shall do my utmost to provide you with all the facts I have to
hand, and I will limit my speculations as best as I may. So, let me say
first that I have had no communication with Zangi-Ragozh, the Worthy
Foreigner who owns the Eclipse Trading Company, since he left Yang-
Chau for Chang'an, nor, to my knowledge, has any other Captain of his
fleet, nor his clerks. Our travels have been severely limited, as you
know, and that has made for much slower transferring of letters, and it
may be that one of the other Captains have heard from him, but no
confirmation of this has been presented to Hu Bi-Da, his senior clerk,
for he would have informed all of us in the city that he had news of
Zangi-Ragozh. Second, I must tell you that the loss of his ships—there
are two that we know of, and there may be more—has been a blow to
the business. Third, I wish to say that Zangi-Ragozh is far from being
the only merchant who has been unable to get word to this city since the
current hardships began, and I put no more significance in his absence
than I do in the missing Jai Mi-Jah or Bo Gan-Lao, who have not been
seen for more than a year, and who were not so provident in their
preparations for being gone.

It may be that Zangi-Ragozh has come to grief, and if that is the
case, I know he has prepared a Will, which must make some arrangement for the distribution of his property and goods. I am certain that
his clerk or his steward may produce the Will if the Council should
require it. You, most respected Councillor, must know that Zangi-
Ragozh has made a great effort to comply with our laws and our customs, and I cannot believe he would be lax in so important a matter as
the distribution of his estate. His steward keeps good accounts for the
household, and I know Jho Chieh-Jen will not balk at surrendering
any information you may require.

To answer your question, no Captain to whom I have spoken has
any news of Zangi-Ragozh in the ports that his ships visit, and that
includes the new office in Saylan; that establishment was badly

damaged by the mountainous waves that struck at the end of winter and marked the beginning of this dark time of yellow snow. The Captains of courier ships have also had no news regarding him, and I have to say that I believe wherever he is, it is not in a port where he is known. Not all merchants travel by sea, and although you may have found that he left Lo-Yang, he might well have taken the Huang Ho north as well as east, to follow a land route rather than the sea-lanes. No one has demanded a ransom for him, but I would not be much surprised if such a demand arrives soon. At such a time, a ransom may be regarded as the only means of securing food and heat for the winter, for all China seems to be still in the relentless grip of cold, and the slow torture of starvation.

It is fortunate that Zangi-Ragozh left so many provisions for his Captains and his household. There is rice in quantity in his warehouses, stipulated for the relief of hunger for us all. Also there are smoked meats and pickled vegetables that will provide enough food to last us into the spring, when we must all hope August Heaven once again allows crops to thrive. You will find that both Clerk Hu and Steward Jho have instructions from Zangi-Ragozh that specify how such stored foodstuffs are to be used, as well as strictures for those who do not honor his wishes. I, myself, know that if we are to survive this terrible time, we must follow his orders on every point, for his foresight has guided his company successfully in prosperous times and I know his policies will do so in hardship.

I submit this to you, with my assurance that what I tell you is accurate, that my opinions are based on reliable information and not wild speculation. I will not give up hope that the Worthy Foreigner is still alive and will eventually return to Yang-Chau when conditions here improve. I will report to you any news I may receive regarding him, as I have stated, and I will do all that I may to assist the Council in preserving his Eclipse Trading Company against his return.

                                              I Mo-Ching
                                Captain of the Morning Star
                                              (his chop)

4

To the north of them, the Tien Shan range rose up, stark and forbidding, the mountains shining gold from the peaks to far down the slopes where the weak sunlight touched them, striking the stinking yellow snow; ahead lay a narrow swath of sere, dust-colored grass where lush green should have been, and only a few clumps of hardy grasses reminded them of what was usually there in profusion. Even the stream they followed gave no comfort, for the waters were cloudy and harsh-tasting and did little to slake the thirst that plagued the Desert Cats clan and their animals as they made their way toward Turfan.

Baru Ksoka was both dismayed and disgusted, for the clan was not making its customary rapid progress, and he was becoming worried, for not only were they behind, but winter was approaching much earlier than ever before. All the hunting that usually kept his clan fed while they traveled had proved disappointing, and as a result, there were many Desert Cats who had begun to mutter about ill-luck, and the danger strangers presented; nothing Baru Ksoka said could stop the insidious whispers, and gradually, he began to listen to the growing complaints. He regarded Zangi-Ragozh, the foreigner in the elaborate black shuba on the cinder-brown pony who had become the nexus of all clan fears, with an emotion compounded of unwilling gratitude and envy as he swung his red pony around to bring him alongside Zangi-Ragozh. "In all your travels, have you seen anything to match this?" Baru Ksoka was a big man with heavily muscled arms and shoulders. His broad, high-cheekboned face was fairly expressionless, but every line of his body revealed strong purpose, and he carried himself in a manner that showed he was used to being obeyed.

"No, Kaigan, I have not." The two spoke an amalgam of Chinese and Jou'an-Jou'an that made their mutual understanding possible. "Not in the West nor in the East."

"Do you think there is going to be an end to it? Is our weather to turn warm again, and our grasslands to flourish, or will it remain cold and arid?" Baru Ksoka asked variations on these questions almost

daily, and over the nearly two fortnights that Zangi-Ragozh and Ro-
shei had been with the clan, the Kaigan had become more insistent.
"How much longer can this continue?"

Zangi-Ragozh paused, thinking back to the hard years of famine
he had seen before, in his homeland, in Egypt, in Rome, in Byzantium, in the wild mountains that lay to the southeast. "Anything I ventured would be speculation at best. I am sorry I have nothing more to
offer you than this—that every dreadful time I have passed through
has eventually ended, and this is probably no different than any other."
He did not entirely believe this, having never before seen such unac-
countable ruin over so much of the earth, but he kept that bleak
thought to himself.

"If it is different, then what is to become of us?" Baru Ksoka
asked Zangi-Ragozh.

"That depends on more than you or I can say."

"Do you think it is magic, or the gods contending?"

"As to your gods, I have no understanding of their might, or their
dispositions. They may have done this, but so might many other powers beyond our reckoning. Other gods, far away, may be the cause of
this, and no appeals to your own will appease them." Zangi-Ragozh
looked up at the high, trailing clouds. "Not even the sky reveals what
has happened."

"The sun is less than it was, that much is certain," said Baru Ksoka.
"I should not be cold at this time of year."

"Yes, the sun has lost its power, and the earth is paying for it. But
why it is so, I cannot tell."

"We must find out what we can do to change this, and soon," said
Baru Ksoka.

"If there is anything that will bring about a change," said Zangi-
Ragozh.

"There must be something," Baru Ksoka said in hard determination. "If Dukkai were stronger, she would attend to it. She must know
what we have to do."

"There might not be any means to implement such a change. This
wretchedness may be like a flood, which must pass before anything
can be done about the damage it has caused," Zangi-Ragozh warned,
wondering if he could persuade the Kaigan not to demand human in-
tervention in this catastrophic time; there had been occasions in the

past when he had witnessed dreadful natural occurrences that led to appalling attempts at solutions that served no purpose but the worsening of the disaster.

"You spent time with Dukkai, our magician, last night," said Baru Ksoka, the sudden change of subject intended to jar Zangi-Ragozh into betraying any shameful act he might have attempted.

"Her pregnancy is not going well," said Zangi-Ragozh, wholly unflustered. "She asked me to come and provide some ease for her."

"That seems to be true, that she is suffering with her growing baby, although why she should be so much burdened, I cannot say; my other children have all been lively and thriving in the womb," said Baru Ksoka heavily. "I regret that we had to give your wagon over to her use."

"The camels carry the chests and crates well enough." He thought of his hidden gold and jewels now in chests carried by camels.

"To have our magician miscarry at such a time would be a dire omen, and all the clan knows it."

Zangi-Ragozh appreciated the warning he heard in the remark, and so he offered a conciliatory answer. "If there is any way to preserve her and her infant, I will do it, to the full limit of my skills. She is in her eighth fortnight, and she should be more accommodated to the pregnancy. If all goes well, she should be over the worst of her weakness in another fortnight, and assuming she is able to sate her hunger, she ought to be able to travel with the rest without more than the usual difficulties of pregnancy."

Baru Ksoka's laugh had no mirth in it. "You speak as carefully as a man facing the Underworld Judge."

"I want to be precise in what I say, so that we understand each other," said Zangi-Ragozh.

"A very commendable intention." Baru Ksoka lowered his head in deep thought. "At Turfan, you will have to decide if you are to continue with us or go your own way. We should not take too much longer to get there, even at our current slow pace. I give it five days, unless we have another mishap." He referred to the hunt of two days ago when one of the men had fallen from his pony at the gallop and broken his shoulder and smashed his ankle. "You were very helpful with Dur Moksal."

"I am not sure I have done that much for him, yet," said Zangi-Ragozh. "He is badly hurt."

"He is alive, and that is more than any of us expected him to be," said Baru Ksoka with finality.

"At Turfan, you and I will decide," said Zangi-Ragozh.

"Yes," he agreed, then tapped his pony's sides with his heels and rode back to the van of the Desert Cats, leaving Zangi-Ragozh to continue on in isolation, for only three of the clan other than the Kaigan and Dukkai ever spoke to him: Imgalas, who supervised the animals; Gotsada, Dukkai's cousin, who had been assigned the task of looking after her; and Jekan Madassi, who was in charge of all cooking when the clan camped, and who had come to Zangi-Ragozh for spices. The rest of the Desert Cats made a point of avoiding contact with the two foreigners, a reserve that was increasing as they traveled.

By nightfall they had reached a small spring surrounded by trees with long, drooping leaves; these were turning as pale yellow as the snow on the mountains, preparing to be shed for the season. The spring was wonderfully fresh, lacking the harsh taste of sulfur that had become common in streams and rivers throughout the region. Most of the women spent the evening filling casks and skins from the spring, and the animals drank deeply of it. Around the central fire, most of the Desert Cats gathered, and a few tried to bring a little jollity to the occasion by getting out their pipes and drums. But very shortly the merry tunes fell flat, and soon the music was abandoned as the clan waited for the side of wild goat to finish cooking over the flames.

"This is not going well," Ro-shei said to Zangi-Ragozh from the tethered camels as he unloaded a small sack of chopped hay he had bought in Kumul from the nearest pack-saddle.

"No, it is not," Zangi-Ragozh agreed; they spoke in Imperial Latin, keeping their voices low.

"I make it mid- to late October, in the Western calendar," said Ro-shei. "It feels nearer mid-December."

"I would say the third week in October, or perhaps the last," said Zangi-Ragozh.

"And winter already under way," said Ro-shei, a hard shine to his faded-blue eyes. "There was snow on the ground at sunrise, two mornings ago."

"With travel going more slowly because of it," Zangi-Ragozh agreed.

Ro-shei spoke into the silence that had fallen between them.

"Have you decided what we are to do in Turfan? Do you plan to winter there?"

"I believe it may be decided for us, and without any reference to our sentiments, or the weather," said Zangi-Ragozh.

"Do you think the Desert Cats might winter there?" Ro-shei persisted.

"I have no notion, but for us, I think it would not be wise, no matter how many foreigners may seek shelter there. I believe foreigners will be unwelcome this winter, for the sun is growing weaker and the cold is spreading, and everyone must look to his own during such perilous times. I have never experienced anything to equal this." Zangi-Ragozh took a long, deep breath. "From what Baru Ksoka said earlier, as soon as we reach Turfan, he will want us gone."

"Unless Dukkai is worse," said Ro-shei. "Or there are more injuries. Or another miscarriage."

"That may yet be attributed to my presence and not the impact of hunger that is at the heart of Dukkai's troubles, and the misery of all the rest. Most of these people are just beginning to grasp what lies ahead next spring. I am particularly worried about Dukkai: she needs better food, and more of it, but there is none to be had." Zangi-Ragozh pressed his lips together.

"Is it, at root, the fault of the child?" Ro-shei looked surprised.

"Perhaps indirectly, because it is as hungry as she is." He held up his hand as Ro-shei began to speak. "Yes, I know. I, too, am hungry. Everyone is hungry."

"You do not need me to remind you, I am certain, that you must feed," said Ro-shei.

"I will continue to take small amounts of blood from the ponies late at night; they can spare it, and it does not weaken them as it would any of the Desert Cats; it may not be very much, but for now, it must suffice," Zangi-Ragozh said with a swift, sardonic smile; he took the sack from Ro-shei, holding it easily as if its weight meant nothing to him. "I will present this to Baru Ksoka, so he may keep his animals in little better fettle than he has been able to."

"And once we are on our own, what then for our ponies and camels? You will have to use them more often, and that will take a toll on them. They will need extra rations, yet you are giving this sack to the Desert Cats. What will we feed the animals if we find nothing for them to graze upon?" Ro-shei did not make this a challenge to him, but let the question remain between them, raw in its impact.

"There are still the hidden sacks under the wagon-floor, grain and chopped hay; six of them, and they appear on no inventory. Assuming no one finds them, and we are permitted to take the wagon contents, we will manage well enough. What we have stored away should give us two more fortnights of food for travel before we have to make our ponies and camels live on scrub brush." He stared over at the clan members, all of them caught up in the smell of the cooking goat. "This is wearing on all of them."

"And on you," said Ro-shei. "At least I have been able to find enough to eat, although the game is becoming scrawny."

"What was it today?" Zangi-Ragozh asked.

"A bird, about the size of a large hen, stringy and tough, but enough to sustain me," said Ro-shei.

Zangi-Ragozh glanced over his shoulder. "At least we are sharing with them, which makes us less strange."

"With their animals, more to the point," said Ro-shei.

"And, with their magician doing poorly, they are glad of my medicaments," said Zangi-Ragozh, as he shouldered the sack of chopped hay. "I will stop to see how Dukkai is doing before I return."

"And what of Dur Moksal? Will you see him, too?"

"If his women permit it," said Zangi-Ragozh. "They are being very protective of him just now and do not want me to taint him any further."

"Then I hope they do not make him worse," said Ro-shei. "These Jou'an-Jou'an do not trust you."

"That, old friend, has occurred to me," said Zangi-Ragozh as he left Ro-shei to go in search of Baru Ksoka; his passage through the camp attracted little attention, for everyone was waiting for the signal for the meal to begin. He found the Kaigan with Imgalas on the far side of the cooking fire, and he stopped at a respectful distance and ducked his head. "Baru Ksoka?"

"What is it?" the Kaigan snapped as he turned to Zangi-Ragozh.

"I have a sack of chopped hay that my companion and I have decided we can spare for you." He swung the sack off his shoulder. "If you would accept this as a gesture of my gratitude for allowing us to accompany you on your travels?"

Baru Ksoka stared at Zangi-Ragozh. "This is . . . most unexpected."

"But still useful, I trust," said Zangi-Ragozh. "Your herds and flocks are on short rations."

"Why are you doing this?" Imgalas demanded after a single look in Baru Ksoka's direction.

"Because you need more food for your animals—" Zangi-Ragozh began.

Imgalas interrupted him, "Your animals need food, as well. Why should you give up any for us, and ours?"

"Imgalas," Baru Ksoka warned. "You overstep yourself."

Imgalas rounded on the Kaigan. "You must want to know, too," he said bluntly.

"I do," said Baru Ksoka. "But I think it is for Zangi-Ragozh to tell us if he wishes. In the meantime, I thank you, foreigner, for your gift. It means much to us."

"That's his intention, isn't it?" Imgalas asked the air. "To make us so indebted to him that we are forced to keep him with us no matter where we go."

"I have no such intention," said Zangi-Ragozh.

"That remains to be seen," said Baru Ksoka pointedly.

"What do you think—that the clan will tolerate strangers among us?" Imgalas glared in Zangi-Ragozh's direction, his expression combining disdain, contempt, and awakening fury.

"They have helped our wounded and shared their food," the Kaigan said, making this bear more weight by speaking with loud authority.

"Only to earn our gratitude," Imgalas said, spitting for emphasis.

"This man is helping us! You will not despise him!" Baru Ksoka barked out his commands, his face flushing to the color of Damascus leather.

"Do not shout," said Imgalas, relenting for the present. "I meant nothing to his discredit." The necessary lie received an automatic nod.

"Take the sack and distribute the chopped hay to the ponies and goats; be sure that all of them have some," said Baru Ksoka, now sounding more tired than angry.

Imgalas frowned as if wanting to say more, then hefted the sack and trudged away toward the large pen of driven posts and heavy rope where the ponies and goats were nominally confined.

"That was a generous act," said Baru Ksoka as soon as Imgalas was beyond hearing range.

"It is also a practical one. Neither your clan nor my companion and I wish to prolong our journey any more than we must." He gave a small, single nod.

Baru Ksoka considered this. "You are correct in that."

"It is not a question of being correct, Kaigan, it is a question of living," said Zangi-Ragozh, and took a step back. "I want to be sure that Jekan Madassi has put aside meat for Dukkai."

"Of course she has," said Baru Ksoka. "She wants no curse on her family."

"I should think not; she is a most sensible woman, and worthy to be the head of her family," said Zangi-Ragozh, and nodded to Baru Ksoka again before turning away and striding off toward the cooking fire again, where he slipped through the crowd of Desert Cats to Jekan Madassi's side, near the spit where the spitted goat turned, and next to the large cauldron in which a stew of dried squashes, herbs, mushrooms, and garlic simmered. "You are fortunate that those markhor are so large."

"For that, the gods have been good to us in hard times," said Jekan Madassi, a short, robust woman with bright blue eyes and deeply marked features. "Though I could wish for another markhor or two, and a serow as well. I would rejoice in having so much as a single animal for my spit: I prefer them good-sized and meaty."

"May your gods give you what you seek," said Zangi-Ragozh.

"They have been reluctant or unable to do so," Jekan Madassi complained, her voice dropping as if to keep from being overheard.

"It is not for you to deprecate the gods," Baru Ksoka warned her.

"Then order the foreigner to make our magician well, and they might grant us their protection again," Jekan Madassi said, adding to Zangi-Ragozh, "I will send meat to her shortly."

"There are some who say her child is stealing her magic, which is what makes her ill." Jekan Madassi gave him a sidelong stare.

"All the more reason to think that the child will be a powerful magician when it is born," said Zangi-Ragozh.

"It may seem so," said Jekan Madassi. "But in such hard times, there are those who will not believe a child can flourish while the mother declines."

Zangi-Ragozh concealed his alarm at this cold-blooded remark. "Once you get beyond the afflicted region, you may find that she, and her infant, will thrive."

"If such a place still exists, and if we do not have to fight too many foes to claim it," said Jekan Madassi.

"May it be so," said Zangi-Ragozh, and made his way through the crowd once more, this time going toward his wagon, which Baru Ksoka had commandeered for Dukkai's use. As he approached, he saw Gotsada climb down from the rear platform and raised his hand in greeting. "How does your cousin today?"

"She is improved, I think," said Gotsada, his voice more hopeful than certain.

"That is encouraging," said Zangi-Ragozh. "Is she awake?"

"Oh, yes; and fretful. She dislikes her confinement." Gotsada tried to maintain an air of friendliness, but anxiety gave his manner a sharp edge.

Zangi-Ragozh nodded toward the rear platform. "I will tend to her for now. You go get your supper."

"I will be back when I have finished," said Gotsada. "I will bring Dukkai her supper so that she may be well and strong again."

"Very good," said Zangi-Ragozh, determined not to be put off by Gotsada's ill-concealed hostility; he watched Gotsada go and then, quickly and lightly, sprang onto the platform and stepped through the heavy silk-canvas cover into the interior of the wagon. He saw Dukkai lying on her back on the hanging cot, her body supported by folded bear-skins, her face lit unsteadily by a small butter-lamp set in the bracket on one of the cover supports. He had to stand slightly stooped to keep from brushing the roof of the cover with his head. "How do I find you, Dukkai?" he asked, nodding to her.

"You find me bored," she said, offering him a wan smile.

"A very good sign," he approved, ignoring her disbelieving snort.

"I don't want to have to live this way until my child is born," she informed him.

"It would trouble me if you did, for it would mean you were losing strength," he said, and went to her side. "Is your cousin giving you good care?"

"Gotsada?" She sighed. "He is doing the best he knows to do."

"You are not satisfied with his efforts?" Zangi-Ragozh asked, dropping down onto his knees beside the cot.

She shook her head. "I know that what he has made is his best effort, too obviously. I tried to explain at first that he didn't need to strive so hard, but it only made him fussier." She waited while he moved his hand from her forehead to her throat, to test the pulse there. "What do you think, Zangi-Ragozh?"

"I think you are a little better, but I also think you need to continue to be careful," he told her. "You are not fully recovered, and you will not be for a while yet."

"A while yet," she repeated.

"I cannot anticipate how well you will do. If your infant is growing rapidly, that may cause you to be tired. If it is not growing quickly enough, it could still become dislodged."

"My limbs are feeling stiff," she said.

"Then work them gently, while you lie in bed. Stretch, and flex your arms and legs. I wouldn't recommend you rising yet, except as you must. But stay in the wagon for a while longer. You are not up to walking about, no matter how much you long to do it."

She looked at him, a long, thoughtful scrutiny. "What do you think is wrong?"

There was a loud shout from outside, and a general scuffle as Jekan Madassi decreed that the markhor was done and that all could eat.

"I told you before—your child is not well-fitted in your womb, and until it is larger, it may be easily dislodged, and that would be a problem for you." He took her hand, holding it gently, sensing her strained vitality.

"You mean I would lose the child?" She shook her head. "That must not happen."

"Then you must remain where you are and keep yourself rested and still for another fortnight, at least." He put his other hand over hers. "It is hard, I know, but you are sensible, and you have self-discipline to serve you." He reached for a small crate and drew it nearer so he could use it as a stool. "It is a pity that you should be pregnant at such a time as we have to endure now."

"There are three other women in the clan who are pregnant," she pointed out. "They are not as weak as I have become."

"Only two are pregnant now. Boksalli lost hers yesterday. And

Meudan's young son died the day before." He had not been allowed to tend Boksalli, but had prepared an infusion for her to drink, and a poultice, to speed the purging of the womb lining. For Meudan he could offer no consolation, not with her loss so agonizingly recent; it would be many days before her grief would allow her to accept the commiseration of her family and clan.

"Poor women," said Dukkai, surprised to feel tears well in her eyes.

"If the infant could not live within her, it certainly could not live outside her; and Meudan's son had been coughing for a fortnight," said Zangi-Ragozh as kindly as he could.

"Could they have been saved?" she asked him. "I would have done my utmost when they asked for my magic to protect them, but as it is, I cannot serve my people as they deserve."

"No, not just now," he said, holding out his hand again.

"Will I regain my strength when my child is born?" There was worry in her ice-blue eyes, and she touched him again as if for reassurance.

"If the weather is better, and you eat well, you should not continue to suffer."

She studied his face again. "Hunger is hurting our clan, isn't it?"

"That, and the cold," said Zangi-Ragozh.

"If it continues, we will lose more than infants, won't we?" Her eyes again filled with tears.

"It is likely," he said gently.

"Then I have failed them." Dukkai swallowed against a fresh bout of weeping. "My magic is needed, and I am a burden instead of a help, lying here in this hanging cot, unable to do more than sit up to piss." She wiped her eyes with the back of her hand. "I wish I could keep from crying. It seems so . . . so fragile a thing to do."

"Women with child often weep readily," said Zangi-Ragozh. "It is no weakness."

She managed a single laugh. "You may think that, but I know my Desert Cats, and I am certain they have a poor opinion of me for it. Their women may cry, but not their magician."

"Even if that magician is a woman," Zangi-Ragozh suggested.

"Especially then," she said. "They want me to be stronger than any of them, so they know my magic has power in it." Dukkai shook her head. "I worry about that, too."

"That you are losing your magic," he said.

"That, and that I am failing my clan." Her tears were falling in earnest now, and she did not bother to wipe them away. "I feel a complete ruin."

"You are not that," Zangi-Ragozh promised her, leaning forward, his dark eyes fixed compellingly on hers. "You are not failing your people. You are providing an example for all of your Desert Cats, an assurance that this appalling time may be survived, and that you and your clan have something to live for, a good reason to do all you can to survive."

Dukkai sniffed and thought about what he said. "It would please me to think this," she said at last.

"You would not deceive yourself if you did," he said, and touched her forehead with his lips.

"That strange Western salute again," she said, fingering the place his mouth had brushed.

"Yes," he said.

"You told me it is a token of honor," she said.

"And affection. The old Romans would call it piety—loyal, fond devotion."

She considered this. "Apostle Lazarus said that piety meant devotion to his God, and the God's Son."

"So his sect uses the word, but the Romans applied it more generally," said Zangi-Ragozh. "I prefer the old definition."

"And you feel this for me? loyal, fond devotion? Piety?" There was more longing in her question than she knew, so she was startled at the warmth of his answer.

"Were you not the woman of Baru Ksoka, and not pregnant, I would want you to be my woman, for as long as it suited you to be."

Staring up at him, she could think of nothing to say to him, and so she shoved herself up and kissed his forehead. "Token for token." She reached for his arm and pulled him down beside her, wrapping her arms around his waist. After a moment she blinked. "I can't hear your heartbeat."

"Never mind," he said, his voice low and melodic as she once again snuggled close to him. "It does not matter."

✧   ✧   ✧

Text of a letter from Chu Sung-Neong, the Undersecretary of the Prefecture of Holin-Gol, to Minister K'an Shao-Shou, at the Wen Emperor's capital at Chang'an; carried by a courier but never delivered.

To the most worthy Minister K'an Shao-Shou at the Wen Emperor's capital of Chang'an, the greetings of Chu Sung-Neong, Undersecretary of the Prefecture of Holin-Gol, on the behest of the Prefect Ting Yu-Huan, with utmost regard for the Wen Emperor and his Minister:

Regretfully, I am charged with the task of informing Your Excellency that we cannot support the company of two hundred soldiers you have dispatched to this city to detain refugees from Chang'an; we are hardly able to provide for our own garrison, which is loyal to the Northern Wei Dynasty, no matter who wields the Vermilion Brush in Da-Tong. Our soldiers here will be willing to apprehend those refugees summoned by your courts to answer criminal charges, but not to keep them as prisoners.

Unfortunately, your soldiers have taken certain matters into their own hands, and that has led to most unwelcome incidents in this town. Five of the suspects seized, including two women, were pulled apart by four oxen, three were subjected to the execution of the bell, and the rest were mutilated and beheaded. None of this is acceptable to the Prefecture, and the new Magistrate, Ngo Hai-Ming, has dispatched his own condemnation of this flouting of law and social order, and his request that the troops be withdrawn at once.

It is my sad duty to inform you that Holin-Gol is very low on civic provisions. We are having difficulty feeding our own people, and the addition of your two hundred soldiers is imposing an intolerable burden on us. Dreadful acts of theft and other outrages have been perpetrated, and the new Magistrate has ordered our local militia to remove your soldiers from the town and not to admit them again, upon pain of death.

Here in our town there has been a very cold summer, and now that the year is closing in to the dark, we are already seeing snow two days out of three. The snow is yellow and it bears an odor that is most offensive. This would be hard enough, but in a time when there have been almost no crops harvested, our Merchants' Council has declared that many businesses in Holin-Gol will not survive the winter without some relief granted them by the Prefecture, which arrangements we are even now attempting to arrange. Another hard year lies ahead, and if we are not to collapse into anarchy, you must exercise prudence and call your soldiers back to Chang'an before something truly disastrous occurs.

Sent this day by courier, the sixth day of the Fortnight of the Dying-Autumn Lanterns, at the order of the Prefecture of Holin-Gol.

Chu Sung-Neong
Undersecretary of the Prefecture of Holin-Gol
(his chop)

5

Nine of the Desert Cats and Zangi-Ragozh rode after the furious sounder of boar; seven of the large, wild pigs ran squealing from the galloping ponies and the armed men who straddled them. Baru Ksoka stood in his metal foot-loops and took careful aim with his powerful bow, loosing his arrow as the leader of the boar swung around to rush at him, his tusks foaming. The boar staggered and his furious attack turned to a limping retreat as the Kaigan sent a second arrow into the boar's flank; the animal tottered, then fell heavily onto his side, his blood spreading through the dusting of yellow snow. The rest of the sounder scattered, the boars keening in fury and dread.

Imgalas rode up, his arrow notched to the string. "Shall we go after the others?" He sank onto his saddle and pulled his pony to a trot.

"Try for at least two more," Baru Ksoka said, and swung around in his saddle to look at Zangi-Ragozh. "Do you want to go with them?"

"I'll chase a boar for you," said Zangi-Ragozh, who carried a Roman boar spear. "I want to see how much better your iron foot-loops let me aim."

Baru Ksoka laughed aloud. "You will be surprised," he promised, and stepped down from his saddle, drawing his curve-bladed Nepalese chilanum to begin the task of gutting and skinning the dying boar. "Bring back a prize."

"I will," Zangi-Ragozh promised as he hastened after Imgalas and the rest. He gathered the cinder-brown pony's reins in his left hand and raised the spear with his right as he caught up with the other hunters.

"See you don't hurt anyone with that . . . that poker of yours," Imgalas shouted to him.

"I would not do such a thing," Zangi-Ragozh called back.

"That is a reckless sort of weapon," Imgalas remarked.

"No doubt it seems that way to one who does not know how to use it," Zangi-Ragozh said, trying to maintain a genial demeanor; he spoke the Jou'an-Jou'an language much better now than he had even a fortnight ago. "If you like, I can show you."

"A spear against a boar when an arrow is possible? What do you take me for? Foreigners!" Imgalas scoffed, then allowed, "Well, why not? Perhaps you can use it well enough." He pointed with his arrow, indicating one of the largest of the wild pigs. "You try to bring down that big one with the tattered ear. You can make a good kill; he'll provide some meat, and enough leather for two saddles." Waving Zangi-Ragozh away, he ordered the other men to follow him, whooping as they hurtled after a pair of boars.

Zangi-Ragozh wheeled his pony and hurried after the boar Imgalas had indicated. He did not feel the harsh wind nor the bite of the cold in the scattered snowflakes. All his attention was on the boar, and on getting his pony close enough to throw the spear. Up ahead the ground rose into a low knoll, and the boar headed directly for it, Zangi-Ragozh and his pony steadily closing the distance between them and the wild pig. As he approached the fleeing animal, Zangi-Ragozh rose in the iron foot-loops and steadied himself for casting his boar spear, a risky and crucial preparation for the plunge. He maneuvered his pony close to the boar, held him there at a steady gallop while he prepared to thrust down with the long spear. His downward thrust rocked him, but his aim was true: the boar shrieked and kicked as he fell, and Zangi-Ragozh pulled in his cinder-brown pony to a walk, then guided him back to the boar, where the black-clad foreigner stepped down from the saddle—another benefit of the iron foot-loops—and approached the twitching boar, a long Darjeeling dao held ready for the final, fatal chop at the boar's neck; the blood that gouted from the wound steamed in the frosty air. Bending down, he drove the blade into the pig's belly as he drank the fountaining blood, wincing in spite of himself as he recalled the disemboweling knives that had killed him twenty-five hundred years ago.

"So you brought him down," exclaimed Imgalas as he rode up, his shearling shuba spattered with new blood.

Zangi-Ragozh straightened up and pulled the spear out of the dead animal. "Do you save the guts?"

"Of course," said Imgalas. "Why should we throw away something so useful?"

"Some others do not," said Zangi-Ragozh, putting the offal in a pile. "Do you have a sack for this?"

"Joksu Guadas has them. I'll send him over as soon as we have dressed the others," Imgalas shouted as he started his pony running back toward the rest of the hunters.

Zangi-Ragozh continued with his chore, setting the boar's organs beside the carcass. As he worked, he became aware of a distant sound of growling, and an instant later, he heard a pony whinny in distress. Straightening up, Zangi-Ragozh looked around and saw that Baru Ksoka, who was in the process of securing his kill to the back of his saddle, had attracted a pack of wolves. The Kaigan had reached for his chilanum, but the knife was beyond his grasp on the ground. He had unstrung his bow and could not brace himself to string it again, for the wolves were closing in around him, and his pony was panicking, rearing and trying to pull away from the powerful hand on the reins, and although Baru Ksoka kept the animal from bolting, he could not quiet him enough to mount. From his vantage point on a slight rise, Zangi-Ragozh realized that the Kaigan was in dreadful danger. Imgalas and the others were a greater distance away than he, making it clear that if he did nothing, Baru Ksoka would be savaged or killed.

Leaving the boar where it lay, Zangi-Ragozh vaulted into the saddle and set his pony galloping down the incline toward the wolves and Baru Ksoka. "Kaigan! Kaigan!" he shouted, hoping to be heard over the wolves and the pony.

One of the wolves rushed in and bit the on-side rear leg of the pony, drawing blood and giving the pony the final jolt of terror; the pony broke free of Baru Ksoka and bolted, the slaughtered pig bouncing on his croup as he fled. Most of the wolves took off after the pony, but five remained to circle the Kaigan, who had no weapons to fight them.

Zangi-Ragozh came pelting the last lengths between the Kaigan and the wolves and him. He had grabbed his boar spear and now began to swing it like a club, knocking one of the wolves with such force that he heard the animal's ribs crack as the flat of the spear-blade struck. As soon as he was sure that the wolf would not be able to continue the fight, he wheeled his pony and drove off another of the pack.

Baru Ksoka dove for his chilanum, shoving it deep into the nearest wolf, shouting as blood spurted over his hand; he pulled out the blade and prepared to stab again just as another wolf fastened on his arm, once, twice, teeth sinking into his flesh; the Kaigan's pony screamed as the wolves pulled him down, falling upon him in a frenzy. Hearing this, Baru Ksoka swore viciously and began to poke at the wolf that held him; his chilanum finally penetrated the wolf's shoulder, making him howl, and giving Baru Ksoka the chance to pull his arm free.

Zangi-Ragozh could see that the Kaigan was bleeding heavily from four serious wounds—three in his legs and one on his arm—and he paused in his attack on the remaining wolves to shout, "Can you stand?"

"For a while," Baru Ksoka said, reeling as he glanced at the damage that had been done.

From some distance away, Imgalas and the rest could be heard rushing toward them.

"Guard the boars!" Baru Ksoka shouted. "We need the meat!"

Zangi-Ragozh drove his boar-spear into the last wolf, then swung out of the saddle, leading his pony and going purposefully toward the Kaigan, who was jabbing at the bodies of the wolves lying around him, some still twitching.

Imgalas and the rest of the hunters appeared around the curve of the rise; they all stood in the foot-loops and had bows raised and arrows notched, ready to bring down the wolves. "Joksu Guadas!" Imgalas brayed. "Save the boars! Stop the wolves!"

Joksu Guadas pulled away from Imgalas, heading toward the surging knot of wolves as they descended on the pony and the slaughtered boar. He began to fire arrows into the mass of hungry wolves, shouting to Demen Ksai to work the other side. "Don't damage the hides any more than you must. They'll fetch a good trade!"

Demen Ksai shouted back his understanding and raised his bow, an arrow notched to the string, as he closed in on the other side of the churning pack. He quickly dispatched three wolves, and then sent an arrow into the pony's skull to end its suffering. Satisfied he had followed orders, he shouted to Joksu Guadas, "The pack is breaking up."

"Kill as many as you can." Joksu Guadas shot another wolf as an example. "They'll trail the clan now that they've found us, and we'll have to keep watch against them. Besides, we can use the skins, though theirs look a little mangy."

"That we can," Demen Ksai agreed, and shot another arrow into the pack.

The wolves roiled around the pony, snapping and growling; they were thin—not even their heavy winter ruffs could disguise how scrawny the bodies beneath the fur had become. As the men bore down on them, more and more fell to the arrow, and those few who broke away did not flee unscathed.

Watching this, Baru Ksoka hobbled a few steps in their direction. He staggered and would have fallen if Zangi-Ragozh had not come to his side and slipped his shoulder under Baru Ksola's arm to support him. "I . . . I don't know what . . ." A film of cool sweat made his face shine in the sere sunlight, and he had to clamp his jaw to keep his teeth from chattering.

Zangi-Ragozh had seen this rush of cold many times in his long life, and he knew it was more dangerous than the bleeding wounds. "Here. Put my shuba over yours," he offered, pulling off the heavy, sleeveless garment. "Then lie down and—"

"No! No Kaigan of the Desert Cats lies down in hunting, or in war!" His voice was shrill and he tried to break away from Zangi-Ragozh's support.

"You will fall down, then," said Zangi-Ragozh calmly, not giving up his bolstering. "If you stand, the blood will more quickly run from your legs. If you recline, you will save more blood."

"How bad are the bites?" His voice lowered as he looked away from Joksu Guadas and Demen Ksai as they finished off as many of the pack as could not flee, yipping and howling.

"They will need to be tended, and quickly." Zangi-Ragozh pulled on the reins of his pony, forcing the reluctant animal to walk through the wolves. "If you will not lie down, will you at least mount? Shorten the foot-loops so that your knees are higher than the pommel? You will not bleed so much."

Baru Ksoka nodded. "I am Kaigan. I should ride."

"Truly, you should." Zangi-Ragozh held the pony still as he assisted Baru Ksoka into the saddle, and then shortened the strap of the iron foot-loop.

Imgalas came cantering up on his lathered pony. "Eleven got away. The rest are dead, Kaigan."

"Then make the boars and pony ready to carry, and start skinning the wolves. Leave the bodies. Let them be food for scavengers." Baru Ksoka swayed a little in the saddle.

"That we will. There are four boars, counting the foreigner's," Imgalas reported.

"Jekan Madassi will be glad of that," said Baru Ksoka, his voice becoming thready.

Zangi-Ragozh spoke up. "Kaigan, your wounds need to be cleaned and closed."

Imgalas finally noticed the blood that was dropping from Baru Ksoka's foot, starting to puddle on the ground. "Our Kaigan is strong."

"Yes, he is, he would be unconscious now if he were not," said Zangi-Ragozh.

"Hardly that," muttered Baru Ksoka.

"If you force him to remain, he will have a more difficult recovery," Zangi-Ragozh warned.

"Foreigners are all so cautious," said Imgalas, his mouth turning with contempt.

"Be glad of it," said Zangi-Ragozh, and vaulted up behind the Kaigan, onto the croup of the pony; he nudged the flanks and set off at a jog-trot. After a short distance, Baru Ksoka slumped back against him, his breath labored. By the time they reached the Desert Cats' camp, Zangi-Ragozh was holding Baru Ksoka to keep him from falling. He turned his pony toward the wagon where Dukkai lay, and the pony slowed to a walk as if relieved that their journey was over. "Ro-shei!" he shouted as he jumped down from the pony.

From all around the camp came shouts and pointing as the Desert Cats saw Zangi-Ragozh ease Baru Ksoka out of the saddle and carry him toward the wagon; Neitis, Baru Ksoka's young nephew, was the first to come running up, shouting, "What happened?" He reached the pony's off-side and took hold of the iron foot-loop, his young face showing intense worry as well as curiosity.

"There were wolves after boar, and there was a fight." Zangi-Ragozh had reached the narrow rear platform and put Baru Ksoka down on it, making sure his shuba, as well as the Kaigan's own, was wrapped securely around him. "Baru Ksoka held off the pack."

"A valiant thing," Neitis approved, but his praise was short-lived as he stared at the deep bite gashes in the legs. "He is badly hurt."

"Yes, he is, which is why I must begin to treat him at once. Tell the others that the Kaigan cannot be disturbed just now." He was about to climb into the wagon, but added, "Dukkai will watch all that I do."

As if in response to her name, Dukkai called out, "Is that you, Zangi-Ragozh?"

"Yes. I am going to bring Baru Ksoka into the wagon, to clean and treat his injuries. Will you guard him while I work?"

Four more of the Desert Cats had reached the wagon, and they all spoke at once as they saw their Kaigan lying unconscious on the wagon's rear platform. The babble grew noisier as more of the clan hurried over and the questions became more insistent.

"Yes," Dukkai called out. "I will do that. I will see that no harm comes to Baru Ksoka."

"Watch closely!" shouted someone in the gathering crowd.

As Ro-shei reached the wagon, he had to push through the press of Desert Cats to reach Zangi-Ragozh. One glance at Baru Ksoka was enough for him to realize how grave the situation was. "Did a boar slash him?"

"No; those are wolf bites," said Zangi-Ragozh. "I need to get to work on him now. You know which direction the hunt went—Imgalas needs five men to ride out to help them bring home the pigs and pony and the wolf-pelts. Those of you who go, tell Imgalas that the Kaigan will live, if his wounds do not fester."

"You must stop that happening!" Neitis sounded terrified.

"If you cannot keep him alive, you had best have a fast pony ready," threatened another voice from the rear of the group.

"Go ahead with what you must do," said Ro-shei quietly. "I'll stand guard and do my best to explain." He noticed Neitis standing very near the back platform and said to him, "Do you want to help your uncle?"

Neitis nodded. "Why is he so quiet?"

"He is hurt," said Ro-shei. "He must have rest, so that he can regain his strength." He nodded over his shoulder to Zangi-Ragozh. "We will handle things, my master."

"Thank you," said Zangi-Ragozh, and climbed onto the rear platform and picked up Baru Ksoka in one easy gesture. He shouldered through the double hanging flap and saw Dukkai sitting on her hanging cot, anxiety carving lines in her countenance. "I suspect it is worse than it looks, but it is bad enough," he told her. "It is important that he stay warm."

"Has he lost a lot of blood?" She held out her hand. "Tell me; I have to know."

"Yes. But he has not lost so much blood or turned so cold that he will die."

"How can you be sure?" She was pale, more from worry than from her own condition.

Zangi-Ragozh stared at her as he put the Kaigan down on a large chest. "If there is one thing I can be certain of, it is blood. The cold is less certain, but he has not become icy."

"Is that a danger?" Dukkai was growing upset.

"Cold is always dangerous to the living," he told her.

She studied him, nodded once more, and lay back on the hanging cot. "Do you have enough light?"

"I see well enough in the dark," he replied, then saw the apprehension in her eyes and went on, "But if you will move that oil-lamp, I will have fewer shadows to deal with, and my work will go more quickly," he said, working to peel back the leather leggings the Kaigan wore. "These are ruined," he said as he dropped the leggings, letting them fall into a basket near the head of the chest where Baru Ksoka lay.

"What happened?" Dukkai wondered aloud.

"He had slain a boar and was gutting it," said Zangi-Ragozh. "So he was by himself when a wolf pack came upon him. His pony bolted, and the wolves caught it." He bent over Baru Ksoka. "I have clean water in that blue cask." He pointed. "If you will hand it to me?"

"That I will," said Dukkai, reaching for it and holding it out to Zangi-Ragozh. "Will water be enough?"

"To clean the wounds? yes," said Zangi-Ragozh, prying up the wide top of the cask. "It is essential that the injuries be washed free of all material so that the medicament may work without impediment." He opened a large container and took out a stack of cotton squares, two of which he put into the water to soak. "He will have to sleep for as long as possible. I will prepare a draft for him when I have done with dressing his injuries. It is made from poppies—"

"We know about poppies," said Dukkai. "They can rob a man of his wits."

"And they are anodyne," said Zangi-Ragozh; he took one of the cotton squares from the water.

"You said—out there—that if his wounds do not fester, he will recover."

"Yes, and so he shall. He has an excellent constitution, and even now, when times are hard, he has kept up his strength and his stamina. Such men do not usually fail in their health unless rot of one kind or another sets in, and I have a sovereign remedy that makes such a development less likely."

"Are you so certain he will—"

"You need not worry, Dukkai." He leaned forward, using the wet cotton square to clean out the savage bites on Baru Ksoka's legs and arm. "He has a deep gash on his arm, and there may be some difficulty in healing."

"Why should that be?" She was becoming agitated, trying not to look away as Zangi-Ragozh continued to bathe the Kaigan's wounds.

"Because tendons are torn, and they often do not knit well, particularly in the arms, for they are so crucial in riding and fighting." This last addition was said as if from a distance as he concentrated on his task. "Those wolves—Baru Ksoka might well have been killed and eaten."

"Eaten?" she asked sharply.

"Of course. The wolves are as hungry as you are. Usually they avoid men in numbers." He put the red-stained cotton square into the basket with the leggings. "If you have any magic to offer him, it would be wise to do so."

"I will chant for him," she said, and began a three-note repetitive pattern of invocation to the gods of the flesh and healing, and to the Lord of the Skies, all the while keeping a wary eye on Zangi-Ragozh.

Taking the second cotton square from the water, Zangi-Ragozh sluiced the wounds thoroughly, then cleaned off Baru Ksoka's hands and face; while he was wiping the Kaigan's brow, the man finally stirred, murmuring disjointed syllables as he tried to shift his position on the chest. Zangi-Ragozh held him down with deceptive ease. "Calmly, Baru Ksoka, calmly," he urged. "Lie still and you will soon feel better." He reached with one hand to his container of medicaments and reached for a vial, and then a small jar, which he set on the end of the chest. Keeping Baru Ksoka still with his right arm, he took a cup from a braced shelf and dipped it in the cask of water, then emptied the contents of the vial into it before adding a dollop of thick, amber-colored syrup to the cup. He stirred the contents with an ivory chopstick and then helped Baru Ksoka to raise his head. "Drink this. It will lessen your pain."

Obediently Baru Ksoka drank, sputtering a little once as he tried to swallow too quickly. When the cup was empty, he looked blearily up at Zangi-Ragozh. "Where am I?"

"In my wagon at your camp. Imgalas and the rest of your men are bringing back boar, pony, and wolf-pelts." He disposed of the cotton square with its fellow in the basket. "I am going to dress your wounds and bind them with cotton."

"I believe his sovereign remedy will help you," Dukkai interjected.

"A sovereign remedy." Baru Ksoka was having trouble fixing his attention as he looked blearily from Dukkai to Zangi-Ragozh. "I need rest. Let me sleep." The last ended on a sigh as Zangi-Ragozh eased his head back down onto the chest.

"Yes. If you will rest, the remedy will do its work." He reached for his container of medicaments again, and this time took out a twist-lidded jar. He opened it, revealing an unguent that was the consistency of rabbit-skin glue. He fingered out a small amount and smeared it on the worst of the Kaigan's leg wounds, then repeated the application on the other. Straightening up, he took a length of cotton from his container and began to wrap the leg, working slowly and methodically. When he had finished with both, he took another fingerful of unguent and spread it over the deep punctures on Baru Ksoka's arm, taking care to work the substance deep into the injury; he paid no heed to the occasional grunts of pain that came from Baru Ksoka. When he was finished, he said, "I do not want you to use your arm or your hand for at least three days."

Baru Ksoka was growing weary, but he sighed, saying, "You must . . . I am not . . . a weakling."

"No, Kaigan, you are not," Zangi-Ragozh agreed. He stepped

back in the confines of the wagon, taking care not to intrude upon Dukkai's chanting. He looked out the double-flap and saw Ro-shei standing nearby. "His wounds are medicated and bandaged. Will you inform his women to make his bed ready? He will be more comfortable among them than lying here."

The Desert Cats who had remained a short distance from the wagon looked up, many emotions on their usually impassive faces. Gotsada held up his hands. "Dukkai, my cousin, is summoning the gods to heal the Kaigan."

"Yes, she is." Zangi-Ragozh surprised the clan members with this statement. "All medicaments are improved by the might of the gods."

"Do you truly endorse her magic?" Gotsada demanded.

"I do." He signaled to Ro-shei. "He will need a carry-pallet."

"How can you know what is best for the Kaigan of the Desert Cats?" young Neitis asked with a little bravado in his manner.

"I can know because he is made of flesh, as are all men. He is strong, and that bodes well for him, but he is not made of anything stronger than flesh," said Zangi-Ragozh in a tranquil tone.

One of the Desert Cats laughed, and this broke the rising tension. Soon all the clan members keeping watch over the wagon were laughing, as much from relief as from mirth.

"I will see to the carry-pallet," said Ro-shei while the Desert Cats were distracted. "I will be ready in a short while."

"Very good; so will he," Zangi-Ragozh answered, then ducked back into the wagon's interior.

"Is it safe to move him?" Dukkai asked, her nervousness now more controlled than before. She had stopped chanting just as Zangi-Ragozh had come back into the wagon.

"It is," said Zangi-Ragozh. "Ro-shei will bring a carrying pallet, and that should be enough for the distance he has to cover."

"Are you sure that you have done all you can for Baru Ksoka? Have you used all your knowledge to aid him?" This bordered on an accusation.

"For the time being, yes. Now he needs a chance to strengthen himself and to be restored. It would be best if he had as few disturbances as possible."

"Is that important?"

Zangi-Ragozh nodded once. "Out here, on the trade route, rest is the most potent medicine of all. If he is bothered, jostled, fussed over, or his rest impeded in any way, it will only serve to slow his re-cuperation. As he improves, there will be more I can do."

"You do expect him to improve, don't you? If you think he will get worse, let me know now so that I may chant for him more diligently."

"He may have some fever, but I have treatments for that if he should need it; however, the sovereign remedy should keep rot at bay. He may have swelling around the bites. But unless the wolves were rabid, he should recover, if his wounds are kept properly dressed." His voice was level and assured, and he looked at Dukkai somberly. "We will know in a day if he will recover: believe this."

"Then I shall chant for as long as I can today, and as long as I can tomorrow," she announced. "It is what the clan expects of me, and what I must give them." She looked from Baru Ksoka to Zangi-Ragozh. "I hope you are right."

Before he could answer, the back flap was lifted and Ro-shei climbed onto the platform. "I have the carrying pallet, and two men to bear it."

"Will that be enough?" Dukkai asked sharply.

"Two men should be sufficient," he told her, "if they are careful."

"Have Gotsada walk with them, to keep the clan away," said Dukkai.

"A very wise precaution," said Zangi-Ragozh. He signaled to Ro-shei. "Leave the carrying pallet here and go find Gotsada, if you would; bring him here quickly. Tell him he is needed to protect the Kaigan." As Ro-shei moved away, Zangi-Ragozh pulled the carrying pallet into position, bracing it in place with a small, heavy chest. "I will make this as easy as I am able," he said to Baru Ksoka, although only Dukkai gave any sign of hearing him. With a swift, powerful mo-tion, he lifted Baru Ksoka and lowered him onto the carrying pallet, then set about securing the two broad belts around him. "There," he said as soon as he was finished. He reached for one of the folded lengths of wool and put it over the Kaigan's recumbent form. "This will keep him warm."

"Is cold really so dangerous?" Dukkai asked as if she expected a different answer than before.

"Men die of it," said Zangi-Ragozh, lifting the carrying pallet with no apparent effort; he moved this to the rear platform and saw two young men—Ksuintol and Erasai—waiting. There was no sign of Ro-shei or Gotsada. "Baru Ksoka is almost ready for you to carry him." Behind him, from the wagon, he heard Dukkai start to chant again. "Carry him as lightly and gently as you can. Let nothing intrude upon him."

Erasai seemed a bit dubious. "Nothing? Not even his family?"

"Only his women, when he is in their care. Otherwise you may interfere with Dukkai's magic."

The two young men exchanged glances, and Ksuintol was about to speak when Gotsada arrived to take charge of the situation. "Your companion told me what must be done. I will see that the Kaigan is undisturbed as we go through the camp."

"Very good," said Zangi-Ragozh, saying to the two young men, "Remember: lightly and gently."

"Take him up," ordered Gotsada, and took up his position at Baru Ksoka's head. "We will not go any faster than a walk."

The young men hefted the carrying pallet and got it balanced between them, then, at Gotsada's nod, they set off toward the Kaigan's large, round tent, Gotsada warning all those who approached to leave Baru Ksoka alone so that he could rest. As they moved through the camp, more and more of the Desert Cats followed them, at a respectful distance.

Zangi-Ragozh remained on the rear platform of the wagon, waiting for Ro-shei to return. As he listened to Dukkai's chanting, he noticed that the pale-yellow snow had started falling once again.

Text of a letter from Hu Bi-Da to Jho Chieh-Jen, both in Yang-Chau, at the end of the Fortnight of the Frost Kings.

To my most esteemed colleague and fellow-employee of the distinguished foreigner Zangi-Ragozh, the most earnest and sincere greetings of Hu Bi-Da, the senior clerk of the Eclipse Trading Company, with the fervent wish that Jho Chien-Jen is faring better than we are here at the offices and warehouses of Zangi-Ragozh's trading enterprise.

Alas, I must begin by reporting that we now have learned from four sources that the Bounteous Fortune, *and all her cargo, are lost. The* Bounteous Fortune *had just left Sangasanga between the Sulu and Celebes Seas, bound for Marakan. Captain So was relieved that the ship had not been damaged by the huge waves and howling winds that had battered the region, saying it was unwise to go to sea with such omens. He ordered canvas shelters be put on deck to guard against the stinging, stinking rain that fell relentlessly and pledged to ride out the storm. But in those narrow waters, what is hardly noticed in the open sea becomes cause for upheaval. The two seas and the Macassar Strait combined the force and confines of the waters, making the waves higher, more irregular and disruptive, and at last, the* Bounteous Fortune *broke apart on the rocks of Borneo and sank in shallow water. All but three of the crew died of injuries or drowning, Captain So succumbing to infections in burns and similar eruptions on his skin, which no one would touch, fearing it would pass to them. Two of the three remaining succumbed to similar lesions; the lone survivor had improvised a turban such as some wear in India and wrapped himself in broad leaves during the rain. He finally came upon a ship belonging to Kao Shai-Ming, who, in the spirit of Yang-Chau, brought the sailor, one Mong-Dja, back home. Now that winter is closing in again, I am very much afraid that no ships from Eclipse Trading will be able to set out again until at least the Fortnight of Flower Rains, and that is ten fortnights away—too long for ships to be idle if any business is to succeed.*

It pains me to add more unfortunate news: the house of Dei-Na, our employer's former concubine, was broken into and ransacked. Dei-Na herself, who has led an exemplary life, was treated with great violence and disrespect and has withdrawn to the house of her father, to tend to him now that his health is failing. She has taken as much of her goods, clothes, and food that can be salvaged. As you must have heard, there was a raid by hooligans in the riverfront area. Twenty-three people were killed and another forty-nine were injured, according to what the Prefecture has announced; I am of the opinion the figure is higher, but I have no means to confirm this suspicion. In the raiding, six ships were set afire, and it was only due to Kuan-Yin that none of this company's ships were lost, although the warehouse on Old Canal Street was a little damaged.

For these reasons, and because of the Gray Cough, I can only spare nine men. You may have to find the remaining six you seek from outside the city. I know that rebuilding the south wall of the compound is essential, and that there have been raids in your area as well as inside the city walls. I regret that we have reached such an impasse, but with the weakness of the sun, the tempestuous weather, the spreading and insidious Gray Cough, and general hunger, no one is free from want, or capable of eliminating danger. You tell me your supplies are low, and you now know that mine are, as well. I wish I were in a position to do more, but I am not, just as you cannot spare anyone to fortify the docks and increase the guards on Zangi-Ragozh's ships. I will beseech August Heaven to aid you, as our Captains must also be aided, at least until such time as our employer returns to make his desires and decisions known to us all.

This Year of Yellow Snow has brought many hardships, not only to the Middle Kingdom, but to many other lands. From the reports of the sea Captains, no port has been untouched by this dreadful cold, and the burning rain. It may be some time before any of us will be able to restore his fortunes, and it may be that, if worse comes, most of us will lose all. It has been reported by a number of trustworthy seamen that Sunda Kalapa has been all but leveled by waves and falls of ash that are higher than a tall man in many places. Such desolation has been spared us, but it may still happen that we may endure greater calamities than have befallen us thus far. It troubles me that we cannot provide suitable offerings to our shrines nor spare more incense for the ancestors, but I also know that this is the Will of Heaven, and that when the worst has been reached, the change will come that, like the seasons, will restore us to better than what we had before, for all nature must ultimately be in balance.

May Kung Fu-Tzu's principles guide you, and Lao-Tsu's comprehension bring you comfort. May your family be spared suffering, and may all this soon be nothing but a terrible memory.

Hu Bi-Da
Senior Clerk, Eclipse Trading Company
(his chop)

6

Outside the mud-brick walls of Turfan where during most winters a sea of Mongol, Uighur, Jou'an-Jou'an, Turkish, and Persian tents besieged the town with merchants and their goods, there were now only a few tents, and a cluster of improvised paddocks for the camels, mules, and ponies of the stalwart or desperate travelers who had arrived there before the snows came. Eight bodies hung on ropes from the city walls, their flesh blackened and becoming mummified in the dreadful cold. The ground was now thigh deep in yellow snow, and there was more coming from the wind-bludgeoned clouds above.

Baru Ksoka halted his clan not far from the entrance to the town. He had taken up the lead position in their numbers only the day before, and it was an effort for him to remain in the saddle. "Everyone hold!" he shouted, barely heard over the wind. "The gate of Turfan is ahead. I and Imgalas will ride to the gate, to secure a place for us, our herds, and flocks. We will try to get places for all of us inside the walls. Zangi-Ragozh, come with me. The officers of the town will want to know about you, since you are not Jou'an-Jou'an."

From his place on the driving-box of his wagon, Zangi-Ragozh signaled with a wave to show he had heard. "We are going to the town gates, Dukkai," he said. He stood up on the box and called back to Ro-shei, who rode immediately behind him, "We're going to the gate."

Dukkai was protected by the double-flap from the worst of the wind, and wrapped in bearskins over her winter clothing. "Then we will have a chance to rest and get warm, and for our animals to be fed and watered. I will chant for their strength and endurance; the gods have demanded much of us." Her pregnancy was going better than it had, and she might have ridden with the other adult women, but she tired quickly, and Baru Ksoka had decreed that for the sake of his child, Dukkai would continue to ride in the wagon.

"So we hope to be restored. If all is well in Turfan." Zangi-Ragozh kept his voice level.

"All well? Nothing is well, here or anywhere. Yet it may be that they will let us stay here and recruit ourselves for the next stage of our travel. At least we will not have to bed down in snowdrifts, as we have done the last four nights." There was a brief, awkward pause, and she spoke more quietly, "I am sorry you won't be going on with us. It was not a decision he made easily, asking you and your companion to leave us."

Zangi-Ragozh gave a shrug she could not see. "Baru Ksoka is taking the northern route, and I am planning to keep to the middle, going through Karashahr to Aksu, which would part us in any case. Turfan is as far as I want to come into the mountains, especially in this winter— I might as well be in the distant northern forests." He knew she wanted something less final, so he added, "We may meet again in Kashgar, if you take the Amber Trail, in Tashkent, or Tok-Kala. I will ask for you and the Desert Cats wherever I go, all the way to Constantine's City, if I push on so far."

"That is a greater journey than any I have traveled. Do you want to go there?"

"I am bound for my native earth, which is some distance from Constantine's City," said Zangi-Ragozh.

"In the Carpa-Ti Mountains, I recall you said," she remarked. "Baru Ksoka said we may reach Kashgar on the Amber Trail, if we find no good pasturage in Dzungaria. The last one of our Kaigans to lead us to Kashgar was Baru Ksoka's great-great-great-uncle. It is a very long way to Kashgar, I think." She was improved from a fortnight ago, but she still had much discomfort, and she had to shift position frequently or risk more aches and cramps; the furs whispered as she adjusted her position behind the driving-box. "I hope it isn't too rigorous, making our way there."

"It may prove more demanding than is usually the case," he said carefully. "Consider how difficult it has been to get to Turfan."

"Surely it will not be so harsh in the West," she said, repeating what the Desert Cats had been saying for three fortnights.

"I hope it is not. But it may be that the desolation is spreading." Zangi-Ragozh waited for her to respond.

She was silent for a long moment, then said, "If you think this is not a wise thing to go so far, then tell the Kaigan."

"I have," said Zangi-Ragozh. "When he informed me he had

decided—much as it embarrassed him—that it would be best if Ro-shei and I left your clan."

"But you saved him. His wounds are healing almost without fever because of you." She was deeply indignant. "How can he serve you such a turn when you have spared him suffering and restored his health? and saved his child within me, for that matter?"

"I think he is worried for the clan, which is what a Kaigan must be; I cannot argue with his decision, for it is what I would have done, I suspect, had our situations been reversed," said Zangi-Ragozh. "Many of the Desert Cats see my companion and me as interlopers."

"Not interlopers," said Dukkai firmly.

"Not to you, perhaps, but to most of the Desert Cats: Ro-shei and I are barely tolerated, and that will not change for the better." He softened his voice still more. "If the winter is as hard as the rest of the year has been, resentment toward our presence will only increase."

She sighed. "I know you're right, for I can feel it as if it were a sandstorm building, just beyond the limits of sight, and I understand that Baru Ksoka did not decide the issue without much reflection, but I am still abashed that you should be made to—" She stopped as a wooden horn sounded and the gates of Turfan began to open.

"I think we had best move up now," said Zangi-Ragozh, and twitched the reins to put the pair of ponies moving. "It seems that Baru Ksoka wants me to present myself."

"You mean he wants you to translate for him, if you can," said Dukkai, sounding disgusted. "In case the men of Turfan no longer know the Silk Road coign."

"Then that will be what I shall do, although he will probably have little use for me. Turfan is more a caravan camp with walls than a real town," said Zangi-Ragozh, taking care not to force any of the clan's carts and wagons aside as he threaded his way toward the head of the line; the snowy road made the way difficult, and it took all Zangi-Ragozh's skill to keep the ponies from floundering in the roadside ditch that lay hidden beyond the uneven furrows left in the snow. At last he drew up behind Baru Ksoka and Imgalas.

Two dozen armed men in bearskin cloaks stood in the mouth of the gate, their spears and bows at the ready; they shouted in ragged unison, "Halt, you Jou'an-Jou'an!" They spoke in the Mogol-Hunnic-Turkic patois of eastern Silk Road merchants. "You may not enter!"

Baru Ksoka stopped his pony and signaled to the rest to slow, as well. "Tell me," he said quietly to Imgalas, "do you suppose they mean to kill us?"

"I think they fear *we* will kill *them*," said Imgalas, deliberately raising his voice enough to carry to the contingent of guards.

"Well, we have no such intention," said Baru Ksoka, and addressed the men barring their way. "I am Baru Ksoka of the Desert Cats clan of Jou'an-Jou'an. We have wolf-pelts and goats to trade, and a few strings of Chinese copper cash to pay for shelter and food."

One of the guards stepped forward. "You will have to surrender your weapons, and you must pay us in gold."

"We need our knives, but if you must have our lances and arrows, you may hold them. We would rather keep our bows. Without arrows, what harm is there in letting us have them?" He studied the guards. "Can we not trade the pelts instead of giving you gold? Gold cannot warm you."

"You are right as far as it goes," said the guard. "But we must think of better days to come, and for that, we must have gold."

"Then," said Baru Ksoka, "we are at an impasse. We do not trade in gold, but in furs and goats and copper cash." He rubbed unthinkingly at his forearm; his half-healed wound was aching from the cold. "If you cannot accept what we have, then I fear we will have to camp outside the walls."

"There is a Uighur caravan outside. Talk to them about your pelts," the chief guardsman recommended.

"We saw them, and the Persians," said Baru Ksoka.

"One of the Persians died yesterday—they found him frozen." The guard laughed harshly.

"I wish you would reconsider. We have children with us, and women with child."

"Then guard them well and ask your gods to bring back the sun," said the guard, stepping back, and motioning to his companions to move as well.

Zangi-Ragozh, who had been watching this with a growing sense of the inevitable, called out, "I have a little gold with me."

Baru Ksoka swung around in his saddle and stared at Zangi-Ragozh. "It is unnecessary for you to—"

"If Dukkai is to deliver a healthy baby, it is," said Zangi-Ragozh. "I am in a position to help her, and you."

"If you do it, it can change nothing," Baru Ksoka warned.

"I realize that," said Zangi-Ragozh. "My companion and I are going on to Aksu and Kashgar, and you are taking the northern route. It is for Dukkai that I do this, so she and her babe will be able to endure the deepening winter." He set the simple brake before sliding back into the wagon and searching for the small strongbox in which he carried as much money as he wanted others to know he had. He opened the lock and drew out three gold bars, saying to Dukkai as he did, "I hope this will give us a little respite from the demands of travel." The gold shone against the heavy black leather of his gloves.

"You do not have to do this," said Dukkai.

"But I think I do," said Zangi-Ragozh. "This may be the last opportunity I have to—" He stopped as he closed the strongbox and set the lock again.

She nodded, color mounting in her face. "I know."

He held up his hand. "Let me give this to Baru Ksoka." He held up the gold as he stepped back into the driving-box. "Ro-shei!" he called. "Will you take this to the Kaigan?"

Ro-shei came up beside the wagon on a red pony and held out his gloved hands. "I will do as you ask," he said.

Handing Ro-shei the gold, Zangi-Ragozh said softly in Imperial Latin, "Have a care—those guards are not in good form, and they are seeking an excuse to attack."

"I think so, too," said Ro-shei, and carried the gold to Baru Ksoka. "My master gives you this for the benefit of your clan."

This generosity was shocking, and the Kaigan hesitated to take the three bars. "This will not be forgotten." He coughed and spoke to the guards again. "Very well. I have two bars of gold. That should secure us lodging and food for four or five days, and shelter and fodder for our animals."

"Two bars of gold is not enough," said the guard, recovering himself enough to bluster. "We must have more."

"Then three strings of copper cash into the bargain," said Baru Ksoka. "It is a handsome sum—twice what you would require in better years."

"But as you say, this is a bad year," said the chief guard, then spat.

"Still, two bars of gold and three strings of copper cash should suffice."
He gestured with his spear. "Go down this street and you will come to
three inns. Choose whichever one you like, and pay the landlord in advance. You will be able to stay for four days. If you must remain longer,
whatever the cause, we will require more gold. Give me your payment
as you enter." The passage the guards formed was hardly wide enough
to let two horses abreast pass, as if the guards were unwilling to give
any leeway to the Desert Cats. "Give your spears and arrows to Nuchcusal there. He is our warden."

Nuchcusal, a brawny man in a vast bearskin cloak, stepped out to
block Baru Ksoka's progress. "I will hold these in the gatehouse. You
may claim them again when you leave."

"We each have our marks on our spears and arrows," Baru Ksoka
declared as he surreptitiously slipped the third bar of gold into the interior sleeve of his tiger-skin mababa. "If you try to substitute any
other, we will know." He handed down his quiver and his spear. "There.
See you keep them safe."

The leader of the guard came up to him. "Two bars of gold and
three strings of copper cash." He held out his hand, all swathed in
shaggy, tahr-skinned gauntlets. "Give them to me."

Baru Ksoka handed over the two gold bars, then made a great
display of taking the strings of cash from his saddle-bags and presenting them to the leader of the guards.

"This will do," the leader announced. "Let them pass." He permitted the Desert Cats to pass into the town, but the guards followed them as they went down the street where they had been told
to go.

Ro-shei brought his pony alongside the wagon. "Those guards are
a suspicious lot." He spoke in Latin again.

"Who can blame them?" Zangi-Ragozh asked. "Think what they
have seen in the last year."

"I think of those bodies hanging over the walls." He waited a
moment, then went on, "It won't take much to turn the guards into
marauders."

"You are remembering Paulinos Oxatres," said Zangi-Ragozh, recalling the Byzantine commander with distaste. "His men were already trained soldiers, not like these guards. They were used to
killing. I doubt such is the case with these men, at least not yet."

"They would be more than willing to learn, by the look of them. I will remain awake tonight, and on alert." Ro-shei allowed the wagon to move ahead.

"What do you think they may do, those guards?" Dukkai asked, and added before Zangi-Ragozh could speak, "I think they may demand more money to permit us to leave."

"That is one possibility," said Zangi-Ragozh. "They may also invent charges to impose upon you and confiscate your trade goods as payment."

Dukkai took a short while to answer. "That is likely," she allowed, and started to chant softly.

The inns were little more than two-story mud-brick houses with a number of small rooms protruding in many directions. All three had stables, barns, and paddocks, and all had a bedraggled look about them, testament to the severity of the weather.

"We will need to occupy two of these inns," Baru Ksoka declared loudly. "Dur Moksal, you and your family, and four other families will go into that inn"—he pointed to the southeast side of the square to a building with a sign that showed a rough-carved bed and cooking fire—"and I and the rest will go to this one." The inn was on the northeast side of the square, a slightly larger edifice with a sign over the door saying in four languages Travelers' Rest.

"Which four families?" asked Imgalas, scowling against the wind.

Baru Ksoka considered, then said, "Joutan, Guadas, Rodomi, and Ksai. The rest, come with me." He dismounted and led his pony to the front of the inn, calling out, "Landlord! You have travelers!"

Dukkai had stopped chanting and was looking out through the double flap. "Is this where we will stay?" she called to Baru Ksoka.

"Yes!" he shouted back. "All of you, turn your animals over to Imgalas, and then go to the inns. Neitis, help Imgalas. You, too, Erasai!"

There was a sudden flurry of activity as the Desert Cats got down from their ponies and wagons and carts and began to gather their animals together. They worked efficiently, each keeping to his assigned task as they did every night making camp. Soon the ponies and goats were separated into two groups and contained with rope enclosures held by the oldest members of the clan while Baru Ksoka sorted his people out for the two landlords who had come out of their inns to deal with the unexpected arrival.

"Where do you wish me to go?" Zangi-Ragozh asked as Baru Ksoka came up to his wagon.

"Since you are treating Dukkai, you had better come with her. She will have a room in the Travelers' Rest. I have arranged it with the landlord. You and your companion may have a chamber to yourselves." Baru Ksoka glanced over his shoulder. "The landlord is demanding a silver bar to lodge us."

"I have enough to pay for it," said Zangi-Ragozh. "And the other landlord? What of him?"

"He has asked for five strings of silver cash," admitted Baru Ksoka. "You know what town-dwellers are. What is the use of gold and silver and copper when it is winter? Can it keep you warm? Can you eat it?"

"You must not mind them," said Zangi-Ragozh. "Most men seek treasure of one sort or another, and gold is sought everywhere."

"By fools," said Baru Ksoka. "Still, I am grateful that you have such metals with you. We would fare badly outside the gates."

"As the Persians are being forced to do," said Zangi-Ragozh, and changed the subject. "My companion will look after our animals and this wagon, if it is all the same to you."

Baru Ksoka held up his hand. "I understand. And I am relieved that you are so careful." He looked at Dukkai. "How do you go on? And how is the infant?"

"It is moving," she said. "It is eager to get out into the world, and that troubles me."

"That is why you ride in the wagon," he reminded her, and gave his attention to Zangi-Ragozh once more. "I thank you for all you have done, and I am sorry that you needed to do anything. I, and my family, and my clan will be obligated to you for at least another generation."

"There is no need," said Zangi-Ragozh. "You have helped Ro-shei and me to travel more safely in this terrible year. I am obliged to you for that."

"You are obliged to Dukkai," said Baru Ksoka, and started to turn away, but hesitated, saying, "You are to be certain that Dukkai is well. I have a lammergeier claw, to help her gain strength."

"Why do you not give it to her?" Zangi-Ragozh asked.

"She is the magician, not I." With that, Baru Ksoka strode off toward the entrance to the largest barn, calling for the goats to be brought "To get them out of the snow tonight!"

Dukkai went back into the wagon. "I don't like being inside rooms," she said. "This wagon is hard enough, but to have solid walls!"

"Do walls bother you?" Zangi-Ragozh asked, already aware that they did.

"They trouble me. With a tent, no matter how fine the skins that cover it, it isn't so very enclosed. With brick walls, a room is more a grave than a room." She fretted at the edge of her bearskin robe.

"They can seem so," he admitted apologetically. "I grew up in a stone castle." It had been not unlike the larger inn, but hewn from living rock high in the fishhook of the Carpathians, more than twenty-five centuries before. "It does not bother me."

"More of your foreign nature, I see," she said, and opened the double flap again to stare at the inn.

"If there is a blizzard coming—and it seems likely that there is—you will want to be inside. Mud brick holds out the cold better than a skin-covered tent." He half-rose, preparing to get down from the driving-box. "I will help you out of the wagon from the rear platform."

She sighed. "I shouldn't let you do so much, but I thank you for the care you give me."

He secured the simple brake and called to Ro-shei, "Will you take the wagon in hand, old friend?"

"That I will," said Ro-shei, dismounting and coming up to the wagon. He gave Zangi-Ragozh's cinder-brown pony a friendly pat as he loosened the lead that had kept it following the wagon for most of the day. "I will groom and feed them and be sure they have water. I will come this evening to report on the ponies and the camels." He stood aside while Zangi-Ragozh helped Dukkai out of the wagon, re-marking to her, "You and your clan will be warm tonight."

"I guess," she said dubiously.

Zangi-Ragozh got into the wagon, took some more gold and silver from his strongbox, then pulled out a small chest, saying to Ro-shei as he emerged from the wagon, "I believe we could both use a change of clothes—what do you say?"

"I would be glad of it," said Ro-shei, and gathered the two riding ponies and the three camels together; he led them and the wagon with its two-pony hitch off toward the stable.

The clan was breaking up into two parts, Gaudas, Moksal, Joutan, Ksai, and Rodomi going with Imgalas, the rest following Baru Ksoka into the Travelers' Rest.

It was a stark place, with an eating room around the central chimney, and three corridors branching out to the various rooms. Two steep staircases gave access to the upper floors. The landlord, engulfed in a wolf-skin cloak, greeted the Kaigan with greedy obsequiousness that would have been comical at a less harrowing time. He promised in three languages to light a fire for his guests, explained that the bath-house was out behind the kitchen, and offered to heat it, as well. "For a string of coppers more."

"I have already promised to pay you," said Baru Ksoka.

The landlord cringed even as he insisted, "You have promised payment for a room and for food, nothing more."

"We will do our own cooking," said Baru Ksoka, motioning to Jekan Madassi. "This woman supervises our meals, and she will do so here."

"Of course you will do your own cooking," said the landlord. "You will also pay for the use of the bath-house."

Baru Ksoka glowered at the landlord. "You are asking too much."

"I want a bath," said Zangi-Ragozh calmly from the rear of the group. "I will pay for heating the bath-house."

Baru Ksoka made a gesture of appreciation, took the string of copper cash Zangi-Ragozh proffered, and pointed him in the direction of the stairs. "Before you bathe, you will want to secure your quarters. I have arranged who is to have which room: your room will be at the end of the upper corridor. There are stairs on the outside of the building, if you would rather go up that way, or so the landlord tells me."

"I will," said Zangi-Ragozh, "though I may use the outside stairs to go to the bath-house." He gave a single nod to the Desert Cats and said to Dukkai, "A bath would do you good. Why not plan to bathe when I am done?"

There was an awkward silence, and then Dukkai answered, "If it will aid my child, I will do it."

"I think it will," said Zangi-Ragozh, and took up the chest he had brought from the wagon as he started up the stairs toward the corridor that would lead to the room he and Ro-shei had been allocated.

The landlord took the string of cash and squirreled it away inside his cloak. "I will have the bath-house heated at once." He studied Jekan Madassi for a short moment, then said, "I will order wood brought for your fires. If you need pots or spits, there will be a charge for them. I will bargain for some of your wolf-pelts."

"We have what we need," said Jekan Madassi brusquely, then clapped her hands to summon her family to assist her.

Watching this as he climbed the stairs, Zangi-Ragozh had a sudden pang of sadness as he realized that he would be parting from the Desert Cats in a few days. As he continued westward toward Europe, he would do as he planned and ask about them, but he found he was already resigning himself to their loss. He went down the corridor, noticing how low the ceiling was; occasionally the beams almost brushed his hat, trying not to listen as the voices of the clan faded behind him.

By the time he emerged from the cramped room to go to the bath-house, many of the Desert Cats had made their way to their quarters, and the first aroma of cooking meat was insinuating itself onto the chilly air. Zangi-Ragozh took his change of clothes with him, along with a wide drying sheet. He used the outer staircase, taking care not to slip on the icy treads, and made his way to the stable before going to bathe. He found Ro-shei securing the wagon by the light of two oil-lamps; the ponies and camels had been brushed and fed, and Ro-shei had a scrawny chicken soaking in a bucket. "You found something to eat," he said in Byzantine Greek.

Ro-shei laughed. "Such as it is."

"I trust you will enjoy it," said Zangi-Ragozh.

"I will, more than you will your taste of pony's blood," Ro-shei responded.

"Are you planning to bathe?"

"Later, yes, I am," he said. "When the Desert Cats are done."

"I have carried the clothes chest to the room."

"I know," said Ro-shei. "I saw you take it." He pulled up a plank stool and dropped onto it. "Are you going to sleep there, or here in the wagon?"

"In the wagon, I think. On my native earth."

"Do you still intend to let the Desert Cats have it for Dukkai?" Ro-shei asked, although he knew the answer.

"Certainly. In this snow, the wagon would only serve to slow us down, and only one box of jewels and gold is still in it; I will move it tonight." Zangi-Ragozh regarded Ro-shei for a short, silent while. "You said you thought it was a good idea."

"I do still," said Ro-shei. "But I wish we had more pack animals. Two ponies to ride, two to pack, and three camels hardly gives us any margin for losses."

"Then I will purchase pack animals, tomorrow." He nodded in the direction of the wagon.

"Good," said Ro-shei, reaching down for the chicken and beginning to pluck it. "Not much meat on these bones."

"Be glad there is any," said Zangi-Ragozh.

"You have not taken anything from the magician, have you." It was not a question.

"No. She is pregnant, and I do not know what of my nature might pass to her child. There have been times when she has come to me for comfort, and that has resulted in a kind of intimacy; she has given me some of herself then, and that provides a little nourishment, tenuous but real." He looked away.

"Do you think she would accept you as you are?" Ro-shei asked, trying to wipe away the wet feathers clinging to his hands.

"I have no notion. She tolerates my foreignness, so she might . . ." He finished his thought with a slight nod.

Ro-shei stopped plucking and looked directly at Zangi-Ragozh. "You are losing flesh."

"So is everyone else," he countered, deliberately oblique.

"But you might not have to; we will be going on soon, and she will remain with her clan. Surely she would not begrudge you what you seek?"

Zangi-Ragozh took a little time to answer. "Whether she would or not, I will not ask her."

Ro-shei shook his head. "She might prefer that you let her decide."

"But what if she does not?" With that for a parting shot, Zangi-Ragozh turned and went off through the densely falling snow toward the bath-house.

Text of a report by Apostle Lazarus in Kumul to Apostle Jude at Cambaluc; carried by Uighurs and delivered six months after it was written.

To my most revered Brother in Christ, Apostle Jude of the Holy Re-deemer Apostlary of Cambaluc, the greetings and Kiss of Peace at the Mass of Christ in the 535th year of Salvation, from the Apostle Lazarus at Holy Trinity Apostlary at Kumul.

Surely, my dear Brother, God has laid His Hand most heavily upon His people and the people of the earth. I have seen for myself the horrendous hardships that many have had to endure since early last spring. I fear that there will be no remedy in the coming months, for the year has been so cold that many crops did not grow at all, and those that did were poor and lacking virtue. In this region, many have asked to be baptized, fearing that the end of the world is come, and wanting to make an offering of their misery as well as to secure their place in the life that is to come. The congregation here is double what it was a year ago. I tell the story of Our Lord to those in need of com-fort, and I pray for the souls of those who died unshriven and in sin, so that they, too, may rise from the toils of Hell to the Glory of Heaven.

I regret to inform you that the six sacks of rice you entrusted to the Celestial Turks have not arrived. The leader of the caravan tells me they were stolen, which may or may not be true, for as much as I wish not to be suspicious of my fellow-men, I am daily reminded of the want around us, and I know the Turks are not above profiting from the misfortunes and wretchedness of others. I wish I could send some token of my appreciation for your concern, but I fear this is im-possible. Kumul has twice been raided, once by Khitan clans, and once by a group of men from the Wu-Wei garrison. I have learned since that in many of the farther regions of the Middle Kingdom, the soldiers have turned raiders and brigands, which does not surprise me, given the capacity for ferocity that marks so many of those who have not yet accepted the promise of redemption that makes it possi-ble for Christians to bear their ordeals without the desperation that those who have not must endure.

If I have any such news to impart to you, you may rest assured that I will do so, using the most trusted couriers I can find, for in these times, when men are tested in their faith and their flesh, I know that even the most devoted may be moved to stray from his duty. In the spirit of this responsibility, I must inform you that the road to Urum-chi has been badly damaged by a landslide and is not safe to traverse. I recommend that anyone traveling the northern route of the Silk

Road wait at Kuldja until a new road has been cut, or an alternate route established, for there may be more slides in that area. I have sent messages about this and related matters to the Magistrate at Wu-Wei, to the Apostles at Khanbalik, Khara-Khoja, and Ning-Hsia, and to the garrison at Chanchi-lah Pass informing them of our situation here and asking that they let us know what their circumstances are. Perhaps, if we remain in contact, we may be spared the worst of this calamity that continues to bring so much distress to the world.

Rarely have I felt more ardently than now the disadvantages of dealing with peoples and clans whose languages have no written form, nor any other means of keeping records than the spoken word. Now, when famine and rapine are upon us, to have no way to make our losses and our numbers known beyond the apostlaries of our Church, I find myself battling dissatisfaction with my fellow-men because of the widespread distrust of writing, and the lack of willingness on the part of so many to carry written messages, for fear that the words may work a magic spell upon those who carry them. If you may prevail upon the Turks and the Jou'an-Jou'an not of our faith to consent to bear written messages, I will number your name with the Saints of God. Barring such success, I ask only that you make every attempt to maintain your records and correspondence as best you may, until this travail ends, or God calls us to Him.

Amen

Lazarus, son of Seraphim, Apostle of Holy Trinity, at Kumul

7

By the time they reached Aksu, they had lost one of the camels and had been forced to improvise a kind of cart on runners to hold all the crates, chests, and barrels the camel had carried; their six ponies, tough and hardy, had to struggle in the face of the relentless fury of winter, while the two remaining camels trudged on, their shaggy coats becoming matted and the pads on their feet cracking from the constant freezing temperatures; Zangi-Ragozh wrapped their feet in straw and rags, which stopped the worst of the chapping but failed to prevent sores from cold entirely. The weather continued to deteriorate, remaining blustery and chilly, the sun moving higher in the sky, but bestowing little heat, still veiled by invisible clouds. Cutting winds and vast eddies of blown snow made travel dangerous and laggard as Zangi-Ragozh and Ro-shei pressed on to the West; they encountered only three groups of travelers, and one of them was a company of Turkish merchants returning from the West with as much bad news from Persia and the Syrian plains as Zangi-Ragozh could give on China. At Aksu they had waited three weeks before setting out again, and when they did, it took them two weeks past the Vernal Equinox to reach Kashgar: the Takla Makan desert lay behind them; ahead was the rising mass of the Pamir Mountains.

"Where are you coming from? Where are you bound?" demanded the guard at Kashgar in bad Persian.

"We come from China and are bound for Constantine's City," said Zangi-Ragozh in much better, but slightly old-fashioned Persian.

"Are you begging?"

"We are merchants, not beggars," said Zangi-Ragozh.

The guard laughed, a high, delirious sound. "They are much the same thing, in these times."

"Except that the beggars have died," said Zangi-Ragozh somberly.

"That they have." The guard glanced at the few tents some distance from the town walls. "There are fewer of them every day."

"The same is true for all of the living," said Zangi-Ragozh.

"Do you have any food?" the guard asked abruptly, as if recalled to his purpose.

"For our animals," said Zangi-Ragozh. "We have been living off whatever we can find."

"Including men?" The question cracked like breaking ice.

Zangi-Ragozh stared at the guard, his compelling eyes fixed on the other man's. "No," he said at last. "We have not fed on men."

"Are there more of you?" The guard was attempting to reestablish his authority, and floundering.

"There are just the two of us, our six ponies, and two camels. We had a third camel, but it got a fever from an injured foot and died." Zangi-Ragozh studied the guard, noticing that the man had scabs on his face and his cheeks were hollow. "What is the condition of your town?"

"What is the condition of any town in these times? The old and the young are dying, and those strong enough to endure hunger are suffering." The guard laughed again, a grating sound like a rake over pebbles. "We can't bury the dead; the ground is frozen and most of the men are too weak for hard labor in the cold. So we stack them beyond the camel-middens, as if they were Towers of Silence, such as they have in Persia; only the lammergeiers will benefit, if they haven't all died." He laughed again, this time with an underlying note of mania. "If any of us remain in the summer, and the ground is warm enough, we will have to make a large, general grave for those who—"

Zangi-Ragozh made a sign to Ro-shei, and they moved back from the gates. "If the town has so much to deal with, we will move on."

"There is snow in the mountains, yellow snow, and it is still deep. We have seen few caravans coming from the West, as you must know." The guard looked at the ponies. "If you wish to remain here, you have to contribute to our welfare. We will let you sleep in a bed in exchange for a pony."

"We need all our ponies," said Zangi-Ragozh, his voice firm and soothing at once.

"Do you? Surely you could do with one less." The guard's stance became pugnacious. "My companions and I have need of one pony, at least, no matter how skinny it may be."

Zangi-Ragozh could see no other men at the gate, and his sense of alarm sharpened. "How many companions do you have."

"Enough," said the guard, making it a threat.

"I think it would be best if we moved on," said Zangi-Ragozh, reaching for his spear, just in case.

"No! You must not!" The guard lifted his bow and fumbled an arrow to the string, drawing hardly far enough to send the arrow across the distance between them. "We are starving! You must leave us something to eat."

"I have nothing I can spare," said Zangi-Ragozh, uncomfortably aware it was true.

"A pony. You can spare a pony!" The guard took a step toward him.

Zangi-Ragozh motioned to Ro-shei to move back. "I regret that I cannot give you what you ask."

"You can, *you can!*" the guard insisted. "Just one pony. We are all going to die, anyway." He pointed accusingly at the two foreigners. "You are keeping what you have for yourselves!"

"That is a great misfortune for you," said Zangi-Ragozh. "If I could alleviate your suffering, I would."

The guard's expression grew crafty. "But you can. If we have a pony, we can—"

"Live to starve another day," said Zangi-Ragozh, pulling his pony around and tugging on the leads of those carrying crates and chests. "Ro-shei! The camels!" He was able to get his ponies to a trot, and they were quickly beyond range of the two arrows fired ineffectively in his direction.

"I have them moving," Ro-shei assured him.

"Then hurry. They may send riders after us!" Zangi-Ragozh glanced back once and saw three men on emaciated ponies attempting to follow them; one of the riders carried a lance, the other two had mauls. It did not take long for Zangi-Ragozh and Ro-shei to outrun them; they slowed as soon as they could, wanting to spare their animals.

"Was that as dire as it appeared?" Ro-shei asked as they pressed on past the walls of Kashgar.

"It may have been much worse," said Zangi-Ragozh, thinking back to his days in the Temple of Imhotep, the battlefields of Dacia, the mal aria in Athens, the worst days of the Roman Circus. "The guard was suffering from lice, which usually means fever, especially if the people are weakened by hunger. He might have been able to attack if he had felt less ill. As it is, I wish I did not find so much relief in his sickness." He turned in his saddle and stared back in the direction of the town. "I wonder if the Desert Cats made it this far."

"If they did, I do not like to think what may have happened to them," said Ro-shei, then waited a long moment. "We are low on food for the animals. Have you thought of what we are to do?"

"Not yet; I had hoped we would have time here to recover our strength and rest before climbing into the Pamir Mountains," said Zangi-Ragozh, turning his back on Kashgar. "As it is, I must find us food of some sort, and shelter so the animals can rest; our travels have taken a toll on them."

"Do you think the guard would have killed us for the ponies?"

Ro-shei had an edge in his question as if he had already made up his mind.

"I think he tried, in any case, and his three comrades," said Zangi-Ragozh. "If it had been possible, I believe he would have done all in his power to take our ponies, and our camels, for his cooking pots. The other three would help him for a share of the spoils."

"Then we may find as bad along the way," said Ro-shei.

Zangi-Ragozh sighed and squinted into the wind. "At least the snow has stopped falling."

"For now," said Ro-shei. He pointed to the irregular furrows in the muddy snow that marked the road. "If this freezes tonight, it will be midmorning before the ice thaws."

"You're right," said Zangi-Ragozh quietly. "I think it may well be that this year may be harder than the last. The famine is under way already, and with the sun lacking in strength, next year might be worse than this one." He pointed to the road ahead of them. "There are no merchants on the road because there is nothing left to trade—a very bad sign."

"Those who travel may well find that there is more danger than snow and scarcity; there may be demands made that no one can meet and still manage to live," Ro-shei observed.

Zangi-Ragozh agreed with a gesture. "I doubt many traders could get from one of the Silk Roads to the other just now without losing much of what they carry to robbers, and worse."

"What could be worse than robbers?" Ro-shei asked.

"Killers, for one," said Zangi-Ragozh distantly. "Desperate men do desperate things."

Ro-shei realized what Zangi-Ragozh was implying. "A risk indeed: you mean that more than ponies might end up in the cooking pot."

"It is a possibility," Zangi-Ragozh said levelly.

They went some little distance in silence; then, "I wonder what sort of meal we would make?" Ro-shei mused aloud.

"Insufficient, I imagine," said Zangi-Ragozh.

"Worse than useless, I would assume," said Ro-shei. "A five-hundred-year-old ghoul, and a two-thousand-five-hundred-year-old vampire! They might as well try to eat mummies."

"It would not surprise me to learn that such had been tried," Zangi-Ragozh said, emptiness of spirit sparing him pain for the time

being; he carefully blocked out the compassion that usually accompanied such insights.

"With that to consider—that everyone is at the limits of their
strength and wits—where are we bound?" Ro-shei asked, his face set
in austere lines.

"For Osarkand. We should be able to reach it in three or four
days, providing there is nothing blocking the road, or any other hazard before us." Zangi-Ragozh looked back at their ponies and camels,
shaking his head once. "There are four bags of grain left, and enough
chopped feed to last another month, if we are careful."

"And if we have no more encounters with thieves or other mis-
creants."

The night was clear; the moon in its third quarter rose in the night
and shed a frosty light over the snow-clad crags. Ro-shei took advantage of the illumination to go hunting and came back after nearly a
quarter of the night had passed with a hare, which he dressed and devoured before the first hint of sunlight limned the eastern horizon. As
he disposed of the skin and guts, he heard a high, wailing howl.

"Wolves," said Zangi-Ragozh unnecessarily.

"A good distance away," said Ro-shei.

"Still, it's just as well that we will be traveling on shortly. The packs
are as treacherous as armed men, and as persistent." Zangi-Ragozh
stopped long enough to string his bow and make sure his quiver was
firmly buckled to his saddle. "At least these iron foot-loops make it easier for us to aim while riding, and that improves our chance of successful hunting."

"As you have said, it is one of the advantages of them." Ro-shei
tossed the bones of the hare far down the slope, into darkness.

For most of the day they climbed along the deep river canyon,
following the muddy track that was the middle fork of the Silk Road.
They spent the night at a goat-farm where the family described the
death of their oldest uncle not three days ago and tried to choose
which of their remaining herd would be sacrificed to the honor of
their dead. Zangi-Ragozh offered the family a little jade statue of the
Four Celestials; after a brief refusal, they accepted the statue and
promised to give it to their gods, along with the prayers that the
power of their gods would be restored.

"The sun has been bled of his vigor, and the earth is deprived of his potency to make her fertile; it is through our offering that the sun—and thus the earth—will be revived, and all the gods of place will once again provide their protection," said the new head of the household. "We have given him kids and two milking goats, but they have not been enough. We have buried sacred images in the ground, but it will not grow anything more than weeds. We have left grain and small amounts of food at the shrines of the smaller gods, but nothing has worked."

"That is unfortunate," said Zangi-Ragozh, seeing the despondency in the householder's cadaverous face. He opened his chest of trade-goods he had brought into the house and poked among the cloth-wrapped objects until he found what he sought. He held out a wooden figure of a water buffalo; he looked through the rest of the items and added a cinnabar horse to the gifts. "This may be useful in your offering: what do you think?"

"If it helps the gods, yes; we will thank you for your aid," said the householder.

"If any of these help the gods," Zangi-Ragozh seconded, and put the two objects on the table before the hearth. He made no mention of the risk of avalanches and landslides rain could bring to the snowy mountains, but only said, "Our travel to Osarkand should be less difficult with the rain." He indicated Ro-shei. "We will leave at first light, to make the most of the day."

The householder pointed to his barn, which was immediately outside his house. "The straw in the barn is a little musty, but it will make a good enough bed." He touched his steepled fingers with his forehead. "May the gods give you a good passage to Osarkand."

"That is very gracious of you, Shamal-pe-Uzmar," said Zangi-Ragozh, rising and heading off for the barn and a night in the straw.

Ro-shei, following close behind him, asked, "Shall you or I remain awake?" in Imperial Latin. He stopped next to the cart and laid his hand protectively on the largest crate in its bed.

"I will," said Zangi-Ragozh.

"You seem wary." Ro-shei went back to close the rough door behind them as they stepped into the barn, which smelled of goats and ponies and camels. "You anticipate some mischief on their part?"

"Oh, yes; I think they may steal our animals' food if we sleep, or perhaps something worse," said Zangi-Ragozh.

"Then we should depart before the family rises," said Ro-shei, resting his hand on the down-turning quillons of his Roman dagger.

By morning they were a good distance from the goat-farm, having left well before dawn. They kept on steadily, avoiding the worst of the mud, and taking great care when passing along a steep or narrow part of the road. Throughout the morning they continued to climb, the river falling away beneath them until it was little more than a frothy stripe at the bottom of the canyon.

Osarkand was tucked into a fold of the mountain, on the leeward side of the rocky flank, which afforded enough protection that there was some small amount of neglected grass growing in the sheltered meadow behind the town, which was protected by high, stone walls and a stout gate of thick planks.

"Do you notice there are no animals grazing, although there is grass?" Ro-shei pointed out as they came around the bend in the road; they stopped to survey any activity around the town; after a half day of observation while their animals did their best to graze on the desiccated grasses at the edge of the remaining swaths of snow, they realized that there was nothing to be seen: no sign of any life, either human or animal. They moved a bit closer to the little town, into the shelter of an overhanging boulder the size of a large building. "You see? No animals. Not even fresh dung."

"They might be in the barns, to stay out of the rain," Zangi-Ragozh said, dubiety coloring his voice.

"So they might, but there is also no smoke from the chimneys, and that is—"

"A bad sign," Zangi-Ragozh finished for him. "Taken with the rest, yes, it is a bad sign."

"What do you want to do?" Ro-shei asked.

"The road goes through the village, and we have no other passage up this canyon."

"There is no road on the other side," Ro-shei reminded him.

"That was my point, old friend," said Zangi-Ragozh with a hard stare toward the little town. "I will go closer. This is most odd."

"Do you think it is a trap?"

"It may be; it may be, but it may also be something else," said Zangi-Ragozh without elaborating. He studied town walls for a short while, then handed the lead he held to Ro-shei. "I should not be long.

If I do not return before sundown, retreat to the deserted way-station and wait there. If I am not back in three days, look for the Amber Trail, and take it into India. If I am able, I will look for you in my ancestral home."

"In the Carpathians? The old castle?" Ro-shei asked, all emotion leached from his demeanor.

"Yes. If I am not there in a year, search out Olivia and remain with her as long as she will have you. She will know if I am still walking the earth." He cocked his head as if listening to a soft, distant conversation. "She, at least, still survives."

Ro-shei had seen Zangi-Ragozh perform that *listening* before, and it no longer perplexed him as it once had. "Hearing with the blood?"

"Yes," said Zangi-Ragozh. "It is the nature of the Blood Bond."

Ro-shei stood aside so that Zangi-Ragozh could pass. "You'll give the usual signal?"

"I will. Watch the gate. It is where I will come to give the signal if the town is safe to enter. If I signal from anywhere else, assume there is danger and go back."

"I will," said Ro-shei, and watched Zangi-Ragozh as he began his climb up the slope, a darker shadow moving through the shadows cast by the mountains.

Zangi-Ragozh approached Osarkand on what he assumed were goat tracks. He ignored the discomfort from the constant film of running water coming from the melting snows above and put all his attention on the cluster of buildings and the vacant pasture. He did his best to concentrate on everything—the sights, the sounds, the smells, the feelings the place evoked in him. He reached the rear of the pasture and climbed over the wall. Then he saw the remains of a goat lying near the base of the wall, and he knew that Osarkand was empty. Still, he remained cautious, for there were other hunters than humans who might be waiting inside the walls; he stopped beside the picked and pulled skeleton and examined the marks on the bones. "Bear," he muttered, "and some kind of bird of prey; an eagle, perhaps—or lammergeier, if they came through the winter." He stayed in the shelter of the wall and walked toward the barns, pausing frequently to listen for any hint of activity in the town. When he reached the first barn, he found a small window to peer in before attempting the door. Satisfied that the barn was empty, he went to ease the door open and found himself staring at a row of empty mangers. He made an inspection of the place and discovered under a heap of old straw, a last sack of old grain. Mice had been at it, but there was enough left that could be salvaged; he took it with him as he went to the next barn, which was larger and emptier than the first. Here there was clear evidence that bears had ransacked the place, for the double row of mangers were broken, and the wood was marked by gouges from long, curved claws.

The sun was starting to slide below the horizon by the time Zangi-Ragozh opened the gate and waved his short, improvised torch in a circle first to the left and then to the right. That done, he braced the gate open and went to light the butter-lamps in the house he had chosen to occupy for the next two days. He had a fire going in the hearth when he heard Ro-shei and their ponies and camels come down the narrow stone street. "In here!" he called out.

"I was beginning to fret," Ro-shei said as he opened the door.

"There are barns behind the houses; take the smallest one—it is the least disturbed." He picked up the half sack of grain. "This was left behind. I reclaimed it from a family of mice and cleaned out most of their droppings. The ponies will need it more than the camels."

"I will; what will you do?"

"Try to secure this house so that you and I can rest. I will try to find a bolt for the gate, for what protection that can provide. You may have the night to sleep—I will take the day." Zangi-Ragozh lowered his head and pointed to a straw-filled mattress on a low pallet. "I will make that usable for you: I will sleep on a chest of my native earth."

"The smaller chest is almost empty," Ro-shei reminded him as he started back for the door.

Zangi-Ragozh thought a moment. "Once we reach the plains of Kushan, if we travel by night and rest during the height of the day, my supply of earth will last longer. At least the sun is not at full strength, or I would have to spend most of the daylight hours resting in whatever dark I could find."

"Then it is fortunate that this calamity has not strengthened the sun," said Ro-shei.

"It is," Zangi-Ragozh said quietly.

Ro-shei went to lead their animals to the smaller barn, where he busied himself unloading them, stowing the cart, stacking their burdens along the wall, except for the chest of clothing and the larger chest of Zangi-Ragozh's native earth, both of which he placed near the door, anticipating carrying them to the house Zangi-Ragozh had selected for their use.

It was dark by the time Ro-shei came back to the house, his chores taken care of; he was moving more slowly than usual, as if the long climb was telling upon him at last. He had washed his hands and face and unclubbed his sandy hair and was using his Byzantine comb as he entered the house, which was now neat and warm. His mababa he carried over his arm, it being too cumbersome for wearing anywhere but in the open or in the saddle. "This is very pleasant," he said to Zangi-Ragozh. "A fire in the furnace, lamps lit, and a good bed ready."

"It should suffice for two or three days, until our ponies and camels have eaten all the grass in the pasture—what little there is of it." Zangi-Ragozh had just finished sorting through a small stack of sectioned wood. "We will have to replenish this supply tomorrow."

"Neither you nor I need heat," Ro-shei remarked.

"We both like it," Zangi-Ragozh said, and put another branch into the stone furnace. "Our clothes and gear should dry out."

"So they should," Ro-shei conceded. "Very well; I will plan to look for wood." He finished combing his hair and clubbed it up again.

"As will I." Zangi-Ragozh went to secure a plank-shutter over the window. "We can keep the house warm until we leave." He pointed to a broken jug that had been left behind, set on the single shelf near the furnace.

"What do you think happened?" Ro-shei asked, curious to know how Zangi-Ragozh had reached that conclusion.

"Everyone fled, or so it appears to me," said Zangi-Ragozh. "You can tell by what little they left behind: there are large items, like that bed and the furnace, and useless items, like this broken jug. I have found a few raw bear-skins; they are half-rotten and not much use, and in the grainery, there was a tub of washed rice; it may have been meant for fermentation, but it is wasted now. The counting-house has a few tally-sticks left. In my search, I discovered nothing that might provide us comfort beyond what you see here. The town packed up what it had and has gone elsewhere. They were not driven out—there is no sign of haste or fighting. There is no evidence of grain illness— the few remaining beds show no sign of sickness, and there are no mass graves outside the walls, as there would be with a deadly fever."

"Then why did they leave?" That was the greater puzzle to Ro-shei. "The walls are sound enough, and the houses look to be sturdy."

Zangi-Ragozh shook his head. "I have been about the town, and I think perhaps their animals were being affected by the weather and inadequate food. Between that sort of trouble, and the sharp decline in merchants passing along the Silk Road, I reckon that the people could no longer sustain themselves here, and so they went to find better pastures."

"May they have good fortune," said Ro-shei, a hint of bitterness in his wish.

"May they, indeed," Zangi-Ragozh said sincerely.

"Do you think they went east, or west?" Ro-shei pursued his piqued interest; he was somewhat surprised that it mattered to him.

"I would guess they went east; that direction is downhill and away from the snow. They may have gone on the Amber Trail, if they reached the desert," said Zangi-Ragozh. "We might have encountered them had we arrived at Kashgar a week earlier."

"Kashgar," said Ro-shei significantly. "Would they have gone into the town, do you think?"

"For their sake, I hope they did not." Zangi-Ragozh answered Ro-shei.

"And I," he said, and held out his mababa, so that Zangi-Ragozh could position it near the furnace to dry. "I will be glad of a chance to sleep."

"It is the result of being hungry, this exhaustion."

"Yes," said Ro-shei as he took off his sen-cha, which he folded and put on the shelf. Next he removed his boots, and last of all, his leather britches. When all these were folded and put on the shelf, he went to stretch out on the bed, pulling two skins around him. "Wake me before dawn."

"I will," Zangi-Ragozh promised, and pulled on his mababa before going out into the cold of the night. He returned in the last quarter of the night, a small pig hanging from thongs. He woke Ro-shei and hefted the pig into view. "I took my portion. The rest is yours."

"And welcome it is," said Ro-shei.

"I have a little wood, as well; enough to keep the house warm until nightfall. I left it by the door outside." He seemed a bit distracted, and he regarded the pig for a short while. "I thought at first that was a shoat, but now I doubt it. The pig is at least a year old. Hardship kept it small." Zangi-Ragozh sat on the chest that contained his native earth. "I saw a temple of sorts near the highest part of the wall, with the remains of five newborn kids on the altar." He fell silent again, watching Ro-shei cut up the little pig.

Ro-shei turned away as he began to cut up the undersized sow. "Pigs and birds are not sufficient for you. They suit me well, but you need more than blood to—"

"I am aware of it," said Zangi-Ragozh, and went to bring in the wood from outside the door before stretching out on his chest of native earth.

Text of a letter from Chu Sung-Neong, Undersecretary of the Prefecture of Holin-Gol, to the Regional Army Commander, General Dan Gieh-Gon, carried by courier; never delivered.

To the most well-reputed and honorable Regional Army Commander General Dan Gieh-Gon, this greeting from Chu Sung-Neong, the Undersecretary of the Prefecture of Holin-Gol, with the authorization of Magistrate Ngo Hai-Ming, the Magistrate of Holin-Gol, acting Prefect of the city and supervisor of the local garrison.

Most worthy General Dan, I am enjoined to implore you to come to Holin-Gol with your troops to deal with the present insurrection that has proven too insistent for the garrison here to control. Four times in the last three fortnights we have had rice riots in the city, and there have been uprisings in the countryside as well. These mutinies have been the result of wide-spread starvation, now made worse by Swine Fever, which has spread through the city and has done what starvation has begun. I have enclosed a record of the deaths within Holin-Gol for the last six fortnights, along with the reasons for the deaths; you will notice that six officials are among their number, as well as more than fifty foreigners. In vain the Prefecture has striven to enforce order, and all times but once has failed badly to accomplish what was attempted. I fear that without more soldiers and the action of many more troops than are quartered here, we may find the city and its vicinity collapsed into anarchy as starvation grows more widespread and the farmers have difficulty bringing crops to harvest.

We have rice enough for two more distributions within the city,

*but then I dread what may come afterward if we have no support
from the Army. Surely you would not deny this entreaty from an official who speaks for all the officials of Holin-Gol when he asks you to
come with all the soldiers you can spare to contain the violence that
has marked this most wretched time. If you fail us, I cannot think
what greater misfortunes we may yet have to endure. For the sake of
us all, come as quickly as you are able.*

Chu Sung-Neong
Undersecretary of the Prefecture of Holin-Gol
(his chop)

8

"I wanted to die," the ragged, gaunt woman protested as Zangi-Ragozh
dismounted and held out his hand to help her to her feet; she winced
and let out a little shriek, and he released her at once, seeing that her
arm was badly injured and only partially healed, with yellowish bruises
marking her skin. "What are you doing? You should have killed me."
Her eyes were dazed and she swayed in her effort to remain upright;
around her the Kokand market did its utmost to appear busy and prosperous, but like the woman herself, it was struggling just to stay alive.

"Throwing yourself under the hooves of our ponies would not ensure that; you are more likely to be hurt than killed," said Zangi-
Ragozh with remarkable calm, trying to soothe the woman; his Persian
was more elegant than hers, and less mixed with the local tongue, and
his manner alone commanded her respect. "If you wanted to do yourself harm, why should you? it appears that you are already in pain."

"I might have died, if you had kept going. Your cart's skids might
have been enough to break my back or crush my chest." She folded
her arms as a means of unobviously supporting the one that hurt and
tried to make out his features with the sun behind him, obscuring his
features and dazzling her at once, as if he were more otherworldly
than foreign. "You should have gone on. Why did you stop?"

"If we had kept on, we would have run over you—"

"No," she said. "You didn't have to stop and talk to me." She was perplexed and a bit irritated that he had done this.

"I would have had to be indifferent to your plight, and I could not be that, not after you made your attempt at our expense," he said slowly and carefully, glancing once at Ro-shei, who remained in the saddle, holding the leads of two ponies and both camels. "Surely you understand that?"

"But that is what you should have done, don't you understand?— run me down and left me," she protested. "I want to die—I still want to."

This was more than an impulsive frenzy, Zangi-Ragozh realized, and he scrutinized the woman's face before saying, "I regret that I have no wish to be your executioner. For that you must look elsewhere." He signaled to Ro-shei. "Go on to the main square and find an inn for us, if you would."

"I will," said Ro-shei, taking the lead for the cart-pony from Zangi-Ragozh as he went past. "I'll expect you before sundown."

"I will find you when I am finished," said Zangi-Ragozh, and turned back to the woman. "Why do you want to die?"

She stared at him blankly and decided to answer him. "You see this place, how it is? Do you see how few merchants have come to trade their goods? This month there should have been many caravans on the Silk Road, but as you see, there are hardly enough to have a market. How am I to earn the money Kasha wants if there are so few merchants in the market, and they are all more interested in finding food than in a woman?" She wrapped her hands across her middle as if to protect herself against more pain. All her talk with this foreigner seemed dreamlike, and she could not rid herself of the impression that she would presently wake up and find herself once again in the small, dark room to which Kasha confined her when she most displeased him. Only her growing discomfort provided her any sense that this was real.

"Kasha is your master?" Zangi-Ragozh asked in a disinterested tone.

"He is," she said.

"By what right?" Zangi-Ragozh asked, so politely that there was no reason the woman could summon up not to answer. The halo the sun made of his head might not be as brilliant as in years past, but it was enough to overwhelm her reticence; answering him seemed to be the same as speaking to a supernatural spirit at Kokand's sacred spring.

"He bought me from my parents when I had nine summers, I served as his household's maid for a time, and then, when my bleeding started, he hired me out, as he does his other women." She regarded him with sour defiance, as if expecting a rebuke. "Why do you want to know?"

"You put yourself in harm's way at my expense, and that, according to many traditions, makes you answerable to me. It is apparent that you need care and medicaments, and that being the case, if Kasha is your master, I will need his permission to treat you," said Zangi-Ragozh. "You have a fever, and it may be from injured bones improperly healed, in which case, you are in grave danger."

"How can you know that?" Her eyes shone with sudden fright; this encounter was as wholly unlike any she had had in the past that its strangeness was as unnerving as what the foreigner in the black shuba had said about her physical condition. "You cannot know such things."

"I am something of a physician; in my younger days, I was trained to treat the injured and the ill," he said, thinking back to his centuries in the Temple of Imhotep. "There is an odor to such inward hurts as you may have that I came to recognize."

"Are you saying I have those inward hurts?" she asked, staring more urgently.

"I am saying you are not well, and it may be that you have such injuries," he responded cautiously. "If that is so, then it would explain why you hoped the cart would kill you."

"Why is that?" she asked, fascinated and repelled at once.

"Many of those who have taken a fever see things others cannot—"

"You mean that are not there?" Her challenge ended with a break in her voice.

"I mean that only the sufferer can see them," said Zangi-Ragozh at his mildest; he saw that she was upset and would need reassurance before she accepted anything from him other than what she expected. "Who can say what is there and is not there?"

"It's the same thing, if no one can see it but one with a fever," she declared, attempting to disguise her rising fright and to get away from him by taking a few steps backward.

"No, it is not," he said, coming after her. "You do need treatment, whatever is the matter with you, especially now, when food is scarce and its quality is bad, for the body cannot heal properly if it is under-nourished."

The woman looked about, her eyes wild. "Are you going to feed me?"

"I am worried that you will do yourself harm, since that was your intention," said Zangi-Ragozh patiently. "Why do you want to die, and why do you need someone to do it for you?"

She regarded him suspiciously. "Why should you want to know?"

"If you want to die, surely you must have more certain ways than falling under the hooves of a caravan as small as mine. By the look of you, you have been badly beaten more than once." He nodded to the side of the road and moved toward it, his pony following close behind, the woman lagging back. "You decided to try to die under the skids and the hooves of my caravan. I still want to know why."

"If I took poison, Kasha would know, and my son would answer for it. If he beat me to death, he would still be angry with me. If I am trampled in the market, he cannot be sure that it was a deliberate act—it could be misadventure, and he might think it was an accident, and my son would not have to suffer on my account," she told him sullenly, moving with him as if compelled by his dark eyes. "I do not want my child to bear any more burdens than he already has."

"And what burdens are these?" Zangi-Ragozh asked as he finally moved into the shadow of a stone-fronted building.

"That I am his mother, and that he does not seem to hear well, or, if not that, he is simple and will be sold to someone needing a fool. I have watched him, and I have observed that he is alert to everything if it happens where he can see," said the woman as if making a shameful admission; she was puzzled that she should speak so openly with a stranger. "Kasha will not make him his son because of what he requires me to do."

Zangi-Ragozh felt a pang of compassion for this woman. "Your child has a very honorable mother," he said gently. "As to the other, that is unfortunate."

"He speaks very little, and I believe it is because he does not hear clearly." She hunched over as if to conceal a defect.

"That may be a good reason to suppose he is somewhat deaf;

simpleness and deafness are often mistaken, each for the other," said Zangi-Ragozh. "Your son has how many summers?"

"The one that is approaching will be his sixth," she said, stepping into the protection of a jutting angle of the building.

"It is a bad time," Zangi-Ragozh agreed, and reached out to pat his cinder-brown pony's neck. "Tell me about this Kasha," he prompted. "I will give you silver for your time, so that you will not have to go to Kasha empty-handed."

She whispered a curse. "You do not want me?"

"Not as you mean," he said with abiding kindness.

She gaped at him. "What manner of man are you? You are not a eunuch—you haven't the look of it." Her face changed, suspicion re-asserting itself. "You aren't one of those Christians, are you? always praising suffering and struggle, and promising perfection in the after-life?"

"No, I am not a Christian," said Zangi-Ragozh.

"There seem to be more of them every day, praying and pro-claiming their salvation because they are miserable, and pestering everyone about their earthly burdens as if they longed for more of them," said the woman darkly, and went on, more to herself than him, "They keep to their own and say that they will be richly rewarded for all the hardships they have endured. Some try to add to their misfor-tunes by giving what little they have to others, thinking they will have more and better recompense in Paradise if they do."

"But you have no such hope," he said, seeing the despondency in her expression.

Her countenance lost what little expression it had, as if the ques-tion had taken away her last refuge from the ordeal of her life. "I have my hopes for this world and no other, and I would rather be quit of this world than have to die slowly for lack of food, and money." She spat.

Zangi-Ragozh reached into the sleeve of his sen-cha and brought out a string of silver cash. "Take this. I know it is foreign money, but the silver is high quality, and it will maintain its value anywhere silver is exchanged. Keep half of it for yourself."

She took the string of cash. "I haven't brought him so much in a fortnight." She touched the silver coins gingerly as if she expected them to evaporate.

"What of his other women? Does he make them go with men as he does you?" Zangi-Ragozh asked.

"Two of the others, yes, but not Farna. Farna was his first, and she is permitted to remain true to herself, being a true wife, with a dowry." She sounded more defeated than bitter. "Amanu, Monshu, and I are the ones who must earn our keep. He is most belligerent with Amanu, because she has no sons."

"He believes Amanu has affronted him?" Zangi-Ragozh asked.

"He prefers sons. Farna has two left. Her youngest died last year, in the winter." She looked away. "He dislikes my son."

"That is a pity; at a time like this, he could find comfort and courage in his living children," said Zangi-Ragozh.

"He will not own my son, will not even speak his name," she said, the complaint an inward one.

"And you are: what is your name?" Zangi-Ragozh inquired politely, holding up a cautioning hand before she could answer. "Not the name you use in the market, please," he went on as he saw her falter, "the name the other members of your household call you."

She hesitated. "Ourisi," she said at last. "My son is Rialat, named for my grandfather, not for Kasha's father, since he is unrecognized."

"Ourisi," he repeated. "And Rialat. I am Zangi-Ragozh."

Her spurt of a giggle surprised him as much as it startled her, rousing her from her deepening reverie. "It is such a funny name," she almost apologized. "I don't think I can pronounce it."

"Would you prefer something less cumbersome?" Zangi-Ragozh asked, thinking of the many names he had had through the centuries.

"If I am to address you beyond *foreigner*," she said, anticipating derision at best.

He pondered a brief moment. "Then, if you would rather, you may call me Ragoczy Franciscus, as I am known in parts of the West," he said.

"That is much better," she said, color rising in her cheeks.

"Then Ragoczy Franciscus it will be." He stood between her and the street as a small party of Persians made their way down the street, headed for the main square.

She watched the camels and asses pass. "Only nine camels and four asses. Usually the caravans from the south have twenty of each."

"Perhaps they chose to have fewer animals to feed than to risk all of them starving," Ragoczy Franciscus suggested.

"Perhaps they did," said Ourisi. "That is bad enough."

"Yes, it is," said Ragoczy Franciscus, and took a chance. "You are in need of treatment of your body: believe this."

Ourisi glanced away. "Kasha might refuse."

"For so much silver cash, I would think he could not mind too much," said Ragoczy Franciscus, a note of world-weariness in his words.

"Yes. He may be persuaded by money," she said, absently rubbing her arm. "He keeps me for money and swears that if I cannot bring in enough for me and my son, he will throw both of us out of his house."

"Does he make similar threats to the other women, or are you the only one?" Ragoczy Franciscus asked, the full force of his gaze on her.

"To Amanu, he does. She has had three daughters, and that displeases Kasha. The Town Leaders have given him permission to disown her, but she still has some value as a whore. When she has none, he will cast her out, and she will have to beg until she starves, or freezes." Ourisi gave a short, angry sigh. "Or until she has enough determination to take her own life."

"If the caravans remain few, and small, what will become of you?" Ragoczy Franciscus knew the answer; he had seen it often enough before.

"Much the same as what becomes of Amanu," said Ourisi. "Kasha must care for Farna—Farna has brothers, who will not permit Kasha to make a whore of their sister. He hasn't got much, particularly now, except the three of us, to support him and his wife as he demands, so that he will not have to answer to Farna's brothers. But those of us who are not wives like Farna but his whores, he may keep or discard us as suits him." She had begun to cry silently, tears on her face unacknowledged and unheeded, as if she were unaware of them. "He cares for his sheep more than us."

"And for that, you are angry."

A loud jangle of camel-bells announced the arrival of three more Persians, stragglers from the caravan that had entered Kokand a short while ago. The lead camel's humps sagged, testament to the hard travel from Persia; one of the men walking beside the well-laden camels limped heavily, his ankle swollen and wrapped in layers of cloth.

"I am not angry," she said with grim determination.

"Then I must suppose you are too frightened to be angry," said Ragoczy Franciscus with abiding kindness. "Take me to Kasha's house, so I may arrange to treat you."

"He will not be pleased that you asked to deal with him," she warned, noticing for the first time that she had a dense, ringing headache and that she was becoming nauseated.

"Then he should not have sent you out to the marketplace," said Ragoczy Franciscus.

This had never occurred to her before, and she strove to think it through in spite of the intense pain in her skull. "You will have to explain it to him," she said at last, and sagged against the building. "But do not tell him I want to kill myself."

"I will do my utmost to oblige you," said Ragoczy Franciscus as he reached out to support her with his arm.

She flinched as if she expected a blow instead of aid. "You have been good to me, Ragoczy Franciscus." She spoke almost by rote, and she looked away toward the nearest side street.

Ragoczy Franciscus patted his pony's neck again. "Do you see the chest secured to the saddle?"

"Yes." She looked at the scruffy animal dubiously.

"It contains my medicaments. I have something more than dead mice and herbs to burn in a brass bowl to cure you," he said, deliberately choosing the favorite remedy used by traders to treat severe bruises. "I will rub no ashes on your skin and tell you it will improve you."

She stared at the chest. "What do you use?"

"That depends upon the nature of the injury, which I cannot yet determine. I have powders and unguents for wounds, poultices to draw infections, syrup of poppies to ease pain, pansy and willow for anodynes, and my sovereign remedy for sickness of many sorts." He wanted to reassure her, and to convince her that he could offer her some chance of improvement, for as she was she would continue to fail.

"Kasha will not pay you for any of your medicaments," said Ourisi with a kind of gloomy satisfaction.

"That does not concern me. If you improve, then perhaps something may be arranged," he offered, knowing he would be gone before she could recover, if indeed she would be able to; he could feel the fever in her as he felt the weakness of the sun overhead.

"Perhaps," said Ourisi with a great lack of conviction.

"If you will take me to where you live, I will speak to Kasha," said Ragoczy Franciscus.

"He may be angry and take your concern amiss," she said, looking about nervously.

"I can be persuasive, when such is needed," Ragoczy Franciscus assured her. "I would be very surprised if he wants you to continue to sicken."

"No; he dislikes having any of us unable to do his bidding," Ourisi said.

"Then take me to him, if you would," said Ragoczy Franciscus.

She raised one shoulder and glanced away down the narrow street. "If we go this way—" She began to walk, a bit slowly, for she had to concentrate to keep from weaving as she went.

Ragoczy Franciscus followed her, leading his pony, picking his way through the littered alleyways. "Has there been much famine here?"

"It is getting worse," Ourisi said. "There were reserves in the city warehouses, but most of it is gone, and there aren't caravans enough to replenish them. The animals do not have strong young, and most of the kids and lambs end up in the cooking pots."

"It is much the same to the east," said Ragoczy Franciscus.

"The city guard collects the dead every morning, and those who can afford to bury their own arrange for it; the rest are put into mass graves." Her voice caught in her throat. "So many of them are dead."

"So many of whom?" Ragoczy Franciscus asked, stepping around a man huddled against the wall, wrapped in a Turkish mababa.

"The farmers and the merchants. They come into the town and they die." She stopped suddenly and swung around to look at him. "You won't die, will you?"

Ragoczy Franciscus smiled sardonically. "I give you my Word I will stay as I am." He saw the now familiar look of emptiness in the crooked little street, the lack of children playing, or women calling from windows. "How much of the population here has died?"

"They say one in three, now. If the local farmers cannot bring in crops this year, then there will be many more." She spoke as if this meant nothing to her, for the sense of unreality that had claimed her was increasing and she was becoming more and more convinced that none of this was real, that she was dreaming, or lost in the fever-haze that had grown stronger during the last several days.

"Were there any farmers who had harvests last autumn?" he asked.

"A few, but their crops were small and the quality was poor, and very little was spared for market." She stopped walking and turned to him. "There are clans raiding out of the east. They take everything they can and move on, for which we should be thankful, but there is often another clan close behind them." Suddenly she began to weep as the illusions that had held her suddenly vanished, leaving her with the starkness of her life rushing in on her.

"Do you know what clans have attacked you?" Ragoczy Franciscus asked, hoping for news—however dire—of the Desert Cats.

"Who knows? They are all mad barbarians." She took a long, shaky breath. "I think we will all starve, and only the strongest will be here in the end, to follow the raiders and to kill one another for meat."

"That is possible," Ragoczy Franciscus said with deep compassion and an abiding grief. "But if that should happen, it will mean that more than Kokand is lost."

"Do you think it will happen?" She wiped her tears with her good hand and studied his attractive, irregular features. She had not noticed until they were in shadow how dark his eyes were, and how they seemed to penetrate to her very soul.

"I trust it will not," he said, and motioned to her to move on. "How far to Kasha's house?"

"Not much farther—just another street to go," she said, and clenched her teeth to stop herself from crying.

Ragoczy Francisus moved a step closer to her. "Is there a place where you can get water?"

"There is water at Kasha's house. It doesn't taste very good, but he has four barrels of it," she said, and brought herself under control once more. "There are also two barrels of wine. It's a little sour, but it's better than the water," said Ourisi, pointing vaguely in the direction of the next street. "He will not give you wine or water if you do not pay for it."

"I will keep that in mind," said Ragoczy Franciscus.

Ourisi felt steady enough to resume walking; she wanted to move a bit more briskly, but found that her energy was insufficient for so much activity. "This way," she mumbled.

Ragoczy Franciscus stayed two steps behind her, willing to cover the last distance at whatever pace she chose to set. As they turned into an even narrower alley, he remarked, "The houses here are older than the first we passed."

"Yes. These were built many centuries ago, or so it's said," she replied. "They say these were here when the Silk Road began." There was no pride in this revelation, only numb acceptance of the unchanging character of the place.

"Certainly a long time," said Ragoczy Franciscus, remembering the first time he had gone into these vast plains and mountains; then he had taken the Amber Trail into India, to the lands of Oshaka; that had been three centuries before he had journeyed into Gaul with Gaius Julius Caesar and his Legions. It had been a long, arduous journey, but no more difficult than this current crossing had been. He vaguely recalled the Stone Tower fortress where merchants carried out their exchanges, the occasional lush meadows, and the many small towns that marked the route: Kokand was just one of many.

"This is Kasha's house," Ourisi said as she stopped in front of a small wooden door. "You can bring your pony into the courtyard if you—"

"—pay for the privilege," Ragoczy Franciscus finished for her. "I am prepared." He fingered three more strings of cash on his arm and was glad they were wrapped in bands of cloth so they would not jingle.

Ourisi tugged a rope by the door, and a chorus of camel-bells sounded. "Someone will come," she said.

"So I expect," said Ragoczy Franciscus, trying to decide how best to approach Kasha when he came to deal with the man. He was deep in thought when the door was pulled open and a youth of no more than twelve shoved the door open and glared out.

"Qasashi, open the door," said Ourisi as she saw the outraged youngster.

"It is you," he responded, making a sign against the Evil Eye. "If you had any wisdom, you would stay away from this house."

"It is where my master lives, and I must stay here unless he shuts me out," said Ourisi wearily. "Open the door and let us in."

For the first time, the young man noticed that Ourisi was not alone. He frowned at Ragoczy Franciscus, saying, "You should not have come here."

Ragoczy Franciscus did not object to being so bluntly confronted; he regarded Qasashi steadily. "If you would let me in, I may be of use to you and your family."

"We have little money, and not much food, so there isn't much to steal," said the youngster defiantly.

"Qasashi," Ourisi said with the authority born of exhaustion. "Let us in."

"My father will be displeased," Qasashi predicted, but held the door to admit Ourisi, Ragoczy Franciscus, and his pony to the small courtyard that fronted the house.

Ourisi held out four silver coins from the string Ragoczy Franciscus had given her. "Not with this," she said, and sank onto a plank bench near the door.

"Silver!" Qasashi exclaimed, all suspicion vanishing. He snatched at the coins, but could not wrest them from Ourisi's closed fist.

"That is for Kasha," said Ourisi.

"You mean he will buy you and take you away with him?" Qasashi asked with unabashed enthusiasm.

Ourisi drooped in her place, but anything she might have said remained unuttered as a large, painfully thin man burst out of the house, cursing and waving his fists.

Ragoczy Franciscus stepped forward and began his mentally rehearsed explanation, all the while aware that his chances of winning Kasha over were much lower than he had assumed; he could not decide how to assess the blank expression on the man's face and remained puzzled until Kasha turned suddenly to Ourisi.

"Your boy died. I've given him to the guards for burial," he announced, ignoring the dreadful wail with which Ourisi received the news. "Just as well," he said to Ragoczy Franciscus. "A simple boy like that—why waste food on him?"

To his inward surprise, Ragoczy Franciscus heard himself say, "Then let me reduce your burden still further: what do you want for Ourisi's freedom?"

Text of a letter from Atta Olivia Clemens in Bononia on the Via Aemilia in Italy to Ragoczy Sanct' Germain Franciscus in Yang-Chau,

written in Imperial Latin and filed as unreadable when delivered four
years later.

*To my most-dear, most-aggravating friend, Ragoczy Sanct' Germain
Franciscus on the far side of the world, the greetings of Olivia on this
the thirteenth day of May in the 1,289th Year of the City, or the 536th
Pope's Year, since so many monks are keeping records now. I have only
a single sheet of parchment and so must be more terse than I would
like to be.*

*As you see, I have left Lago Comus and am now bound for Roma,
and a return to my estate, as well as the direct care of yours. The entire Comus region has been mired in cold, and the sun has been unable to bring enough warmth to the earth to end the chill. All of last
year we had frost, and that, while less consistent this spring, is still
enough to cause profound worry amongst the farmers and peasants
working the land. I have granted access to the Lago Comus property
to the local growers and forgiven them their rents-in-kind for the next
five years. I am sure you will not object to such measures, for if you
were here, you could see for yourself what a dreadful hardship this
cold has been. It has been worse to the north of the Alps, for they say
that they are going to have another year with almost no harvest, and
they also say the boars and aurochs are dying in the forests, for want
of food, so only the vultures and the wolves have fared well.*

*When last spring was so disappointing, I bred only a few of my
better brood mares, and now I am glad that I did, for only three foals
have survived beyond their sixth week, and they are not as hearty as I
would like. I am bringing them south with me, and I am hoping that in
the slightly warmer and brighter environs of Roma, I will be able to
save at least one of them, for I know another hard summer will be
more than these foals can deal with, young as they are. I have taken to
feeding them raisins from the vines we could not get wine from last autumn, and that seems to have a little benefit, as do the dried apples you
had stored at the villa's stables. We have been able to travel at twelve
thousand paces a day—hardly any speed at all compared to the days
of my breathing youth, when messengers could cover eighty-five thousand paces a day, and troops could march for twenty-one thousand
paces a day. Still, given the weather and the poor state of the roads,
twelve thousand paces is acceptable, or so Niklos informs me. He is*

going ahead to Roma to make my estate ready, and to see to yours. I have not had word from Romulus Ursinus in more than eight months, and that is beginning to worry me, what with the raids on Roma and the problems of scarcity, for in such times, even the most upright man may be driven to steal and maraud for the sake of his family.

For that reason, I am taking as little with me as I providentially can. Those with much in the way of food and goods require armed men for protection, which only serves to alert desperate men that there are things of value to be seized. I have two small carpeta, drawn by mules, and six riding horses, and the mares with their foals at their sides—not very rich pickings for anyone. I am planning to spend the summer putting our estates in order and then working on building up my stud again, but that is for later, when I am once again on my native Roman earth and have access to my three casks of gold, which you so generously provided me before you left for distant lands. Not even Niklos knows where the casks are hidden, and that inclines me to believe that at least two of them are intact, since they are not hidden together, but, as you recommended, are secreted in separate locations.

There are two minor advantages to these horrendous times: mal aria has not struck in over a year, some say because of the cold, which has kept the miasma from rising; and the Byzantine army in Italia has not made as much progress toward conquest as the Emperor in Constantinople has ordered. General Belisarius has been delayed in the far south, and that has given the people some opportunity to prepare for his coming. The barbarians from the north are retreating, which I, for one, view with mixed emotions, for it may be that we are trading one ill for another. I would like to see Roma returned to Roman hands, but I am afraid that will not be possible.

I have finally had it confirmed that it is true: Emperor Justinian has ordered the Academy in Athens—Plato's school—closed because its teachings do not all conform to Christian dogma. I was saddened to hear this from a reputable scholar, bound for Pisae, who had gone there in its last two years to improve his knowledge of geography and ethics, neither of which meet with Justinian's approval. I know the loss of that school will distress you, and I am sure that many others will share your grief, but I cannot think that such useful knowledge will be forgotten.

This is going into the hands of Brother Servus, who is leaving on a mission to the churches in the East, to report on how this cold has

*affected the Christians in those foreign climes. I have asked him to put
this into the hands of Chinese merchants bound to the south and the
city of Yang-Chau. I have done my best to copy the scratches you told
me in your last letter—years ago—were proper writing for that place.
I hope I have done a good enough rendition of the lines to get this into
your hands, just as I hope you have not had to endure all the vicissitudes that have been visited upon us.*

   In haste but with affection, nonetheless,
Olivia

PART III

RAGOCZY FRANCISCUS

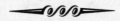

*T*ext of a report from the Apostle Gideon of the apostlary of Kuldja-and-Almalyk; sent to the apostlaries of Cambaluc, Khara-Khoja, Kumul, Khanbalik, Kuldja, Kashgar, Ning-Hsia, and Wu-Wei; written in vernacular Latin.

To my most esteemed, most highly valued Brothers in Christ, the greetings of the Apostle Gideon from the apostlary of the Most Sacred Crucifix in Almalyk, where God has seen fit to strand me for the winter, and where I am prepared to depart this world, if that should be His Will.

For the last eleven fortnights I have had no news from anyone, Christian or pagan, due to the remaining depth of the snow and the bad condition of the road leading to this place. We have had avalanches and rock slides at many places along the Silk Road, and that has impeded progress for all caravans. But there is now a way around the worst of the slippage, and the snow is retreating a little, all of which has meant that I have at last been able to read your accounts of the autumn past; nothing more recent has arrived, although we are well past the Feast of Resurrection, and for that reason, I will strive to tell you as much as I can of what we have endured in this place, and how it has shown God's Hand to us.

I must inform each and all of you that the past winter has been worse than any in living memory or in the records of any region that has them to consult. God had already made demands upon us, and that has only increased in the last year and a half. We have borne all in patience, offering our affliction to God, with thanks for His Mercy, but we have had to bear hunger and the continuing raids of unbelieving clans. Turks are the most persistent, but there have been Jou'an-Jou'an and Mongols as well, though the groups have been smaller and their damage less extreme. One of the small clans of Jou'an-Jou'an did little more than steal three goats and two sheep before going on to the West. They said their magician—a woman with white hair—had warned them against shedding human blood, for which we are grateful to God for so moving her pagan heart. Others were not so charitably inspired: twenty-six of our congregation have died from wounds received in resisting the pagan attacks. Another forty-three have starved to death, four as a show of sacrifice, giving up their food to those in greater need of it, by which example all of us have gained in the strength of our faith. We have defended the apostlary and the town, in the hope that if we prevail by force of arms we will also demonstrate the Power of God that is bestowed on all true Christians in the face of danger.

How have we failed in our efforts, that God has so greatly reclaimed our stewardship over the earth? In what way have we sinned, but in our inability to bring all souls to God? Since we have received God's mandate to care for the world, it is our responsibility to deal with the new conditions He has created, and to see our lands in good heart again, with flourishing crops and fruitful herds and flocks. By giving us this new world, which is harsher than the one we have lost, we are punished for our lapses and our pride and provided the opportunity to bring our sins and our failures to God in our devotion to repairing and restoring the earth. It is for us to fix what has been broken before we will be sufficiently worthy of the salvation bestowed so lovingly upon us, to return the land to the natural garden God intended, not to let it languish in this state of decay and infertility. Those who run from such burdens are not deserving of Redemption or a place in Heaven, and so I have told my congregation. I can only thank God for His Goodness in bringing the consolation of faith to those mired in want and despair.

Not that our condition has been relieved: our supplies are all but gone—I have only a dozen sheets of paper left when this report is dispatched, and a single ink cake remaining, which is commensurate with the state of our other supplies—and what little we have left at Most Sacred Crucifix has been carefully rationed and will be so until God sees fit to provide us with food and sweet water again, for although not so odious as the water of a year ago, there is still a yellow tinge in the stream and in the snow, and a faint odor of rotten eggs. We have done all that we may to extend charity and shelter to those in need and, in so doing, have brought more souls to Salvation, although many have proved obdurate because of their dread of writing. If any of you have supplies that could be added to our stores, we would bless you and give thanks to God for your charity. We are almost at Midsummer Festival, but so far there is little to celebrate; I have ordered that the lamps we light burn only until midnight, not through the night, so that we may not squander what little oil is left. I hope that the Four Evangelists, whose Feast the festival is, will understand and forgive our decision. We will go to bless the fields, but it will be a sad occasion, for we have almost nothing growing in them, and our prayers may have more of despair than thankfulness in them. If you have any new crops that have been strong enough to thrive under this cold sun, then I beseech you in the Name of Christ to send as many shoots as you can spare so that we may have some degree of harvest. Our crops are not developing in spite of all our efforts, and even our trees are dying. If you have it within your power to aid us in this effort, I ask you to lend us your aid, for God's Glory and your joy in Paradise.

May God show you His Favor and may He bring you to triumph, if not in this world, in the next,

Gideon, Apostle of Kuldja-and-Almalyk
At the apostlary of the Most Sacred Crucifix

1

In the dusty marketplace of Tok-Kala a small crowd had gathered to marvel at what the foreigner in black had brought in from a camp on the eastern branch of the Kushan Road; the afternoon sun had dropped low enough in the west to cast long, purple shadows from brilliant yellow skies, making the huge, stone bone appear more impressive than it was, and it was remarkable on its own merits. The marketplace was surrounded by two- and three-story buildings of clay bricks, most without decoration of any kind, but with two marked by ominous swaths of dark-reddish brown stains and ornamented with racks of skulls, now shining in the spectacular colors of early sunset.

"How did you find it?" asked a Byzantine merchant in a tattered paragaudion of dark-blue, nubby Antioch silk. He spoke the dialect of Silk Road merchants in the West—an amalgam of Persian, Byzantine Greek, and the local vernacular.

"There was a landslide, coming into Ferghana, that brought down a long section of the hillside, and the bone was exposed; there were bits of what I suspect were other bones, but I could not wrest them from the earth; they were all of great size," said Ragoczy Franciscus in excellent Byzantine Greek; the merchant gave a hearty sigh of relief as he heard his native tongue, and he nodded his thanks to Ragoczy Franciscus. "I also found two teeth," he added, taking the sharp, triangular objects from the sleeve of his sen-gai; they were nearly as long as the palm of his small, elegant hand. He cast his mind back to the early morning three days since when he and Rojeh had come upon the swath of fallen rocks that blocked the road. The work of clearing the slide away had taken most of the morning and half the afternoon, and in the process they had come upon the great stone bone, which, when stood on end, came up to the middle of Ragoczy Franciscus' chest. He had struggled to load it onto one of the camels, after adding the camel's chests and sacks and barrels to the other animals' pack saddles; at the time it had seemed a very important thing to take with them. "Whatever this being is, it is ancient."

248 Chelsea Quinn Yarbro

"Ancient? I should say so! What manner of creature has such teeth, if they are truly teeth?" the merchant exclaimed. "They could be arrowheads, or spear-points, from an ancient battle."

"Both with no means to fasten them to a shaft?" Ragoczy Franciscus inquired gently. "No, I must suppose they are teeth, but I cannot imagine what creature has such teeth."

"A giant, whatever it was," said the Byzantine merchant.

"I think we must assume that," said Ragoczy Franciscus.

"How could such a creature manage to—?" The Byzantine merchant looked about. "They say strange beasts have come down from the northern forests."

"It could be one," said Ragoczy Franciscus quietly, and prepared to join Rojeh at the inn they had chosen. "But I have heard nothing of anything like this, and I would expect news to travel quickly about such a beast."

"Very true; very true. I would like to discuss it with you, later, if I may?" He slapped his chest. "I am Vermakrides, from Kaffa. I may still do some trading before I return home." He grinned, his openness a deliberate ploy to encourage Ragoczy Franciscus to volunteer as much about himself and what goods he might have. "That bone of yours interests me."

Ragoczy Franciscus ignored the last. "Then I wish you a successful end of your journey."

Vermakrides nodded. "Yes, it is almost done, and never have I been more glad to see the end of travel ahead. Have you far to go?"

"I, too, am returning to my native earth," said Ragoczy Franciscus with a slight, formal reverence, aware he was being prodded for information.

"And where might that be?" Vermakrides asked, annoyed that he had to press for information.

"In the Carpathians," said Ragoczy Franciscus in a formidably polite tone that discouraged more inquiry. "Very high in the eastern crook."

"Have you been gone long?" Vermakrides realized he was pushing his luck to ask, but the habits of his trading were too strong to be broken.

"More than a decade," said Ragoczy Franciscus; he did not mention that his absence from his homeland would be correctly calculated in multiple decades—nine of them since his last visit there.

"A considerable time," said Vermakrides, prepared to embark on more conversation.

But Ragoczy Franciscus cut him short. "If you will excuse me?" He sketched a reverence to Vermakrides and went to where Rojeh was standing, next to the enormous bone. "Have you found a place for the night?"

"The inn at the corner of the market? The one with the blue shutters? It is called the Wayfarers' Refuge. The innkeeper has taken our animals into his barns and is preparing a room even now." He spoke in the language of Egypt, fairly certain that only Ragoczy Franciscus would understand him.

"For a price," said Ragoczy Franciscus drily in a slightly older version of the same tongue.

"Naturally for a price, luckily one that can be paid in silver," said Rojeh; he paused a moment and finally broached a matter that had been niggling at him. "I hope the bar of silver you gave Ourisi will be enough to keep her safe."

"So do I."

"Will she survive?" Rojeh persisted.

"Will any of us? At least with silver and her freedom, she has a chance, unlike she would have, had she remained with Kasha. There was nothing more I could do: she was too ill to travel." He reached down and touched the stone bone and said in Persian, "Hire some of the marketplace men to help you move this to the stable at the inn. Speaking of silver, give them a silver coin each—that should help to encourage them."

"I will," Rojeh said loudly enough to be overheard. "One silver coin each."

Ragoczy Franciscus began to walk toward the inn, but stopped and turned back to Vermakrides, who was exchanging jokes with a group of camel-drovers from the south. "Why are you interested in the bone?"

"It is a wonder. I would like to display it," said Vermakrides promptly. "Many would pay to see it, I think."

"Pay to see it," Ragoczy Franciscus echoed. "What a notion." He paused. "I will consider it."

"Well and good; I will come to your inn after supper, to make you an offer; you are at the Wayfarers' Refuge, are you not?" said Ver-makrides, and turned back to the camel-drovers.

"Yes; come there when you like," said Ragoczy Franciscus, and continued on his way.

The interior of the Wayfarers' Refuge smelled of smoke and wet leather, with a hint of slightly rancid cooking oil. The innkeeper—a man who had once been rotund but was now so thin that his flesh hung on him like an inner garment and whose face was so sunken that he resembled the Chinese fighting dogs—reverenced Ragoczy Franciscus, indicating the flight of stairs behind him. "Be welcome, Man from the West. Your servant has already prepared your quarters."

"That is very good of you," said Ragoczy Franciscus.

The innkeeper set a scale on the counter and waited. "Do you want feed for your animals, Man from the West?"

Ragoczy Franciscus considered for a moment, then said, "Yes." He saw the greed in the innkeeper's eyes and asked, "Has my traveling companion paid for our accommodations yet?"

"He has given me the initial payment for the rooms. Anything else must be paid when requested." The innkeeper looked narrowly at Ragoczy Franciscus. "You have come from far to the east, your man told me: they say that the clans from the east are coming in greater numbers now. What have you seen?"

"Why do you ask?" Ragoczy Franciscus inquired.

"Travelers who stop here ask for advice; I want to have good information to provide them, for their sake. Traders pay well for such news."

"Of course. They pay."

"You do not give your goods away, foreigner," said the innkeeper brusquely. "News is as valuable as goods in this town, and more so now, the last year and a half being so hard."

"I will tell you as much as I can, for the protection of other travelers." Thinking back to the Desert Cats, Ragoczy Franciscus answered carefully, "I would reckon that if the clans are on the move, it is because their own regions can no longer support them."

"But where will they go? There is nothing for them here, and Ferghana is already overrun by clans looking for horses to steal."

"The scrub is dying, giving way to moving sands," said Ragoczy Franciscus, reporting what he had learned from Baru Ksoka as well as what he had seen. "They cannot survive on sand."

"Nor can anyone," said the innkeeper. He pointed to the window. "The wastes between the seas are doing much the same thing, the grass and scrub drying up and giving way to shifting sands. At least we have the Amu Darya to give us water, or we might have to abandon our homes, too. We are fortunate to have the river." He glowered, his head down. "As it is, many of us have starved already."

"It is much the same everywhere we have been," said Ragoczy Franciscus. "Starvation and its companions—illness and desperation."

"We gave foals and kids to the gods, and when they did not suffice, we gave sons and daughters. It has not been enough." The innkeeper looked at Ragoczy Franciscus. "What have you lost, foreigner?"

"All my family," said Ragoczy Franciscus, accurately but misleadingly.

"I have only one wife and two children left. I could not bear to part with any of them," said the innkeeper in a sudden burst of overwrought emotion. "Those coming from the West say that there the sun remains weak and the cold is everywhere."

Ragoczy Franciscus took money from the string of cash in his sleeve. "Here are coins enough for the food, the feed, and something extra so you may make other offerings to the gods."

The innkeeper took the cash and did his best to smile. "This is most generous."

"May it bring you what you seek," said Ragoczy Franciscus, ducking his head before going off toward the stairs. "Which rooms are assigned to my companion and me?"

"The two at the end of the north arm."

"Thank you," said Ragoczy Franciscus as he began to climb. "Oh," he said, stopping on the third riser, "there is a Byzantine merchant coming later in the evening to talk with me."

"It will cost you to receive him," said the innkeeper automatically.

"Of course it will," said Ragoczy Franciscus, resuming his climb to the unusually wide corridor that led to the north arm of the building.

Some little time later, one of the slaves came up to Ragoczy Franciscus's room to announce, "There is a Byzantine merchant waiting in the visitors' room."

Ragoczy Franciscus tapped on Rojeh's door and said he would return shortly. "He and I may strike a bargain."

"For the bone," Rojeh said incredulously.

Vermakrides was waiting in the visitors' room, seated on a pile of cushions near the newly lit fire. He had a cup of wine in his hand, and he nearly spilled its contents when Ragoczy Franciscus came through the door. "May the Saints be praised!" he exclaimed.

Ragoczy Franciscus reverenced Vermakrides. "You said you wanted to discuss the bone I brought to—"

"To the point. Yes. Yes, I do," Vermakrides said impulsively. "I very much want to discuss the bone. You say you came upon it in a land-slide?"

"I did," said Ragoczy Franciscus.

"You said this was in Ferghana?" Vermakrides persisted.

"Yes. On the road from Kokand and Tashkent." He regarded Ver-makrides for a short while. "Do you plan to look for the place?"

"It had occurred to me," the Byzantine admitted.

"I will hope you have good fortune, if you try," Ragoczy Francis-cus said cordially. "There was a second landslide shortly after my trav-eling companion and I removed the bone, and all that had been uncovered by the first was buried again by the second."

"If what you say is true—" Vermakrides began, and stopped short as he glanced at Ragoczy Franciscus.

"Why should I speak false? If I wished to conceal the place I found the bone, there are many easier ways to dissemble. I could have claimed to have found it anywhere from here to China, on an-other branch of the Silk Road." His voice remained genial, but there was something in his eyes that held the attention of the mer-chant.

"It could be that your account is fanciful," he said cautiously.

"It could be," seconded Ragoczy Franciscus, a slight emphasis on *could,* "but as it happens, I am telling the truth. You will have to take my Word for it."

"If I must, I will," said Vermakrides. "I will also accept that I might not be able to find it."

Ragoczy Franciscus shrugged. "You may find other bones, if you decide to look for them."

Vermakrides tapped his fingers on the rim of his wine cup, and then looked up, startled. "I should have offered as soon as you came in: let me buy you a cup of wine."

"Thank you; it is a most gracious offer, but I do not drink wine," said Ragoczy Franciscus.

There was a brief silence between them, then Vermakrides coughed and said, "About the bone? Do you have a price in mind?"

"I do," said Ragoczy Franciscus.

Vermakrides blinked. "What might it be?"

"Four Ferghana horses of my choosing," said Ragoczy Franciscus, "and one full measure of gold."

"That is a substantial amount," said Vermakrides.

"So it is," said Ragoczy Franciscus. "The bone is unique."

Vermakrides pulled at his lower lip, twisting his beard as he did. "Three horses and a three-quarter measure of gold."

This was a larger counteroffer than Ragoczy Franciscus had been expecting; he covered his surprise by saying, "Four horses and a three-quarter measure of gold."

Fiddling with his beard, Vermakrides set his cup aside and took a short time to ponder. "That is a very tempting proposition," he admitted, and gulped down the last of his wine while Ragoczy Franciscus waited calmly for the Byzantine merchant to decide.

Vermakrides gave him a careful look. "I will not offer a higher price than the one we have discussed."

"Let me see the horses before I decide." Ragoczy Franciscus gestured toward the door. "We will fix the matter shortly."

Rising, Vermakrides smiled. "I can see you are a careful man," he approved, and led the way out of the inn to the horse-market to conclude their transaction.

The three horses Ragoczy Franciscus chose were young, strengthy animals: a copper-dun mare, a black-and-white-spotted stallion that Rojeh favored, and a splendid blue roan mare that Ragoczy Franciscus had selected as his own. The ponies—now each carrying lighter loads as their burdens were spread over more backs and some of the crates and barrels were growing lighter as the food and water they contained was depleted—were able to pick up their pace. They made rapid progress along the Kushan Road toward the Volga Delta at the north side of the Caspian Sea.

"I estimate our speed at nineteen thousand paces yesterday and this morning," said Rojeh as they broke camp in midafternoon.

Ragoczy Franciscus was gathering up their bedding and setting it in place on the pack saddles, using heavy hempen nets to hold all in place, when he allowed himself the luxury of a single chuckle. "What a strange trophy to want."

Rojeh realized Ragoczy Franciscus meant the Byzantine merchant. "What sort of an exhibit do you think he will make of it?"

Ragoczy Franciscus considered his answer. "I have no idea."

"Didn't he say he wanted to display it and charge for people to see it?" Rojeh could sense Ragoczy Franciscus' disinterest. "When he took it, he said he would show it as a giant's bone, or a dragon's."

"Yes, he did. An odd notion."

"That Byzantine merchant may succeed in his plan, if he can bring the bone to Trebizond without mishap. Who knows what people may make of it if he actually displays it?" With a quick, tight smile, Rojeh went to work on the riding horses. "You took sustenance from the copper-dun, did you?"

"Yes. Two nights from now it will be a pony I drink from, and then, two nights later, my blue roan, and after that, the cinder-brown pony, then the black-and-white. I have adhered to that routine since we left Tok-Kala." He patted his mare's neck. "It is sufficient to keep me alive, but it puts no flesh on my bones."

"So I see," said Rojeh, reaching into their grooming box and handing a stiff-bristled brush to Ragoczy Franciscus.

"Just as well, being a bit gaunt just now. A man with abundant flesh in these times would become the object of envy and suspicion." He looked at Rojeh, his face unreadable.

Rojeh, nonplussed, began to groom the copper-dun, his austere features showing little of his thoughts. Finally, as he started brushing their ponies, he remarked, "Have you wondered at all about what has happened in Yang-Chau since we left? You haven't said much about it."

"There is little to say. With such harsh weather along the Silk Road, if the ports of China and India were not badly compromised, they would be bringing foodstuffs and other necessities with them, for there would be handsome profits to be made, if such things were available." He squinted up at the sky. "Though it shines, the sun is still veiled—I can feel its lack of power as I have since shortly after we crossed the Crane River. It may be that wherever the sun shines, its weakness has taken a toll." He got his saddle.

"But Yang-Chau is very far away," said Rojeh, pulling out saddle pads for their riding horses, and handing one to Ragoczy Franciscus.

"And we have come a great distance without finding the sun any stronger, and there is evidence everywhere that the last year has been unusually cold and stormy everywhere, judging from what we have heard. There are no accounts of good harvests or flourishing land," said Ragoczy Franciscus as he finished securing the girths.

Rojeh began to saddle his black-and-white stallion, remarking as he did, "I hope the mares will not come into season anytime soon."

"And I. But they may not, since they have been on short rations for so long," said Ragoczy Franciscus. "Hunger delays such things."

"Truly," said Rojeh as he tightened the girths on his Jou'an-Jou'an saddle. "We will have to replace the foot-loop straps soon. They are showing too much wear."

"I agree," said Ragoczy Franciscus as he took his bridle from the tack trunk. He slipped the headstall over the mare's ears and reached for the throat-latch to buckle it. "I may have to fashion new foot-loops; the iron of these is beginning to rust. When we reach Sarai, perhaps I can arrange something. There must be at least one smithy there where I may work." He put his foot into the iron foot-loop and stepped up into his saddle.

It was sixteen days later that they saw the many mouths of the Volga glistening ahead, and the expanse of the Caspian Sea beyond, flat and glossy as a shield of polished brass. A few small ships moved upon it, but there was a lack of activity that boded ill for the people of the stone-walled town of Sarai, which stood on the last rocky spit of land in the delta; it rose steeply from the sea's edge to a crag. A single, steep road led up to the gate, midway up the slope, an approach that discouraged attackers. Beyond the high stone walls, the town was surrounded by marsh, the waterways marked with reeds and occasional low docks where boats were tied. There was a quantity of islands created by the river, which just now were filled with tents of all sorts, from small cloth tents of the wandering beggars to the skin-covered tents of the clans and peoples from as far away as the Atlai Mountains and the expanses of the Gobi Desert. A maze of fords and low bridges connected the islands to the approach to the town. A faint odor of decay hung over the marshes, and a low, clinging mist was just beginning to rise from the profusion of waterways, sinister in the glistening midday light.

There was very little activity in the various encampments, which added a second apprehension to the appearance of the delta islands.

"Look. Some of those tents are Jou'an-Jou'an; goat-hide over a wooden frame with horses painted on them, and horse-tail standards," Rojeh remarked as he came up to Ragoczy Franciscus, who, this day, was on the copper-dun mare. Both men wore heavy silken Byzantine paragaudions—procured from Vermakrides—over thick, Persian leggings of wool, and tooled-and-heeled Scythian-style boots. The day was warm enough that neither man had bothered to don a cloak or a sen-gai.

"So they are," said Ragoczy Franciscus. "But that might not be significant."

"I didn't mean that the Desert Cats are here," said Rojeh quickly.

"They may be," Ragoczy Franciscus allowed. "And perhaps, if we are taken into the town, I will come and see which clans are among those gathered on the islands. If we must pass on tomorrow, then—" He shook his head once.

By midafternoon they had climbed the road to reach the gates of Sarai and had been admitted, but with immediate restriction, imposed upon them by a single guard who confronted them immediately inside the gates. "You must remain over there, you and your animals," the officer who let them in ordered, pointing to a large pen to the side of the gate. He spoke an outlandish tongue that was the regional language with an admixture of Silk Road Greek and Persian. His weapon was a long, menacing spear with a hook where the point should be, in contrast to the guard, who carried a Persian shimtare and a mace.

"We will; but why?" Ragoczy Franciscus asked in Byzantine Greek.

"Our Master of Foreigners must speak with you," said the officer, annoyed at having to answer. "Emrach Sarai'af has been notified of your coming. He will decide if you may be admitted, and how long you may stay, if you are."

"I understand and accept these terms," said Ragoczy Franciscus, his manner distantly polite.

The officer coughed. "From where do you come?" He was spared more inquiry as a large, bearded man in Byzantine clothing approached in a chariot of western design. He hailed the officer as his slave halted the pair of horses drawing the vehicle. Seen at this nearer vantage, his height was impressive and there was a deep scar running from his forehead, through his eyebrow, to his cheek, disappearing into his beard; his nose was aquiline and his mouth was wide. He stepped down from the chariot and came toward the officer. "What is it you want? The Volgamen haven't arrived yet, have they?" His Byzantine Greek was reasonably good, but his accent would have been laughable in Constantinople.

"No, not the Volgamen," said the officer. "This merchant and a traveling companion have come."

Ermach Sarai'af stalked up to Ragoczy Franciscus, making the most of his size, his hands on his hips to make his shoulders look bigger. Yet loom as he would, his usual intimidation had no effect on the foreigner in the black paragaudion. Flustered, he walked around Ragoczy Franciscus, glaring at him. "I am the Master of Foreigners. All strangers here are here on my sufferance."

Ragoczy Franciscus remained unperturbed by this scrutiny. "I am Ragoczy Franciscus; he is Rojeh. My companion and I have come from China. We are returning to my home in the Carpathian Mountains." His demeanor was deferential but cool; he reverenced Ermach Sarai'af. "My companion and I seek permission to stay here for a month, if we may, to recuperate from the rigors of our travels."

"How much can you pay?" The question came abruptly and without finesse. "We cannot have anyone here who cannot pay," said Ermach Sarai'af.

"I have some gold, and some silver," said Ragoczy Franciscus. "What amount would do?"

"If you have a tent, the amount would be less; you could claim a plot at the rear of the town. If you take a house in the Foreigners' Quarter, the amount would be greater, and separate from any arrangement you may make with the owner of the house." Ermach Sarai'af folded his big arms and made another attempt to hector Ragoczy Franciscus. "You must pay for the right to be inside these walls for the night."

Ragoczy Franciscus gave a single nod. "I am willing to pay the amount if I have enough gold and silver with me."

Perplexed, Ermach Sarai'af paced around Ragoczy Franciscus

one more time, then declared, "I will have to receive two Byzantine bars of gold if you, your companion, and your animals are to remain here for—How long do you plan to remain here, again?"

"A month," said Ragoczy Franciscus. "Perhaps more."

"The two bars of gold will be paid for a month. If you stay longer, I will have the same again from you, whether you remain here a month or a day." Ermach Sarai'af stopped directly in front of Ragoczy Franciscus, challenging him.

"It is a large amount," said Ragoczy Franciscus.

"If you cannot meet it, then—"

"It is a large sum," said Ragoczy Franciscus affably, waited a moment, then added, "And if you would direct me and my companion to an inn where we may spend a few days while choosing a house in the Foreigners' Quarter, I would be most grateful."

Emrach Sarai'af, who had been expecting a long wrangle over the amount he was charging the foreigners, snorted. "You must have had a very profitable journey, to be so accommodating." After a brooding silence, Emrach Sarai'af said, "The Birch House will have rooms for you, and paddocks and stalls for your animals."

"Excellent," said Ragoczy Franciscus as if he were actually delighted. "If you will tell us how this inn is to be found, we will go there at once and expect you shortly before sunset." He signaled to Rojeh. "The Birch House. We will go there at once."

"I will be along before sundown to collect your money," Emrach Sarai'af warned before turning on his heel and striding back to his waiting chariot. "If you do not pay the amount due, the guards will escort you out of the gates, and you will not be allowed to return, not for double the price."

"Yes; I understand," said Ragoczy Franciscus as he swung around to face Rojeh. "Are we ready?"

"If you are, so are we all," said Rojeh, mounting his stallion again and preparing to lead the other animals.

"Excellent," Ragoczy Franciscus repeated. "I will have money waiting for you shortly," he added to Emrach Sarai'af as he mounted his blue roan.

Text of a letter from Tsa Tsa-Si, professor of calendars and geography at the University of Yang-Chau to his brother Tsa Wa-Tso at Chang'an, carried by courier and delivered ten months after being written and two months after Tsa Tsa-Si's death.

The most devoted greetings, Elder Brother, the most worthy Tsa Wa-Tso, now serving the Wen Emperor at Chang'an in the capacity of Translator of Documents to the August Personage, on this the ninth day of the Fortnight of the Fruitful Fields, from your faithful younger brother, Tsa Tsa-Si, from the most pitiful city of Yang-Chau.

    Would that I could tell you, Elder Brother, that the many privations and difficulties of the Year of Yellow Snow have ended, but, alas, such is not the case. We continue to struggle under a sun that has become less than an oil-lamp in the heavens, and because of the lack of such virtue as the sun is wont to provide, trade and life suffer. The University is all but deserted. I have only four pupils left, and were it not for the generosity of the Worthy Foreigner Zangi-Ragozh, and the compassion of Professor Min Cho-Zhi, who supervises his personal affairs, I would be a beggar on the street, or worse. I now have thirty-one years, but I feel as if I had double that. I have consulted a physician, who has given me herbs to treat these conditions, which has provided some relief, but I am far from being what I would expect of myself, and I have had to delegate some of my duties to others, notably Councillor Ko She-Hsieh, who has taken over dealing with the accounts of the enterprises of the absent Worthy Foreigner and will do so until I am sufficiently recovered to resume the work for myself. I have been unable to assist Professor Min as I would like, for he has recently withdrawn to a small house at the rear of the compound and has devoted himself to reading the classic teachings of Mo-Tzu, in the hope that his philosophy will ease passage through these difficult days.

    I have not heard anything from Zangi-Ragozh and so cannot provide any of the information you requested. I have learned—as you must have as well—that the men traveling with him, Yao, Gien, and Jong, have been enrolled in the army at Lo-Yang, and that Zangi-Ragozh and his manservant, Ro-shei, went on up the Huang Ho, but where they went is still a mystery. No word has come from him, and if any has been sent, it has not yet reached its destination—not an uncommon fate of messages at present. It is all due to the lessening of the sun's power, for the Powers of Water are not kept in check, as seen in the tremendous amount of rain we have had since the great clap of thunder of thirty-nine fortnights ago. We saw great waves soon after that did great damage and caused many deaths, and darkness engulfed the sun shortly after they struck. Since then the balance of yin and yang has been disturbed, and evidence of this is everywhere evident.

That does not mean that I have abandoned my duties. I am continuing to accomplish as much as I might, and I am still supported by Zangi-Ragozh's household, as he stipulated in his instructions to Min when he left. No matter what becomes of Min, I have an obligation and I will not disgrace our name by failing to execute every particular of my assigned tasks to the limit of my capacity. I wish I could say that the rest of Zangi-Ragozh's household has displayed equal probity, but that is not the case. Meng, his cook, was caught stealing from the larder and selling the food he took at vastly inflated prices. Jho took him before the Magistrate, who ordered Meng's hands be struck off. Meng's injuries were cauterized and treated, but the stumps became infected, and his arms blackened and he died. Also, some of the furniture of the house has been stolen—by whom we cannot determine—and the losses reported, but so far no one has been apprehended with the items in his possession. I realize that unless some object of very high value is taken, we will have to accept the losses and account for them as best we can if Zangi-Ragozh should ever return.

Thank you, Elder Brother, for informing me of our nephew's death and the illness of our sister. I know that since her husband died, three years since, she has been much put-upon and has struggled with imperfect health. I have burned incense for the boy's soul, and I have listed his name among the tablets in my Ancestor Shrine. I realize that it is an imposition upon you to take our sister into your household, particularly since your wife has said she is not in favor of having our sister with you, which is not an unexpected response, for no woman likes to give over her position to a sister or mother. Perhaps our youngest brother, Tsa Tsi-La, would be willing to have our sister with him, unless he has been posted to some barbarian station where no one bathes and the winters are harder than cold iron. I could contribute to her maintenance, not a great deal, but an amount that could ease the burden on Tsa Tsi-La; if you were willing to do the same, it may render her life more endurable.

They are saying that when the weather improves, the Emperor at

Chang'an is going to take to the field with his Army and bring the Middle Kingdom back to unity. If this is truly the case, I hope he will reconsider and wait a year, for no part of the Middle Kingdom has brought in a good harvest, so the new-planted crops are especially vulnerable. Much ground lies fallow, producing only occasional weeds, and even they are stunted and burned. The yellow rain has blighted many farms. The fields are not the only sufferers: what livestock is left is thin and pathetic, unsuitable to labor or the pot. Because of all the rain, everything is sodden, and cloth decays while it is worn. For the peasants, life is much more demanding than before the thunderclap. There has been Swine Fever and Gray Cough among them, and some horses have succumbed to Black Sores, which has meant that many peasants and farmers have fled in terror, for the Black Sores touches men as well as horses and sheep and hogs. There has been no trace of Black Sores in Yang-Chau, but we have seen Lice Fever as well as other fevers, from tainted air and the sweat of foreigners. We will endure more fevers before this onerous time is done and hope that the Immortals do not desert us entirely.

> *Your most devoted younger brother,*
> *Tsa Tsa-Si, Professor*
> *(his chop)*

2

"There are more tents on the islands," Rojeh said in Imperial Latin as he came into the makeshift laboratory Ragoczy Franciscus had established in the house he had hired. He had paid an outrageous price for three months' residence, and additional sums for furnishings and other supplies; he made no complaint, aware that the Master of Foreigners would support the landlord in any situation.

"Ah? Whose, do you know?" He was in the process of sifting the whitest sand through a silken sieve, removing every imperfection.

"They are Jou'an-Jou'an," Rojeh told him, watching him closely to see his reaction.

Ragoczy Franciscus continued his work, but his fine brows lifted, an indication of curiosity. "Do you know which clan?"

"They appear to be the Desert Cats; I recognized Baru Ksoka's tent, in any case, so either they have come, or they were vanquished by a rival clan and their goods seized." Rojeh stopped by the plank table and studied Ragoczy Franciscus' face. "Do you think it strange that they should come here?"

"Not particularly. It is far more likely that we should meet in a place like this than on one of the stretches of trade route that cross this region." He glanced toward the window. "I am more curious about why they have come so far west than that, having done so, they have come to this place."

"Does it bode well?" Rojeh asked.

"How can I tell until I have seen them? if the new clan is the Desert Cats." He set his sieve aside, straightened up, and added, "This will keep for now."

"You are making glass?" Rojeh asked.

"Three of my vessels are broken and I cannot do half of what I would like to do without having the necessary instruments, including glass vessels," Ragoczy Franciscus said. "Pragmatic necessity, old friend."

"The athanor you're building isn't ready yet," Rojeh pointed out.

"I know, but I am aware that I must make the most of it as soon as it is," Ragoczy Franciscus said, wiping his hands on a cotton cloth. "Is the blue roan in her stall or in the paddock?"

"In her stall. I was planning to turn her out at midday." Rojeh paused. "Would you rather wait until late afternoon to—"

"I still have my native earth in my soles, and the sun is still feeble; between those factors, I should do very well, at least for as long as I will require to investigate the Jou'an-Jou'an." He rubbed his chin, testing his newly trimmed beard and nodding with satisfaction. "I had best wear a sen-gai."

"Most of them are looking shabby," said Rojeh. "But the one with the dark-red piping is quite presentable. Would you like me to lay it out for you?"

"No need," said Ragoczy Franciscus, "I can find it well enough." He set down the cloth and started toward the door. "Make sure this room is locked when you leave."

"Certainly," said Rojeh.

Ragoczy Franciscus left his laboratory and went to the rooms set aside for his use in the sprawling house. Since he had hired the house some nine days since, he had been working to make it into a suitable residence without doing anything to alarm the landlord or his neighbors, one of whom was a Hunnic trader, the other of whom was the widow of a wealthy Constantinopolitan with three surviving children. His comings and goings occasioned no observation, particularly those private expeditions he made very late at night, so he knew his departure now would not give cause for alarm. He reached his apartments and went to the chest containing the clothespress. Unfastening the sturdy boards, he looked through the various garments and finally pulled out the sen-gai he had been seeking. He closed and buckled the press and took off his Persian caftan of heavy black cotton, which he wore over leather leggings; he tossed this onto the back of the single chair in the room, then pulled on the sen-gai, securing the belt before looking for his silver-and-black-sapphire pectoral; since arriving in Sarai, he had made a point of wearing jewelry to indicate he was a man of rank as well as fortune. He found his chilanum and its scabbard; he secured these to his belt. Now that he was suitably armed, he went to the stable to groom and saddle the blue roan.

The guards no longer stopped him at the gate, and he rode out of Sarai without incident, letting his roan set the pace down the low hill to the delta islands. Threading his way along the narrow tracks, he noticed that there were five more bodies wrapped in reeds and left out for cremation on ground already blackened by repeated fires. He continued along the tangle of paths toward the island Rojeh had indicated, and as he rode, he began to consider what he would say if this were indeed the Desert Cats clan who had arrived here. He chided himself for anticipating an answer and put his concentration on the narrow track ahead.

Three children were playing at the edge of the camp, one of them Baru Ksoka's son Zumir; the boy looked up from pursuing a rough leather ball as he heard Ragoczy Franciscus' horse approach; there was an angular scar on his jaw that had not been there when Ragoczy Franciscus had last seen him. He took a defensive stance and shaded his eyes. "Who are you?" he shouted in dreadful Persian. "What do you want here?"

Ragoczy Franciscus answered in the Jou'an-Jou'an tongue, "I am an old friend of this clan, though a foreigner, Zumir. Is your father about?"

Zumir peered up at him. "No. He's not. Neitis Ksoka is Kaigan now."

"Neitis?" said Ragoczy Franciscus. "What happened?"

The boy glared at him. "Why should I tell you, foreigner? You are not one of us."

"I would like to know what became of him." He spoke evenly, his dark eyes on the youngster.

"There was a landslide," said Zumir cautiously, trying to make out the stranger's features, his young countenance twisted with concentration. "He and four others perished, along with their ponies. Nine more were hurt." His face cleared suddenly. "Zangi-Ragozh. I know you. How do you come to be here?" He ran impulsively toward the blue roan, only stopping as the horse backed up a few steps.

"I stayed on the middle branch of the Silk Road when you went north," said Ragoczy Franciscus. "Did you reach Dzungaria?"

"Yes," said Zumir as the other boys came up beside him, their curiosity outweighing their trepidation.

"How long did you remain there?" Ragoczy Franciscus asked patiently. "It can't have been long."

"It wasn't." Heaving a prodigious sigh, Zumir began his account. "We went between the Tien Shan and the Atlai Mountains, searching for a region with grass enough for the ponies and goats. We eventually found a sheltered valley where we tried to make a place for our clan; most of the grass in other areas had dried up, but there enough grew for our needs, and that made the valley we found a good place for us; but another, larger clan of Uighurs found the valley as well—they drove us out by main force, killing ten of us before my father decided we had best abandon our site. We went northwest for many days and came to the Aral Route. We were crossing the pass southeast of Lake Balkhash when the landslide came. Most of the clan thought it was an omen and wanted to turn back, but Dukkai said we must go on. She read the smoke and said that the way forward was the only safe course for us to take."

"Then Dukkai is with you," said Ragoczy Franciscus.

"Yes," said Zumir, with a sly look at Ragoczy Franciscus. "She is as much our leader as Neitis Ksoka is. He makes no decisions until she reads the smoke for him." He clapped his hands once and turned around to his companions. "Go fetch Dukkai," he said. "Bring her here. At once. Muksi, don't tell her who has come, just bring her." He shooed them on with a gesture, then turned back to Ragoczy Franciscus. "What happened to your ponies? I haven't seen that horse before."

"I have the ponies still, three of them. I acquired this horse since I and my companion parted from you." He was amused by the question. "What of my wagon? Do you have it still?"

Zumir glowered. "The Uighurs took it during their fiercest raid." He squinted up at Ragoczy Franciscus. "Do you have another?"

"I did, but no longer." He swung down from his horse and walked up to the boy. "How have you fared in the last year, Zumir?"

"We have had lean times," he admitted as if confessing an error, "and the Lord of the Skies no longer hears our prayers, or, if he does, the God of the Day does not obey him anymore. Plants no longer thrive, and even the trees of the forests are withering."

"It has been a hard time," Ragoczy Franciscus said, kindness in his eyes.

"Nothing changes it. We have had so much to—" Zumir's face crumpled. "We have given sacrifice, and we have done all that Dukkai has said must be done, but nothing avails us. When our men are killed, we make food of them, so that we may live and be strong."

Ragoczy Franciscus was not shocked by this revelation, but he was saddened. "Did that happen with your father?"

Zumir nodded. "As much of him as we could recover." He coughed to hide a sob, and then stared hard at Ragoczy Franciscus. "It is necessary. We all know it."

"When you are starving, you must take what there is to eat," said Ragoczy Franciscus with a slow nod, glancing up as the two boys came hurrying toward them, all but dragging Dukkai between them.

"I only had a little," Zumir muttered, as if to reassure himself.

"See?" the taller of the two boys with Dukkai shouted. "A surprise!"

Dukkai halted, her face gone pale, her blue eyes wide. "Zangi-Ragozh," she exclaimed, one hand to her eyes as if she might rub the sight of him away. "How? Why are you here?"

"Dukkai," he said; he could see she was thinner, and her skin had taken on the fragile look of paper. He started toward her. "Zumir tells me things are much changed for the Desert Cats."

"Oh, yes. As the world is much changed. We are here, where we have never been before." She took a step toward him. "Zangi-Ragozh. I thought I would never see you again alive."

His smile was quick and ironic. "I am as alive now as you have ever known me to be."

"I had no message of your coming," she said a bit distractedly. "The smoke should have shown me."

"Perhaps because I came another way than the roads you took," he suggested gently. "How could your smoke know that I would remain in Sarai, as I have done? I might well have moved on by now, and our paths would never have crossed." He studied her features, noticing how much deeper the lines were, and how much more removed her gaze was.

"I have looked for signs, asked the gods and the Lord of the Skies and the Lords of the Earth for them, but all have been silent. The smoke should have—" She stopped. "My daughter died. She came too soon, and she struggled to live, but it was not enough."

"I am very sorry to hear that," said Ragoczy Franciscus, his concern genuine.

"So all you did to help me carry her turned out to be for nothing," she said remotely. "I should have read the smoke, but I could not believe that my child would be born only to die." She blinked twice and knotted her hands together.

"We are all born only to die," said Ragoczy Franciscus as gently as he could.

She gave him a hard, startled stare, then fixed her eyes on a point well beyond his head. "But later, not sooner." Her voice caught in her throat. "I mourn Baru Ksoka, but I know he lived out his life. My daughter did not live long enough to be given a name."

Ragoczy Franciscus recalled that the Desert Cats did not name their children officially until they had taken their first step. "So she is only Dukkai's Daughter?"

Dukkai nodded. "I had a name for her, but it will never be spoken. I wonder if Apostle Lazarus is right, and there must be suffering on earth for anyone to be worthy of joy in Paradise."

"There is a church in Sarai, not far from the Foreigners' Quarter.

The priest will talk to you, if you like." He made the suggestion without expecting her to accept it.

"When we return to our territory, Apostle Lazarus may explain it to me, if he is still alive, and if I ever see him again," she said as if speaking of something in a distant time.

"I am sure he would be pleased to instruct you," said Ragoczy Franciscus as if speaking to child. "Are you planning to return to Kumul?"

She shook her head. "The smoke has not shown that as coming. I cannot tell when we shall go that way again."

Ragoczy Franciscus stopped himself for asking her more; instead he said, "This camp is very near the water, and much affected by damp. I have secured a house in the town, inside the walls. If you would like to stay there . . . ?"

"In a house? With walls of brick or stone?" She stared at him in disbelief. "No. My place is here, with my clan, whether there is dampness or dryness."

Ragoczy Franciscus regarded her with a combination of anguish and tenderness. "You will find a place to make your own, Dukkai."

"But not with houses," she declared. "Houses keep the Lords of the Earth from speaking, and they turn against those who will not listen, and shut out the gifts the Lords of the Earth provide. The smoke has revealed that the houses and walls of the Middle Kingdom so blocked the Lords of the Earth that the lands became barren and the sun was robbed of his strength. The Lord of the Snows has taken the place of the Lords of the Earth, and we must warm the land with blood of our enemies to drive back the Lord of the Snows."

The three boys were staring at her raptly, their expressions revealing how totally captivated they were by her pronouncements. Zumir spoke for the three of them when he said, "We will bring the offerings the Lords of the Earth demand. We will find our enemies and drain their blood." He poked Muksi in the side. "We will find our enemies and drain their blood—won't we?"

Muksi gulped and held up his small, bony fist. "And ponies. We will take the blood of their ponies and give it to the Lords of the Earth."

Dukkai motioned to the youngsters to be quiet. "I want to talk with Zangi-Ragozh. Leave us. And tell the rest not to disturb us." She pointed to the line of ponies a short distance away. "Imgalas could use your help. He is still weak from fever."

Zumir frowned down at his feet. "But we want to stay with you."

"Go help Imgalas," said Dukkai more firmly.

With every indication of sulking, the three boys ambled away, making it as plain as possible that they had no use for the task Dukkai had given them.

"Imgalas has had fever?" Ragoczy Franciscus asked.

"Yes. I have given him boiled willow-bark and prepared as much broth as we might make from our skinny goats, but he is slow to improve, and he is often taken with chills." She seemed almost herself again, but for the way in which her eyes flickered from object to object, rarely lingering on him for very long. "We have lost ponies, as well. Some have got too weak to work, wolves took four, and seven goats. Three were wounded in our last fight with the Uighurs. Four children have died since Baru Ksoka died, and two nameless infants beyond my own." She stifled a sob. "We gave three goats to the Lords of the Earth a few days ago, and it was enough to bring us safely here. Now we will have to find something else to offer them, so that we may travel on and find a new place to stay, at least as long as winter lasts."

"Winter is still several fortnights away," Ragoczy Franciscus reminded her.

"But it is coming. The days are shortening, and in five fortnights, the nights will be longer than the days, and the year will close in again." She stared into the distance, as if she could see winter lurking at the northern horizon. "I never thought I would see you again, except in the Sky World of Spirits."

There was a flurry of activity near the second line of tents, and then Gotsada came rushing toward Dukkai, his hands raised protectively as if to wrest Dukkai out of harm's way. "Stand back, foreigner!" he warned in bad Persian.

"Foreigner I am," said Ragoczy Franciscus cordially, "but not even you, Gotsada, can call me a stranger." He stood still while he watched Gotsada wrestle with his various impulses. "I am here to discover how you have fared since we parted company."

Gotsada was puzzled. "Zangi-Ragozh? How do you come to be here?"

"Much the same way you do," he answered. "I came along the trade routes." He saw Dukkai's cousin falter and went on, "You went north and west, I stayed to the westbound roads until the Kushan Road, and then I came north." He was aware of a dozen sets of eyes upon him from vantage points around the camp, and he could sense the wariness in their scrutiny.

"He has been here a short while, I gather," said Dukkai.

"That I have. My companion and I have come a very long way, and our animals need rest, as do we," said Ragoczy Franciscus. "I have hired a house in the town."

Dukkai pressed her lips together tightly, then made herself ask, "Do you still have your sovereign remedy?"

"That is one I must make more of; I have only a very small portion left—not enough to treat any serious malady or injury," said Ragoczy Franciscus. "I am surprised you remember it."

"A very odd liquid," Dukkai said. "I was curious about its properties, but—" She closed her mouth abruptly once more.

Gotsada came up to Ragoczy Franciscus, his manner pugnacious. "He has not brought us anything but trouble. Before he joined us, we had our own lands to travel, and our herds were thriving. Once he began to move with us, adversity came upon us relentlessly. And here he is again."

"It was the darkening of the sun that brought our hardships," Dukkai said with strong conviction. "Had Zangi-Ragozh not helped us, we would have suffered more."

"You may think that," said Gotsada. "But you know he is part of the misfortunes that have been heaped upon us."

"Those same misfortunes have touched all the world," said Ragoczy Franciscus at his most reasonable. "I have seen suffering everywhere—"

"You bring it with you," said Gotsada, his ire mounting. "Leave us alone, you interloper." There was a scuffle of activity at the far side of the camp, and a curse bellowed, then hushed. "You see? We know, if you do not, that this foreigner is trouble."

Dukkai made a gesture and rounded on her cousin. "If there is any danger in Zangi-Ragozh, I will know of it, and I can see no miasma around him. No," she said as Gotsada attempted to speak. "I want to hear nothing from you. You have already said too much."

"I only speak what our clan thinks." Saying this, he turned on his heel and stomped off.

Dukkai spoke when Gotsada was gone. "He had no cause. No one has accused you of bringing us trouble."

"At least not where you could hear them," said Ragoczy Franciscus.

Dukkai laughed bitterly. "There are too few of us to keep secrets. Gotsada is discontented and often surly, and usually he finds an explanation for himself in what others have done. The clan would receive you well, if you want to join us once more."

Ragoczy Franciscus shook his head. "No; Gotsada is probably right—perhaps I should not linger here." He looked about the camp, still aware of being under surveillance. "I have no desire to impose upon any of you, but when Ro-shei told me that there were Jou'an-Jou'an on this island, I had to come and see for myself." He took a step back toward his horse. "I am glad to see you are well. I am truly sorry that your infant died. I hope you will be spared further trials." He reverenced her before he turned to mount his blue roan.

"You must come again," Dukkai exclaimed, a wild note in her voice. "Promise me you will come again."

Ragoczy Franciscus paused, one foot in the metal foot-loop. "Is that what you want?"

"Oh, yes," she said a bit breathlessly. "If you will come again, I will be truly grateful."

"All right," he said as he mounted. "When shall I come?"

"Tomorrow night, or the night after. Come when the fires burn low. You remember which tent is mine?"

"The one with the basin in front of the door, for offerings," said Ragoczy Franciscus, taking the reins in hand and ready to depart.

She stared at him, an unspoken plea in her blue eyes. "Yes. Come in two nights. I will wait for you."

He nodded. "I will come." Then, with a tap of his heel, he swung the blue roan around and let her canter out of the Desert Cats camp.

Text of a letter from Vermakrides at Ecbatana in Persia to his father, Phocadoros Vermakrides, in Trebizond, carried by courier and delivered in December of 536.

To my father, the greetings of your most devoted son, from Ecbatana, where I will spend the winter. You may anticipate my arrival in the spring, in the Paschal Season, if God favors me.

You may question the wisdom of my decision to remain here for so long, but I have two reasons to do so: first is that I am recovering from an illness that has only recently begun to abate. I doubt that traveling in winter, given the severity of the winter of last year and the cold of the summer before, would help in the restoration of my health, and might bring about another onset of this sickness, which could prove more harrowing if it should strike while we are on the road in the more desolate stretches through the mountains. My second reason I will explain after I tell you what has befallen my companions.

This journey has been the most difficult of any I have undertaken, and not because of my illness, or the vicissitudes of weather. No, the reasons strike closer to home: I regret to inform you that my two cousins—Theocrates, living at Kokand, and Themistokles, who traveled with me—are dead, Theocrates from fever, Themistokles from the infection of a broken arm. I have seen them both buried with Christian ceremony and marked their graves with crosses so that no evil force can call them forth before Christ comes again. I have also lost three men from my caravan, one of whom was killed by marauding outlaws who attempted to steal our goods, and the other two from drinking polluted water. In addition, two mules died, and two camels. I have had to purchase ponies and donkeys to carry most of our goods home, and for one extraordinary find, I have also purchased a wagon.

I must tell you of this treasure: it is a bone wholly of rock, but such a bone as you have never seen! Stood on end, it reaches almost to my shoulder. It resembles a thighbone, but nothing like any other thigh, for it is massive. I am of the opinion it must be from a dragon, perhaps the very dragon that the Devil became when the Rebel Angels fell from Paradise. In any case, I have been exhibiting it as we go along, and I have made a tidy sum from those eager to see this prodigious relic. I secured it from a foreigner who was returning to the West from a long sojourn in China. He spoke of dreadful times in that faraway place, and many difficulties in his journey westward. He came upon this bone, he claimed, in a landslide and dug it out. Whatever the truth may be, I have seen nothing like this in my journey, and I believe I am most fortunate to have this astonishing object to display.

This town is much reduced in size from when I was last here. I was dumbfounded to see so many houses left empty, and the markets reduced to less than a third of their wonted size. I hope this does not continue, for I am certain that if it is allowed to go on much longer, the establishments along the Silk Road that contribute so much to our trade will wither as surely as the grass has done. For that reason, I am going to purchase a house here, so that when members of our family set out for the East, they will not be at the mercy of the whims of innkeepers and village tax collectors. I have already selected one of my companions to remain here until we relieve him. By having a house here, we will lessen the taxes that can be demanded of us, and it will let us be able to resupply our caravans on the same terms the locals do, which should shortly balance the price paid for the house.

I attended the gem-market two days ago and was able to secure amber, sapphires, and a number of lesser stones, all for less than I would expect to pay. This is another sign of the vicissitudes of the times—that the price of these jewels has lessened even while the difficulty of bringing them to the towns has increased. This speaks of a scarcity that has touched every trade route in Asia, and that may spread into the ports of the Mediterranean Sea as time goes by. I would urge you to have ships ready to sail as soon as the worst of the winter storms have passed, for I believe that we may find an advantage if we act swiftly, but if we falter, the returns on our efforts will drop as they have for so many others who have been laggard.

May this find you well, and all our family in good health. I ask you to inform my wife that I anticipate our reunion with joy, and the hope that she and our children have not endured any malady or loss of fortune in my absence. I ask you also to give three gold coins to our church for prayers for our safe return.

Basilios Vermakrides
Merchant of Trebizond

3

Fragrant smoke wreathed Dukkai's head, making her appear ghostly in the twilight, on this the night of the dark of the moon. She held up her arms and began a long invocation of the Lords of the Earth, with the remaining Desert Cats encircling her at the edge of the firelight. "Tonight, O Lords of the Earth, we give you blood, to strengthen you, and to ask you to spare our clan more losses. We are still hungry—all the world is hungry. We find death everywhere, from want, from war, from cold. Accidents have ravaged us. Raiders have come and taken our smoked meats. Three more of our numbers have taken ill with Marsh Fever, and they are in need of your succor, as are we all." She lapsed into chanting, the words unclear to Ragoczy Franciscus, who stood outside the cluster of the tents, his blue roan behind him.

Neitis Ksoka approached Dukkai carrying a bleating, half-grown goat, its legs trussed so it would not kick too much. He held out a long, straight knife, saying as he did, "For the honor and the power of the Lords of the Earth and the safety of our clan."

Dukkai took the kid from Neitis Ksoka and swung it over the fire three times, continuing her chanting as she did. Then she caught the young animal close against her and in a quick, graceful movement cut its throat but took great care not to sever its head or touch the spine, for such a clumsy act would sully the sacrifice. Satisfied with her work, she swung the kid once, twice, three times more to fling the gouting blood onto as many clan members as possible. She herself was soon soaked in it, and her face had become a gory mask. As the kid went limp in her grasp, she once again held it over the fire so that it was engulfed in smoke; she remained there, chanting and swinging the kid as the smoke roiled. "The offering is accepted," she announced, and staggered backward as if suddenly bereft of all her strength.

"I have it!" Neitis Ksoka cried, springing forward to keep the kid from falling into the fire—a dreadful omen if allowed to happen—while Demen Ksai rushed forward to steady Dukkai.

"Let the fire burn down of its own," said Dukkai weakly. "The blood isn't enough to put it out."

Neitis Ksoka carried the kid away from the fire to a wooden stand, where he cut off the head, putting it into a leather bag, then began to skin and gut the little goat. He sliced small bits of raw meat from the bones and offered this to his clan members, making sure everyone had a taste of this pledge between them and the Lords of the Earth.

From his vantage point beyond the tents, Ragoczy Franciscus watched, his thoughts on the sacrificial animal. He had witnessed such offerings from his own youth to the altars of Nineveh and Babylon, to the Temple of Imhotep. He had also seen the slaughter in the Roman arena during the Great Games and the maddened hunting of the Goths, and every time he felt sympathy for the animal giving its blood.

Standing on her own again, Dukkai approached the sacrificial fire once more, her arms extended. "Sweet is the life given to the Lords of the Earth," she intoned. "Let all of us give thanks for the bounty they provide." There was a thudding of a drum from the edge of the light; Zumir was pounding it with a leather-wrapped stick. "This, like the heart of the Earth, shows the Lords of the Earth our devotion."

The Desert Cats began to move with the drumbeat, a slow, sideways stamp then a shuffle, all gradually moving to the right around the fire. After a short while most of the clan had joined the dance, many of them chewing their bit of goat in time to their dance.

"I will read the smoke," Dukkai announced, and half-closed her eyes, rocking in place with the throb of the drum. She was soon caught up in the drumming and the fragrant smoke, and after a short while, she began again to speak. "Hear the Gods of the Smoke, Desert Cats: there is more traveling to come, always to the West," she murmured. "There are more raiders and greater dangers ahead, but we cannot remain here long, for the Lords of the Earth are weakened by so much water, and we will have more fever among us if we stay here more than two fortnights—long enough to repair our tents. The Lords of the Earth will desert us if we stay too long." She began to hum, a ululating, soft wail without melody. "There is no rest for us before we reach the high plains in the crook of the mountains. We will lose more of our own before we arrive there, and our herds and flocks will be more reduced. I will fall before the place is found. If we do not continue on, all of us must surely die, from hunger, from fever, from raiders, from the loss of the favor of the Lords of the Earth. So say the Gods of the Smoke, and the Lords of the Earth." She swayed in place, but soon stepped back, her hand to her head, her face pale beneath the blood drying on it.

The drumming stopped abruptly; the dancers broke their circle and moved away. Dukkai motioned to Neitis Ksoka, who doused the fire with the last of the kid's blood mixed with the powerful liquor of the clan, and a new billow of smoke arose. Dukkai watched it with intense concentration, all her attention fixed on the rising cloud. Finally she shook her head and stared at Neitis Ksoka. "Speak to me in the morning, and I will tell you, for what the Lords of the Earth imparted in your regard are for your ears alone," she said, her voice dropping to an exhausted whisper. She rubbed her face, smearing what damp blood there still was on her skin, and flaking off some of the dried. "The Lords of the Earth are pacified for now, but they will not be neglected."

"So far from our own territory, how can they reach us?" Zumir dared to ask.

Dukkai answered him, "There are veins in the earth, as there are in our bodies; we see them in the rivers, and in the roads. The veins in the earth are everywhere, including deep within the earth, where the Lords of the Earth reside, and the Lords of the Earth are the bodies of those veins. That is why the head must remain with the sacrifice, or the Lords of the Earth would be cut off from us. The mountains are their spine, and when they fall, all the world is fallen." She drew a long breath, going on in a sing-song, "When we travel the roads, we walk their bodies, the bodies of the Lords of the Earth. When we drink from the lakes and the rivers, we have their surface blood, which is clear when it is wholesome, because it is near the air. When the rain comes, it is the Lord of the Skies rewarding or punishing or guiding the Lords of the Earth. When snow blankets the roads and the rivers, it is so the Lords of the Earth may sink back into their deep veins and rest, just as the stars go beyond the God of the Sky to rest. All things need rest, Zumir, and if they tire too much, they die." She sank down onto her knees; no one moved to touch her.

Zumir suddenly abandoned his drum and fled.

Neitis Ksoka took the bag containing the head and held it out to Dukkai. "Where is this to be buried?"

"Under the enclosure for our ponies." She was barely audible, but purpose shone in her bright blue eyes. "See that you dig deep. A shallow scratch will insult the Lords of the Earth."

"Very good," said Neitis Ksoka, and went to fetch a shovel before he began his assigned task.

The rest of the Desert Cats milled about near the fire, a few of them still chewing on the raw goat meat. The air smelled of copper and smoke, and the people of the clan seemed uneasy. Finally one of the women—Ragoczy Franciscus recognized the first wife of Demen Ksai—approached Dukkai, bending down to her. "Can you stand?"

"In a moment," she said flatly. "The Lords of the Earth are near. I must attend to what they say." She bent over and put her ear to the ground.

Demen Ksai's wife looked about uneasily. "So we must prepare for what they may demand."

"They have had enough already," said Jekan Medassi, who now had to lean heavily on a stick when she walked and coughed much too often. "Isn't it enough that they have taken our best men and sickened our children?"

Ragoczy Franciscus heard this with apprehension, for he was aware of the sharply increased desperation among the people of the clan. He moved back a half dozen steps, pushing his horse with his shoulder. He could not help but remember the other times—in Babylon, in Nineveh, in his homeland, in the nameless wastes of the Persian mountains, in Byzantium—when he had seen chaos erupt out of prolonged privation, and this was building up to be another such instance.

"You there!" a voice challenged him from the path behind him.

Ragoczy Franciscus turned around, his hand on his short Byzantine dagger, the only weapon he had brought. "Yes?"

"Step forward where I can see you," the voice demanded.

Doing as he was ordered, Ragoczy Franciscus found a vantage place where the spill of the firelight brought his face into sharp relief. His composure was unruffled although all his senses were on the alert, and he moved very little. "I think you know me," he said in a calm voice.

Losdi Moksal came into view, his scarred cheek looking ferocious as the surface of the desert. He was not yet used to his position of family leadership, and so he blustered to make up for his unease.

"Zangi-Ragozh. You have no business being here. This is a sacred oc- casion."

"Dukkai sent for me," Ragoczy Franciscus said with diffidence. "I meant no disrespect."

"You stay here," Losdi Moksal told him. "I will speak with her di- rectly."

"Well and good," said Ragoczy Franciscus. "It is fitting that she should have the right to decide about my presence." He patted the neck of his blue roan. "My horse and I will wait here."

Losdi Moksal made an abrupt nod, then strode off toward the fire where Dukkai was still crouched on the ground, her head pressed to the earth. "Dukkai," he said as he neared her.

Very slowly she looked up, her eyes dazed. "What is it?"

"I found Zangi-Ragozh out there"—he gestured in the general direction—"and he said you asked him to come tonight. Surely you didn't want him here?"

She rubbed her eyes and rose. "Yes. I did. He has a great strength and I have need of it." She tottered a little as she got to her feet, but steadied herself; when she spoke again, her voice was clearer. "I am grateful that he came." As Losdi Moksal turned away, Dukkai peered into the deepening night. "Zangi-Ragozh?"

"I am here," he said, and raised his hand to provide movement for her to see.

"You did come," she said, stumbling toward him. "You, of all I have ever known, are one with the Lords of the Earth."

"I might not have said it that way, but I agree," he said, a sugges- tion of a smile in the depths of his eyes.

She held out her bloodstained hands to him. "I knew you would help me. You gave me more force than the sacrifice alone could pro- vide."

"Then I am richly rewarded," he said, touching her shoulder lightly; the blood spattered there was still slightly damp and tacky. He studied her face, seeing fatigue and a deeper exhaustion than he had perceived before. Trying not to be alarmed, he glanced toward the fire. "I do not recall you reading the smoke while I traveled with your clan."

She gave a short, wild laugh. "How could I read the smoke while I was pregnant?"

"Ah. I did not understand this." He waited for her to speak; when she only sighed, he said, "You read the smoke tonight."

"You must have seen," she said.

"I did, but why?" He let this suggestion hang between them for a short while.

She shook her head. "I have need of your strength."

"Do you? With all your clan around you, what difference can I make."

"You need nothing from me, you seek nothing from me, so your strength is untrammeled." She wiped her brow, leaving streaks in the dried blood. "I am too worn to be able to support them all."

Ragoczy Franciscus regarded her with recondite understanding. "Then I am honored you sent for me." He held out his hand to her. "You and your clan have had much to bear."

"That is the reason we have made this sacrifice," she said, adding in a whisper, "There is more misfortune to come."

"Is that what you saw?" he asked with concern, his dark eyes searching her face.

"No. Or that was not the whole of it." She finally laid her hand in his; her fingers were hot, feverish, and dry. "Some of our ponies are failing, and that worries me, given what I saw in the smoke. They must all be sound and strong for us to continue our journey."

"Certainly they must," he said, grasping the enormity of this new problem.

"It was bad enough when we were only hungry. But then we lost Baru Ksoka and the rest, and their ponies, and his flesh did not sustain us long. I thought we would regain our vigor here, but that has not been the case. Yet the Lords of the Earth led us here." She glowered at him. "You are of them, of the Lords of the Earth, but you are not one of us."

This last startled him. "No, I am not," he said, a shade too quickly.

"But you know the Lords of the Earth of old," she went on dreamily. "You have seen how they work in the world, and you know their power. And you will know what must be done so that our ponies will not fail. We must be able to hunt, and we cannot do it from goat-carts." She pulled away from him suddenly. "If you have anything to help our ponies thrive, I ask you to provide it, for the sake of the Lords of the Earth."

"I hope I can help," said Ragoczy Franciscus. "You have come so far and sustained so much, it is hardly conceivable that you should have to bear more."

She stared at him. "The Lords of the Earth are demanding. It is because the sun is so weak."

"But the sun is getting stronger; it is slight now, but over time, it will become apparent," he said.

"How can you say this?" She rounded on him, her temper in tatters. "The world is dark, the earth is parched, there is not enough grass, the seasons are too cold. Yet you say the sun is stronger. How is it possible?" She stood panting, her mouth square with fury, her hands hooked into claws. "Tell me, foreigner."

Ragoczy Franciscus waited a short moment until he was certain she would listen; then he said, "Those of my blood are, as you have said, allied with the earth. Because we are, we have a keen awareness of the sun, as well, just as the earth does. I know the sun is not as . . . as veiled as it was." He remained where he was, very still, the whole of his concentration upon her. "Believe this."

Her face went blank, and she sank to the ground. "Lords of the Earth," she muttered; she gestured to him to keep back as she stretched out on the ground, listening intently. Finally she raised her head. "There is a sickness in the earth. The Lords of the Earth are engulfed in a plague for lack of the sun." She pushed herself up on her elbow. "You know this. You must know this."

"All things in nature are bound to the sun, as all things in nature are drawn by the moon." He sought for some means to comfort her. "I have lived a long time, Dukkai, and I have seen hard years and bountiful years, wars, plagues, and calamities of all sorts, and the one thing I have learned from it all is that eventually it all comes to an end—the good times and the bad ones never last."

She began to chant, softly, her face turned away from him. Finally she got to her feet and brushed her hands on her long goat-hair robe. "You mean well," she said distantly. "I thank you for that. But these hard years will not be over next spring, or the next, or the next."

He saw she was caught at the edge of a trance once again. "Dukkai. Do not—"

She held up her hand. "If you have something for the ponies, I will thank you for it, and so will all the clan." Her eyes sharpened and she took a few uncertain steps toward him. "Is there anything you can provide to help our ponies?"

"I will have to see them for myself," said Ragoczy Franciscus. "Not tonight: tomorrow. I will come early in the morning, to see how they eat and how they are behaving."

Her countenance showed no emotion of any kind. "That is good of you, Zangi-Ragozh. I am grateful to you for doing so much." Her voice was flat, lending no credibility to her words.

"Will you join me in the morning?" he asked.

"I will have to. None of Imgalas' family will let you near the ponies without me." She tossed her head and without a backward glance walked away from him.

When he was sure she was not going to return, Ragoczy Franciscus swung up into the saddle and turned his horse toward the gates of Sarai. He watched the path ahead, but his thoughts were elsewhere: what had Dukkai experienced in reading the smoke that had so much aggrieved her that she was unable to speak of it directly? As he reached the gate, the guard who had let him out challenged him.

"It is three coppers to enter," he called out through the small, high opening in the gate.

Ragoczy Franciscus had expected something like this, and so he said, "I have that. Open the gates and you will be paid."

"Hand the coins in, and I will," the guard countered.

"Oh, no," said Ragoczy Franciscus, "You must admit me. Otherwise you will demand another three coppers, and another, and I will not get inside the walls."

The guard barked a laugh, and then the bolt scraped open and the gate swung back. "Enter," he said.

Ragoczy Franciscus rode into Sarai, handing three copper coins to the guard as he did. "Thank you," he said, and continued on toward the Foreigners' Quarter, where he made his way to his house. He found Rojeh waiting for him in the rear yard where the small paddock was. "You did not have to remain up," he said as he dismounted.

"I thought it might be wise," said Rojeh, lifting his oil-lamp high to allow its small puddle of light to spread as far as possible.

"In case I was delayed overlong?" Ragoczy Franciscus guessed as he led the blue roan toward the small stable. "Did you expect me to be detained?"

"That had occurred to me," said Rojeh.

"I thank you for your concern, old friend, but I was as safe as we ever were while we were with the Desert Cats. Dukkai is not apt to summon me and then turn that against me." He pulled the horse up at a grooming hook, secured the reins, then went to unfasten the girth.

"Are you certain of that?" Rojeh asked.

"Because she commands the clan's magic, do you mean, and might read some omen that would link bad cess with me?" Ragoczy Franciscus laid the girth on top of the saddle, swung them off the horse, and put them on the simple rack at his elbow. He reached for the box of brushes and began to groom the glossy neck.

"Dukkai may not be as trustworthy as you assume she is," Rojeh warned.

"Meaning you have reservations about her," said Ragoczy Franciscus. "I am not wholly . . . sanguine about her state of mind." He paused, then added, "I am going back to their camp in the morning."

"Why?" Rojeh asked.

"Dukkai is worried about their ponies. Something may be ailing them. She has asked me to help," he said, keeping on with his brushing.

Rojeh thought for a long moment. "Is there anything you can do?"

"I cannot tell, not until I have seen the ponies. They are hardy creatures, but they have had poor fodder for so long, it may have taken a toll on them." Ragoczy Franciscus was working over the rump now, and down past the stifle.

"Can you improve their food?" Rojeh inquired skeptically.

"How, when there is no good fodder to be had?" Ragoczy Franciscus sounded dubious as he began on the off-side of the blue roan.

"Do you think they will take your suggestions to heart?" Rojeh waited for Ragoczy Franciscus' answer.

He stood very still. "She sacrificed a goat—cut its throat."

"And that troubles you?" Rojeh knew it did, but kept his awareness to himself.

"It does," Ragoczy Franciscus admitted. "Most rites demand blood in some form, but I find I cannot—" He stopped talking.

"You find you cannot watch killing—even ritual killing—as you once did." Rojeh wondered if Ragoczy Franciscus would be angered by these observations and steeled himself for his employer's wrath.

Ragoczy Franciscus gave Rojeh's comments quiet attention and said levelly, "Perhaps you are right." He added nothing more as he combed the blue roan's mane, then changed the roan's bridle for the halter. "Is there any grain left?"

"Very little," said Rojeh. "I have tried to find more, but without success. If the Volgamen come soon, they may bring some—I understand they did the last time."

"Very good; I will speak with Emrach Sarai'af to arrange for purchasing priority; I am sure he will consent to letting us have a high position on his list if I give him a gold bar or two," said Ragoczy Franciscus, going to one of the barrels standing against the far wall. He scooped out a handful of the mixed grain and brought this back to the roan, holding it under the horse's nose, waiting while the soft tongue licked up the last of the treat. "We may need to open that cask of gold yet," he said as he wiped his palm on a rough cloth.

"To buy feed?" Rojeh sounded worried. "Or to pay bribes to the Master of Foreigners?"

"It is all part of keeping our animals sound," Ragoczy Franciscus pointed out.

"And Emrach Sarai'af knows it," Rojeh protested, adding sadly, "Since you will not do more than visit women in dreams, and that very rarely, you must depend on the animals."

"This is hardly the time to seek out a lover," said Ragoczy Franciscus.

"It may be just the time," said Rojeh. "That Constantinopolitan widow would be glad of someone to protect her and her children. She would not begrudge you what you require."

"Are you so certain of that?" Ragoczy Franciscus asked in dismay.

"She has spoken to me on three occasions. I know she would like to speak with you, but has no acceptable reason to do so." Rojeh folded his arms. "You will do nothing with Dukkai, will you?" He allowed no time for an answer. "Then think about Thetis Krisanthemenis. She may well prove to be precisely what you seek."

"I seek more than blood," Ragoczy Franciscus reminded him. "I seek acceptance. I seek the touch of intimacy. Do you think the widow is willing to provide that?"

"I cannot say," Rojeh replied. "And neither can you until you try."

*   *   *

Text of a dispatch from Hsai Wilung at Khotan to Ogulijen the Ax at An-Hsi; carried by personal courier and delivered five fortnights after it was written.

To the most estimable warlord Ogulijen the Ax, the greetings of Hsai Wilung, who, with his private company of soldiers, has arrived at Khotan at the foot of the Kunlun Range, according to the instructions issued by the great warlord Ogulijen, whose name is revered by all Mongols, as well as by all who hear of his deeds.

I am assuming that your scribe, Manun-Tsuj, will read this for you and send any answer you may wish to give us, your contracted men, in this far place where we have found so much despair and suffering that very little fighting was required to claim this place in your name. Not many others have succeeded in coming here since the Yellow Snows began because there have been avalanches on both sides of the town that have cut it off from the commerce that has kept it thriving for so many decades. We managed to make our way around the slides, and thus we have arrived here, according to your orders, and are now in possession of the town, although it is not much of a victory we have achieved.

We are low on food, and I am sending my men out in search of wandering clans who still have flocks and herds so that we may have food enough for the soldiers and those in the town willing to help us. I was able to lay my hands on a few pigs, but they were very thin and their meat had little savor, being tough and tasteless, and they did not last long. We must find a better source of food, or we will have to eat our horses, which is not to be thought of. There have been some fish in the streams, of course, and some birds as well, which will hold us until we can find more substantial food. It is unfortunate that there is so little grass growing here, for there is hardly any grazing possible, and that puts a fresh burden on us all, as food that we might well use must be given to our horses.

The town has had many disasters befall it, including Swine Fever and Gray Cough, and there has been almost no one here who is able to treat these diseases. We have seen houses left empty by the deaths of all the families who lived within them. Already I have lost two men to Wet Lungs, and I do not want to lose more. It has been a time of starvation, as you know, but also of sickness, and that is troubling my men, for they fear that the fevers are not ended and that they may succumb to them. I have ordered them all to drink strengthening herbs, if we can find them, and to eat grasshoppers if there are any to be caught. That may help to keep them well while we establish our control of the town and the region.

This being the time of year when there would usually be a harvest, the Fortnight of the White Dew, we have tried to find fields that we could reap, but in this place such farms as there are do not have a great deal of planting in good years, and in this year, not even the beans are doing well. I have sent men up the slopes of the mountains to see what they might find for us. They have killed mountain goats and sheep, and some spotted deer as well, but their hunting has exposed them to danger from other raiders, some of whom are of your people, judging by their clothes. In a good year, I would capture them and hold them for slaves, but since slaves must be fed if they are to work, my men have wanted to kill them instead.

There has been some difficulty regarding the women in the town. My men, being men, are eager to have women, but very few of the women here are willing to give themselves to them, so I must condone their selecting the women they want and permitting them to force the women into concubinage. I regret that we could come to no other arrangement with the people of the town, and I know they will complain of it to you when you finally come here, but I have no other solution to propose, and the men cannot be expected to go without the solace of female flesh, as you know. I have established a heavy fine for any murder committed on an unwilling woman, and that appears to have lessened the deaths that were occurring too often when we first entered the town.

I have worked to establish a customs center to tax the caravans that must eventually return to this place. I have talked with the two remaining leaders of the town to discover how much they had charged in the past, and I have increased those rates by half again as much, a quarter of which will go to repairing and securing the town and paying my men, the rest of which will be yours. According to the people here, the last caravan coming through this town was here more than three fortnights ago, when summer—such as it was—was still present. Now that autumn is beginning, I have been told that it is unlikely that we will see any more merchants before spring, and that is not what you had hoped for. If there had been no avalanche on the

Chanchi-Lah Pass, men might come from the Land of Snows, but with the pass blocked, we cannot expect those traders, either. In the spring, I will send part of my company to help clear the pass if I deem it safe enough to do, or if you order us to do it.

There may be more trouble coming from the wandering peoples of Takla Makan, for some of them are banding together for safety, and they are all searching for pastures for their flocks and herds. I believe that in time we will need more than this company if we are to hold on to this town. I ask you to consider sending us another company of fighting men—they needn't be Chinese like us, but it would make it easier if they were—to help man the town, for the spring will surely bring more trouble to us all.

In all duty and supreme respect, and with thanks for the nine bars of gold to guarantee the payment of me and my men, I pledge our continuing loyalty.

Hsai Wilung
(his chop)

4

Rain seethed down on Sarai, washing the fine sand out of the air and leaving the streets streaked with grit that made the paving stones slippery; the first storm of winter had arrived with exuberant ferocity. The wind rioted among the buildings, sending unlatched shutters and loose roofing planks flying; with insistent, cacophonous fingers, it tugged at the oiled-parchment windows, snatching a few from the security of their frames and sending them careening. Anyone venturing out of doors was shoved and buffeted along while being drenched, which accounted for the bedraggled appearance Thetis Krisanthemenis presented when she came to Ragoczy Franciscus' hired house at the height of the storm. She had attempted to protect herself with a vast woolen talaris with only a single, small tablion inserted in the front, but it was soaked through, her dark-blond hair dripping steadily, serving to give her an appearance of waiflike hopelessness.

She lowered her head apologetically, preparing to explain her errand, and struggled to find the words she needed to engage the occupant's sympathy. Her shivering was completely authentic, although her demeanor was a bit forced.

Rojeh came to the door to answer her third pull on the bell. "Neighbor Krisanthemenis," he exclaimed in Byzantine Greek. "What is so urgent that you come out in such weather?"

"I fear I come to ask a favor." She stepped into the shelter of the inner court, under the broad eaves; she twisted the long cuff of the talaris' sleeve, then spoke in a rush. "Actually, it's more than that: I have to ask for your help. It is not something I can take to the Master of Foreigners myself, at least not now." She faltered, then went gamely on, "You see, a portion of my roof has been blown away by this storm, and I and my children are in need of shelter."

"What a terrible thing," said Rojeh sympathetically. "Come in, and tell me what my master and I may do."

"We cannot stay in our house, not with half the rooms ruined, and our belongings." She took a deep breath. "We have to leave the house, and we must have a safe place to go." She said this last more bluntly than she had intended. "I don't mean to be brusque, but I am nearly beside myself with worry. I am afraid we are in a most precarious situation: with my husband dead, there is very little I can do to tend to the house without Emrach Sarai'af's approval, and he is not going to extend himself while the storm is blowing. But my need is present—it is immediate—and I cannot pretend that the loss of the roof is only an inconvenience." She shook her head as if suddenly bereft of strength. "We can work, do household chores, if your master requires it."

"You may discuss that with him, when you know more about what you may do for your home," said Rojeh, certain that Ragoczy Franciscus would never make servants of this woman or her children.

"I wish I could be permitted to make my own arrangements for the house, as my husband would do if he were still alive." She pressed her lips together, then went on, "It is much the same for widows in Constantinople, but at least there my brother could supervise our needs."

"We are not your relatives," Rojeh pointed out. "Emrach might not permit us to do more than shelter you until your house is sound."

Thetis flung up her hand. "For now, that is enough."

Rojeh stared at the raging rain and the flotsam on the wind and listened to the hiss and howl. "Then, if it suits you, I will send our houseman and our man-of-all-work to bring your children and such goods as you need into this house," he said, making up his mind.

"And your master? What will he say?" Thetis glanced about uneasily, as if she expected to be disappointed.

"He is with the Jou'an-Jou'an just now and will likely remain there until the rain has passed," said Rojeh, knowing what agony running water could be to Ragoczy Franciscus; he hoped his master would spend the storm in that stupor that masqueraded for sleep, safe in one of the Desert Cats' tents.

"He is out of the town?" Thetis seemed shocked.

"Yes. The clan he is visiting has had many troubles with their ponies, and he has gone to help them as much he can." His austere features revealed little, but his faded-blue eyes were worried. "If you will come into the house?"

She sneezed. "Oh. Yes. Thank you."

He indicated the door to the reception room. "You will find an upholstered bench and a table. The lamps are already burning. I will have some mint tea sent in to you." Fortunately, mint was hardy enough to still be available, and Dasur Shiraz'af, the Persian cook, used it frequently in the five-person household.

She looked startled. "Mint tea? Hot tea, with honey? Yes, if you would."

"I will instruct the cook," said Rojeh, and left Thetis in the reception room. He decided he would ask Aethalric, the houseman, to build up a fire for her—in those wet clothes she could easily become chilled, and the chill could bring aches and sickness.

Both the Persian and the Goth were in the kitchen, huddled in front of the great, open hearth where a single lamb's carcass turned on a huge spit intended for oxen, and both men looked about guiltily as they heard Rojeh enter the echoing chamber. Dasur scrambled to his feet and reached for another log, thrusting it into the burning stack in the huge fireplace.

"I will begin the afternoon meal shortly," Dasur said as if he had only just become aware of Rojeh.

"I have another task for you," said Rojeh calmly. "For both of you, and for Chtavo, as well."

"He's in the stables, cleaning tack," said Aethalric.

"Then he won't mind having to stop awhile; the stable is drafty as a tree, and as damp as sitting under one," said Rojeh. "You, Aethalric, are to build up the fire in the reception room, where you will find our neighbor, and then you and Chtavo are to take the covered handcart and go to her house. You are to gather such items as clothing and personal possessions as they might need and bring those things, and her children, to this house. Take blankets of oiled muslin with you, to protect you from the storm." He paid no attention to the incredulous stares of the two men, but went on, "Dasur, if you will make a good portion of mint tea with honey, and provide whatever we have in the way of breads for the widow and her children?"

Aethalric stared in astonishment. "Why should we have those Byzantines with us?"

"Because, as I understand it, their house is damaged, and they are in need of a place to stay while it is repaired. You cannot expect her to remain there with the storm still at full cry, not if there is no shelter to be had." Rojeh gave both men a hard glance. "Not that it is for you to question such a decision."

"It may not be," said Dasur, "but it is not the usual thing."

"This storm is not the usual thing, either, from what I have heard," Rojeh observed. "Nothing in the last"—he calculated the length of time since he and Ragoczy Franciscus had left Yang-Chau—"nearly two years has been."

"You may think this excuses what you do, but it may not," Aethalric warned. "It is dangerous to take strangers into the house."

Rojeh regarded him in silence, then said, "My master brought you into the household, and you both are strangers."

"The law provides that you cannot employ natives of Sarai," said Dasur.

"Even they are strangers to Ragoczy Franciscus and me," Rojeh observed. "The times have made demands on all of us—this is no exception."

Dasur added his own note of caution: "Taking in a widow and her children, there will be talk."

"Particularly about the odd habits of foreigners." This remark of Rojeh's got the men's attention; Dasur went to fill a pot from the water barrel, and Aethalric started for the door. "Let me know when you and Chtavo are back."

"All you will have to do is listen; children are never quiet, and you haven't special accommodations for them," replied Aethalric as he went out into the gushing rain toward the shed containing the household supply of wood. He came back with five cut logs in his embrace, two of which he shoved at Dasur before he headed up the stairs toward the reception room.

"Mint tea with honey?" Dasur asked Rojeh as he hung the pot of water on a hook and pushed it over the fire. "Enough for the women and her children?"

"Yes. There are three still living, as I understand it," said Rojeh. "I have seen the boy walking with his mother. He's about ten or eleven, by the look of him."

"Oh, yes," said Dasur. "He is a well-mannered youth, reserved and trying to be grown-up, now his father is dead." He retrieved a large, metal, spouted pot from the utensil shelf, set it on the trestle table in the center of the room, then went to his spice chest to take out a handful of dried mint leaves; these he put into the pot, then went to the pantry to get the honeycomb. As he brought back the sticky box containing it, he said to Rojeh, his face showing disapproval, "Take care that the widow does not take greater advantage of your hospitality." He acknowledged Rojeh's nod as he set about pouring off a generous portion of honey into the spouted pot. "When it is ready, I will bring it. A pity we have no dried figs or dates, but no one has had any for well over a year."

"They will probably return, in time," said Rojeh, and went to the rear door to secure it against the blustering wind.

"May you prove right," said Dasur as he returned to the pantry. "I haven't much in the way of breads, just a few sesame cakes I made this morning, with a bit of chopped egg to garnish them. And I have an oil-loaf with a few raisins. I can cut some of that, if you think it will do."

"Both sound adequate." Rojeh wanted to add that at other times such spartan fare would seem the height of inhospitality, but in these days, this bordered on lavish. "Put them on a tray and bring them up when the tea is ready."

"I will," said Dasur, going to choose a platter for the food and cups for the tea.

Rojeh returned to the reception room and found Thetis huddled next to the fire, her talaris tented about her to make the most of the heat from the blazing logs. "I could get a blanket for you, if you like," he said as he came a few steps into the room.

She managed not to jump, although she was startled. "I am sorry," she said, moving back from the fire. "Your man brought more wood, and I was making the most of it. The warmth is so . . ."

"You needn't move on my account; take all the advantage you can of the fire," said Rojeh, choosing a chair some distance from the hearth for his seat. "I've sent two servants to fetch your children and your clothes from your house. When they arrive, you may have this room to yourselves until chambers may be prepared for you."

"I have two servants," said Thetis. She scowled briefly. "When my husband was alive, we had two more, but they were provided manumission in his Will." Her voice became more peevish. "In such times as these, you'd think we could offer work to one of those many unfortunates who are native to this town, just so they have lodging and food, but the Master of Foreigners still refuses to allow it."

"It is their tradition," said Rojeh. "Tell me about your servants?"

"Sinu is a Hun; she maintains the house and does our cooking. All other work is done by Herakles, whom my husband brought with him from Constantinople. He is getting on now and suffers from stiffness, but I promised Eleutherios that I would keep him with us as long as he wished to remain." She did her best to produce a brave smile, but she could not sustain it, and so she looked away from Rojeh. "It is bad enough I have to ask shelter for me and my children. It is inexcusable to ask for my servants as well."

"Servants are as much *famiglia* as any child," said Rojeh, deliberately using the old Roman word for household. "If your Sinu is willing to sleep in the same room with your daughters, there should be no trouble."

Thetis looked about in confusion. "I suppose . . . I think my girls would agree."

"Very good. In a household such as this one, where only males have been permitted, keeping females together will lessen any comments that might be to your detriment." Rojeh stopped as something clattered into the courtyard. "I had better see what that was," he said, rising and reverencing Thetis.

"I hope I have caused you no difficulty with your employer," she said as if suddenly recalling her manners.

"You and your children, and your servants, have nothing to fear," said Rojeh, and left her to the heat of the fire while he went out to check on the small courtyard. A wooden plank with a long break in the grain lay by the gate to the stable-yard. Rojeh picked it up and moved it under the eaves; he squinted up at the sky, noticing that the afternoon was growing darker. He made a quick calculation and decided that it was growing late in the afternoon, which meant to him that the storm might last into the night. His thoughts turned to Ragoczy Franciscus with the Desert Cats, and his concern increased, for with such heavy rain, the low-lying islands could well be swamped, which would be horribly debilitating to the vampire. A rattle of wheels on paving stones barely penetrated the roar of the storm, but it alerted Rojeh to the arrival of Aethalric and Chtavo with Thetis' children and servants, and he went to admit them to the courtyard, handing the Goth and the Volgaman a copper coin each for their service.

Pentefilia, the older daughter, had disdained riding in the cart; she walked ahead of the sodden household, her talaris gathered around her like a shroud; if she was aware of the storm, she was determined to ignore it. She hardly glanced at Rojeh as they started toward the main door of the house, as if acknowledging him would end what little dignity she had left. Aristion, her brother, came down from the cart with alacrity, a small box of his possessions clutched to his chest, his face set with concentration as he looked around him. He squinted anxiously toward the roof, as if to be certain it was intact. Next the Hunnic servant Sinu climbed down from the covered interior of the cart, then turned to lift out Hrisoula, the youngest child, who was doing her best not to cry; she burrowed her head into Sinu's shoulder, muffling her whimpers with her fist, allowing the squat-bodied Hun to protect her with a flap of her rough-woven cloak. Herakles brought up the rear, his rolling gait revealing the pain of a stiff hip.

"I am taking the cart to the stable," said Chtavo to Rojeh. "I'll bring in their cases later."

"Just so they have them tonight," said Rojeh, knowing the Volgaman rarely bothered with the convenience of others. "I will tell you which rooms they are assigned when you come in for your evening meal."

Chtavo shrugged. "As you like." He hefted the double handles of the cart and lugged it away.

Dasur was just climbing the steps from the kitchen as Rojeh came into the vestibule to direct the new arrivals to the reception room. After Dasur set his burden down on the table there, he reached for the spouted pot, saying, "Mint tea with honey," before he selected a cup and poured the steaming liquid into it. "I have fare for your servants in the kitchen."

Thetis had risen to greet her children, but now she regarded Dasur with anticipation. "This is wonderful. So much better than the millet-cakes we have been eating of late." She looked toward Rojeh. "Will your master mind that you have given us so much?"

"If he does, it will be most unlike him," Rojeh said.

Thetis took up her cup of tea, letting the heat warm her hands. "This smells wonderful," she said to Rojeh.

"Then it is Dasur you should thank. All I did was tell him to prepare it." He nodded toward the Persian cook.

Dasur was busy filling cups for the three children, but he stopped his efforts to say, "I am glad it pleases you."

"And the cakes look delicious," Thetis added, this time speaking directly to Dasur, who nodded, suddenly speechless, and went back to pouring tea.

As she carried Hrisoula into the reception room, Sinu was embarrassed to have intruded so far into the house. She muttered something to Thetis as she set the frightened little girl down on the upholstered bench, then said to Dasur, "Where shall I go?"

"To the kitchen," said Dasur. "Wait a moment and I'll show you the way." He took a last look around the room, and satisfied with what he had done, he spoke to Rojeh. "I will feed these two with the rest of us." His gesture took in both Sinu and Herakles.

"Very good," said Rojeh. "I will call upon you later, but for now, give yourself a little rest."

Dasur motioned to Herakles and Sinu to follow him; they trooped off toward the lower level of the house and the kitchen.

The two older children had taken cups of tea and wedges of cakes and were settling down to eat, Pentefilia near the fireplace, Aristion near the central table. Only Hrisoula remained huddled where Sinu had put her, her eyes enormous, her face pale; Rojeh went to the youngest child and sat down at the other end of the bench. "Don't you like oil-loaf? I could bring you a bit of it, if you like."

Hrisoula stared at him in silence, then slowly nodded her head once.

In response to this sign, Rojeh got up and went to the table and broke off a small portion of oil-loaf, then picked up the last unclaimed cup of tea. "Here you are," he said, offering the child the oil-loaf. "And some tea to wash it down." He went back to his place at the far end of the bench. "Storms like this don't happen very often." He had intended this to reassure Hrisoula, but it was Pentefilia who spoke.

"I know. I'm fourteen, and I can't remember anything like this for as long as I've been alive." She took a large, defiant bite of her wedge of sesame-cake.

"Things like this didn't happen when my father was alive. There was no cold, there was enough food, and the town was busy," said Aristion suddenly. He had got up and gone to sit beside his mother, his full attention on the fire as he picked at his food.

"It must surely seem so," Rojeh agreed. He looked at the simple food on the table. "In the past, my master would have been ashamed to have so little to offer you; he has long made a habit of having the best fare for his guests."

"I am sure this is the best he has," said Thetis, shooting a warning glance at her children.

"It's better than what we've been eating," Pentefilia muttered.

"Pentefilia. Mind your tongue." Thetis turned to Rojeh. "You said your master went to the Jou'an-Jou'an camp?" she asked, then chewed a little of the oil-loaf.

"Yes. When we reached the Silk Road last year, we covered some of the distance with that clan. Since chance had brought us together again, my master is inclined to do his utmost to help these people. They have borne much travail—their leader was killed in a fall, along with his most senior men. The clan has been near starvation, and there has been illness among their numbers."

"What kind of thing does he do?" Pentefilia asked, an imperious tilt to her chin.

"Pentefilia!" her mother admonished her more sharply than before.

"It's all right," said Rojeh. He gazed at Thetis' oldest child, speaking calmly and with no indication of disrespect for her inquiry. "My master has some skill with medicaments. The Jou'an-Jou'an have their own traditional treatments, but it seems these have failed. So my master has gone to see if he has any information gleaned in his travels that might serve to help the Desert Cats—for so the clan is called—treat their ponies."

Pentefilia considered this and nodded slowly. "He is not above working in the rain and mud. That says he has humility. Patriarch Stavros says we all must strive for humility."

"He is the Patriarch of the Most Holy Dormition," Thetis explained. "He advises the other two Byzantine churches here." She colored slightly. "He is truly a godly man. I asked him if we might have shelter at the Most Holy Dormition, before I came here. Patriarch Stavros said he would have to refuse me because my husband is dead and I have no brother or father to vouch for me and my family, and Aristion is still too young to serve in that capacity." She reached out and put her hand on her son's head; Aristion winced. "So you see, I didn't simply fling myself on you without thought."

"It would be all right if you had," said Rojeh.

"I will have to tell Patriarch Stavros where we are. I don't think he will entirely approve, particularly since you and your employer are not Orthodox Christians." This last made her uncomfortable to admit, and as soon as she had spoken, she turned away from him, ostensibly to straighten Aristion's paragaudion, but in fact to avoid Rojeh's scrutiny.

"It may be best to wait until the storm is over." He put his hand on the side of the spouted pot. "The tea is still warm. Shall I pour you another cup?"

Flustered, she hesitated, then extended the cup. "I would like that."

As he poured the tea, Rojeh said, "I gather you have had a difficult time since you were widowed."

She shrugged impatiently. "I have sent word to my brother, so that he will send for us, but conditions have been so harsh that I begin to fear that my message may not have arrived."

"It may be a wise precaution to send a second," said Rojeh, and began to explain the allocation of private rooms he had decided upon for their use. By the time Sinu reappeared with Aethalric to escort them to the upper floor, the tea was gone and all that was left of the oil-loaf and sesame cake were crumbs. Rojeh rose and reverenced Thetis. "You may go to settle yourselves into your quarters. Aethalric, see that there are lamps in their rooms and provide them any bedding they may lack."

"Of course," said Aethalric, as if Ragoczy Franciscus entertained guests every day. "If you will allow me to show you the way?" he offered, and led the way toward the steep, narrow stairs.

Rojeh went off to the pantry to determine how much more food he would need while Thetis, her children, and her servants were in the household. He found the cook finishing the last of his cleaning up following the evening meal. "Tomorrow, if the storm is over, I want you to go to the butcher and secure meat for all the household for four days."

Dasur laughed. "That will be a very costly purchase."

"I realize that. I have sixteen silver pieces for you to spend." He held up the small leather purse.

"A goodly amount," said Dasur, recovering from his surprise.

"At least the butcher has some meat to sell," said Rojeh. "There are many places—so I hear—where no sum could buy meat for there is none to be had."

"True enough," said Dasur, going somber. "All right. Sixteen pieces of silver for meat." He thought about the amount. "You know, for a few pieces more, you could buy a boat and fish."

"If my employer were planning to remain here, he might want to do that," said Rojeh, privately amused. "But the Master of Foreigners has said he will extend our residency only once more, for three months, and then we must go on."

"That's unfortunate, for all of us," said Dasur.

"He will not leave you wholly without means," said Rojeh.

"How can you be sure of that?" Dasur asked sharply.

"Because he has never done so in the past," said Rojeh, and left Dasur to his duties.

Text of a letter from Eimonthoris of Hydros, Captain of the merchant-ship *Demeter* at Trebizond to Lucius Valentius Gnaeo at Brundisium; carried by the Byzantine courier ship *Archangel Rafael* and delivered in January of 537.

Greetings to Lucius Valentius Gnaeo, factor at Brundisium, from Eimonthoris of Hydros, now, by Grace of God, lying in port at Trebizond. I have news that may make up for the delay in my sailing from this place, which I think now must have been the Will of God, for the one extra day we had to wait for repair of the rudder was enough to spare us the perils of the processions of wind and rain that have been visited upon us.

Once the rain and wind began, I could not set out, and we have had three weeks of tempests. I am grateful to Saint Luke and Saint Spyridion for preserving us, for if we had sailed when we intended, surely we would have been lost. During this time of forced idleness, I have gone amongst the various warehouses and stalls of other merchants, and I believe I may have hit upon an opportunity that you will want to seize; with that in mind, I am giving you the first opportunity to bid on what I have purchased from the heirs of a Silk Road merchant who succumbed to Marsh Fever a month ago, shortly after his return from a three-year journey. Their rejoicing upon his triumphant return was soon turned to lamentation, for he became ill and died within a month of his reaching Trebizond. The family of Vermakrides has allowed me to purchase what must surely be the strangest item of trade I have ever seen. It has been displayed here, and for a modest charge, the people of the town could view it.

I must tell you I have never seen the like of this item, not in all my travels. Nothing out of Africa can equal it but the tusks of elephants, and this is more remarkable than any of those: it is a huge bone, made of stone, and unlike anything I have found before. I am told Vermakrides had it from a merchant from Cathay, and that it was reputed to come from the body of a dragon, for what other creature could have a skeleton of stone? The bone is easily recognized as belonging to a leg that was longer than a man is tall, for this bone, stood on end, reaches almost to my shoulder, and it is from the thigh of the monster. It provides much occasion for speculation, as well as being a reminder that Creation has taken many forms.

The supply of silk has diminished sadly, since fewer caravans are setting out from the distant East. There is so little food to be found along the way that most merchants are unwilling to take the risk of venturing into the wastes of the Silk Road. One report spoke of a walled town where more than half the inhabitants starved, and where foreigners were slaughtered for meals. Such desperation is present in this region, and if it is so widespread as these accounts would suggest, it is not surprising that no one is willing to undertake the hazards of

*such journeys. I have little more to offer you than this dragon bone,
but I believe it may prove to be the most valuable thing I have ever encountered.*

*I await your answer when I come to Brundisium. Pray that God
gives us a safe passage and that no further harm comes to me or my
crew.*

Eimonthoris of Hydros
Captain of the Demeter

On the fifteenth day after the Autumnal Equinox, at Trebizond

5

"Another storm," Pentefilia said in obvious disgust as she turned away
from the shuttered window; it was chilly in the reception room in
spite of the fire, and the rising whine of wind served only to chafe at
the nerves of the three children, who had been confined to the house
for the whole day.

"Not so bad as the last one; it is dying down, the Mercy of God
be thanked," said Thetis, looking up from her sewing. She was nursing the last of a cold, and although she was relieved that it had become nothing worse, she had reached the peevish stage, where small
annoyances nettled her. A cup of honey with wine and ginger stood
at her elbow, still steaming, and she was trying to drink it all while it
was still hot. Dutifully she picked it up now and drank a third of the
contents, then said, "I'm sorry you've had to stay in so much."

"What is *wrong* with God, doing this to us?" Pentefilia burst out.
"It's boring, and it doesn't stop, even though the Patriarch is coming."

Thetis raised her hand. "Don't say such things, Pentefilia. People
might not understand." She looked about the room as if she expected
to discover eavesdroppers. "God has His reasons, as the Patriarch has
said."

"God may be seeking our deaths, and everyone's," muttered
Aristion.

Pentefilia folded her arms. "I wish you hadn't asked the Patriarch to come here: if he does, all he'll do is tell us that we have to pray and suffer, suffer and pray."

"Don't say that," Thetis warned. "It is an honor when the Patriarch accepts an invitation to visit."

"He isn't here yet," Pentefilia said as if preparing to do battle on the point.

"Rojeh said I could go help in the stable," said Aristion, breaking in to stop the argument. "I don't have to stay here with you."

Ordinarily Thetis would have been glad of a reason to let the fretful boy go, but now she pursed her lips in displeasure. "He has said nothing of it to me, and the Patriarch is coming."

"I want to go to the stable," Aristion announced in a dangerous tone.

"Keep this up and you'll go to your room," said Thetis, and turned as she saw Sinu in the doorway. "Oh, thank goodness. Please tell me you have a visitor to announce."

"Patriarch Stavros has come," said the Hunnic woman. "Shall I tell him you will receive him?"

"Is Ragoczy Franciscus in the house?" Thetis asked suddenly; as host, he would be likely to want to receive this newcomer.

"He is in his study, or so Rojeh says, and would dislike being disturbed," said Sinu.

"Then I suppose the welcome is mine?" Thetis said uncertainly; she was not used to the degree of liberty her host allowed her, and she took a long moment to think what the Patriarch would prefer.

"If he does not see you now, he will probably come again," said Pentefilia, surprising her mother by this sign of her attention.

"Certainly I shall, then," Thetis said, smoothing the front of her talaris and touching her hair. "Ask him to enter." As soon as Sinu left, she fixed her children with quelling gazes. "Remember what I told you: I want you all to conduct yourselves properly for the Patriarch."

"Oh, Mother," said Pentefilia with an impatient sigh.

"See you keep your place there," Thetis warned. "I want nothing to upset the Patriarch." She settled herself on the upholstered bench and tried to look at ease as she heard the approach of Sinu with Patriarch Stavros.

Hrisoula gave a little shriek as the Patriarch came into the reception room; her mother quelled any greater outburst with a single glance.

The Patriarch was tall and bearded, in a paragaudion of dark dull-blue damask edged in bands of rusty red embroidered with Orthodox crosses. His hair was steel gray and his face was dominated by a large, hooked nose and prominent, fleshy ears. He paused in the doorway and made a general blessing on the occupants of the room at the same time subjecting the chamber to intense, critical scrutiny. "No iconostasis," he said at last. "It is bad enough that you are widowed without a brother or a father to care for you, but that you should have to be in the household of unbelievers in so perilous a time—no wonder you have need of my instruction."

"No, there is no iconostasis," said Thetis uneasily. "You are correct: Ragoczy Franciscus is not one of our faith. But he is a man of good conduct." She rose so that she could kneel for his blessing. "He has permitted me to have an iconostasis in my own chamber, and he has provided a covered chariot to carry me to services."

Patriarch Stavros sniffed. "Concessions, at least, which are to his credit. There are those in Sarai who would not be so willing to—" He frowned at a place in the empty air about an arm's length in front of him. "It is a pity that you had to appeal to him for his charity."

This annoyed Thetis, who looked up at the Patriarch with an air of barely concealed indignation. "If you had taken us in, it would not have been necessary for us to come to this house at all. Emrach Sarai'af would not let us take rooms at an inn, and none of our other neighbors would welcome us. What were we to do? live in a hut?" She lowered her head to lessen the impact of her defiance. "It is most fortunate that Ragoczy Franciscus is willing to let us stay here."

"Has he said why he has done this?" the Patriarch inquired.

"Not directly, nor have I inquired too closely, for as a guest it would ill become me to do so." She stared directly at the Patriarch as if anticipating an argument. "He has said that he is willing to have us here until our house is repaired."

"A very generous act. One has to wonder why he, a stranger and not a Christian, would do this?" His bushy eyebrow raised, punctuating his doubts.

"He has done what we most need," said Thetis, getting to her feet and returning to her place on the bench. "If you would like to rest awhile, Patriarch?" She noticed her children were unabashedly staring at her, and color mounted in her face.

"I will do so," he said grandly, and chose a fine wooden chair from Edessa, the largest in the room. "Have you been treated well?"

"As you see, we are shown the same courtesy as any guest would receive here, and without any let or hindrance in our hospitality." She drank the last of her hot, honied wine.

"Yes, but it is also undesirable that a widow like you should remain in the house of an unmarried man who is no blood relation," said the Patriarch. "If my wife were still alive, I would have been able to receive you, but as it is, no one would countenance having you in my compound."

Aethalric appeared in the doorway and reverenced the Patriarch. "I have been asked what refreshment you might want, Patriarch." He made no apology for interrupting, but his manner was servile enough to make his arrival acceptable.

"Does your master make this offer?" Patriarch Stavros asked.

"He does," said Aethalric, as if the order was a specific one and not a general household policy.

"Then, if you have some good goat cheese and wine, I have my cup with me, and my knife." He waved Aethalric away. "Has your host shown inappropriate interests in your children?"

This ungracious question ruffled Thetis' temper, and she rose to Ragoczy Franciscus' defense. "No, he has done nothing of the sort. Why do you persist in thinking the worst of him because he is not a Christian! May not a man do good in the world for more than reasons of faith?"

The Patriarch studied her for a long moment, then said, "It is commendable that you are grateful, but you do not need to be wholly suborned by him. It is your duty to bring him to the worship of Christ and redemption." He laced his long, thick fingers together over his paunch; his expression was stern and his voice rumbled like wooden wheels on cobblestones. "Barring conversion, you have a grave obligation, woman, to uphold the virtue of this household. If you fail to do so, there may be serious consequences that I cannot mitigate."

"If you think I would make myself a harlot in order to keep my family from penury, you have no cognizance of how I have lived, or how I was instructed by my mother. Do you think I came here expecting to make myself a whore?" This blunt word so shocked those in the room that the resulting silence lasted for several heart-beats. Then Thetis said, "I do not mean to offend you, Patriarch, but what you have said has cast aspersions on my honor and I cannot per-mit such allegations to go unchallenged."

"I understand that," the Patriarch said, his brow beetled. "It is wor-thy in you that you have such a high regard for your reputation. For that reason alone I would recommend that you find another dwelling to oc-cupy as soon as possible. I will put in a word on your behalf with the Master of Foreigners, and that should incline him to aid you."

"How kind of you," she said, an edge in her humility that took the subservience from her words.

"It should ease your mind to know that I will defend you against any gossip or accusations," Patriarch Stavros said magnanimously.

Thetis had recovered herself enough to say, "Yes, I would appre-ciate your efforts to put an end to any defamation my character may suffer because of this current difficulty."

"If your husband had not been so devout, there would be less pe-rusal as to what you experience, and fewer of the congregation would see your present situation in such a troublesome light. But as Eleuthe-rios Panayiotos was as devoted as any in the congregation, you and his children are held to standards he established, and for that reason even the appearance of a lapse would seem an error of vast significance. You must not allow your husband's memory to be tarnished by your actions, Thetis." He lifted his hand and sketched a blessing in her direction. "And, in these sad days, you must always be ready to appear before the Throne of God to answer for your life."

"I will keep all you say in mind," Thetis mumbled, and tried to come up with an excuse to send her children out of the room.

"God is often revealed in privation and the offering we make in the name of Christ," said Patriarch Stavros. "You know that sin brings its own price, and that it is paid in suffering, either in this world or the next. A virtuous life promises glory in Paradise."

"I understand that," said Thetis, "and I thank God for His Com-passion every day that my children and I remain safe in this world."

"It is right that you should do so," approved the Patriarch. "We are being put through the fire, my daughter. It is the obligations of Christians to find solace in our faith when God shows His love of us in the burdens He expects us to carry. You have had much to contend with, but so have almost all others. Daily I am asked to condole with those whose belief is faltering, and I help restore their courage by showing that through the ordeals God has imposed upon us, we gain strength and our place at His Throne," said the Patriarch. "All those who have been touched by these days must see the Hand of God in what is happening."

"I trust that God will not impose the end of the world upon us," said Thetis with a protective motion toward her children.

"It is not for you or me to say when God may summon us to Him," Patriarch Stavros said with conviction, then softened his observation, adding, "And remember that God does not make demands upon His worshipers but that He also provides some relief. For all the severity of the weather, He has given us the most refulgent sunsets that have ever graced the world."

"When we can see them," said Pentefilia, and ducked away from the pointed glance her mother sent her.

"That is also a reminder of the sorrow of earthly existence," said the Patriarch. "You must be aware that in this realm of tears and lamentation, God gives joy to those who trust in Him. And you, my daughter, by striving to live in grace in spite of the exigencies of your life: many women have not had the fortitude to preserve themselves as you have done. I would like to thank God now for all he has spared you." He held out one hand as if to direct Thetis in formal prayer.

She was spared the trouble of complying with the Patriarch by the arrival of Ragoczy Franciscus, who came to the door of the room. He was resplendent in a kandys of heavy black silk edged in red and embroidered with silver eclipses; his dark hair had been cut short in the old Roman style, and he wore a ruby ring on the first finger of his left hand. With no sign of distress, he addressed the newcomer cordially, "Good day to you, Patriarch. It is a pleasure to welcome you to my house." He reverenced the Patriarch and turned to Thetis. "You have done well, permitting me to extend my hospitality to this worthy man."

Thetis stared at him and finally managed to say, "I am sorry we have disturbed your studies."

"I can study at any time. I do not often have the opportunity to converse with so distinguished a man as Patriarch Stavros." He came a few steps into the room.

The three children remained silent, all of them attending to what was happening with fervent concentration.

The Patriarch started to bless him, then stopped. "Would you permit me to—"

"I have no objections to blessings," said Ragoczy Franciscus, going down on one knee before the Patriarch. "I will esteem your office and your faith; do not be vexed that I do not share it, for that would insult my family and the gods of my people."

"They may desert you in your hour of need, not being God as He has been revealed to us," said the Patriarch.

"Then your blessing may provide what my gods lack," said Ragoczy Franciscus, keeping the irony out of his voice.

Patriarch Stavros completed the blessing and then shifted his chair a short distance as if to lessen his contact with Ragoczy Franciscus. "May God show you favor."

Ragoczy Franciscus rose and went to stand beside the fireplace. "I would have been most upset not to have had the opportunity to make your acquaintance while you were here, Patriarch Stavros."

Hrisoula giggled and was shushed by her brother.

"You have shown this woman and her family much benefaction, foreigner," said the Patriarch, not quite making this an accusation.

"They are my neighbors and we are all foreigners in this town, subjected to the Master of Foreigners." Ragoczy Franciscus glanced once at Thetis. "I would not like to see a widow of this woman's quality turned out of her house in winter."

"Nor would anyone who knows her, or knew her husband," said Patriarch Stavros.

Aethalric came into the reception room bearing a tray. "There is food for all here; come and take your pick of what I've brought," he announced, with a swift flick of his eyes toward Ragoczy Franciscus as he set down his burden. "Wine, and almond milk. Two kinds of cheese, flat bread, eggplant crushed with garlic and herbs, butter, smoked duck sausages." He pointed out various dishes, then reverenced the Patriarch, Ragoczy Franciscus, and Thetis before he withdrew.

"Patriarch, if you will take what you want?" Ragoczy Franciscus invited. "Enjoy what my house can offer you."

Patriarch Stavros took his cup and his knife from his sleeve and pulled his chair nearer the table where the large tray waited. "How do you manage so much when most of us are forced to live on nuns' rations?" The suspicion was back in his voice, and he made no apology for it.

"My wants are few and very simple," said Ragoczy Franciscus. "It allows me to provide well for my household and my guests."

"Commendable," the Patriarch said as if by rote as he cut himself a wedge of cheese.

"My cook is very pleased to have those in the house who appreciate his skills," Ragoczy Franciscus went on. "I fear he despairs of me."

Thetis rose, her self-possession once again secure. "I will give the children sausages and butter," she said to Ragoczy Franciscus as she reached down. "They may pour almond milk for themselves."

Ragoczy Franciscus said, "You may do just as you like."

She nodded to him, taking care not to make too much of this offer, for fear that Patriarch Stavros would misread her intentions. "I think Dasur has done well."

"He will be glad to know you are satisfied," said Ragoczy Franciscus, stepping away from the tray; he soon made his excuses to the Patriarch, saying that he had work in his study that required his immediate attention. Returning to his study, he checked on the two flasks of moldy bread that were sitting on the trestle table where he worked. The process was coming along satisfactorily; he moved the flasks to a rack he had improvised. "Another two weeks and it will be finished," he remarked to the air. Sitting down on the single stool in the room, he brought out the parchment sheet on which he had been drawing a map of his westward journey, making notes of events and observations along the course he had traveled. Soon he was caught up in his labors, and the time passed swiftly.

"Ragoczy Franciscus?" The voice at his door surprised him.

"Thetis Krisanthemenis?" he replied, setting his quill aside and rising from the stool. The study was sunk in evening shadows, and he took flint-and-steel to spark the wicks of his oil-lamps before opening the door.

Her eyes were wide with curiosity and something more intense. She favored him with an automatic smile, saying, "I wanted to thank you for the hospitality you extended to Patriarch Stavros. He is a well-meaning man, but the trials of the last two years have worn him down."

"He has a difficult task," said Ragoczy Franciscus, standing aside so that she could see his study. "Would you like to come in?"

"May I?" Her face brightened with excitement.

"Do, please," said Ragoczy Franciscus with a casual reverence. "As you see, there is nothing compromising here, no matter what they say in the kitchen."

Her confusion revealed she had heard the speculation of the servants; she shook her head once. "I do not listen to gossip."

"Of course you do," he said, no suggestion of condemnation in his remark. "It would be unwise not to, considering that you are my guest." He paused. "Is it gossip that brings you here?"

"No, it does not," she said too quickly. "And if you fear that my coming would lead to rumors, it should not."

He smiled, his dark eyes softening. "I am sorry, however, that you have decided to forgo the evening meal in order to speak with me privately."

"I wanted to see you."

"You are not hungry?" he asked.

"Not very. We had a lot to eat while the Patriarch was here, all of it excellent," she said. "You have fed us very well, given what there is in the markets."

"This last year, no one has fed well," said Ragoczy Franciscus with feeling.

She hesitated. "You do not join us at table. Rojeh says it is the custom of those of your blood to dine privately."

"Yes; it is," he said.

"I have wondered if you would sometime allow me to join you," she ventured, uncertainty making her speak softly. "I used to dine privately with my husband upon occasion, and I find I miss the—"

Ragoczy Franciscus shook his head. "I regret to tell you: I believe you would find the experience not what you expect."

She mustered her courage and looked him directly in the eye. "That doesn't concern me. It's all coming to an end, isn't it? Well, I would like to have a little companionship with a man before I die."

"We must be speaking of two different things, you and I," he said with a slight, sardonic smile.

"No," she said, reaching up to put her fingers against his lips, silencing him. "I don't care anymore. I have been a prudent woman all my life. I have lived as I have been expected to live and earned the good opinion of others for doing it." Sighing suddenly, she moved away from him. "I thought that was what I had to do to be safe, but I have learned it is not."

"The death of your husband came at a bad time," he said, watching her move about the room; she reminded him of a caged animal.

"There would have been no good time for it," she declared, stopping abruptly and rounding on him. "I was fond of him, and I respected him. He was a good man; my father chose well for me when he married me to Eleutherios Panayiotos. He cared for me and for our children with kindness and affection, which is more than many wives and children receive." Thetis crossed her arms and gripped her elbows. "I thought there would be no reason for me to have to worry about what would become of us. My husband had money and position. But I haven't the authority to use the money: my brother will have to do that, and he is in Constantinople. Only the smallest allowance is granted me. So I am wholly at the mercy of those willing to help me. You have been willing." She came up to him again.

He did not speak for a while. "You owe me nothing, Thetis."

"On the contrary, I owe you everything. Now that I fear death is coming, I long for—" She blushed. "I did not understand how rare a thing benevolence is until I had need of it."

"You owe me nothing," he repeated.

"I am grateful to you, Ragoczy Franciscus: whether the Patriarch approves or not, I am grateful." She was half a head shorter than he, so she rose on tiptoe as she leaned forward to kiss him, lightly, on the mouth. "I would like to show you how grateful, to touch some measure of hope, or—"

"Gratitude can be burdensome," he said.

"You have given us so much, the least I can do is offer as much as I have in return." She looked at him. "And I don't want to die completely alone. If only for comfort, would you?"

"I do not ask that of you," he said gently, all the while feeling her desire fueling his own.

"I know." She kissed him again, this time longer and with more intensity.

Slowly he embraced her, his esurience surging in response to her long-denied ardor. When they broke apart, he whispered, "You do not know what you are playing with."

"It doesn't matter," she said, wrapping her arms around him as if he were a floating log and she a drowning sailor. "I want you, and I want you to take me."

He put his hand on her shoulder. "Thetis, I have no wish to impose on you," he said, his fervor now completely banked; he had not visited her in her dreams, and now he realized it might have been better if he had. "It would serve neither of us if I tried."

"I am not a clumsy woman in such arts. My husband taught me skills that should please you," she said, on her mettle.

He regarded her steadily. "I do not seek . . . entertainment."

"I wouldn't mind if you wanted me to please you in strange ways—foreigners often have such desires, or so my husband told me." She tried to kiss his lips again and got his cheek. "You would not trouble me if you—"

He shook his head once more. "No, Thetis. As desirable as you are—and you are very desirable—my bed is not a marketplace, where you may barter your security with your flesh and blood." His face revealed very little of his emotions.

She considered him as if trying to decide if she had been insulted. "That wasn't why I came to you."

"Very well: why did you come?"

She remained clinging to him. "You must know why. I know you understand what I'm enduring. Do not tell me you aren't lonely. I can see it in your eyes. I know what it is because I am lonely, too."

"Ah, Thetis," he said, kissing her forehead.

"Why not assuage your loneliness, and mine, before we die?" she persisted, her hold on him unbroken. "What is the harm in that?"

"What of your husband's memory?" he asked when he could. "You revere him. I would become an interloper."

"No, you wouldn't," she insisted, holding him as tightly as she could. "You would be anodyne to my grieving if you would but—" She attempted another kiss but without success.

"Are you so sure of that?" He touched her cheek, his fingers soft as the brush of a feather.

"I know I don't want to remain alone, on the eve of dying," she said, continuing in a strained way. "If you don't lie with me, I will tell Patriarch Stavros you've made advances to me."

"That would be a mistake," said Ragoczy Franciscus, taking a step back from her and moving out of her arms without any apparent difficulty.

"Would being your lover be as much a mistake?" she asked, trying not to be dismayed.

"If you fear more than you love, very possibly," he said.

"But—" She began to weep. "I am so afraid. Can't you let me have some respite from it?"

"If I thought I could." He took her hand. "I wish I could banish your fear, but that is beyond my skills."

With a little cry of dismay, she shied away from him. "If you do not want me, then say so and spare me any more embarrassment."

"It is not a question of wanting you," he said. "Never think that."

"What else am I to assume, since I am willing?" She had begun to weep and now made an exasperated swipe at her eyes. "Am I repugnant to you, or do you think I would demand more than you are able to give?"

"Neither of those things," he said. "I am afraid that what I want you would not want to part with."

She laughed suddenly. "What could that be? What would I refuse you?"

"Your blood," he said deliberately peremptorily.

She stood still, her eyes fixed upon him. "Blood?" she echoed at last. "Why?"

"Because it is the essence of you." He managed a lopsided smile and his voice had become deeper and more mellifluous.

"What do you do with the blood?" she asked.

"Drink it," he said, offering no softening, no disguising of his especial requirement. "Not very much; enough to convey the knowledge of you to me."

Staring at him with eyes huge, Thetis stammered, "I . . . What . . . what knowledge?"

"The knowledge of what you are, all of you," he said.

"You taste my . . . *soul?*" It was impossible to determine if this prospect fascinated or repelled her.

"It is the culmination of touching, of intimacy, taking some of your blood." He waited while a log in the fireplace spat sparks, crackling. "So you see, it is not something I would ask of you."

She blinked twice as if waking from sleep. "Does it hurt when you take it?"

"A little, I suspect," he answered.

"Then have what you want," she said, thrusting her arms toward him, wrists exposed. "If it will bring you joy, then have what you need."

"It is I who must bring you joy, or the blood is nothing more than metallic water." He stared down at the sheet of parchment on the table. "I trust you will keep what I have said in confidence."

"Oh. Yes. Of course." She took a step closer to him. "What do you mean, that you would bring me joy?"

His enigmatic gaze rested on her face as if he were discerning hidden treasure. "The virtue of the blood is in what it carries. If you have no fulfillment, I have none."

"I hoped you meant that," she said, and clasped her arms around his neck. "Do what you will," she exclaimed as she tightened her hold. "I have had so little joy of late I hardly remember what it is like. All I can think about is dying. You would do me a service if you helped me to rediscover my joy. A little blood is a good bargain." She kissed his mouth eagerly.

"Thetis, this is not a bargain," he warned her when she released him.

"I know; your bed is not a marketplace. You told me," she said, and drew him down to her lips again.

Text of a letter from the trader Choijun-Sonal on the Silk Road near Tashkent to his sales agent, Kai Wo-Heh in Chang'an, written in Chinese, carried by courier, and lost in a flood on the Nor River.

To my most worthy sales agent, Kai Wo-Heh, this report, written by the cleric Pajret the Christian of the local church, Holiest Incarnation, where we have spent the last three fortnights while the worst of the rains continue.

It is my sad duty to inform you that your nephew, Kai Tung-Ba, has died of Marsh Fever; I had not realized how ill he had become, for it took him suddenly, while we were traveling, filling him with heat and all signs of an invasion of dryness. He lingered for four days, then lapsed into the stupor that comes when death is near. The Christians here have given him burial and offered prayers for his soul. I can only thank the Gods of the Air that I have remained untouched by this scourge, and I have made gifts of baby camels and incense to them so that I might remain strong and fit, as I intend to resume my journey as soon as the rain lets up.

For it is raining steadily here. Never have I seen such a downpour in this region, nor have I encountered such dangerously swollen rivers. Even the streams are over their banks. Many bridges and other crossings have been washed out, and so I cannot tell you with any certainty which route I will have to travel in order to reach you. I have been speaking with the few merchants I have encountered coming from the East, and they all say it is not safe to venture beyond Kashgar.

The mountains are also unsafe because of the heavy rains. Portions of the roads have been washed away, or avalanches have covered them, making travel difficult. I have decided to take on a scout so that we may not be trapped on the road, as I have heard has happened to others. The reports of stranded merchants are heard everywhere, and in all instances, what is said of them does not encourage great confidence. There has been a sharp increase in banditry, and many merchants who were fortunate enough to cross the desert and the mountains without harm have ultimately lost all to raiders.

The asses have not held up as well as I had hoped, and even the camels are having difficulties in this weather, and with poor rations. Most men traveling with horses have lost stock. Cattle have fared badly as well, and I have seen many head reduced to near-skeletons by the poor quality of their feed. Goats have managed better, but they, as you know, will eat anything. If the rain brings grass in the spring, the remaining herds and flocks may be saved, but if there is another year of parched grass, I doubt many of the animals will survive. One of the northern hunters has said he has seen tigers starve in the last year, and bears fight wolves for the carcass of a bony pig.

It has been a difficult time in all manner of ways, what with trade being down, and so many places still feeling the lack that the darkened sun has brought. Food has been hard come-by, and costly. I have spent more to keep the camels fed than I have for the amber I have got from the men from the north who have traveled the Amber Trail down from their forests to trade amber and furs for our spices and jade. One of these amber traders said he had lost all his family but one sister. He has sacrificed a bear to his gods, but he is still in great distress. A few nights ago he became so drunk that he could barely walk, and he attacked one of my drovers, who had to use a club on the man to keep from being badly hurt. The companions of this trader demanded that my drover's hand be struck off for clubbing the man. But as it is, everyone is becoming strict and vengeful, so it may still be that the drover will lose a hand, and then I will have to decide if he is any use to me.

Assuming there are no more problems to deal with foisted upon me, I have decided to travel from church and apostlary to other Christian outposts, for they will always take in strangers, offer them shelter and such food as they have, and they keep scribes in every location, so that I may continue to inform you of my progress, for that may be less certain now than it has been in the past. I intend to make as much haste as we may, but I will not press on at the cost of my men and our merchandise. I have had to endure too much already to let this journey end in nothing. You have markets waiting for what we carry, and it is fundamental to our endeavor that we do not fail to deliver these goods to the markets you have found. You may rest assured that I will make every effort to preserve our goods and our men and our animals, for loss of more of any of them would be a terrible toll to pay for our success.

I will send another letter within two fortnights, and I will prepare an accounting for you when we have reached An-Hsi, for then I will be close enough to Chang'an to be able to make a reasonable estimate of what the last leg of our journey will cost. I am planning to make at least one more journey to Ecbatana before I retire to raise hemp in Wu-Tu, and to do that, I must have goods to trade. I will leave those arrangements to you, and thank you for your diligence now, while so many others have abandoned their work. May the Immortals bring you long years, many honors, and many sons.

Choijun-Sonal

By the hand of the scribe Pajret the Christian

6

Thetis rolled back on the pile of pillows and announced to the ceiling, "I am replete." She lifted her arms, shoving aside the muffling blankets stuffed with goat-hair as she reached for Ragoczy Franciscus. "Thoroughly, deliciously replete." She cocked her head. "If I am replete, you must be, too." She had not wanted to come to this place at first, not knowing what she would find in this withdrawing room. The bed—which also served as a couch—with its heaps of silk-covered pillows and heavy, soft blankets, had surprised her as much as the two oil-lamps that smelled of roses and jasmine.

"What you have, I share; I thank you for what you have given me," he said from the alcove near the window where he had gone to look out at the night sky; satisfied, he turned back toward her. "There could be more, if you wanted."

"More?" she said speculatively, eyeing him with roguish satisfaction. "You say we can only do this twice more before I am at risk to become like you?"

He leaned over and kissed her lightly, the heavy black silk of his kandys whispering luxuriously as he moved. "Yes."

"But if I should change my mind? What if I should want to be like you after all? To rise after death?" She caught his wrist, holding him purposefully.

"It is not something I would advise you to do, not without careful reflection. This life is not for everyone, especially for a woman like you: you have more than yourself to think about." He brushed her dark-blond hair back from her face, watching the firelight play on her features. "It is not a life that would please you, Thetis, and I would not like to lose you to the True Death." Again he felt a pang of grief for Nicoris.

"Such a dramatic warning," she chided him teasingly.

"Not dramatic, simply accurate. It has happened before," he said softly.

She offered a tentative smile. "Will you tell me? When I'm not so satisfied?" She lay back, her arms flung up to hug the pillow behind her.

"When the life of those of my blood seems less enticing than it does at this moment," he said, regarding her with abiding thoughtfulness.

"You've told me what to avoid, and how to deal with the most pressing difficulties," she reminded him. "Most of them are not so difficult—no worse than being a widow alone."

"Those lessons were hard-won, and nothing to be made light of," he said, a slight frown between his fine brows.

"You manage your life well enough," she pointed out.

"But I have had centuries to learn, and I have no children, which—"

She tugged him toward her. "You have those of your blood; aren't they like children?"

"They are very few, and at great distances from here. We do not often come together once we enter this life. It increases our risks and offers little compensation." As he spoke, he found himself missing Olivia, and wondering how she was faring in her distant Roman estate. Had this harsh weather touched her at all, or had she remained unscathed?

"Those who come to your life cannot make love with another of your kind; you must seek the living," she said as if reciting a foolish lesson. "I did listen."

He took her face in his hands, gazing into her face as he said, "You have nothing to fear from me. Nothing."

"But what you are," she said, and sank one hand into the short waves of his dark hair so she could pull his head to her mouth.

"How does that frighten you now, when you have seen what it is to be a vampire?" He showed no distress at her remark, and his manner remained attentive.

"It is dying that frightens me, not you," she said with conviction. "You are so much that is truly wonderful that I wonder if you are also terrible." She sought his lips with her own, as if to set her seal upon him. When she released him, her eyes were serious. "I am grateful to you for so much."

"I have told you repeatedly you have no reason to be." He kissed her again, his lips persuasive, unhurried, and evocative.

"Can you . . . will you pleasure me again?" she asked in a rush.

"If it is what you want. Dawn is still a long way off, and the night is clear and calm." He ran his finger along her brow, his touch light and passionate at once. "If you wish to have pleasure once more, you will have it."

She reached out for him. "Oh, yes. I do want to have pleasure. I wish I could have it every night from now until the end of time."

"That is not possible," he reminded her when he had kissed her once more.

"Then I want to spend the night in full ardor," she said at once, and drew him nearer, pulling the blanket off her so that he could see most of her body. "All this is yours, to do with as you like."

He touched her shoulder with delicate care, as if she were made of the most fragile porcelain. "Tell me what delights you most." He continued along her clavicle, then down to the swell of her breast. "Where are your sensations the sweetest?"

She wriggled with anticipation. "Everything you do is sweet to me." She stretched, making more of her flesh accessible. "I would like you to . . . to use your lips as well as your hands."

"Certainly," said Ragoczy Franciscus, beginning a series of little tongue-flick nibbles along the same route his fingers had just taken, making his way down toward the hardening nipple of her breast.

"Oh, yes," she whispered, shivering blissfully as her body awakened to the transports to come. "That's . . ." Her sigh expressed her increasing arousal. She tried to hold her breath so that she could feel the whole of what he did without the distraction of breathing; she finally had to inhale, and as she did, his mouth touched her breast, creating another surge of sensitivity that left her superbly weak, and each subsequent breath renewed the coursing thrill of his skillful caresses. As he continued to feel his way along the rises and curves of her flesh, Thetis began to succumb to the rapture that welled from the inmost part of her. She could feel her body gather as if readying for release. "Not yet, not yet," she murmured as he reached the sea-scented recesses at the apex of her thighs. "Not yet; not yet." This time she was a bit more forceful. "I am not ready."

"Then I will explore farther afield," he said, the musical quality of his voice as enticing as what his hands were doing to her hips.

"If I had more flesh, you would be better pleased," she said as she glanced down at her body. "I am all bones and sinew."

"That does not matter, so long as you are fulfilled," he said, stopping his expert ministrations. "It is your delectation that signifies, not how your body is formed."

She closed her eyes. "I will imagine I am voluptuous as a Tunisian dancing girl," she said. She had seen one once, when she was still unmarried in Constantinople; then the woman's luxurious black skin and ample curves had seemed unimaginably sensual, opulent and enticing, a feast for the senses and sensations; now, the memory provided her with an unhappy comparison to her current state.

To her astonishment, he said, "No. Do not yearn for anything but for yourself. It is you, as you are, that I seek. That is the reason blood is so important to our touching: nothing is as uniquely you as your blood, and nothing else is so truly alive." He bent and kissed the sharp rise of her hip. "This is you, and your hands are you, and all your skin is you, contains you." He resumed his tantalizing stroking of her flanks and legs, causing tingles wherever he touched.

"Why does this gratify you?" She was growing curious, and her excitement added to the urgency of her question. "You could demand so much more."

He moved up her body and kissed her; it was a long, complex kiss, calming and inflaming at once, bringing both tranquillity and ecstasy to her; the restlessness that had been increasing within her was replaced with serene anticipation, and a feeling of equanimity that she had not known since the birth of her first child. When they finished the kiss, he moved back just far enough to be able to speak. "It gratifies me because you accept what I can give to you. You permit me to know a quality of your soul, not simply a spasm of the flesh."

Her lips formed words, but no sound came until she began to weep. "I didn't understand. I thought I did, but I didn't." There was a kind of anguish in her that she could not express and it made her crying worse. Kissing the tears from her face, he sheltered her in his arms, his whole attention on her; he held her until her sobs abated and she clung to him with more ardor than misery, and her heartbeat once again revealed a return of sensual rapture. Gradually, he began to stroke her as he had before, and to ignite the many fervid responses he had discovered in her; she wakened quickly to the promise of answered need. "Yes," she exulted as he finally moved between her legs, using his tongue to set off minute explosions of ineffable transports that suddenly burgeoned into a pulsing release that amazed her with its intensity as much as its vastness. It took her a short while to come to herself, and when she did, she felt Ragoczy Franciscus' mouth still on her throat. "Remarkable," she said slowly.

"Yes, it was," he said, rolling onto his back and giving her his chest to rest upon.

"I never felt anything like that," she said a bit later. "I didn't know I could—did you?"

He kissed her forehead. "I hoped," he told her.

"Oh," she said, closing her eyes for a brief rest while the last of her excitation faded from her body. When she opened her eyes again, the room was awash in pallid sunshine and Ragoczy Franciscus was fully dressed in a kandys of black silk topped with a curly, black-shearling shuba. She sat up quickly, pulling the blanket about her. "I must have fallen asleep."

"You did," he said, his eyes affectionate. "I sent word to Sinu that you had come into this withdrawing room to get warm. There is a very cold, high wind coming out of the northeast."

Her alarm increased. "Do they know . . . anything?"

"You mean about our time together? I doubt it. Rojeh has taken good care that any speculation is quashed at the outset; I am sure he has offset most suspicions." He indicated a woolen talaris laid over the back of a rosewood chair. "I asked Sinu to bring your clothes here. I told her you would want to have her help dressing when you awoke," he went on. "It is your usual custom, and she would think it odd if I had not asked."

"I have done something reckless, coming to you as I did, and the falling asleep where I could be found by anyone in the household," she muttered, preparing to get up. "You had better leave me alone or the servants will talk, no matter what your Rojeh does."

"He laughs at any suggestions that there is any unbecoming conduct in this house. He boasts of my remoteness and my inclination to hold apart from foreigners. So far, your servants, and mine, are persuaded."

She glared at him. "You had best leave, then, or no one will—"

He started toward the door. "I will ask Sinu to assist you, and to bring you your breakfast. I am sorry that we have only millet-loaf and butter for you to eat, but food is growing scarcer as the year winds down." Saying this, he slipped out into the corridor, where he found Pentefilia waiting, her thin arms crossed and a sharp expression in her hazel-green eyes. "Good day to you" was his unflustered greeting.

"You shouldn't be alone with my mother," she criticized.

"I was worried that she might have taken ill," said Ragoczy Franciscus. "She was cold in the night and went into the withdrawing room to make the most of the fire there."

"Still, you shouldn't be with her. She's a widow, and you are not my father. Patriarch Stavros says that it could lead to temptation and torment." Her expression did not soften, nor did she show any inclination to move from her post. "I saw you go into the withdrawing room, just after Sinu left."

"I have a jar of lamp-oil I keep there, and I wanted to refill the lamps so that your mother would have a pleasant scent to waken her." He could see that Pentefilia had no intention of departing, so he said, "Do you know where Sinu is? Your mother wants to get dressed."

"I am not leaving," said Pentefilia defiantly. "You cannot make me leave."

"No. I do not suppose I could do that," said Ragoczy Franciscus mendaciously but with an accommodating smile. "That is why I plan to seek her out."

"Sinu is in the washing room, doing our clothes," said Pentefilia as if parting with a military secret.

"Thank you," said Ragoczy Franciscus, adding as he turned away, "You may want to knock on the door and assure yourself that all is well."

"I will," said Pentefilia.

Ragoczy Franciscus made his way down to the lowest level of the house; in the kitchen he ordered Dasur to heat up a wedge of millet-loaf and prepare a pot of mint tea. "She is finally rising."

"Just as well. Herakles is fretting, and not just because his hip is giving him pain." Dasur gestured to the shelves across from the open hearth. "Look at that! It is almost as bare as a stork's nest in winter."

"I can arrange for a goat or two from the Jou'an-Jou'an camp,"

Ragoczy Franciscus offered. "It is not much, but as there has been no market for ten days, everyone is short on food."

"Will the Jou'an-Jou'an give you any?" Dasur asked. "Most of those camped around the town keep their food and their livestock for themselves."

"I have been treating their horses for cracked, peeling hooves; they have lost nine head to the condition and I hope they will not lose more. So long as the herd improves, I doubt they will begrudge me a goat or two," he said with a slight raising of his brows.

"Then take them," said Dasur.

"I must go to the Jou'an-Jou'an camp today, and I will fetch a goat or two."

"The goats will hardly be fat, but it is better than nothing but millet-cake and cheese." Dasur took a tray from the plateboard. "How much longer will the Jou'an-Jou'an remain?"

Ragoczy Franciscus nodded. "They meant to move on before now, but many of their ponies cannot walk, and that has kept them where they are. As soon as they can do so, I know they will leave."

Dasur went to get the millet-cake. "Then I must look for another source of meat, against their going." He cut two deep wedges from the round loaf. "The widow's breakfast will be ready shortly."

"Then I had best summon her woman," said Ragoczy Franciscus, and left the kitchen, finding his way through the dim, narrow corridors without hesitation. He had almost reached the washing room when he heard a commotion beyond the walls of the house, and a rising chorus of shouts. Pausing, he tried to make out what he heard and realized that people in the street were crying, *Fire! Fire!* Quickly he retraced his steps to the kitchen, demanding, "Where is Rojeh? Where is Aethalric? Chtavo?"

"They are with the mason at the widow's house, with Herakles," said Dasur. "Is something wrong?"

"I fear so," said Ragoczy Franciscus. "I want you to put one of the children to watch in my study"—it was the highest room in the house—"and then I want you to ready a cart, in case you have to leave."

"Why should I leave?" Dasur asked.

"Because there is a fire somewhere in Sarai," said Ragoczy Franciscus bluntly. "Do not wait until you see flames at the door: leave if the fire turns in this direction."

Dasur paled visibly. "I will do as you order."

"Good. I will return when I can, but I must rely upon you to protect the people in this house. Do you understand?" He saw Dasur duck his head. "Good." With that, he rushed toward the stable-yard and, after a swift glance around to be sure he was not seen, vaulted over the high wall and into the side-yard of Eleutherios Panayiotos' house. A quick glimpse of the sky told him that the fire was still some distance away, for the smoke sliding on the brisk wind was not dense enough to indicate close proximity. He rushed through the yard toward the house itself, calling to Rojeh and the others as he went.

"My master?" Rojeh answered, stepping out of a partially demolished shed where workmen's tools were stored.

"There is a fire. We must go help fight it," he said curtly. He pointed toward the sky.

"So that is what the clamor is all about," said Aethalric. "I wondered why the din—"

"A bad thing," said Herakles. "It could damage fishing, being down toward the docks."

"So it might," said Ragoczy Franciscus as the others came up to him. "I will provide two silver pieces for any of you who decide to help battle the fire."

At that Aethalric grinned. "I would cross the Serpent Sea if the pay was good enough," he announced, and surveyed the others. "What about you?"

Chtavo rubbed his hands together. "I am with you."

"Those of you who want to come, come. If you would rather stay here, then guard the widow and her children, and protect her house," said Ragoczy Franciscus, heading for the main gate. "Bring buckets and rakes."

The mason, a powerful, squat man with spatulate hands and a much-broken nose, spoke up. "I have my wagon behind the house. It has all manner of tools."

"Very good," Ragoczy Franciscus called over his shoulder. "Bring it and all you have." As he reached the gate, he pulled back the bolt and shoved it open. "Hurry."

The sound of urgent voices was rising, becoming a howl in counterpoint to the wind; in the south, smoke was billowing out over the high stone wall of the town, roiling along the two long piers, and hugging the shore of the sea beyond. From all over Sarai people were running toward the smoke, creating confusion in the street and the first stirrings of panic in the town's inhabitants.

"Is there anyone in the house?" Aethalric shouted as he came to the gate, rake in one hand, bucket in the other.

"There is no one that I know of," said Ragoczy Franciscus. "I will offer to help fight the fire." He disliked fire intensely and had to steel himself to face it; fire had licked most of the skin from his body two centuries earlier, and the experience was still fresh in his memory; had it taken hold of him then, he would have died the True Death: for a time after it happened, he wished he had, so agonizing was the damage it did. He set his teeth and called out to Rojeh, "Fetch me pails."

"I will, my master," Rojeh answered, and came from the shed carrying an array of buckets, pails, and a small barrel. "Which do you want?"

"Leave the barrel, give the two metal buckets to me, and find me a rake," Ragoczy Franciscus said as Chtavo and Herakles hurried out the gate, armed with pails and shovels.

Rojeh appeared with a long rake and an ax. "We may need both of these."

"Give me the ax. You keep the rake," Ragoczy Franciscus said, moving aside as the mason and his apprentice moved the donkey-drawn cart through the gate.

The apprentice nodded, his young face showing stark dread. "Famine, a dying sun, and now this. The world is ending."

"Then you will have nothing to worry about when this is over," snapped the mason, and all but shoved the young man into the street; the donkey and the cart lurched after him.

Satisfied that no one remained at Eleutherios Panayiotos' house, Ragoczy Franciscus motioned Rojeh out into the street, stepped out beside him, and pulled the gate closed behind them. "I think the Street of the Water Temple would be the quickest. Not too many will use it."

"And it goes directly to the waterfront, and the Fishermen's Market," Rojeh said, agreeing. "If that square isn't burning yet, it is a good staging area for fighting the fire."

Ragoczy Franciscus hefted the ax so that the handle lay on his shoulder, and taking the bucket in his other hand, he set out at a rapid walk. "Be careful as you go."

As they started down the narrow, ancient street, they saw people teeming out of their houses, many with valuables clutched in their arms, some with children around them clinging to their clothes. Women struggled with infants in their arms, and older children tugged along younger ones, all of them making for the western gate of the town, which was the farthest away from the fire. In amongst them ran men with chests and other booty in their arms; which were rightful owners salvaging treasure and which were thieves making off with plunder was impossible to determine. Everywhere shouts and wails of alarm created an incomprehensible din, and the confusion increased steadily as Ragoczy Franciscus and Rojeh made their way toward the ominous clouds of dark-gray smoke.

From a side street, a man in Armenian clothing came running, arms windmilling, his face contorted in a rictus of fear. He careened into Ragoczy Franciscus, cursed, shoved himself free, and went on at a more frantic pace, shouting incoherently as he went.

"He is frightened," said Ragoczy Franciscus as he brushed himself off. "More than I am."

They reached the livestock-market square and found that this was the main staging area for those willing to fight the fire. Emrach Sarai'af was standing to one side, shouting for foreigners to come to him. His big arms were crossed over his barrel chest as if to help him shout more loudly. As he caught sight of Ragoczy Franciscus, he pointed to him. "You are here! I have sent your servants to the bucket line."

"Very good. Would you like me to join them?" Ragoczy Franciscus assumed a sang-froid he did not feel. "My manservant and I are at your disposal. What is burning, and how far has it spread?"

"One of the wharves is burning, and the warehouses next to it. They contain furs and wood, which also burn, which makes it much worse," said Emrach. "A few of the smaller buildings adjoining the warehouses have also started to burn, and sparks are setting small fires near the main blaze. At least the wind is not blowing the flames deeper into the town. That is something in our favor." His eyes narrowed. "Do you think you could help take down the small houses between the fire and this square? We are going to pull down as many as we can. Most of them are poor and made only of wood." His eyes narrowed. "Well? It has to be done quickly."

"Whose houses are they?" Ragoczy Franciscus asked.

"The dockworkers and other laborers. Don't worry about damaging them. They are poor folks' houses, and those who live in them haven't much to lose." He glared at the foreigner in black. "Do you say it should not be done?"

"No," said Ragoczy Franciscus. "But I regret the necessity. When you have little, it is a terrible thing to have that taken from you."

"Oh, I realize that. With winter coming, it will be hard on those workers who have lost houses." Emrach pointed toward a small cluster of shacks. "If you want to start there?"

"Very well," said Ragoczy Franciscus. "With whom will we work?"

"For now, you and your man are on your own," Emrach declared, and looked past Ragoczy Franciscus to a group of Volgamen who were approaching. "You men. Go down to the wharf that isn't burning and see that the boats there are safe. If they have to be towed out to sea, you must arrange that."

Realizing that he had been dismissed, Ragoczy Franciscus signaled to Rojeh. "Let us start."

"Are those houses empty?" Rojeh asked.

"I sincerely hope so," said Ragoczy Franciscus, and trudged toward the huts. "Rough planking like that burns easily," he said as they reached the rickety structures, seeing how they leaned together for support. "For the safety of the town, they should be razed."

"But you worry about the dockworkers who live in them," said Rojeh with conviction.

"There is another hard winter coming," said Ragoczy Franciscus as he swung his ax down from his shoulder and faced the simple wood buildings. "I will try to find the main beams and the walls carrying the most weight. Once we get those down, the rest should be simple."

Rojeh knew better than to question this assertion. Ragoczy Franciscus set his bucket down, saying as he did, "There is a water trough near the Christian compound. Fill this and your pail there, and bring them back. We will need water—"

"—if anything begins to smolder," Rojeh finished, hastening to obey.

Confronting the small wooden houses, Ragoczy Franciscus felt a pang of sorrow for these buildings, so forlorn to begin with, and now given as sacrifices to the advancing fire. Looking about, he realized that the houses were vacant, that the workers who had lived in them had abandoned them some time ago. Reluctantly he swung his ax at the nearest door and felt the planks splinter under his first blow. He tugged the ax free and struck again, this time destroying the door. He went into the small house, making a quick inspection of its interior, noticing a crudely painted Christian icon on the wall over the single window. A swift survey of the two rooms showed him where the weight of the house was centered, and he began his calculations.

"My master," Rojeh called from outside. "Where are you?"

"In here. I've found the trunk of the roof," he said. "If I bring down the north wall, I should be able to fell the house like a tree."

"How do you wish me to help?" Rojeh asked.

"Pull the rubble away as I knock down the wall," said Ragoczy Franciscus, and chopped at the main supports of the wall, hearing the wood crack on his third blow.

The single bell at the Most Holy Dormition was tolling out the call to midday worship when the group of five houses finally collapsed. The fire had come closer, and the air was acrid with smoke. Cinders floated on the rising wind, many of them igniting small fires where they landed, whether on wood, on clothing, or on debris.

"I'll get us more water!" Rojeh shouted as Ragoczy Franciscus struggled to pull a large beam out of the confusion of the wrecked building at the edge of the square.

"Good!" He was beginning to tire. "And then help me stack all this."

Rojeh said nothing; he brought the water, saying as he neared Ragoczy Franciscus, "The wharf is not burning any longer. What's left of the fire is confined to the south end of the town."

Ragoczy Franciscus nodded to show he had heard. "I hope we did not demolish these houses for no reason."

"The fire isn't out yet," Rojeh reminded him, and took up his rake again to clear away the wreckage. He rubbed his face and left a smear of soot and grime across his forehead and cheek; then he took up his ax and looked about. "Where next?"

"To where the last of the fire is." Saying this, he turned on his heel and started across the wide market-square through the scudding smoke and the hectic disorder of the afternoon.

*   *   *

Text of a letter from Brother Theofeo in Antioch to Pope Silverius in Roma, carried by pilgrims and delivered at Easter in 537.

Hail, Silverius, true and only Pope of Christians, our source of inter-cession in this world, and the means of the salvation of all souls on earth, this from your most humble servant, Brother Theofeo, currently in Antioch, but bound, as you have ordered, for the trade routes of the East, on this the last day of November in the 536th year of Redemption.

I have at last arrived in this city, and I regret to tell you that most of the churches here remain stubborn in their adherence to the East-ern Rite, preferring the teachings from Constantinople to those from Roma, thus showing their lack of comprehension of all that Christ sacrificed for us, and for which they will pay dearly when He comes again in glory to judge the living and the dead. There have been many conversions of late, but not to the True Church, which may mean that in the name of Christ many are led from Grace to Perdition. Amen.

For surely the end of the world is at hand. Many have starved, and others have suffered from fevers. Some have lost their wits, while others have had to give up every possession in order to get enough to eat. The sun has not given life to the fields, and the farms show sparse growth, so that there is talk of another year of famine in the coming winter, which must surely mean that the end of the world has arrived and the Messiah is coming to purge away the sins of the world. Amen.

Sailors here have said that the sea has continued to be turbulent, and if my crossing was an example, then I must accept what they told me as truth, for I have rarely encountered so many days of squalls and tempests as I found coming here. And now we are subjected to rain, as if Noah were needed again. One man I spoke with told me that he had lost his house, his barns, his wife, and three of his chil-dren to floods. Amen.

I have been informed that in some parts of the city there has been a dramatic upswelling of rats, that these fell creatures, rather than hiding in the shadows, have taken to the streets in chittering swarms, devouring all that they encounter, including children. Some have lost donkeys to them, as well as the dogs and cats that roam the streets. Some say this is another plague, as there were in Egypt, and that lo-custs may soon be upon us. There have also been many mad dogs seen, and a few have bitten men and given them their madness. Now any stray dog is in danger of being stoned to death, for fear of the mad-ness. The carcasses are left for carrion birds and rats to eat, and that has led to fights among these scavengers that remind us that Mercy is often most lacking where it is most needed. Amen.

There is a hermitage established not far from here, in the desert, where it is said a hundred holy men are in constant prayer for the sal-vation of all souls. I have determined to find these hermits and discover what they know of these hard years, for they must have garnered wis-dom through their long years of prayer. Amen.

Marsh Fever is increasing in this city, and there are makeshift shelters for the afflicted. Some of the Christians, in charity, have de-voted themselves to tending those with Marsh Fever, and there is now a Patriarch assigned to supervise the activities of those nurses, for many of them are ill-prepared for what they must do to succor the sufferers. I myself have given three days to attend Brother Maurinios, who had taken Marsh Fever, and who passed beyond this life to Glory in Paradise two days since. I have benefited from the Patriarch's in-structions. Amen.

Travelers from the East—and there are fewer of them than there have been in the past—tell of similar harsh conditions as far as the Fortress of the Stone Tower and beyond. There are accounts of whole tribes of grassland peoples moving westward with herds and flocks, because their pasturage has dried to nothing and they must find other ground or starve. I am making a point of seeking out various travelers to discover what they have seen for themselves, to be sure that the chronicles I have been given are not rendered more exciting by the addition of calamities beyond what they may have experienced. Amen.

One of the Patriarchs from the Church of the Annunciation led a procession of penitents through the streets not three days since, all singing the Dance of Jesus, and exhorting all they encountered to join with them in prayer and contrition, to Confess past errors and em-brace humility and their faith for the sake of their souls. Many of those who saw them joined with them, proclaiming that they would forsake sin and live in virtue for the life that is to come. I saw this with my own eyes, and I was touched by their fervor and saddened by their error in following the Eastern Rite. Amen.

I shall await your instructions, Holy Father, and I will pray for the triumph of Faith before we are all Judged. This tribulation can only bring greater joy in Paradise, and so we must bow to God's Will and dedicate ourselves to emulating the sacrifice made for the atonement of our sins, and for our Salvation. Your courier may find me at the Church of the Apostle Luke in the Street of the Saddle-Makers here in Antioch. Amen.

Brother Theofeo
At the end of November in the 536ᵗʰ Year of Salvation

7

"The ponies are no better; you can see that they are not improving," Dukkai accused as Ragoczy Franciscus rose from inspecting the peeling hooves of the latest victims of the crippling condition. "We will have to kill these four. It is meat for us, but we must save some of our ponies or we will never leave this place."

Ragoczy Franciscus brushed off his hands. "You have had fever—especially Wet Lungs and Gray Cough—among your people, and your animals are sick."

"We are punished by the Lords of the Earth. The Underworld Judge is one of them, and he is calling us to account." She put her hand to her eyes, whether to hide her tears or to block out the sight of the miserable animals, not even she knew. "We will die here, just like those in the town are dying. As all the world is dying."

"Are more of your people ill?" Ragoczy Franciscus asked, trying not to give in to the worry that was building within him. "Shall I make you more of the sovereign remedy?"

She studied him briefly. "No; you needn't bother. They won't take anything from foreigners now."

"Yet they will let me treat their livestock," said Ragoczy Franciscus with a slight shrug, coming across the icy path to her side.

"I had a dream of Tejamksa, and it troubles me," Dukkai said unexpectedly. "She has appeared to me, to guide me," she added, slowly.

"Has her guidance been useful?" Ragoczy Franciscus asked.

"I fear it may be," she said. "If you would be willing to let me tell you about it before you leave this evening?"

He saw the hopefulness in her blue eyes and said, "I will be at your disposal."

She made a gesture of relief. "Thank you."

"I have done nothing yet," he reminded her.

"You will help. You always have," she said, and pointed toward the marsh. "There is ice forming in the reeds tonight."

He accepted her change of subject without challenge. "The winter is going to be a hard one. Perhaps not as severe as last year, but worse than usual."

"Yes. All the signs are for it. I have told Neitis Ksoka to make sure there are shelters for our animals as well as for us. He has ordered more tent frames made so that we can put the ponies and the goats inside if there is another ice storm. And there will be—more than one." She closed her eyes hard, the deep wrinkles around them standing out in sharp relief.

"Did you see that in the smoke?" Ragoczy Franciscus asked, keeping his voice as level as he could.

"Yes. If we do not resume our journey, and soon, it is more likely that we will have to suffer for our stubbornness. The Lords of the Earth are in need of our travel. The longer we remain fixed here, the more they must undergo for our sake."

"That is asking much of you in a difficult time," Ragoczy Franciscus observed in a deliberately neutral tone.

"There were many years when the Lords of the Earth asked little and gave much. Now the stream flows the other way, and we must give more for less. If we honor them, the Lords of the Earth will once again restore us to plenty. If we do not show our respect, they will abandon us and we will perish." She pointed out over the marsh, now glowing in the feeble sunlight on the low-lying mist. "The Water Spirits are strong here, and the Lords of the Earth are as weak as the sun has been for two years."

"Ah," said Ragoczy Franciscus. "You have not changed your vision of your circumstances, then?"

She shuddered as the wind picked up, cold and unforgiving. "I have eaten the Fingers of Truth—I brought them with me, in a box made of jade—and hoped for more knowledge to be imparted to me, but it hasn't happened; I have sought out the most remote parts of the marsh where the Water Spirits hover in orbs of light and have ascertained nothing from them. The Lords of the Earth still ail, and I cannot learn more from them until I offer them healing, and the strength of blood to fortify them."

"You will give them another sacrifice?" Ragoczy Franciscus walked a half step behind her as they went back toward the cluster of tents where most of the Desert Cats were busy sewing second layers of skins to the tent frames.

"I must," she said, avoiding his penetrating gaze. "I have a duty to my people and to the Lords of the Earth. They expect me to provide more." She glanced over her shoulder toward the line of ponies, then back at him. "You have done as much as you can."

"I hope I have helped ease your burdens," he said. "I am willing to do more, if you require it."

She went a short distance in silence. "Are you planning to leave Sarai soon?"

"The Master of Foreigners has ordered that I depart within a week after the spring thaw." He thought a moment. "Your visions: what do they tell you is ahead?"

"I'm unsure. The dream of my aunt has made what is coming more difficult." She turned as a dark smear issued from the caves beneath the walls of Sarai. "Bats. They fly every sundown."

"They do little harm," said Ragoczy Franciscus, pausing by the midden.

"The midden gathers heat to itself."

"I will arrange for a cartload of wood-shavings to be brought to you. If you do not want them, burn them in your cooking fires. Otherwise, use them in your middens."

"You have no need of them?" She sounded dubious and studied his face for his answer.

"Considering that Sarai has had two fires in the last month, I believe it would be wiser to bring the shavings to you. If you would rather not have them, I will tell the builders to dispose of the shavings as they like." He smiled at her.

She thought about her response, then said, "If Neitis Ksoka approves, it is acceptable to me."

"Then where is he? I would like to ask him if he would permit me to do this for you."

"He has gone with two of the men, hunting for meat. They said there were wild pigs to be had along the marsh, if the tigers haven't gotten them first." This last was a dark afterthought, one that brought a frown back to her face.

Ragoczy Franciscus understood her fears; attacks by wolves, bears, lions, and tigers were increasing as the amount of food available dwindled. "He is a clever hunter, and he and his men are well armed, I doubt he is going to be hurt."

"It would be a very bad omen if anything were to happen to him. Ksoka would have no leader and the clan no Kaigan. Zumir is too young to lead, and he is not going to guide Ksoka, in any case, not with his fits. You have not seen him have one, but he is taken with dreadful twitching and spasms from time to time, and he is lethargic for days afterward, when he cannot ride." She pressed her lips closed as if afraid of what more she might say.

"Why did you never tell me about this?" Ragoczy Franciscus asked.

"It is a shameful thing. The clan would not like to know I've told you." She lowered her voice. "Do not tell anyone about this."

He knew she was utterly serious. "Very well. But if you change your mind—"

"I will not," she interrupted. "I give him Fingers of Truth brewed in a tea, and it provides some relief."

"Then I hope he may be safe." He went around the end of the makeshift pen where the goats were gathered. All of them were thin, and a number had patchy coats where the hair had fallen out. "Have you done anything about that?" he asked, indicating the exposed skin of the goats. "With the weather turning so cold, you need to protect them."

"They will go into a tent tonight, with two guards with them," said Dukkai.

"A good beginning, but not enough to keep them from hurt, not with their hair falling out in that way," said Ragoczy Franciscus. "I have an unguent that may help them—it is made of herbs infused with wool-fat and olive oil." He could sense her reluctance, so he added, "If you have treatments of your own, I will not impose mine upon you."

She shook her head. "No. The treatments we have tried have done nothing. I will be glad to use yours, but there are those in my clan who would not be."

He held out his hand to her to help her over a broad swath of un-melted ice. "Come. I want to make sure you can use the new cooking pot I bring you."

"Another gift," she said, wagging a finger at him, refusing his help. "You continue to do us service, Zangi-Ragozh. It is not an easy thing to explain to the clan."

"It is what Neitis Ksoka said you lacked when I was here two days ago. He said your old one had become rusted and it was no longer reliable." He stopped as he saw two young men approaching, one of them carrying the bodies of two limp ducks, the other holding a stick from which depended four small fish. "You will be glad of a new pot to cook those in."

"Yes. So I will accept it." She folded her arms and addressed the young men. "Have you brought those for our evening meal?"

The two exchanged quick glances, then the one with the fish said, "Yes, Dukkai," with an exaggerated show of deference. "We intend these for everyone."

"Very good," Dukkai approved, adding in an undervoice to Ragoczy Franciscus, "Some of the boys have been catching birds and fish, then going off into the marsh and eating it all themselves."

"Are you surprised?" Ragoczy Franciscus asked.

"No, but I cannot allow it to continue." She raised her voice. "Your game may be the first into the new pot."

The young man with the ducks sighed. "We'll clean them and bring them to Tokatis."

"He will be glad to have them," said Dukkai, and tugged Ragoczy Franciscus' sleeve. "Show me this wondrous pot."

"It is with the other items on the mule I have just purchased," he said.

"I saw it as you rode in. Your mare is a much finer animal." She took a long moment to look at Ragoczy Franciscus, as if she was committing his face to memory.

"The mule is tougher, however," he said.

She thought about what he said. "As tough as our ponies—when they are well?"

"Certainly their match," said Ragoczy Franciscus. "I bought this one from a Goth, who arrived just before the ice-storm with a small train of mules from the Black Sea. You might find what he has to say useful, if you are planning on continuing west: I certainly did."

"A Goth merchant, from a place called the Black Sea. Does it exist, or is it a tale? If you know, you must tell me." She rounded on him. "If you lie to me, the Lords of the Earth will punish us all for your prevarication."

Ragoczy Franciscus was startled by the vehemence of her challenge, but did his best to answer reasonably. "There is a Black Sea. I have seen it many times." The first time had been while he was still alive, more than thirty-five centuries earlier. "There are towns and cities with ports around it, all of which are benefited by the Black Sea, and the trade that is conducted on its sea-lanes."

Dukkai scrutinized his face, then took a step back, satisfied. "You have spoken truth."

Very seriously, Ragoczy Franciscus held her eyes with his own. "Dukkai, I have no reason to lie to you, and every reason to tell you the truth. If you have questions about what I say, you have only to ask me to clarify what I have said and I will do it."

She had the grace to look abashed. "It isn't that," she mumbled. "I don't doubt you, for I have found that what you say is trustworthy, although it is often beyond my imagining." For a short while she said nothing, then slapped her heavy sleeves with her gloved hands and said as heartily as she could, "Show me this pot. There are fish and ducks to cook—and pig, if we are fortunate. Perhaps pony if we are not."

"It will please me to do so," he assured her, and took her to the edge of the cluster of tents where his horse and mule were tied. "The pot is of heavy copper. You will have to clean it by scouring it with sand between uses, but you will find, I think, that it will serve you well." He took the cauldron from the pack saddle and held it out to her. "From me to your clan, for extending your hospitality to me for all those fortnights."

She held the large pot, both her arms wrapped around it as if around a barrel, for the cauldron was much the same size as one. She resisted the impulse to smile, making instead a moue of discreet smugness. "This will be most welcome, and it is an omen of good to come. If no one else will thank you for it, I will. It is a kindness that you do this, and it shows you a most worthy man. I will let everyone know that you gave this to us without demanding anything in return."

"Is that necessary?" He was not surprised, but he could not conceal his disappointment.

"In hard times, there is always carping," she said, turning and trudging off toward the center of the encampment. "I wish Jekan Madassi had not died of Wet Lungs. This would delight her."

"I am sorry she is dead, too," he said, following Dukkai toward the center of the camp. "Your clan had need of her."

"That we did, and the need is growing, for she knew more of edible plants than anyone else, and now I wish more of us had her knowledge," she said, and stopped near to the main fire-pit. "I will put this here, and shortly we will begin our cooking for the night."

Ragoczy Franciscus stood for a moment, then asked, "Would you like me to wait, or leave?"

She did not answer at once, then said, "If you would wait a while, we will finish what was begun."

"I will go back to my animals, then, so you can deal with your people without my intrusion," he said, starting to turn away.

"Where is Ro-shei?" The question came so suddenly that it stopped him.

"He is at my house in Sarai."

"You have taken in a family, I am told," she said.

"A Constantinopolitan widow and her children," said Ragoczy Franciscus.

Dukkai thought for a long moment, then said, "He knows you have come here."

"Ro-shei? Yes, of course," said Ragoczy Franciscus.

"Of course," she repeated, then looked up as Tokatis came toward her. "Look! A new cauldron, of copper."

"A fine vessel," the butcher announced as he inspected the pot. "And a fine omen." He glanced at Ragoczy Franciscus, then angled his shoulders so that his next remarks were clearly intended for Dukkai alone. "I have some fish and ducks I had not expected. I understand that was your doing."

"I reminded them of their duty," said Dukkai, and called out to Ragoczy Franciscus, "I will call you shortly, Zangi-Ragozh, when I will have a task for you. Let me attend to this now."

Ragoczy Franciscus ducked his head to show he would comply and made his way through the tents back to where his mare and mule stood. He found the Jou'an-Jou'an camp profoundly sad and troubling, for the Desert Cats had lost more than a quarter of their numbers since he had first encountered them in Kumul. He came up to his mare and patted her neck, thinking that her mane needed brushing. Even in her thick winter coat, she was that remarkable shade of dark-blue coat with black mane and tail that caught the attention of all who saw her. The mule was stolid and remote, accepting a bit of dried fruit from Ragoczy Franciscus with the air of boredom his owner had come to expect.

Shouts of children erupted from somewhere within the Desert Cats' group of tents, the cries nearer shrieks than whoops. This commotion began to move, marking the progress of the children as they rushed from one tent to another, shouting the names of the occupants, and chanting some doggerel about the Lords of the Earth. Gradually they made their way to every tent in the encampment.

"They are excited," said Neitis Ksoka, appearing out of the mists near where Ragoczy Franciscus waited.

"They are hungry," said Ragoczy Franciscus, thinking that this young Kaigan was only a few years older than most of those busy children.

"That they are," Neitis Ksoka said. "We all are."

"It is the nature of this new age," said Ragoczy Franciscus, noticing how rapidly the light was fading; at this time of year the days closed in quickly.

"I fear you are right," said Neitis Ksoka. "I am told you are to be thanked for the copper pot."

"I hope you find it useful," said Ragoczy Franciscus.

"You know we will," he said, and strolled away toward the burgeoning glow of the main fire. He swung around to address Ragoczy Franciscus again, all the while walking backward toward his destination. "The mists will be thick tonight. Can your mare find her way back to her stable?"

"We've come here enough that it should not be a problem; she will know the path," said Ragoczy Franciscus, startled by this indication of concern; he had not expected anything so amicable from Neitis Ksoka. He did not add that for those of his blood, darkness was not a serious impediment to sight.

Neitis Ksoka nodded and continued on his way,

Soon it was obvious that all the Jou'an-Jou'an who were able to had now gathered to watch the preparation of their evening meal. Two large pails of water were brought and poured into the pot, which was then placed ceremoniously on the rack above the fire. Each family head brought forward the contribution he was making to the meal, and Tokatis came forward with a tray laden with gobbets of meat, poultry, and fish. These were ceremoniously dumped into the new pot, accompanied by cheers and the steady beating of a drum—Zumir was at his post again. As darkness thickened around them, and the shine of the mist became a glimmerance over the water, Dukkai began to chant, summoning the Lords of the Earth to attend their feast, promising them a feast of their own. Someone threw bitter herbs onto the fire, and the smoke that rose from them blew toward Dukkai.

"Bring our sacrifice," she intoned. The drum became louder, and some of the older men droned a two-note chant. "Bring our sacrifice," she repeated emphatically.

There was a flurry of activity as a number of the young men left the blaze of firelight and hurried off to their appointed collection of the offering.

"It is probably one of the ponies with peeling hooves," Ragoczy Franciscus said to his mare as if apologizing to her. He was about to lead her and the mule back several paces when he felt a sharp blow to the back of his head. This staggered him, and as he fell, he could feel ropes going around him, and he heard the urgent, whispered instructions his captors gave one another as they fixed their knots and strove to lift him to their shoulders. "Release me!" He squirmed in his bonds, comprehension coming over him so abruptly that he almost feared he had been knocked unconscious and this was his dream. The jostling of the young men bearing him toward the fire warned him that all this was as real as the band of scars across his abdomen. He forced himself to be calm and spoke as evenly as he could. "You must put me down. This is an error. Dukkai has—"

"She told us to bring you, and bring you we will," said one of the young men, and slapped the rump of the blue roan to set her moving on the road back to the town.

"She told you?" Ragoczy Franciscus wished he were more astonished than he was. He understood now the reasons for Dukkai's occasional shifts of conversation, her unexpected silences, and her odd explanations: she had known when he arrived that she would make him a gift to the Lords of the Earth. At least, he thought, it had troubled her.

The space around the fire-pit was empty but for Dukkai, who stood, smoke rising around her face, a distant stare in her eyes as if she saw impossibly distant vistas. In her hand was the same knife she had used on the goat.

As the drumming grew louder, the young men put Ragoczy Franciscus down in front of her and then backed away, one of them tripping and almost falling as he did.

Taking advantage of this distraction, Ragoczy Franciscus struggled against his bonds, his strength sufficient to loosen two of the knots, but not enough to break the ropes that held him. He began to twist his confined hands, working at the rope to gain enough purchase to slip free.

"Stand!" Dukkai ordered the youth. "To fall is an ill omen."

"Yes, Dukkai," the young man muttered, and slid back toward the shadows of the tents.

Ragoczy Franciscus schooled himself to calm and spoke with patient authority. "Dukkai. This is not going to please the Lords of the Earth. My blood is not worthy: believe this."

She did not look down. "Lords of the Earth, this is the blood demanded by Tejamksa for your solace and strength. The Gods of the Smoke confirm the choice. This foreigner has been along your veins farther than any of us, and he has seen how you shape the earth. So it is fitting that his blood should be shed for your benefit." Leaning forward, she sank her hands in Ragoczy Franciscus' hair and tugged his head back, and in the same notion, slit his throat, taking care not to sever the spine, for such mutilation would render the offering unacceptable. She brought up her hand to protect her face from the pulsing fountain of blood she expected, then stared as only a small amount oozed from the deep cut and soaked into the thick woolen collar of his shuba and kandys.

The assault was so sudden that at first all he felt was a blow; there was little pain. Then the agony hit him and he fell heavily to the side, feeling disoriented and verging on panic. He felt a small amount of blood run down his throat as comprehension burst upon him. In spite of his determination to hang on to consciousness, he began to grow dizzy from shock, and his whole body ached from the insult that had been done to him.

"Look!" someone said in awe. "There is no blood in him."

"It isn't right," said another.

The drumming stopped just before a wail went up from the Desert Cats, and one of the older women screamed, "The offering is refused!"

Neitis Ksoka came up to Ragoczy Franciscus and bent over him. "His eyes are open, and they are moving." He made a sign against sorcery, then kicked the foreigner in the back. He pointed at Dukkai. "You said the Lords of the Earth wanted him. You said the Gods of the Smoke wanted him. You said Tejamksa singled him out!"

"She . . . she did," Dukkai faltered. "It was . . ."

"It was *what*?" Neitis Ksoka demanded. "What have you done?"

Even if Ragoczy Franciscus could have drawn enough breath to speak, with his throat cut he could not. He thrashed where he lay, sensing that things would shortly become much worse. With an effort that left him weak with exhaustion, he pulled one hand free from the ropes and felt his neck to determine how much damage had been done. The cut crossed the front of his throat and had sunk slightly more than halfway through skin, muscles, and windpipe, toward his spine, more than enough to be quickly fatal to any living man. To the undead, it would mean many long months of misery while the wounds knitted slowly—that was assuming he was able to get out of the Jou'an-Jou'an camp without further injury and had the opportunity to heal. He lay on his side, fighting to remain alert, his attention fully on Dukkai as Neitis Ksoka continued to rant at her.

"I have done what had to be done," she said woodenly.

"You have brought disaster upon us. We have come to this horrible place because you said we should find pasture here! It was your guidance that put us on this wretched island, that doomed our ponies to die from ruined feet, that let fever loose among us!" He was being supported by growls of agreement. He strode around the fire. "We had to continue west, you said! The Lords of the Earth required it, or the sun would remain weak and we would suffer!"

Dukkai was backing away from him. "No . . . I . . . No."

"Look at the foreigner! He gives no blood!" Neitis Ksoka pursued.

"Cast him from the camp," shouted one of the men. "Get him away from here!"

"I will remove him," volunteered another.

Ragoczy Franciscus, lost in a haze of pain and turmoil, hardly felt the hands that grabbed his arms and legs and scrambled him out of the camp, casting him toward the edge of the marsh. With every jolt and jounce, excruciation engulfed him, so that by the time he landed with this feet in the water among the weeds, he was unaware of any-thing but agony, and that soon faded as he fell into a torpor that shut out all the world.

Text of a letter from one of the Imperial secretaries, Shai Ho-Jhi, in Chang'an to Hu Bi-Da in Yang-Chau, carried by Imperial courier and delivered nine fortnights after it was written.

To the most respectable senior clerk of the Eclipse Trading Company in Yang-Chau, the greetings from the court of the Most Illustrious Wen Emperor, Yuan Buo-Ju, the Exquisite Wielder of the Vermilion Brush, at the behest of Hse Hsia-Dju, the Minister of Trade and Mon-etary Transactions, on this the twelfth day of the Fortnight of the Frost Kings, regarding the current disposition of the affairs of the foreigner Zangi-Ragozh, who is your employer, and the owner of ships and master of caravans throughout all the Middle of the World.

Although summoned to this court more than a year ago, Zangi-Ragozh and his companions have not yet reached this capital nor has any word of them been heard officially since he departed from Lo-Yang. There is an unconfirmed report that he and his personal servant crossed the Great Wall at Holin-Gol, but circumstances in that region have become so chaotic that no reliable information has reached this Ministry concerning this foreigner, and we cannot confirm or discount any intelligence we have. In terms of taxations and customs duties, any caravans of his trading company will be counted against the funds held here in trust for him or his duly appointed heirs.

A copy of this letter will be provided to the Prefecture of Yang-Chau so that there can be no question as to how matters stand in terms of his company, should Zangi-Ragozh return. It is fitting that we do this, for the peace of the Middle Kingdom and the success of our continuing commerce in all parts of the greater world. We ask that you provide this Ministry with accounts of all ships, caravans, and similar trading ventures held by this foreigner, so that no merchant will be taxed unfairly in his name, and nothing of his shall be given away due to lack of information or sufficient records to make a fair assignment of title and worth to such goods as may come through Chang'an from the distant cities of the West.

There are many merchants whose businesses have been reduced to little more than local peddling since the Year of Yellow Snow. With the sun still dark in the sky, there is little hope that trade can resume next spring, or the spring after, if what is said of the state of the trade roads is true, and much of the way has been damaged by floods and other perturbations of nature. For that reason, the Minister, Hse Hsia-Dju, has stated that taxes on merchants may be postponed for a period of up to four years, at the conclusion of which time the principal sum must be paid, although any interest may be defrayed for another two years. If these provisions will in any way help your employer, I ask you to provide me with such accounts as will have bearing on this ruling, along with itineraries of the caravans, when such can be determined, due to the disruption of trade.

I also ask, on behalf of the Minister, that you notify us should Zangi-Ragozh return and at that time provide any necessary documentation to accompany his return. Also, should you be provided irrefutable proof of his death, this Ministry would like to know of it so that a proper record may be made, any death duties levied, and an appropriate record of all registrations made for the benefit of his heirs as well as those with whom he has done business over the years.

Whatever holdings are on record here in Chang'an may be inspected by you or your appointed deputy at any time, providing all taxes and duties are current and the accounts maintained by Zangi-Ragozh are sufficient to cover the cost of such an inspection. The Ministry of Trading and Monetary Transactions receives such petitions for inspections on the fifth, ninth, and thirteenth day of every fortnight, between the Hour of the Cock and the Hour of the Dragon. You or your deputy may leave credentials at the Ministry any day and arrange an appointment for the next available inspection day. It would be my honor to assist you in such an inspection, if that is in accord with

Zangi-Ragozh's instructions to you, or the nature of your business transactions determines this is a prudent course.

Your cooperation will be noted and appreciated and will reflect well upon any member of your family residing in the bounds of the Wen Emperor's rule.

Shai Ho-Jhi
Secretary to Hse Hsia-Dju
Imperial Ministry of Trade and Monetary Transactions
Chang'an
(his chop)
(the chop of Shai Ho-Jhi)

PART IV

Rojeh

*T*ext of a letter from Eustasios Krisanthemenis in Constantinople to his uncle, Porphyry Cantheos, in Sinope, carried by merchant ship and delivered two months after it was dispatched.

The greetings of Eustasios Krisanthemenis to his well-regarded uncle, Porphyry Cantheos, in the handsome port of Sinope on this the 537th anniversary of the beginning of the season of the Birth of Christ, which blessed day will come at the end of this dark, miserable month: may Heaven bless you and send you many good things in the year to come, commensurate with your worth and in forms that need no explication to understand. This letter will not be long, for I want to confine it to both sides of a single page; the Captain of the Diadem will charge me by the sheet of parchment, and so I apologize for the necessarily brusque tone of my communication.

I am writing to you to ask a favor of you, dear uncle, one that may be something of an imposition upon you, and for which I am more than willing to compensate you. I have recently received yet another missive from my sister, dictated to and written by the Patriarch of her local church. She, you will recall, is a widow and presently living in Sarai, on the Caspian Sea, where her late husband had his business. She sent a letter to inform me that her house has been damaged in a storm, and since she has no male relations beyond her young son in that town who can order the repairs required and command the monies to pay for them, she has been forced to seek out her neighbor to provide housing and food for her and her family until his forthcoming departure. She cannot not sell her children, for as their mother she has not the authority to do so, and so they are in a most precarious position, and she has said that she must have the promise of some protection soon, or risk everything. She has told me she would like to return to Constantinople, but just at present that is neither possible nor desirable, for the city is much affected with hunger and illness, which makes it an unhealthy place for anyone.

In two previous letters my remonstrations have made no impact upon her, for she is persisting in soliciting my help. It would be a significant task to attempt to bring her and her family safely to Constantinople at this time, but it would be possible to send her and her three children to you, at least until things are less unstable here. This is the proposition I lay before you, and I hope you will consider this request in the spirit in which it is made—as a plea for our family. I am prepared to send you money twice a year to contribute to the maintenance of my sister and her children. We may decide on a reasonable sum if you are willing to take on this responsibility of housing and feeding my sister and her children. I would propose the amount of ten gold Apostles for the year for my sister and six Apostles each for her children. It is not an extravagant amount, I agree, but in these days, it is the most generous sum I can offer. My circumstances have never been affluent, and with the privations of the last two years, I have had to reduce my household and keep my business in much more frugal fashion than I have in the past, which has displeased my wife and children, but has been necessary. I have sold three of the household slaves, keeping only eight to tend to my wife and children as well as my stable and racing teams, which have been idle for almost a year and a half due to this blight God has visited upon us.

I look to hear from you in the spring, and I pray that you will show your family loyalty as well as true Christian charity and say you are willing to bring Thetis and her son and daughters into your house. I also pray that you and your family enjoy good health and as much good fortune as there is to be had in these hard days. May God reward you on earth as well as in Paradise for the kindness you extend to my sister now.

> Eustasios Krisanthemenis
> Horse-breeder and merchant of Constantinople

1

Chtavo rushed into the kitchen, his face white with alarm. "The blue roan's come back," he said, panting between each word. He stood in the kitchen door, bits of icy damp clinging to his hair and the collar of his bearskin cloak. "And the weather is turning nasty."

Dasur looked up from his kneading-board, a rough round of dough lying under his hand. "What do you mean?"

"I mean the master's mare is here, and the mule. But he isn't. And it is coming on to sleet." Chtavo went toward the hearth, his hands extended as if for comfort as much as warmth.

"You know what those Jou'an-Jou'an are, and the master *will* go among those people," said Dasur, not sounding as confident as he would like, and paying no attention to Chtavo's last remark. "The two probably broke away when the barbarians became too wild."

"They never have before," said Chtavo, his frown increasing to a glower.

"But it is starting to blow; and cold rain with high winds can make horses wild," said Dasur.

"The mare wasn't lathered," Chtavo said, mulling this over as he spoke. "Not that the mule would be rushed."

"If there had been real trouble, wouldn't the mule run?" Dasur asked.

Chtavo shrugged. "You can never tell with a mule. Lucky thing they got to the gate before it was closed for the night, or they might have been outside the walls until dawn."

This bothered Dasur; he wiped his hands on a rag and said, "I will inform Rojeh of what has happened: he can decide what is to be done."

"Yes," said Chtavo. "Rojeh will know what is best to do." He looked around. "Is there any wine left?"

"There's a jar of it on the shelf next to the herb chest," said Dasur, trying to decide how to tell Rojeh about the horse and the mule. He gathered his thoughts and started for the corridor to the floor above. "Is the mare in her stall? And the mule?"

"Of course," said Chtavo, offended at such a notion. "Do you think I would leave them standing tacked in the stable?" He had taken his cup from his capacious sleeve and was pouring wine into it.

Dasur nodded and continued on. The more he climbed, the less he liked the news he carried, and the more reluctant he became. Only the certain knowledge that keeping such information to himself might earn him a whipping kept him at his errand—not, he reminded himself, that anyone in this house had ever whipped him, but he had never had to give such worrisome news. He first sought Rojeh in Ragoczy Franciscus' study, but found the room unlit and empty. His second attempt met with more success, for he discovered Rojeh in the room where cloth and clothing were stored. "You should have Aethalric do that," he said to announce his presence.

"Aethalric is busy with the children, and I would not want to take him from them," said Rojeh, making a mark on his wax tablet with his iron stylus. "What is it?"

"I . . . I have a word to offer from Chtavo," said Dasur hesitantly.

"Is there some reason Chtavo could not deliver it himself?" Rojeh asked, his austere features showing little more than polite interest.

Dasur avoided answering that question. "I thought you ought to know, so I have come to tell you." He cleared his throat. "Chtavo reports that the master's horse and mule came back to the stable without him."

Rojeh's demeanor changed at once; he put his tablet and stylus aside and confronted Dasur. "When?"

"A short while ago. It had to have been in the hour after sunset, or how would the animals get through the gate?" Dasur was beginning to feel a cold lump of fear settling in his chest.

Not bothering to reply, Rojeh rapped out a brisk order. "Have Chtavo saddle my horse for me and buckle on a scabbard for my longsword. I am going to change and get my weapon; I will be down very soon." He all but shoved Dasur out of the room, then halted him. "Not a word to the widow or her children. They mustn't know anything about this."

Dasur nodded and bolted for the kitchen, where he found Chtavo on his second cup of wine. "Rojeh says you are to saddle his horse. At once. Oh, and the scabbard for his long-sword."

Chtavo gave Dasur a long, puzzled stare. "Then he thinks something is wrong?"

"Do as he says. Now." Dasur clapped his hands for emphasis. "He won't like being kept waiting."

"Oh, all right," Chtavo grumbled, and set his cup down. "I'll come back as soon as I've done. Don't touch that."

"I won't," said Dasur, beginning to worry in earnest. Chtavo left the kitchen, the plank door slamming behind him as he went out into the worsening weather; an icy breeze writhed through the kitchen, justifying the shivering that had taken hold of Dasur. He went to pour himself a cup of wine and had just taken a long first sip when Rojeh arrived in riding gear, a vast muffling mababa secured around him, his long-sword in one hand and a small case in the other. "Chtavo is saddling your horse."

"Excellent. If I am not back by midnight, have someone carry a message to Emrach Sarai'af that Ragoczy Franciscus may have met with an accident. If I am back before then, depending upon what I find, I will inform you what must be done. See you remember what I have told you," said Rojeh, not allowing Dasur to dither. "And nothing to the widow."

Dasur blundered on, "Do you really think he could be dead?"

"I hope he is not," said Rojeh with great feeling as he reached the outer door and let in another insidious draft as he went on toward the stable, where he found Chtavo just finishing securing the scabbard to the saddle. The spotted stallion was restive, and Chtavo had to keep one hand on the bridle as he worked, swearing under his breath by all the gods of his Volgamen people.

"He's ready, and then some," said Chtavo as he saw Rojeh approaching.

"Fine." Rojeh handed him his sword. "Put this in the scabbard, will you?" He did not bother to see if Chtavo obeyed; he secured the case to the cantle and tested the metal foot-loop. "A good length."

"The sword's in place," said Chtavo. "I'll open the gate."

"And keep watch for my return," Rojeh ordered. "Dasur has my orders in that regard." Saying this, he swung up into the saddle, gathered the reins, and turned the horse toward the door, pausing only long enough to raise the hood of his mababa before going out into the rising storm.

Chtavo hurried ahead of him to open the gate, hunching as he jogged to keep the sleeting rain from getting down the neck of his cloak. He drew back the bolt and tugged the gate, pulling it back enough to allow Rojeh to ride out into the street. Then he pressed the gate closed, set the bolt, and made his way back to the kitchen, all the while trying to keep from worrying about his employer.

The streets of Sarai were almost empty, and those few people not indoors either scurried along, cloaks drawn close about them, or huddled in doorways, trying to stay out of the stinging sleet. At the gate, the guard accepted a silver coin to open the gate and two more to ensure he would open it again upon Rojeh's return, saying to him as he released the counterweight to open the door, "It must be a very important thing, to take you out at this hour on such a night."

"Yes. A matter of some urgency." Once outside the gate, Rojeh held the stallion to a walk down the long slope to the low-lying islands; the last thing he wanted was for his horse to be injured before he could find Ragoczy Franciscus. Rojeh could feel the constant tug on the reins from the bit, and he could sense the horse's uneasiness in his mincing walk, and the stiffness of his neck; in spite of the cold, the horse was sweating, his head coming up at sudden noises, nostrils flared. It was difficult to find and follow the pathways through the maze of small islands to the one on which the Desert Cats were camped; Rojeh kept the spotted stallion moving forward. Twice he took a wrong turn and had to retrace his way back to the poorly marked trails and bridges.

The Jou'an-Jou'an camp was completely dark, the tents like gigantic mushrooms around the cold fire-pit. Rojeh went into the camp very slowly, peering into the dark. At the fire-pit he dismounted, buckled a long, braided-leather lead to the chin strap of his stallion's bridle, and proceeded on foot, leading the horse. He saw the new cooking pot standing empty next to the fire-pit and knew that Ragoczy Franciscus had reached the camp. As carefully as he could, Rojeh began a methodical search, hoping as he did that Ragoczy Franciscus was not in one of the tents. "Do this first," he whispered to himself. "The camp, and around the camp, then the tents, if it is necessary." Steadied by the sound of his own voice, Rojeh continued his explorations; he began to circle the camp, moving out from the tents to the reeds that marked the boundaries of the island. On his sixth circuit, a startled whicker from his horse alerted him to something at the edge of the water; going forward carefully, he found Ragoczy Franciscus lying facedown, his feet in the water, his body limp and cold. Knowing that the icy, slow-moving water had leached the little strength Ragoczy Franciscus' native earth in his soles might have imparted, Rojeh admitted to himself that Ragoczy Franciscus had almost fallen into the stupor that overcomes badly injured vampires, and that would make moving him a difficult proposition. With an oath to the gods of his youth, Rojeh dropped to his knees beside Ragoczy Franciscus and strove to determine what had been done to him. Working as quickly as he could, he was relieved that Ragoczy Franciscus had no broken bones, but that relief was short-lived, for as soon as he touched the edge of the deep cut in the vampire's neck, he gasped. Sitting back on his heels and staring at Ragoczy Franciscus' body, he tried to decide how to deal with this appalling situation.

Then he saw Ragoczy Franciscus' hand move.

That single, small motion ended his doubts. He bent forward. "Holy Jermen Franzic Ragosh-ski," he said, using Ragoczy Franciscus' name from his breathing years. "You have been badly hurt. You are lying at the edge of a marsh stream. This is Rogerian. I am going to take you back to your house here in Sarai."

The hand moved again, not much, but enough to confirm he had heard.

"I may cause you some pain when I move you," Rojeh went on, as much to explain to himself as to Ragoczy Franciscus. "I will bind your neck when I have you on my horse."

This time the hand was more emphatic, the fingers closing into a loose fist.

"Do you think you can hold on, or should I put you up before me?" As he asked, he realized there was no way for Ragoczy Franciscus to answer. "If you should be in front, move one finger. If you can ride behind—" He broke off, knowing that Ragoczy Franciscus would not yet know how much his strength had been compromised. "I'll put you ahead of me, in the saddle."

One finger tapped.

"Then make yourself ready and I will lift you," said Rojeh, "after I turn you over."

The finger tapped again, twice.

At that, Rojeh faltered. "I know you are badly hurt, but your spine is intact. You would have died the True Death if it were not. If you want me to stop at any point, open your hand wide and I will."

The finger tapped a single time.

"I'll take that for agreement," said Rojeh, and crouched next to Ragoczy Franciscus, trying to determine how best to roll him onto his back; Ragoczy Franciscus could not endure much more harm to his neck without risking far greater damage. At last, Rojeh put one hand on his shoulder and the other on his head. "I'll start with the top; I'll try to move your head and shoulder at the same time. Once your shoulders are squarely on the ground, your legs will follow, and I can turn them when this first part is done. If something seems wrong, wave your hand and I'll stop at once." Taking a deep breath, he began a careful, deliberate turn of Ragoczy Franciscus' head and shoulders toward him, making a point not to look at the wound in his neck, for fear of shaking his resolve. He managed to get Ragoczy Franciscus onto his back, and then tugged at his hip to bring his legs over as well.

The spotted horse snorted, startled by the sudden odor of old blood. He pawed uneasily and tried to toss his head to show his distress.

Rojeh pulled sharply on the lead, forcing the animal to stand still. "You have to carry him," he said firmly. He straddled Ragoczy Franciscus, leaning over him to try to determine how much he could take from the travel ahead of them. "I'd best do your neck now," he decided aloud, and without waiting for a signal from his employer, he went to unstrap the small wooden case from the cantle. Opening it as he walked, he took out cotton bandages, three times the length of the height of a tall man, and a handbreadth wide, thinking of how best to employ them. As he reached Ragoczy Franciscus' side, he said, "I will wrap these around your throat and over your head. That should give you a little support and keep your head from lolling." He knelt down again, and working quickly but with as little disruption as he could manage, he swathed Ragoczy Franciscus' neck and then his head in the bandages. "This is the best I can do until we are indoors again." He set the little case down, knowing he would have to leave it. "I am going to help you sit up now," he said to Ragoczy Franciscus, and saw his hand clench. Doing as much as he could to brace his employer's head from behind, he levered him to a sitting position, then stopped as the sleet increased on a sudden gust of wind. "We'll be moving shortly." He prepared to help Ragoczy Franciscus to get to his feet. "I will take you under your arms and stand up with you; if you can assist me, so much the better," he said, wanting Ragoczy Franciscus to know what was coming. "If you will stay balanced, I should be able to get you up."

The hand tightened.

"All right," said Rojeh, positioning himself to lift Ragoczy Franciscus. "Let's try." It took a steady effort, but there was a little strength still left in Ragoczy Franciscus, and he was able to get to his feet with less effort than Rojeh had anticipated. "Can you stand?"

Ragoczy Franciscus swayed a little but he moved a clenched hand.

"Do you think you can walk?"

The hand did not move.

"No, I didn't suppose you could," said Rojeh, tugging on the lead to bring the horse up to them. "I am going to mount first and then haul you into the saddle, if I can."

Ragoczy Franciscus closed his hand.

Rojeh positioned the spotted stallion carefully so that the horse could give Ragoczy Franciscus something to lean upon. Then he mounted behind the saddle and reached down to take Ragoczy Franciscus by the hands and began the struggle to haul him aboard the restive horse. Ragoczy Franciscus was a considerable weight to lift, and Rojeh lacked his preternatural strength, so the effort this required was great, demanding his full concentration and force; gradually he raised Ragoczy Franciscus off the ground without unbalancing his own seat and finally lugged him into place, panting with the exertion this feat demanded.

Ragoczy Franciscus' hand closed on Rojeh's wrist in a gesture of thanks.

"We'll return to Sarai, my master," Rojeh said quietly, and tapped his heels to start the horse moving.

The journey back to the town gate seemed interminable, with the roaring wind blowing sleet in their faces; the cold cut through their clothes and sank into their bones. Even Ragoczy Franciscus, who was rarely bothered by cold, began to shiver, which made his seat less steadied than Rojeh would have liked, and that slowed their progress even more, for Rojeh had to continue to hold Ragoczy Franciscus upright while he also guided the horse. By the time they reached the long ascent to the town, Rojeh was as fatigued as he was cold, and as he summoned the guard, he had to hang on to the saddle as well as the reins to remain in place on the horse's croup.

"You are back after all," said the guard as he opened the gate.

"Close the gate. I am taking my employer back to the Foreigners' Quarter. He has sustained a bad wound and I must dress it properly."

"Judging by that bandage, he must have been waylaid by thieves," said the guard as he worked the device that closed the gate.

"I will know when he is able to speak again," said Rojeh, and continued away from the gate to the far side of the town. As he passed the rubble from the most recent fire, he felt Ragoczy Franciscus twist in the saddle, and he had to halt in order to seat him properly once more. "We are nearly there. You haven't long to wait."

A small lamp burned fitfully beside the gate to Ragoczy Franciscus' house, a sign that encouraged Rojeh as he caught sight of it. He dismounted and took the lead, going up to the gate and tugging once on the bell-pull. He hoped that Chtavo was still awake and sober enough to help him with the horse. He rang a second time and heard the bolt slide back almost as the second toll sounded; the gate swung open, and Rojeh led his horse into the entry court, halting the stallion so that he could drag Ragoczy Franciscus out of the saddle.

Chtavo was beside him, bleary-eyed and a little drunk. He peered at Ragoczy Franciscus. "Been hurt?"

"I'm afraid so. I am taking him to his apartment, and I will need Aethalric to join me promptly. I trust he hasn't gone to bed?" He was keeping Ragoczy Franciscus on his feet by shoving him against the stallion's shoulder.

"Aethalric and Dasur are in the kitchen, drinking hot wine and telling each other what may have happened to the master; their tales are becoming preposterous." He kicked at a loose paving stone as if to underscore his point.

Rojeh nodded. "If you will tend to the horse. Is there enough grain to give him some warm mash when he's cooled down and been groomed?"

"I can find a handful for him," said Chtavo, taking the lead from Rojeh. "Have you any need of me once the horse is stalled?"

"No. You have done well, Chtavo. Ragoczy Franciscus will be grateful." Rojeh wedged his shoulder under Ragoczy Franciscus' arm and started toward the kitchen door, supporting Ragoczy Franciscus' feeble efforts with his own tired body. He gave the kitchen door a single blow, then waited for it to be opened, occupying himself with determining how much of Ragoczy Franciscus' remaining vitality had been vitiated during their ride back; that process left him uneasy, so he was pleased when Dasur opened the door, staring into the darkness and clearly anticipating the worst.

"The master!" he exclaimed. "Is he—"

"He is not truly dead. As you see, he is attempting to stand," said Rojeh, pushing past Dasur into the house.

"By the Djinns," said Dasur, fumbling to close the door even as he strove to lend a hand to Rojeh's struggles. "You have wrapped his head!"

"To protect his wound. It is such that he cannot speak." Rojeh was pleased that Dasur had noticed that instead of the heavy swathing of Ragoczy Franciscus' throat. He looked over his shoulder to be sure the door was fully closed. "He is going to need careful nursing to recover. I want the fire in the master's rooms built up. Now, Dasur."

Dasur was wringing his hands in distress. "This is dreadful. This is terrible. He'll die, and then we'll be cast out into—"

"He is not dead yet, and if we are quick about it, he will not die," said Rojeh, and saw Aethalric coming toward them, his face stark with dismay. "Will you help me carry him?"

"Oh, yes. I will," said Aethalric in the slightly thickened voice of one suddenly struck sober. "How do you want it done?"

"I will carry his shoulders, and you will take his legs. We must go slowly—I will take the lead up the stairs, walking backward. You will have to guide me." He glanced at Dasur. "The fire? In his rooms?"

Dasur nodded repeatedly and hastened to load up a large basket with lengths of wood. "Right away, right away," he kept repeating as he worked.

The warmth of the kitchen finally penetrated Ragoczy Franciscus' daze; he half-opened his eyes and stared at the hearth. His lips moved but no sound came from them, and Rojeh saw anguish in his face.

"That will come, in time," Rojeh said, and watched Dasur scurry from the kitchen with his basket of logs. He looked at Aethalric. "If you will help me?" He turned to Ragoczy Franciscus. "We are going to carry you upstairs. We'll go slowly, but if you are pained too much, signal with your hand."

Ragoczy Franciscus closed both his hands to fists; Aethalric saw this and gasped.

"Very good," said Rojeh, preparing himself as he went on, "If you will lean back against me, I will take your shoulders, and Aethalric will take your feet. We will make this as easy a climb as we can, but I fear there may be some problems."

Ragoczy Franciscus complied, and after a brief jostling, Rojeh and Aethalric were bearing him out of the kitchen and toward the stairs, which were steep, and they curved in unexpected places. By the time they reached the main floor, Aethalric was sweating, and Rojeh ordered a brief halt. As they resumed the upward climb, Ragoczy Franciscus kept lapsing into unconsciousness, which made carrying him trickier, for not only was he dead weight, he could communicate nothing about his state.

Dasur admitted them to Ragoczy Franciscus' room. His hands were sooty from building up the fire, but he seemed relieved to be able to do something useful. "What more do you want?"

"There is a chest of rosewood in his study, banded with brass. Would you fetch that, please," Rojeh said, doing his best to keep his tone level and his manner confident.

"Where do you want him?" Aethalric asked, his cheeks flushed from his exertions.

"On his bed. Just put him on top." He backed in that direction. "Lift him carefully." He hefted Ragoczy Franciscus' shoulders, taking care not to let his head go unsupported.

Aethalric took an awkward step back and almost collided with a low, brass-topped table. He opened his hands to show apology and said, "I had better get back to my quarters. The children will rise at dawn, and Herakles has been feeling ill, so dealing with them falls to me."

"You seem to enjoy that task," said Rojeh, making sure Ragoczy Franciscus was lying squarely on the bed. "If you will spare a little more time and help me remove his boots?"

Nodding, Aethalric stepped up to the foot of the bed and took hold of the left boot. "If you hold his shoulders again, this should be simple."

Rojeh agreed. "Pull by the heel; they'll come off more easily."

Following these instructions, Aethalric tugged off the left boot and then the right, letting them drop to the floor. "There. Is that enough?"

"Yes. Thank you for your help. And don't let the children overwhelm you," Rojeh advised. "I had a family, many years ago. I know how children can require more than we anticipate."

Aethalric gave Rojeh a startled look. "You had children?"

"And a wife. But they have been lost to me many, many years and were far away from here." He changed the subject, not wanting to divulge much more information. "In the morning, neither my master nor I should be disturbed."

"And the widow? She'll want to see him, I'm sure," said Aethalric.

"No doubt," said Rojeh. "Tell her she may talk to me when I rise, but that Ragoczy Franciscus is to remain undisturbed until he himself says that he is ready to receive company." Rojeh motioned to the door. "That goes for all the household."

"I will tell Dasur and Chtavo," said Aethalric.

"If you like. Inform Sinu as well. The widow may want to assign her to my master, but that would not be wise." Rojeh heard Dasur approaching. "Go along now, and know that you have Ragoczy Franciscus' gratitude." Aethalric bolted from the room, and as soon as he was gone, Dasur brought the rosewood chest into the chamber; Rojeh pointed to the brass-topped table. "If you would put it down?"

"May I go bank the kitchen fire and prepare to sleep?" Dasur's cot was in the little pantry, to guard the food from any thieves that might sneak into the house.

"Yes. I appreciate what you have done," said Rojeh, as he knew Ragoczy Franciscus expected him to. "When I wake in the morning, I will provide proof of gratitude." He had decided that all three servants would be given a gold Byzantine Apostle for their extra service this night. "A formal report hasn't been made yet, and until it is, gossip could have unpleasant ramifications."

"Nothing leaves this house. I will see to it," said Dasur just before he left the room, closing the door firmly behind him.

Rojeh went to the rosewood chest and unfastened its locks and took from the upper compartment a pair of shears made of fabulously valuable steel. He used these to cut the clothes of Ragoczy Franciscus, and then to sever the knot on the bandages. Putting the ruined clothes aside, he drew a silk-stuffed blanket over Ragoczy Franciscus, then went to the chest and took out the first compartment, revealing two more beneath. From the second compartment, he took one of the three needles he found there, threaded it with fine silk from a reel of the shiny strands, then went to begin the exacting work on Ragoczy Franciscus' throat. He had seen his master do repairs on appalling injuries and had assisted him more than once to reunite vessels and muscles and skin; he had never had to do it on his own, and with Ragoczy Franciscus for a patient. He began the painstaking work of stitching the severed tissues together again.

It was nearly dawn when Rojeh finished. The snow was falling heavily but the wind had slacked off, and sunrise promised only a slight diminishing of darkness, but for Rojeh, it was as splendid a morning as any he had known, for he was sure that as horribly as Ragoczy Franciscus had been hurt, he would recover.

Text of a letter from Atta Olivia Clemens in Roma to Abbot Helieri at Santus Spiritu in Gaul, carried by the merchant Voramalch of Vindobon, journeying north from Roma, and delivered three months after it was written.

To the esteemed Abbot of Santus Spiritu monastery in Gaul, the greetings of Atta Olivia Clemens in Roma, on this the tenth day of January in the 1290th Year of the City, and the 537th Year of the Christian faith, in the hope that this finds you and your monks in better circumstances than prevailed a year ago.

In answer to your question, I have very little news of the world beyond the region we both inhabit; you in Gaul, and I now in Roma. With the restrictions placed on me as a widow, I have to depend on Niklos Aulirios to obtain gossip and reports circulating in the city; he is diligent in procuring all the latest intelligence, but there are a few things I know for myself: trade with foreign ports has remained inactive, and the weather continues to be to blame. And I have had no word from my blood relative, who is in China, at a place called Yang-Chau, or was the last time I heard from him, a decade ago. Lacking news of him, I can find no one whose opinion I consider reliable who

can provide accurate information regarding what has transpired in
those remote parts of the world, so I cannot advise you on any points
of your inquiry. The merchant who bears the letter, Voramalch of
Vindobon, claims that he has heard that there are orchards and fields
in the East that are flourishing, protected by mighty sorcerers whose
spells have brought the people of those places rich harvests and fe-
cund herds, but I must tell you, I put no stock in such tales. What little I have heard suggests that the East has been as hard-hit as the
West in regard to the weakened sun and the lingering cold. I apologize
for not having anything more definite or more optimistic than this to
report, but to tell you otherwise would be to bear false witness.

The Church continues to gain converts, and in such a time as this,
it is hardly a wonder, for with so much uncertainty in the world, and
with conditions that may appear to be the end of the world—as many
of the Bishops here preach—many people believe that the promise of
the life after death is more dependable than this life. Daily Roma is
filled with funeral processions, and the incense from the churches all
but blots out the sun. Those who venture to the old temples do so circumspectly, for there are bands of Christian youths who go about the
streets with cudgels, attacking any who seek to worship at places other
than their churches. Already they have appropriated some of the old
temples for their own use, changing the dedications to those of Christian Saints instead of the older gods of Roma. For many Romans, the
changing of the Pantheon to Santa Maria ad Martyres was a final blow
to the old ways of Roma, when many faiths were practiced and many
gods were welcome. I have seen the temple of the Bona Dea usurped in
the name of the Virgin Mary, and surely the statue of a pregnant
woman is suitable both to Mary and the Magna Mater.

You have asked about the Pope, and I regret to tell you that I have
very little knowledge about the current state of Silverius, except to say
that the Pope is at odds with the Emperor Justinian in Constantinople.
Now that the Ostrogoths no longer have the strong leadership and
their so-called nobles contend for power, the Emperor in Constantinople can act almost with impunity here, for the Ostrogoths will not
agree to unite long enough to throw back so powerful an opponent as
Justinian's General Belisarius. In this disarray the Church is left to
flounder. For all the prestige that was gained when Pope Leo bribed the
Huns to save Roma, the Church has assumed a position that it cannot

fulfill with the support of the Ostrogothic army, which is not theirs to command. Because the Church is without military champions in Roma, the Eastern Church has increased its pressure on the Pope, attempting to reunify all Christians, under their leadership, of course. There is a convocation of churchmen ordered to take place in Constantinople, but it is not at all certain that Pope Silverius may attend. It is said he is in poor health and that such a journey may be enough to bring about his death. I have no direct information to confirm this; I am only repeating what has been propounded by Senators and other officials. Since the Eastern and Roman Churches broke apart, each has tried to gain ascendancy over the other, and that is detrimental to both, for it means that conflicts within the Churches become more important than what is transpiring in the world. Those prestigious Archbishops would gain more support and assistance if they were to leave spiritual politics to God and extend themselves to their people with charity and succor. I am sorry if this distresses you, but if you think I say this to cast aspersions on the Church, come to Roma and see for yourself. I have no reason to deceive you, but, of course, as I am a woman, I am not privy to the inner workings of the Papal court and must tell you only what I have gleaned from knowledgeable sources.

As part of Justinian's plan, his army is still in the south, not very active at present because of the weather. Some of the companies of soldiers have been recalled to help contain the increasing troubles on the eastern borders of the Byzantine Empire, but many still remain, and it has been the sad lot of the peasants of the south to have to house and feed these interlopers. Some have taken this much to heart and have appealed to the Senate to provide some relief for what they have endured. But the Senate has little to give and even less authority to give it, and so the people in the south languish under a double yoke—that of Roma and Constantinople. With food so scarce, I have been hearing stories of peasants capturing Byzantine soldiers and slaughtering them. I know of no one who has actually witnessed such a meal, but the tales are everywhere, and they are increasing. I have no doubt that men on the edge of starvation have eaten other men, but in this case, the stories have an air of convenience about them—peasants not only getting a meal, but striking back against an enemy—that makes them less plausible than if the peasants were said to have devoured their neighbors.

They say that bears and wolves have been coming down out of the hills to the north of Roma and attacking villages for food. If this is so, and not some often-repeated rumor, it does not augur well for the year to come. I cannot put full credence in it, for I know that bears sleep in the winter and do not venture out until spring. But it may be that in the fall there were instances of lone farms being attacked, for such has happened before after a hard year. I would not put too much stock in such reports, but I would not go abroad alone, either, and not just because of wolves and bears: there are many desperate men who have turned to outlawry and who prey upon the unprotected. You may dislike the notion, but I would advise you to take at least six men, properly armed, as escort when you go abroad in the country, for I fear you are far more likely to fall to a brigand's arrow or spear than to the jaws of a wolf. I would also require your monks to travel in groups of at least ten, for much the same reason. I know they may carry knives and staves, both of which are useful weapons.

I will look forward to your next letter. If I learn anything that may be useful to you, I will send a message to you as soon as I may, if the roads are not still so muddy that the courier would risk ending up in a quagmire. I will hope that the spring is kind to us all, and that you and your monks are spared more tragedies than you have suffered already, that our crops become bountiful once again, and our livestock flourish. I thank you for the good service you have rendered me, and I trust that in time, the service I render you will prove of equal worth.

Atta Olivia Clemens

2

Emrach Sarai'af scratched his beard and contemplated the sheet of parchment on the table in front of him. "You say this is written in the Byzantine tongue? You know the language, do you?" he asked Rojeh suspiciously. He was reclining in a padded-leather chair, but not at rest.

"Yes, it is in Byzantine Greek. Ask Patriarch Stavros if you doubt me. I would offer to read it, but I suppose you would prefer your translator be a disinterested party," Rojeh answered blandly. He had dressed in a long paragaudion of a deep green shade with a Roman-style abolla of heavy, rust-colored wool hung artfully around his shoulders, giving him a somewhat formal appearance for this occasion. His Persian leggings were a deep brown, almost the same shade as his boots.

"Perhaps tomorrow; I have too much to attend to today," said Emrach, stretching out and staring off into the distance. "The last storm was the worst so far—more than a dozen houses have been destroyed and all the builders are busy, as is most of the town. Who knows when we will have such a break in the weather again? I must see as many of you foreigners as I can until the next storm comes."

Rojeh preserved an unperturbed manner, continuing, "My employer would appreciate knowing what your final disposition will be in regard to this—"

"What can it be? I am powerless in this situation. It is a Jou'an-Jou'an matter, surely?" Emrach asked with an elaborate shrug. "The Jou'an-Jou'an are camped outside the walls, where I have no authority."

"You could admit her to the town," Rojeh said patiently; he saw the obstinate set of Emrach's jaw, and he strove to keep his tone level. "If my employer can pardon her for her attempt on his life, surely you can let her into the town. Otherwise she is likely to die."

"But your master is just the problem, don't you see?—she made an attempt on his life, and that would mean I could be permitting a would-be murderer to enter our gates, which would not be accepted by those whose town this is. You are a foreigner, your master is a foreigner, and you will soon be gone, and what would we do with the woman then? With the prison burned down, we have no secure place to put her, and her people have already forbidden her to shelter and eat with them. It would not be wise for me to allow her to come into Sarai, for not only is she dangerous, she might not want to leave, and what then?" He shook his head. "No. No. If the Jou'an-Jou'an have decided to be shut of her, why should I countermand their decision?"

Rojeh sighed. "You have made up your mind."

"I have," said Emrach with vast satisfaction. "I think it is fitting that you should bear in mind the obligation I have to all Sarai, particularly to those who live here, for as Master of Foreigners I must answer for what the foreigners do. Your Jou'an-Jou'an woman is no different than the rest. If she is allowed inside the walls, she might well begin to attack the people of the town, and that would not do. You have said that in this account, your master pardons her. I must not be guided by leniency, but by the strictures of my position."

"My employer is willing to vouch for her," Rojeh persisted. "He would offer her a place but—"

"Exactly. But! He cannot take so bloodthirsty a creature into his house." Emrach held up an admonishing finger, clearly enjoying the exercise of his authority. "You say your master has no fear, and that may well be true, but he cannot be allowed to conduct himself in such a lax manner."

"He is able to protect himself; the staff has been sufficient for his needs. There is no need for guards," said Rojeh, for the first time feeling the pluck of fear in his viscera.

"And who is he that I should pay him any mind?" Emrach challenged, his black eyes brightening.

"He is a man of vast experience who has been about the world for most of his life. He has witnessed things you and I can only imagine— and I say it, though I have been with him for a time." Rojeh tried to be as accommodating as possible, but he was having difficulty keeping his annoyance from his demeanor.

"Do the Jou'an-Jou'an think so?" Emrach asked, appreciating his power tremendously. "How can you tell me they have a high regard for him if they permit one of their own to—"

"My employer is not a man to demand satisfaction of those who do him injury, but he seeks a just resolution to disputes. Even the Jou'an-Jou'an woman has said she is deeply saddened about what her gods demanded of her," Rojeh pointed out. "She cannot long survive without shelter, let alone food."

"No, she can't." Emrach slapped his hand on the arm of his chair. "And why should your master offer to provide either food or shelter for her, considering what she has done? Is it his own pride, or is it truly his idea of justice, to permit an offender to go free?"

"My employer explains that in his report," said Rojeh. "He has said that she was forced to make a decision that redounded badly—"

"And you expect me to heed his request in regard to the woman Dukkau?"

"Dukkai," Rojeh corrected. "That is the reason I am here."

"Yes, so you said at the beginning," said Emrach. "Do you think the Jou'an-Jou'an master—what do they call him?"

"Kaigan. His name is Neitis Ksoka," Rojeh supplied.

"Terrible names," Emrach declared. "Would the Kaigan see it as your master does?"

Rojeh sighed, unwilling to argue. "This is my employer's account: I am ordered to leave it with you."

Emrach sighed his gratification at such an acknowledgment. "If that is what Ragoczy Franciscus has told you to do, then you have fulfilled your mission. I will assume he is giving a truthful report, and I will make a decision shortly."

"If I may ask, why are you so reluctant to extend mercy to this woman?" Rojeh asked.

"Ah, you see, Sarai is a funnel, and everyone traveling on the northern routes comes here one way or another. For that reason I must maintain order here that will extend protection not only to the town, but to anyone living within the walls, whether or not it is to their liking. Otherwise Sarai would be visited by more scoundrels than you can imagine, and no one in the town could maintain order." Emrach's smile was wide and shallow. "I am sure your master will understand when you explain it to him."

"This woman will not endanger that," Rojeh said.

"Perhaps not, but the next one might. And there is always a next one." Emrach laid his hand on the parchment. "I will speak to Patriarch Stavros later today and ask him to read this to me and assess what has been asked of me. That much I assure you I will do." He coughed delicately. "Your master must know that I have a duty to the town before any I have to foreigners."

Rojeh reverenced him. "Then I am most appreciative that you are willing to receive me at all."

"Very gracious—just what I would expect from your master." Emrach sighed and pointed to the side door. "I fear I must attend to the next petitioners. I have three Armenians to deal with, and they would not be pleased that you got here before them."

"As you wish," said Rojeh, not at all certain this was the true reason for Emrach's ordering him to leave in this atypical fashion. The door opened onto a small corridor, which led to a door opening onto an alleyway. Rojeh closed the door and stepped out into the street, walking with care on the rough paving stones covered in slushy snow.

"Ehi! Foreigner!" a scrawny youth called from the wall of the nearest house and, before Rojeh could respond, shied a rock at him. "That's for taking our food!" He scrambled out of sight, his derisive laughter echoing along the stones of the alley.

Rojeh inspected his shoulder where the rock had struck, using his fingers to ascertain how much harm he had sustained; satisfied no real damage had been done, he continued on as the path curved and twisted among the buildings, some of which had been damaged by fire and smoke, but most of which were still fairly sound. As he walked, he realized he had lost his sense of direction and now had no idea where the alley would take him.

A mangy, emaciated dog slunk across the road a short distance ahead of Rojeh. Its hair was patchy, but what there was looked matted. There were rat bites half-healed on its shoulders and flank, and its tail had been broken and now hung at a disconsolate angle. It growled miserably and slipped away through a gap in a blackened wall.

Rojeh was feeling distinctly edgy; he considered retracing his steps and trying the other direction from Emrach Sarai'af's house. He listened closely to the mingled sounds that the walls magnified and melded to a roar like a waterfall. The pale winter light provided little more than shadows, so narrow was the path among the buildings. Now Rojeh was glad he had slipped a dagger into his sleeve, for although it was forbidden to carry weapons into meetings with the Master of Foreigners, he had not been searched and now was ready to face any unexpected opponent he might encounter, he told himself as he pulled the dagger out. The alley made a jog to the right and ended abruptly at a little square near the east wall of the town, where a small knot of men stood about a fountain-trough, leading all manner of animals to drink: horses, ponies, donkeys, mules, camels, goats, and two pair of oxen. Sliding his dagger back into the sheath buckled to his forearm, Rojeh looked about for a wide street that would take him to the Foreigners' Quarter.

"The Westerner is lost," scoffed one of the men at the trough, a Volgaman by the look of him.

"I believe that will take me to the Foreigners' Quarter," said Rojeh calmly, pointing to one of the two broadest streets entering the square.

"Anyone who ventures into the Crooked Lane has to be lost," said another of the men, this one a Uighur with a string of shaggy ponies.

"That's what it's for," said a man with a string of goats.

"Do you still have all your fingers and toes, or were they taken from you?" This from an Armenian with oxen.

Rojeh laughed as much because it was expected of him as from amusement. "It is a strange byway."

"It doubles back twice," said a Sarai native with a pair of skinny horses. "How did you come to take such a route?"

"I mistook it for another alley," said Rojeh. "I must have misunderstood the directions I was given."

This time the laughter was less jeering, and the Armenian nodded emphatically. "It is always thus. In a place like Sarai, only the true natives can find anything." He waved at the road Rojeh had decided to take.

Rojeh went up the street toward the Foreigners' Quarter, all the while wondering what sort of prank Emrach had played on him. By the time he reached Ragoczy Franciscus' house, he was torn between deepening worry and mild exasperation with the Master of Foreigners. He found Thetis and her children in the kitchen, watching Dasur prepare their midday meal; jointed fowl lay in a heap along with onions, two tiny cloves of garlic, and a small cabbage.

"These all go into the pot. If we had any, I would add slices of pork and lentils and use olive oil to give it body, but none can be found in the markets, so we make do with this and be thankful for it. It would also be tastier if we had pepper." He opened a jar of rough wine from Edessa. "This is almost the last of what I could buy. It will make the food taste better—wine and salt, to bring out the flavor. It's a pity about the wharves; there is not much fish to be had since all fishing has been confined to the shore and to the smallest craft, ones that can be launched into the streams of the Delta."

"I would like fish," said Aristion wistfully.

"So would we all," said Thetis in a tone that discouraged complaint.

Dasur caught sight of Rojeh and became much less genial toward the widow and her children. "This meal will be ready on time, not that you will notice." He tittered. "The Master of Foreigners has sent two men to this house. They are in the slaves' room"—he cocked his head in the direction of the room behind the pantry—"for now."

"Two guards," said Rojeh, deciding that he understood the reason for sending him the wrong way out of Emrach's headquarters. "When did they arrive?"

"Not long ago. The fire Aethalric started for them has only just begun to burn, and he is putting the room in order." Dasur fidgeted. "I will have to feed them, I suppose."

Rojeh ignored the intended barb. "Since I have told you that I fend for myself, and my master cannot yet eat anything, providing food for the guards should not be a problem. Failure to do so could make for trouble for all of us." He came a few steps farther into the kitchen. "Whatever Ragoczy Franciscus and I might do, the rest of you are entitled to a proper meal twice a day, and cheese or bread to break your fast in the morning."

Dasur heard him out with an air of long-suffering patience. "Speaking of your meals, I was able to purchase a duck for you. It's alive and in the side-passage to the herb-garden." Dasur stared in Rojeh's direction, not quite daring a direct confrontation.

"That was good of you," said Rojeh, paying no heed to the cook's rancor, which had been increasing since Rojeh had refused his help in nursing Ragoczy Franciscus. "I will deal with it a little later." He looked about the kitchen. "So: Aethalric is busy with sweeping the slaves' room for two guards to use, and Chtavo is still mucking out the stalls?"

"So far as I know," Dasur said stringently.

"Sinu is making a new talaris for me," said Pentefilia, unable to contain herself in silence any longer. "My old one is too worn, and Ragoczy Franciscus provided beautiful cloth—"

Hrisoula began to wail, her face screwed into a grimace. "I want a new talaris," she complained, and began to weep noisily, glaring at her older sister as her sense of injustice increased.

"Stop it," Thetis said. "At once. This isn't the time."

The two girls glowered, Pentefilia smugly, Hrisoula pouting; Aristion seemed to want to be invisible, staring down at his feet and refusing to meet the eyes of any of his relatives.

"And Herakles?" Rojeh asked as if he was not aware of the disruption.

"He is at my husband's house, trying to find anything that may be useful: cloth, utensils, food, anything." Thetis cleared her throat. "So that we may, at least in some small part, repay the generosity of your master, while we may."

"I will inform him, but he does not expect such considerations." Rojeh then addressed Dasur. "The duck is in the side-passage, you said?"

"Sitting on an old reed mat when I left her," Dasur said, and returned his full attention to his cooking. "I gave her a handful of grubs from the edge of the stable sweepings, and she ate them greedily."

"I will claim her shortly," said Rojeh. "For now I must go to my master." He left the kitchen accompanied by the quarrelsome sounds of Hrisoula and Pentefilia talking about their clothes, with occasional admonitions to stop from Thetis, and punctuated by Dasur's efforts to restore peace. The dispute was so wonderfully ordinary that he found himself relishing its commonplaceness as he climbed upward.

Ragoczy Franciscus sat at his small writing table, his long, black-silk kaftan flowing around him, swathing him in a scrap of night. He had a broad, dark-red scarf of Chinese silk wrapped around his throat, which was held in place by a silver fibula embellished with his eclipse sigil. His dark hair was neat, his face unusually pale, and although he needed a shave, he presented a good appearance. As Rojeh entered the room, he looked up from the map spread before him, moving with deliberate care, and gave a slight nod of greeting.

"Are you sure you're ready to be up?" Rojeh asked, making no mention of his surprise at seeing Ragoczy Franciscus off his bed. "Your sinews are just beginning to knit again."

Ragoczy Franciscus put his hand to the scarf and reached for his improvised wax tablet and stylus, writing in Latin in his small, precise hand, *I need to be doing something.*

"More than you know," said Rojeh darkly. He went to the fireplace and shoved a negligent small branch back into the flames with his toe. "There are two guards posted to this house, ostensibly to protect you."

From what, or whom? Ragoczy Franciscus held up the wax tablet.

"They say, from Dukkai, or perhaps one of her clan. Emrach seems to think that a single act of leniency will bring every rogue on the trade-routes that converge here down on Sarai in an unruly pack."

Ragoczy Franciscus made a palms-up gesture of incomprehension.

"It is the excuse he is using to send guards here."

But they are spies, Ragoczy Franciscus wrote.

"I think so," said Rojeh, and described the trick Emrach had played upon him. "I think he used the time to dispatch the guards. I thought at first it was only meant to irk me, but once Dasur told me about the guards, I knew I had been subjected to a diversion. He wanted no opposition to his posting."

What did Emrach say? Ragoczy Franciscus wrote in the wax.

"I doubt he is going to permit Dukkai into the town. He told me that Sarai is a funnel and implied that every traveler must eventually come here. If he knows Sarai survives on trade, he managed to give no indication of it," said Rojeh, pursing his lips in disgust; Ragoczy Franciscus got up from the desk and went to the fireplace to take the smoothing iron from the hob, placed it on the wax to make an unused surface, then set the tablet on the mantel so that the wax could cool enough to use again. He tapped his stylus on the stone ledge of the mantel and shook his head in futility. "It is inconvenient, your not talking," Rojeh agreed. "But you will heal and your voice will be as it was." He took a turn about the room and came back to the hearth. "I believe you may have more to fear from the guards than Dukkai when it comes to possible attack. For that reason, you are safer with her outside the walls than in."

Ragoczy Franciscus nodded emphatically twice and gave a quick frown of pain.

"But questioning the guards' purpose may be more dangerous still," said Rojeh.

Again Ragoczy Franciscus nodded his agreement and reached for the wax tablet. *We have to leave,* he wrote in the wax. *Soon.*

"At this time of year it isn't safe to travel, not with the storms and the cold, to say nothing of the hunger and want everywhere." Rojeh guessed that what he said was useless, but he continued on, determined to make all his reservations known. "There are hazards on the road that—"

Writing quickly, Ragoczy held up the tablet. *There are greater hazards here.*

Rojeh said carefully, "I think that going out into the winter might entail too much risk. We can watch the guards, and—"

But we cannot feed, Ragoczy Franciscus wrote. *Neither of us can.*

Attempting to make light of this caution, Rojeh said, "With your throat cut, you cannot feed in any case."

Ragoczy Franciscus pointed with his stylus to where he had written, *We have to leave. Soon.*

"As soon as the ice begins to withdraw, we should be away." He saw Ragoczy Franciscus point to *Soon* one more time. "Is that why you had the map out?"

The answer was a single nod.

"If you think we should leave while it is still winter, you must be more worried than I am about the guards," said Rojeh, his faded-blue eyes somber. "Why are you so troubled?"

After wiping a bead of accumulated wax from the tip of the stylus, Ragoczy Franciscus wrote, *Emrach is greedy and he is a martinet. It would be useful to him to make himself appear a hero in the town's eyes, and what better way to do that than to have his men strive to thwart a murder?—not just a murder, but one of a foreigner that can be blamed on a foreigner. It would assure him an impregnable position and it would warn all foreigners to hold Emrach in properly high regard.*

Rojeh read this twice. "Are you certain he is so dangerous that he would do this?"

I think he knows an advantage when one presents itself, Ragoczy Franciscus wrote, and added, in very small letters in the little room that was left, *We must establish signs. This is too cumbersome.* Then he reached for the smoothing iron and put it on the tablet.

"You're right. We need a better means of communication than this." Rojeh glanced toward the door. "Has anyone been up here since I left?"

With exaggerated care, Ragoczy Franciscus mouthed *Aristion and Sinu.*

"That must have been awkward," said Rojeh, curious about the two visitors. As Ragoczy Franciscus nodded, moving his head gingerly, Rojeh pondered briefly, then said, "In terms of how I intend to deal with obtaining this information, I will handle the questions adroitly, as a general inquiry into how the house has been run on the first sunny day in five. I will ask each in turn, starting with your household servants, then going on to the widow, her children, and her servants. I have made similar inquiries before. I will ask Dasur about the markets he visited and what he found. I'll ask Chtavo about the health of the mules and the horses. I'll ask the widow if she has anything that needs household attention, and how the progress on her own dwelling is progressing. Who knows—I may even come upon something useful beyond what I ask during this delving. If the guards should hear any of this, or all of it, they will have nothing to notice in it, for it will be what anyone might expect. Is there anything in what I have said that distresses you?"

Yes and no, Ragoczy Franciscus mouthed.

Rojeh looked across the room to Ragoczy Franciscus' bed. "It might be as well for you to rest until I come back from the kitchen."

Ragoczy Franciscus reached for one of the six books he had carried from China; he opened it with care, holding it up for Rojeh to see.

Rojeh accepted this. "If you become tired, or your head or neck aches—"

Ragoczy Franciscus pointed toward the bed.

"Exactly," said Rojeh.

Taking hold of the wax tablet, Ragoczy Franciscus wrote again. *Do not let the guards know how I am doing.*

"I'll be careful," said Rojeh, and went out of the room. Descending the stairs to the kitchen again, he found Chtavo, Herakles, and Aethalric there with the others. All three of them were drinking hot wine, and Chtavo was still in his bearskin cloak; he hunkered down before the fire, his cup held in both his hands for warmth. Herakles had taken a seat on the bench next to the hearth and was rubbing his swollen knees as he downed his wine. Aethalric had seated himself across the main table from Dasur, at the opposite end of the table from Thetis and her children. "Where's Sinu, and the guards?"

"Sinu's working on my talaris," said Pentefilia with a wicked, covert glance at her sister. "My mother says it will look well when I die. They can dress me in it."

"Pentefilia," Thetis cautioned, blanching.

"Well, you *said,*" Hrisoula reminded her mother.

"The guards are still in the slaves' room, making up their pallets, I think," said Aethalric.

"We are all going to eat together," Dasur announced, putting a stop to any wrangling and successfully shifting the subject. "It makes little sense to do two tables in the dining room, one for the widow alone, and another for her children."

"I would have to build a fire and sweep the floor," said Aethalric. "Here, the room is warm, and all of us may have the food we want."

"As much as is available," Pentefilia sniffed.

Rojeh said, "Remember that the widow and her family are our guests and must be treated as such."

Thetis shot him a look of earnest gratitude. "You are always courteous, Rojeh. You remind me of the majordomi in Constantinople: gracious and calm. I never supposed I would die here."

"Why should you die here?" Rojeh asked as the rest pretended not to have heard her.

"If Ragoczy Franciscus is going to die, then who of us is safe?" she whispered.

"He is not going to die," Rojeh said. "His wound will heal."

"Will it?" She daubed the cuff of her tablion at her eyes. "It's hopeless."

"Mama," said Hrisoula, panic in her young eyes.

Immediately Thetis made a reassuring gesture. "You mustn't mind what I say. I am . . . worried. Ragoczy Franciscus is in grave danger, and what is to become of us?"

"You will not be cast on the world, whatever happens," Rojeh said, looking at the girl, not her mother.

Thetis choked back a sob and put her hand on his. "I thank you for saying that."

Aristion ground his fists together. "Why do those guards have to be here?"

"Because the Master of Foreigners wishes it," said Rojeh in his calmest voice.

"I don't like it," said the boy.

"Neither do I," Rojeh agreed, and would have said more, but the inside door opened and the two guards stepped into the kitchen. Both of them had daggers in their belts; their stance was inhospitable. Rojeh reverenced them and pointed to the unoccupied benches next to the main table. "We are preparing for our evening meal. I hope you will share our fare," he invited cordially.

One of the guards grunted an acceptance for them both; they sat down.

"Would you like some hot wine?" Dasur asked with a quick glance at Rojeh. "I think we can provide cups for you."

"It would be nice," said one of the guards.

"I'll fill the cups," Aethalric volunteered, and rose before anyone could object.

"I fear we have only a simple meal, but you may find it adequate," said Dasur nervously.

"Probably better than what we get usually," said the second guard, whose teeth were either missing or nearly black.

Rojeh stepped away from the table. "Then may you have good appetite."

"Do you not eat with us?" The first guard was instantly suspicious.

"No, he does not," said Dasur, intervening. "He follows the customs of our master, he says."

The second guard glared. "Strange custom, to eat apart. It is not what happens in this town."

"Nevertheless," said Thetis suddenly, "that is what happens in this house."

Aethalric came back to the table, carefully holding two steaming cups by their rims. "You should like this."

Abandoning their questions for the time being, the guards took the cups and drank eagerly, no longer paying attention to Rojeh, who was once again on his way up the stairs to Ragoczy Franciscus.

Text of a writ by Ragcozy Franciscus in Byzantine Greek, witnessed by two merchants of Byzantium remaining in Sarai for the winter, with instructions to file these dispositions with Emrach Sarai'af and Patriarch Stavros in Sarai upon my departure from the town.

As closely as I can fix the date of this authorization, I make it the first week of February by the revised Roman calendar, in the 1290th Year of the City; it is the first week of the New Year in China, although I am not certain which animal is in charge of this one; it is the tenth year of the reign of the Byzantine Emperor Justinian, and the eleventh year since Theodoric, King of the Ostrogoths, died, and what is set down here was written in the sixth week since the Winter Solstice, and to which I set my sigil as token of my intent.

Upon my departure from this city, I have arranged for Thetis Krisanthemenis, the widow of Eleutherios Panayiotos, along with her three children, Pentefilia, Aristion, and Hrisoula, to be given tenancy in the house I have occupied until such time as her family arranges to bring her to them. I have provided the money for a year of occupancy and left funds to pay the wages of the staff, so that she need not be at any disadvantage imposed upon her because of the limitations law puts upon her access to her late husband's fortune. The monies have been put in the hands of Patriarch Stavros with my specific instructions regarding how they are to be used, and an authorization for providing money to Thetis Krisanthemenis as she has need of it. I will leave a single horse, a copper-dun, for the use of the widow and the household, with funds for its upkeep. Chtavo may continue in his present work, so long as he is in Sarai. None of my servants are bonded and thus may depart or stay as they choose. Aethalric has already declared he has no wish to leave, so he may continue to head the household servants, with his wages paid for another six months, and sufficient monies provided to cover the next six, if they are needed. I leave one restriction for the staff and Thetis Krisanthemenis: that they buy no slaves.

Should Thetis Krisanthemenis decide to leave Sarai, the sums that would have supported the household are to be provided to her for travel expenses, so that she and her children need not endure more hardships on the road beyond what the journey itself provides. I also leave with Patriarch Stavros a sum of money that will allow her to hire three armed men to escort her, and I admonish her to travel only with a larger caravan, so that her escort may not become her captors.

All household goods left must be inventoried and kept for the use of Thetis Krisanthemenis and the household until she and her children depart, at which time the goods are to be sold and the monies divided in this way: half for Thetis Krisathemenis and her children to offset the costs of travel, the remainder to be distributed equally among the servants, Sinu and Herakles sharing a portion. So as to leave no burden upon her, I have provided two diamonds for such taxes as the town may impose upon my household and the current tenants of the house; one is for the Master of Foreigners and should cover the sum of my exit tax, the second is for Patriarch Stavros, who has undertaken to serve as administrator of the widow's affairs.

The landlords of the Foreigners' Quarter will have much to repair and restore before the Quarter can be fully occupied again, and to that end, I have set aside one gold and one silver bar for the purpose of helping to pay for such rebuilding as may be required. In return for *this sum, I ask that supplies for a shelter be provided to Dukkai, the Jou'an-Jou'an woman who has been exiled. Failure to comply with this request will result in a withdrawal of all remaining money, which will then be put in the hands of the innkeeper at the Birch House to dispose of in some manner that benefits the town but without helping any construction in the Foreigners' Quarter.*

I set my hand and sigil to this before witnesses and in the conviction that when it is presented, its terms will be honored.

Ragoczy Franciscus
Merchant
(his sigil, the eclipse)
Nicodemus Daniatos, merchant of Amisus, witness
Evagelos Tomi, merchant of Chersonesus, witness

3

Rojeh stared out at the wet snow pelting down from a black sky. "Are you sure you want to leave now?" he asked Ragoczy Franciscus as he stood in the door of the stable and stared out at the chaotic night.

Ragoczy Franciscus gave the sign for *yes*. He pulled on the lead of the mules and put his foot in the foot-loop of his saddle, preparing to mount, making a last adjustment on the rough-woven blanket that was buckled onto his horse to provide warmth.

"It could be a very hard ride," Rojeh said as he went to get his stallion, who was standing tied to a stanchion, fretting at the bit; he, too, was blanketed against the bone-piercing cold. "Just two mules and two horses provides little margin for trouble," Rojeh pointed out, knowing his argument would not change Ragoczy Franciscus' mind.

Ready? Ragoczy Franciscus signaled, then swung up into the saddle.

"I'm worried about the widow and her children," said Rojeh.

With a long, steady look, Ragoczy Franciscus mouthed, *Our staying cannot help her.*

"Still, it could go hard for her, if the guards really do have orders to kill us," said Rojeh, and went on in vexation, "Do you think you will be able to get the guard to open the gate?" He unfastened the lead.

Ragoczy Franciscus held up three silver coins in his gloved hand.

"He will not keep silent for that amount, if that is what you would want," Rojeh warned as he mounted. "You'll need double that to buy silence."

The response was a restive shrug, followed by the sign *Go.*

"We'll have to leave the gate unbolted," Rojeh reminded him, taking the lead on his mule. He started his horse out of the stable, saying, "Chtavo and the rest of the servants may be blamed for our departure, if not the widow. The guards will think he helped us, since he lives over the stable."

Ragoczy Franciscus made their sign for *How?*

"You and I know that he could not stop us, but he could be expected to close doors and gates and ask where we would be going." He reached the gate and kneed the horse over so he could draw back the bolt so they could go out into the street; since night was more than half over, there was no one else abroad. "When I think of what we had when we left China and what we are reduced to now . . ." He stopped while Ragoczy Francisus maneuvered his mare to allow him to close the gate.

Ragoczy Franciscus drew his mare up alongside Rojeh's stallion and handed him the coins. *Take them,* he signaled, and pulled his mule into line behind his blue roan, then put his finger to his lips as they started down the street.

"Of course I'll be quiet." Rojeh kept his horse on a tight rein; the stallion disliked having to follow any other animal. Once or twice, the horses and mules slithered on the steep, icy street, but they made their way to the main gate without any serious mishap or disturbance.

The guard was half-asleep and largely drunk; he took the coins and opened the gate with no questions, and closed it with a promptness that bespoke finality, leaving Ragoczy Franciscus and Rojeh to inch their way down the sharp slope of the approach road to the snowy islands and the paths that connected them.

Rojeh knew from Ragoczy Franciscus' notes to him earlier that evening that they were to go to the Jou'an-Jou'an camp to see what had become of Dukkai. He kept his dagger near to hand and patted the sheath containing his shimtare, reassured by the closeness of the curved cavalry sword. The heavily laden mules kept their progress to a walk, and the steady plodding was almost sleep-inducing. Rojeh had not realized how far they had come until he saw the snow-covered mounds of the Jou'an-Jou'an tents and heard a single bark from one of the dogs in the camp.

Ragoczy Franciscus rode through the encampment to the far side, out on a spit of land that poked a sandy finger into the marsh where the reeds did not grow, and the water was an obsidian smear against the falling snow; it was the place Dukkai had been sent in lieu of shelter, to crouch in the ruin of an old boat that had been drawn up onto the spit. He rode as near as was safe, then tied the mule's lead to his saddle, dismounted, and secured his blue roan's reins to a scrubby bush half-submerged in snow. That done, he stood still for a short while, then started toward the boat, tapping on it before lifting its bow to look at what lay beneath.

It was impossible to say how long she had been dead, for her freezing had prevented any decomposition. Frost crystals had formed on her eyelashes and her white hair was brittle with ice. Her gaunt face had a bluish tinge, and her lips were a chalky-purple shade. She lay on her side, her head pillowed on her leather sleeve, as if she had fallen asleep and failed to waken.

Dukkai, Ragoczy Franciscus mouthed as he bent over her body.

Rojeh did not dismount; he kept watch from the saddle, in case their presence should be noticed and they were forced to fight their way out of the Jou'an-Jou'an camp. His thoughts were bleak as he surveyed the cluster of tents and the marsh beyond. "We cannot linger," he said as loudly as he dared.

Ragoczy Franciscus held up his hand in the sign for *Wait.* Then he reached for the rotted length of rope that held the boat in place, tugged at it, struggling to pull the boat free of the icy sand so it could float again; a slow trickle of water began to fill it, crystals forming along the inner curve of the hull as the water rose. Taking Dukkai in his arms, he laid her in the boat as gently as he could; since he was unable to bend her limbs, he did what he could to place her as if she had fallen asleep and, stepping back, shoved the old, leaky craft away from the shore and into the stream, watching as the boat and its frozen cargo drifted away.

"Why did you do that?" Rojeh asked as Ragoczy Franciscus came back to his horse.

After releasing the blue roan's lead, Ragoczy Franciscus got into the saddle and gestured, *Later,* before he started his horse moving, going back through the Jou'an-Jou'an encampment and turning westward in the direction of the Sea of Azov and the Byzantine Empire.

By the time the leaden clouds lightened with the coming of the feeble day, Ragoczy Franciscus and Rojeh were at the edge of a small defile in which stood a small fortress that had clearly been abandoned for some time; some of the battlements had fallen away without any indication of repairs, and an empty eagle's nest crowned the watchtower. The gate was little more than a few lengths of wood hanging on ancient iron hinges, and the building itself showed signs of extreme neglect; Ragoczy Franciscus and Rojeh dismounted as they went through the stone maw into the marshaling yard, leading their horses and mules into the shelter the squat stone walls offered. There were a few thorny, snow-shrouded bushes growing through the old flagging in the main court, and when they found the stable, the stalls smelled more of mice than horses.

Ragoczy Franciscus gestured, *We stay*.

"For how long?" Rojeh asked.

One day and one night, Ragoczy Franciscus signed.

"The horses and mules could use the rest, and the storm is beginning to die down," said Rojeh, and seeing Ragoczy Franciscus nod endorsement, he went on, "If you rest on your native earth for a day and a night, you will be strong enough to travel by day: is that your purpose?"

Yes, Ragoczy Franciscus confirmed, and began to look for a rake or some other implement to clean out the debris from the stalls along the inner wall.

"Do you want to sleep in a stall?" Rojeh found a shovel and went to work.

No was Ragoczy Franciscus' response; he mouthed *Mice* for explanation. *Rats.*

Somewhat later, Rojeh remarked, "This looks like a Byzantine fort, doesn't it? The watchtower is Byzantine design, not Roman, and the peoples in this region weren't making fortresses of stone." He was working on a second stall, and the advancing light revealed more about the place than had been apparent at first; the stable accommodated as many as twenty horses, but three of the stalls were so dilapidated as to be entirely useless. The water trough near the door was empty, and almost all the hinges on the stall gates had rusted.

Ragoczy Franciscus nodded and motioned to the much-faded icons painted on the stable beams, images that were clearly of Eastern Rite origin.

"It doesn't seem that there was a hard fight, and it hasn't the look of a siege. Why would the defenders leave?" Rojeh asked, and was about to apologize, when he saw Ragoczy Franiscus mouth *Huns* and stared at the lance shaft Ragoczy Franciscus pulled from the manger. He took this and turned it over in his hands. "It is Hunnic, isn't it?" Shaking his head, Rojeh said, "Then I pity the men who were here."

Taking back the lance shaft, Ragoczy Franciscus dropped it into one of the unused stalls, then sagged against the wall between it and the one he was cleaning.

"It must have been more than a century ago; the Huns were advancing on Byzantine territory then," said Rojeh, recalling the unremitting assault the Huns had made on the little castle in Greece, and the long ordeal he and Ragoczy Franciscus had faced, repelling them only with the help of Niklos Aulirios and an old Roman ballista loaded frequently with hives of angry bees.

There was a long silence broken only by the stamping of one of the mules; it was enough to remind the two that they had not quite finished cleaning the stalls.

As he resumed working, Rojeh said, "There isn't any bedding, and probably nothing we can give as food, not with so many mice about."

Ragoczy Franciscus pointed to the chest that contained grain and some chopped hay.

"Of course. But it isn't enough to last more than a week," Rojeh reminded him.

The nod that answered Rojeh's observation was slow and accompanied by a covert wince.

"The wound is paining you, isn't it? You are having trouble moving your head?" Rojeh asked, putting down his shovel and starting toward Ragoczy Franciscus, who held up his hand authoritatively to stop him.

This time Ragoczy Franciscus made the sign for negation, mouthing, *It does not matter,* as he did.

"But it does," said Rojeh, taking up his shovel once more. "Let's finish up in here and get you onto your native earth. I won't ask you not to work," he went on, working more determinedly than he had done.

Ragoczy Franciscus plied his rake energetically, cleaning out the rest of the stall quickly. When he was done, he put the rake on a hook near what must have been the tack-room, then he went to unsaddle his mare; he left the blanket in place when he turned her into the stall and did much the same with the mule after he unloaded the well-laden pack saddle. Taking a measure of grain from the case that contained it, he fed the horse, then the mule, and handed the scoop to Rojeh, who had just finished stalling his two animals.

"I'll have this taken care of quickly," said Rojeh, looking for something to secure the stall doors.

I will look, Ragoczy Franciscus gestured. A quick check of the other stalls revealed nothing useful, so Ragoczy Franciscus sought out the tack-room. The light was provided by a single window set high in the wall in a double-thickness of stones, hardly big enough to contain a saddle rack. Making the most of the poor illumination, he commenced his search where the light was strongest and progressed through the room toward the more shadowed parts, going carefully in case there should be some danger, for his dark-seeing eyes could not pick out what lay beneath the scattered bits of leather and tangled wisps of ancient straw. He found a length of old rope coiled in one of the corners, so obscured that it was all but invisible. As Ragoczy Franciscus approached, he saw that in it lay a skull, part of a spine and ribs, and one set of arm bones. He dropped to one knee and had a closer look, noticing the deep gouges axes had made in the lower ribs and the spine; he hoped the man had been dead before those ruthless hacks had fallen. Skull in hand, he rose, absentmindedly taking the rope in the other hand. *It never ends,* he said silently. Carefully he set the skull down in the stone window embrasure, then left the tack-room.

"This can be tied across the doors at two levels," Rojeh said as Ragoczy Franciscus used his dagger to saw the thick hemp length in half. "It should do well enough."

Agreeing with a nod, Ragoczy Franciscus leaned back against one of the four stone pillars in the stable while Rojeh strung the ropes across the gates of the stalls. Rojeh was right: his neck did ache, the kind of hurt that gnawed at him, sapping his strength and wearing down his endurance far more than the difficult ride or the harsh

weather did. Glancing toward one of the three small windows lighting the stable, he saw that the clouds were not as thick as they had
been and that the storm was breaking up.

"My master?" Rojeh asked, seeing the shadow of fatigue on
Ragoczy Francisus' face.

He straightened up, waving aside Rojeh's question. He signaled, *I
will look* and *Sleep*. Slowly he started toward the entrance to the stable.

"As soon as you decide where you want to rest, I'll hunt." Rojeh
tied his last knot. "We should take this rope with us when we go."

Ragoczy Franciscus nodded as he went back into the marshaling
yard. He stood, undecided, for a short while, then went toward the
watchtower that stood next to the gate. The sagging door was wedged
closed, and it took two powerful kicks to open it. Carefully, he
stepped inside the marshaling room at the base of the tower, making
note of everything he saw: two small stools, a bucket, a pail, some
spears with their points rusted away, a cooking tripod—without a
cauldron—to fit into the long-cold fireplace that stood on the east
wall, and on the west a large rack of various weapons, most of them
crumbled or rusted. He paced off the size of the room—eight
strides east-west, almost eleven north-south—and decided it was
as good a place as any. He went back across the marshaling yard, taking the time to study the sky before he ducked into the dark of the
stable; the clouds were starting to tatter, and the snowfall had diminished to an occasional random flake. Already a glary brightness
marked the place of the sun as it climbed the morning sky, and
Ragoczy Franciscus could feel a little of its pull, not as he had done
two years ago, but enough to tell him that it was gradually regaining
its power.

Rojeh was stacking their chests and crates and boxes; he had set
aside the chest of Ragoczy Franciscus' native earth and was inspecting the thick leather straps on the box containing their spare clothing;
he recognized the purpose in Ragoczy Franciscus' stance and said,
"You have found a place that will do."

Yes, Ragoczy Franciscus signaled. *We carry*.

"Of course," said Rojeh, going to the chest of native earth. "If I
take the wood from those wrecked stalls, we could build a fire."

Ragoczy Franciscus considered his answer, finally gesturing, *No.
Attention*.

"You mean you think this place could be under surveillance?" Rojeh said as he and Ragoczy Franciscus hefted the chest between them; the tablet and stylus rested on top of it.

Since he could not shrug or signal, Ragoczy Franciscus was unable to respond. He kept walking steadily toward the marshaling room, trying to find some way to express himself.

"You are concerned that this place could serve as a trap. Whose? Look at it. Cobwebs everywhere. No doubt the chimneys are full of rats' nests and mice, possibly birds' as well." They were almost to the marshaling room, and Rojeh faltered as the shadow of a large bird crossed over him. Peering upward into the shattering morning light, he could just make out a raptor soaring against the brilliance; then the darkness of the tower blocked bird and sun from sight, and a few steps later they put the chest down in front of the unused fireplace. "Oh. I found a cistern behind the stable. It has water."

Ragoczy Franciscus signaled, *Good,* as he sat down on the chest and picked up the tablet and stylus, but did nothing with them as he stared at the opposite wall with extreme blankness, his thoughts more distant than the Yang-Tse River.

Rojeh studied him, saying at last, "You're losing flesh again." He turned his attention to the fireplace. "I suppose it would smoke if I tried to lay a fire."

Putting both hands to his throat, Ragoczy Franciscus mimed coughing.

"Well, neither you nor I are much troubled by cold—that's useful," said Rojeh, searching for something to sit on; he found an old stool and tested it by putting his foot on it and transferring half his weight onto it; the stool held.

Good, Ragoczy Franciscus signed, and stretched his arms above his head, arching his back.

"You're tired. So am I," said Rojeh. "You rest first, and I will rest after you wake. While you sleep, I'll see if I can find something to eat." His expression clouded. "How much longer before your throat is healed enough to take sustenance? If hunger is enervating to me, it is debilitating to you, for more than your body is compromised." He sank down onto the stool. "I'll go hunting shortly, when the sky is finally clear."

Ragoczy Franciscus moved the tablet and stylus to the end of the chest near where he intended to rest his head. As he stretched out on the leather-strapped wood, he signaled Rojeh, *We will talk*.

"Later," said Rojeh. "When we're both more rested."

Lying on his back, Ragoczy Franciscus almost seemed laid out for burial, so completely still was he. His light olive skin was lunar-pale and his eyes were sunk in dark sockets. Had Rojeh not seen this state before, he would have been troubled by it, but being familiar with Ragoczy Franciscus, he saw this stillness with relief, for it meant that Ragoczy Franciscus would be imbued with the power of his native earth when he woke, which would sustain him until he was able to seek more living nourishment. "No wonder he wants to go back to the Carpathians," Rojeh whispered as he went out to hunt, returning shortly before sunset with a brace of pigeons hanging from a thong over his shoulder. He went to the marshaling room to see how Ragoczy Franciscus fared, and to improvise a table where he could eat. During his hunt, he had decided he needed to make a small fire to boil water so he could scald the pigeons to make plucking easier. He searched out an old tin pail in the far recesses of the stable, which he went to fill with rainwater from the cistern at the rear of the stable. Gathering up bits of old planking, and other scraps of wood, he found a sheltered place in the marshaling yard and began the tedious business of lighting the fire. As soon as the first tiny plume of smoke rose, he added more kindling to the pile and soon had a small but serviceable blaze going. This he framed with stones and set the pail on top of them, then shoved a few more lengths of wood in through the gaps in the stones. Satisfied that this would bring the water to a boil, he went to lead the horses and mules to the cistern to drink, then returned them to their stalls. He took grain from the case of it and measured out enough for the mash, and returned to the fire in time to add another broken plank to the fuel.

The scrape of the door being thrust open caught Rojeh's attention; he turned to see Ragoczy Franciscus standing just outside the marshaling room, his demeanor much restored. "You're awake."

Yes, he signed.

"You look rested."

Yes, again.

"Good. If you sleep once more before we go on, you should be able to—"

Ride long. Ragoczy Franciscus pointed to the scalding pigeons. *Help you?*

"No, I can manage," said Rojeh, surprised at the offer. "But if you will bring my heavy knife from my personal case in the stable?"

Ragoczy Franciscus nodded and went off with easy, crisp strides to the stable, only to return shortly with the long, slender skinning knife Rojeh used to prepare his food. He handed this to Rojeh, who was busy plucking feathers from the pigeons; he sat in a flurry of gray and white as if he had been caught in a miniature snowstorm.

"Thanks," said Rojeh as he took the knife in his befeathered hand. "When I've finished my meal, perhaps then we can talk—or you can write and I will talk," he added. "Are there any oil-lamps in this place?"

Not find, Ragoczy Franciscus gestured. *We have.*

"In the blue chest, yes, we do. Lamps and oil to power them." Rojeh sluiced slightly bloody water over one of the pigeons, showing it had been completely fletched; he went to work finishing the other while Ragoczy Franciscus went to the stable to bring the oil-lamps and the oil-jar from the blue chest, along with flint-and-steel.

While Rojeh cut up and ate his two pigeons, Ragoczy Franciscus set about filling and lighting the oil-lamps in the marshaling room, finally providing enough illumination to make reading what he wrote on the wax tablet possible.

"I'm finished," Rojeh announced from the door. "The guts and bones are buried, and the fire has been drowned."

Good, Ragoczy Franciscus gestured, and pointed to the stool that Rojeh had found earlier. *We talk.* Before Ragoczy Franciscus could begin to use his stylus, Rojeh suddenly got up and went out into the marshaling yard to where he had made his fire. Bending down, he selected three sticks of blackened wood, then carried these back to Ragoczy Franciscus, pausing as he went to stare at the vivid and glorious sunset that ornamented the western sky with a range of colors from crimson to persimmon, purple to lilac; the sun itself was a disk of brilliant red, splendid as anything Justinian, Emperor of Byzantium, ever adorned himself with or used to aggrandize his Empress or his court. Breaking away from the impressive celestial display as from a transfixing spell, Rojeh shook himself and went into the marshaling room and the soft glow of the oil-lamps. "Here. You can write on the floor with this," he said, handing the charcoal to Ragoczy Franciscus.

Very good, signaled Ragoczy Franciscus, setting aside his tablet and stylus and getting down on one knee to wipe a section of the floor free of dust and the small detritus of the vanished occupants. When he had a stretch of pale-gray stone exposed, he looked at Rojeh. *Ready,* he gestured.

"You said you would explain why you set Dukkai adrift." There was a faint hint of accusation in this reminder, as if Rojeh wanted the complete answer, and not some simple abstraction. When Ragoczy Franciscus hesitated, Rojeh prodded, "Well? Why did you do it?"

Ragoczy Franciscus held up his hand, a request for patience; after a long moment, he began to write with the longest of the three charcoal sticks. *I hoped that by setting her adrift as I did that she would vanish by the time the rest of her clan awoke.*

"The boat probably sank," said Rojeh.

I would assume it did. If the clan did not see it, they would not know what had become of her. As a shaman, vanishing would restore her reputation, and it would permit the rest of her family to remain with the Desert Cats. Dukkai is dead, and nothing can change that. But her death need not be a defeat. Ragoczy Franciscus wiped another swath of stone and prepared to go on. *The Desert Cats are at less than half their strength and numbers than when we first encountered them, and they are still losing people. Fever, hunger, cold, age, all have depleted their ranks and will continue to do so for as long as the sun remains weak. To lose their shaman shamefully adds a burden that many of them cannot endure. If they have no one to speak to the Lords of the Earth, they will be in danger of fragmenting, and if that happens, most of them will die.*

"Do you think having Dukkai vanish will keep them together?" Rojeh was puzzled, and he leaned over the answer as Ragoczy Franciscus wrote.

I trust they will believe her magic took her to the Underworld Judge, and that she will become one with the Gods of the Smoke. This could not happen if they found her body.

Rojeh read the last answer twice. "Why do you care what becomes of them? Dukkai cut your throat and was prepared to offer your life to her gods."

For the living, life is so very short, and the dead slip away so quickly. I have the luxury of time—centuries and centuries of it; how can I live among living humans and not do what I can to make their brief lives less precipitous? I will be here far longer than any of them, and I must not abuse my long life, for if I did, I would lose all claim to humanity; I have worked much too hard to maintain it to want to relinquish all I have sought.

"How long do you think you have to make up for the years you hunted men as fodder, as vengeance for the slaughter of your family?" Rojeh asked with more bluntness than he intended.

That is so far in the past that I doubt I could. What I do now I do because I know the souls of people through the intimacy I have with— His charcoal stick broke. Dusting his hands on his thick leather leggings, Ragoczy Franciscus rose to his feet and pointed toward the chest, gesturing, *You. Sleep.*

Knowing it was useless to pursue this any longer, Rojeh took a deep breath. "We should travel at first light. Will you wake me before dawn?"

Yes, Ragoczy Franciscus gestured, moving over to the stool to sit guard while Rojeh slept.

Text of a letter from the Roman merchant Antoninus Octavianus Stellens in Ostia to the merchant Lucius Valentius Gnaeo, expected in the port of Salonae, carried by merchant ship and delivered on the nineteenth of May.

To the renowned merchant Lucius Valentius Gnaeo, at his warehouse in Salonae, the greetings and good wishes of Antoninus Octavianus Stellens, presently in Ostia, on this, the twenty-fourth of February in the year 537 of the Pope's calendar, with thanks for your communication of last autumn, and the hope that your ventures have prospered since then, that your family has suffered no further losses, and that no contract you have entered upon has been compromised.

I am pleased to tell you that I have come upon a supply of raisins and dried plums from a peasant living to the north of Roma. He has kept four barrels of each in reserve and has started to offer them for sale. He also grows the apples of Api, which can be stored much longer than most of that sort of fruit, and he has a few trees that are bearing still in his orchard. He has named a price that I, by myself, would find hard to meet, but if you were to go shares with me on the purchase, I believe that both of us would profit from the transaction. If this holds any interest for you, notify me as quickly as you may, and I will tell him that he has found a buyer. I hope the storms of winter will abate in time for you to receive this and make your decision.

As to your offer to go partners on the Armenian grains, given the sad state of farming here around Roma, I will dispatch a courier with the amount you quoted to me, so that you may secure as much of the coming harvest as you may. It is unfortunate that the reason they have grain to sell is because there have been so many deaths among the people of the region, but that is true everywhere. Even my old uncle has succumbed, although he did live almost fifty-two years—an ancient, indeed.

You must tell me more about this stone bone. I have read your description of it and still find it too incredible to believe. Is it from the dragon that fell from Heaven when the Rebel Angels were cast out? If it is truly of the size you say it is, no doubt it would attract fascination and wonder. In difficult times, the people of the world cling to those marvels that remove them from their misery, if only for a short while. I am interested in helping you bring this treasure to Roma, if it is truly as remarkable as you have said it is. Tell me what you will need to transport it safely, and I will see you have it, in exchange for an equal share in your profits.

I have made arrangements with a group of weavers near Neapolis for the fine wool they have been making. I would like to think that the terms we have established will serve us all well. Should you wish to participate, receiving shipped woolens and selling them in the ports of the Adriatic and the Black Seas, I will be more than happy to introduce this possibility to the weavers to see if it suits them, both in market and in their own shares of such sales. I know they are not as numerous as they once were, but I am sure some degree of accommodation may be reached, especially if you can guarantee markets that they have not been able to reach in the past.

I am pleased to learn that you are coming to Roma. While you are in Ostia, you must be my guest. I have an enclosed villa; it has only been attacked once in the last decade, and it came through the battle with only minor damage, which has since been repaired. It may be wrong to pray for profits in this precipitous time, but if not now, when should we pray for more goods to sell, and more markets in which to *sell them, for if these two things are granted, then the world will once again bask in God's favor. While we languish, I will offer to God all the sorrow and misery that I endure, but I will rejoice when my daily litany does not reflect the weight of affliction and turns again to praise for bounty and success. To that end, I engage to continue our business together, and to expand it as the opportunities arise. I will continue to search out goods to sell and ask that you find markets in which to sell them, to which end you will remain in my prayers.*

Antoninus Octavianus Stellens
Merchant of Ostia

4

"We haven't seen any lions since we left Tok-Kala, nor their skins for sale," Rojeh observed as they halted beside a carcass of a wild boar. It was the fourth clear day in a row, and the snows were beginning to melt; only under the trees did the drifts remain, and the boar was lying half-covered in the shade of a pine.

Ragoczy Franciscus nodded and mouthed, *No tigers, either.*

"But we have heard tigers," Rojeh reminded him. "Just two nights ago. And a few of the fur traders have their hides to sell." They were eight days away from the stone fortress and were traveling through a stand of scrub forest, with thick-barked pine trees and thickets of close-growing brush. They had been on the road since before dawn, and now that half the morning had slid by, they were looking for a place to rest through the height of the day.

"And wolves—we have heard wolves and seen their pelts," Ragoczy Franciscus said silently. He stared down the ill-defined track ahead of them and with a considerable effort whispered, "Be alert."

"For wolves? With the sun up?" Rojech asked with a slight, humorous smile.

"The human kind of packs, I fear." There was a hint of sound in the words, faint and rough, but as audible as a leaf skittering over the ground.

"You think we could be in danger here? From animals and men?" Rojeh tugged on his mule's lead and tapped his horse's sides with his heels; the stallion was as tired as any of them. The mule was equally recalcitrant, forcing Rojeh to tug on his lead. "What killed the boar, do you think?"

"Probably hunger. It has killed many others," whispered Ragoczy Franciscus, his hand going to the high shearling collar of his shuba; what little speech he had regained came in short bursts and quickly overburdened his slow-healing throat. "That is probably why we have seen no lions." He could manage nothing more.

"You mean they have died, famished?" Rojeh asked.

Or moved on, Ragoczy Franciscus motioned broadly so that Rojeh could understand.

"Like the Jou'an-Jou'an and the Uighurs," said Rojeh.

Yes. Ragoczy Franciscus turned back toward the track through the forest.

"Are we far from the Don?" Rojeh asked when they had gone half a league.

Ragoczy Franciscus gestured his uncertainty and pointed to a curve in the descent of the trail and made the signs for *Robbers* followed by *Possibly.*

"It could be a place to lie in wait," Rojeh said, calculating the distance as he laid his hand on his shimtare. "I'm ready for—" He did not finish that thought.

They continued down the slope, following the way marked by the patches of hard-trodden earth that were revealed where the watery sunlight had melted the snow. The woods around them rustled and shook in the gusty wind, making the place seem emptier than quiet would have done. As Ragoczy Franciscus led the way into the hidden curve, he tugged his Chinese mace with the stellated head out of the sheath he had tied to his saddle that morning. The heavy weapon hummed on the air as he swung it, testing its heft.

Negotiating the declining bend, they entered a stand of mixed pines and birch; no outlaws surged out to meet them, no shouts of challenge or warning interrupted the steady clop of hooves. A creek chortling over stones was the only new sound among the trees, many of which looked bedraggled, with stunted ends to their branches, and bare twigs where the first, faint furls of leaves should have been.

Here and there lay recently fallen logs, a few with the beginning of moss on them. Snow was thick on the ground, but broken here and there by melting, leaving damp edges to the heaps of white.

"We're doing well so far," Rojeh called out.

Ragoczy Franciscus raised his hand to acknowledge his comment, then slipped the mace back into the sheath, making sure the closing was secure. He was in need of shelter; the sun was marginally stronger this spring than it had been the previous year, but for him, it was enough to wear on him, particularly since he had not been able to take nourishment, not even from the horses, since Dukkai had cut his throat and so was wholly dependent on his native earth and shelter. With the advancing day, he felt more and more debilitated.

"Is there any likely place you can see ahead?" Rojeh called up to him. "You're worn-out. And so are the animals."

Shaking his head no, Ragoczy Franciscus straightened himself and made himself maintain a correct seat, but it took more of an effort than he wanted to expend. As the trail continued its zigzag way down the slope, he made a point of peering into the trees in the hope of seeing a cabin or other shelter. They had covered almost a league when he noticed something that might be a barn some distance from the track, and he motioned for a halt, making the sign for *Shelter* before pointing to what he had seen.

Rojeh came up beside Ragoczy Franciscus, saying as he did, "I hope you're right." After a rueful pause, he said, "We should have stopped before midnight."

"But we did not," whispered Ragoczy Franciscus.

"No." Rojeh handed his mule's lead to Ragoczy Franciscus, saying, "I'll ride over to see what is there."

"Keep your weapons to hand," Ragoczy Franciscus soughed as he took the lead.

"I will," said Rojeh, and set his spotted horse jogging toward what might be a barn. He drew in to a walk as he approached the building— for it was surely that—so that he could listen for any telltale sounds that might reveal something about the place. He took a long breath, hoping he might detect the characteristic scents of livestock. As soon as he did, he knew that nothing alive waited there; the metallically sweet odor of decay hung about the barn that fronted on a paddock, in which four shaggy ponies lay, dead at least five days. Rojeh rode near enough to see how they had died and pulled back his horse at once. "Black Sores!" Neither he nor Ragoczy Franciscus had anything to fear from that disease, but their horses and mules did. He swung the stallion around and started back toward where Ragoczy Franciscus waited on the trail, then stopped. "It is Black Sores!" he shouted, then realized that Ragoczy Franciscus could not answer. "Did you hear?" he called when he could see Ragoczy Franciscus again.

Yes, he gestured.

"Should I approach, or must I dismount and kill my horse?" Rojeh loathed the very notion of having to put an end to the stallion's life.

No, Ragoczy Franciscus gestured emphatically, and then added, *Come*.

Hesitantly, Rojeh complied, saying as he rode up to Ragoczy Franciscus and the two mules, "Are you sure this animal is safe?"

"No," whispered Ragoczy Franciscus, "but if there has been contagion, we have all been touched by it. We must find a place to rest, and I will give each of the animals a dose of the sovereign remedy, and it may guard them against the Black Sores." This taxed him to the limits of his voice, and he made a gesture of apology, then touched his throat, a movement of frustration and fatalism. He kept his mouth firmly closed. *We go on*.

"Yes. We must," said Rojeh, and continued to keep looking for a place they might rest safely; the downward path led to a narrow valley that was beginning to show a little promise of spring: there were shoots of the hardiest grasses poking up through the loamy soil, and a few of the willows hanging over the fast-running stream appeared to be trying to produce new verdure. The track followed the stream, stopping at a ford that had obviously been damaged during the storms of the winter. "We can get across, but we'll have to watch for drop-offs."

The way Ragoczy Franciscus nodded showed that he was not pleased by what he saw. He pointed down into the deep hole by the head of the ford. *Rocks. Deep water*, he motioned, and pointed to the narrow band of shallows that now made up the ford. *Stay careful*.

"You have my pledge I will," said Rojeh, only partly in jest. He watched Ragoczy Franciscus start across the ford, keeping the mule drawn up close to the blue roan; running water always gave Ragoczy Franciscus vertigo, and Rojeh was prepared to follow closely after him if he showed any signs of succumbing to light-headedness;

Ragoczy Franciscus kept erect in the saddle, showing no indication of distress from the water. Rojeh started across after Ragoczy Franciscus; his horse and his mule had reached the far shore. Rojeh's horse tried to pull free of the bit so he could plunge across the ford, but the footing was wobbly enough to force the spotted stallion to keep to a steady walk, which he did, constantly tossing his head to indicate his displeasure; the stolid mule followed behind with the determination of his kind. As they came out of the stream, Rojeh said to Ragoczy Franciscus, "It could have gone worse."

Very slowly Ragoczy Franciscus nodded and pointed toward the trail winding ahead. *Go,* he signaled. He was about to give his blue roan the office when a loud whistle announced the arrival of a goatherd and his flock. The goatherd was possibly twenty-five but looked forty, with sun-leathered face and hair starting to go white; his beard was long and unkempt, and the odor of his body was as strong as that of the goats. He wore a heavy sleeved dalmatica of poor-quality wool, and over it a tunica of leather that was so old some portions of the front had almost worn away; his leggings were of patched goat hide with laces crossed over them to keep them in place. He carried a staff and was accompanied by two dogs, which busied themselves directing the goats.

"Something for the ford," the goatherd said in a nearly incomprehensible dialect that had Persian and Khazar elements in it, as well as the tongue of the Byzantines. He held up a grubby hand and turned his huge eyes on first Ragoczy Franciscus, then on Rojeh. "We keep it up for travelers, my cousin and I."

Not knowing if it was wise or foolish, Rojeh reached into the wallet hung from his belt and pulled out a silver coin, which he handed to the goatherd. "For your work."

The goatherd was dazzled; he stood staring at the coin as if entranced. "Too much," he crooned to the coin. "Too much."

"Then you will use it for the benefit of others," said Rojeh.

The goatherd mumbled something incomprehensible to the silver, then slipped it into his leather wallet that hung from a thong strapped around his waist. "God give you safe travel and may your branch ever bloom," he said as if he suddenly recalled what was expected.

Rojeh actually laughed once, then said, "Thank you."

Ragoczy Franciscus sketched a reverence in the goatherd's

direction and started his blue roan moving carefully through the throng of goats, even as he loosened the closure on the top of his mace's sheath. Then he made a quick motion of *Beware* to Rojeh as they threaded their way through the goats.

The goatherd shouted something, and ahead on the trail three large dogs rushed from cover, teeth bared, and rushed at the two travelers, their horses and mules. Behind them the two dogs rushed toward them, scattering the goats, their snarls joining with those of the first three.

Rojeh pulled his shimtare and raised it to strike, saying loudly, "I hate having to kill dogs." His blow did not fall, for the stallion kicked out, sending the nearest dog tumbling away with a single shriek before it dropped in a heap. The mules had laid back their long ears and were in defensive stances; one of the dogs reached Ragoczy Franciscus' blue roan, raking a double furrow in the slope of her shoulder with his teeth. The mare reared and lashed out with her front hooves even as Ragoczy Franciscus brought his mace into play and, with a long, sweeping drub, sent the dog that had hurt the mare flying. Rojeh had managed to cut the flank of another dog, and it had slunk off, limping and whimpering. Rojeh's mule let out a squeal of equine rage, swung around, and bit the dog attempting to gouge his rump.

Standing in appalled stupefaction, the goatherd finally realized that his dogs were taking a beating, and he shouted two short syllables. The dogs retreated, all but one, and he did not move from where he had fallen. The goatherd let out a bellow of grief and held out his arms to the four remaining dogs, who slunk up to him, tails tucked and heads down, ashamed of their failure.

Shelter, Ragoczy Franciscus signaled. *Now.*

Rojeh tugged on the lead to get his mule moving and only then realized that the animal had sustained a gash on its foreleg, a wound that was bleeding freely. "Yes. We must," called Rojeh, forcing the mule to limp along with his jogging horse.

They had gone perhaps a league when they finally came upon a small cabin that had clearly been used by slavers, for there were heavy bars on the windows and stanchions for chains. A crude painting on the side of the small building showed a procession of men all linked together.

We must, gestured Ragoczy Franciscus reluctantly, and nudged his mare off the trail toward the cabin.

"Yes. The animals need treatment before they tie up or take Black Sores," said Rojeh.

Ragoczy Franciscus made no response as they neared the cabin. A short distance from the place, he dismounted and led his horse and mule on foot. At the door he stopped to take stock of the cabin and its surroundings. Noticing a little creek near the rear of the cabin, he led his mare and mule there to drink, and when they had, he went back to the cabin and forced the door open, stepping inside with his two animals. He signaled to Rojeh, *Water. Come in.*

"My animals, too," Rojeh said, just to be sure.

Yes. All in.

The interior was cramped, but there were sleeping shelves around the walls that accommodated more than twenty grown men and women; these were separated by stanchions to which chains could be locked. Deliberately ignoring the purpose for which all this was intended, Ragoczy Franciscus knelt down to look at the gashes that the dog had made in his mare's hide; the injuries were fairly superficial, but they had bled steadily for some little while, which troubled Ragoczy Franciscus. He took his blue roan's lead and knotted it to one of the stanchions in the wall. Then he led the mule to the other side of the cabin and tied it to another of the stanchions before removing his small chest of medicaments from the pack saddle. He opened it and took out his longest needle, threaded it with twisted silk, and went to stitch the mare's cuts closed.

"At least this looks deserted," Rojeh said as he came in with his spotted horse and mule; he secured his horse and his mule to stanchions, saying as he did, "If the slavers are coming, they won't be here until late in the spring, and by the look of it, no one else has used the cabin."

No, Ragoczy Franciscus agreed as he set his last stitch. He patted his mare's neck to reassure her, then took a jar of ointment from his case and smeared a generous amount of the odd-smelling compound over the closed gashes. "Which of your animals is—" he said in an undervoice.

"The mule. One of the dogs got to his on-side fore pastern and cannon bone," Rojeh said. "He's been bleeding most of the way here, and favoring his foot." He caught the sharp look Ragoczy Franciscus gave him. "Yes. Between your mare and this mule, there's a clear path any hungry hunter could follow."

"Wolves," Ragoczy Franciscus whispered. "Or tigers."

"I'm afraid so," said Rojeh, stepping aside to allow Ragoczy Franciscus sufficient room to kneel down and examine the slashes; the mule cocked his hoof and gave a dispirited kick before allowing Ragoczy Franciscus to touch the messy wounds that were still oozing blood. "Is there any risk of Black Sores?" This possibility distressed Rojeh as much as his worries about predators.

Ragoczy Franciscus turned his palms up to show he had no answer to offer. He brought his case next to the mule and squatted down again, brushed the wound clean with a bit of cotton bandage, then brought out his needle again, threaded it, and set to work. When he finished, he dressed the injuries with the same ointment he had used on his mare, then wrapped a bandage around the pastern and up the leg, tying it off with care. As he got to his feet, he managed to murmur, "I will dose all four of them."

"With the sovereign remedy? Do you think it will be enough?" Rojeh asked.

"I hope so," Ragoczy Franciscus said silently, and removed two vials from the case.

Rojeh started to unload the pack saddles, but had trouble making a place for the chests, cases, and crates in the confines of the cabin. He finally put most of the items on the sleeping shelves, thus leaving the four animals a small amount of room to move. As he reached for his grooming supplies, Ragoczy Franciscus came back into the cabin. "How was the exploring?"

Ragoczy Franciscus sat down on the chest of his native earth, patting the cover with affection. *Rest,* he signaled, and rubbed his eyes. *Midafternoon.*

"Midafternoon it is," said Rojeh. "You can deal with the animals then."

When he had finished with the horses and mules, Rojeh left the cabin to hunt for something to eat. He found what he sought in a large hare, which he killed, gutted, and skinned before going back to the cabin, where he sat on a stump where he could watch the door, and sliced collops of meat from the skeleton, eating them off the blade of his knife; when he was done, he carried the bones a fair distance from the cabin to discourage predators. Then he went to wake Ragoczy Franciscus and to get some rest of his own.

Ragoczy Franciscus rose promptly and motioned his *Thank you* as soon as he got to his feet. He had benefited from the respite from the sun, and he was no longer weighed down with exhaustion. *You fed.* There was approval and a tinge of wistfulness in his demeanor.

"Yes. I caught a hare; thin and stringy, but still satisfactory," said Rojeh.

Very good. Looking down at the chest on which he had slept, he said without sound, "When this is gone, I will have to move only at night."

"I've thought about that," said Rojeh. "I believe there are ways to accommodate your problem. Think how we have managed before. What we did then—"

"My throat was not cut," Ragoczy Franciscus breathed.

"No, but we can try some of the same methods, if we plan carefully." He broke off, recalling what had happened the last time Ragoczy Franciscus had endured long hunger.

Good, Ragoczy Franciscus gestured, then left Rojeh to nap while he did his various chores. When Ragoczy Franciscus was done, he began to saddle the animals, beginning with the mules. He had time enough to balance the loads they carried, and to adjust and tighten the ropes, thongs, and nets that held their chests, crates, casks, and cases in place. Next, he saddled Rojeh's spotted stallion, and last, he saddled his blue roan mare and gave each animal a small amount of grain to eat.

Rojeh came awake without prompting and went to check the buckles on his horse's bridle. "I don't know why I always do this."

"Habit," Ragoczy Franciscus said with his lips.

"Certainly; habit." Rojeh untied the leads of his mule and then his horse.

Yes, said Ragoczy Franciscus, leading his horse and mule to the door.

"We should be able to ride until after sundown; there are no clouds in the sky, and the moon should be bright." He was immediately behind Ragoczy Franciscus.

"We will not be the only creatures abroad tonight," Ragoczy Franciscus warned, raising his voice to a soft mutter, then coughing from the strain of it.

"No, probably not," said Rojeh as he put his foot in the iron foot-loop and swung up into the saddle.

Ragoczy Franciscus mounted and came up next to Rojeh. "I smelled smoke earlier," he whispered.

"Not fire?" said Rojeh at once.

"Oh, fire, most certainly," Ragoczy Franciscus murmured. "But not a wild one."

"You mean there are others in this part of the forest, perhaps on the same trail," said Rojeh.

"I cannot say," Ragoczy Fanciscus whispered. "But be vigilant."

"I am, my master." Rojeh put his hand on the hilt of his shimtare.

I know, Ragoczy Franciscus signed, and moved ahead, his dark-seeing eyes unhampered by the lengthening shadows.

Dusk had given way to night by the time they found the shepherd's hut at the edge of the trail, a market sign painted in badly faded blue on the side of the building, indicating it was intended for those driving sheep to be sold. It had a good-sized fold behind the hut, and a water trough that was full to overflowing by a long flume from a spring up the hill. By the smell of it, it had been used fairly recently.

"It looks sound enough for a night," said Rojeh as he rode up to the hut.

Not certain, Ragoczy Franciscus gestured; he sat very still, listening intently. *Something,* he signaled. *Close.*

"Men or creatures?" Rojeh asked, paying close attention to the gathering night.

Both, came the gestured response.

"All the more reason for us to be careful," said Rojeh, raising his voice so it would carry to anything or anyone lurking nearby.

A loud rustling from the undergrowth suggested a night hunter—perhaps a fox or wild cat or a badger—had hurried away; the crackling of twigs marked its progress into the deeper forest.

More danger, Ragoczy Franciscus indicated.

"You mean the woods are too quiet?" Rojeh listened.

"We are being followed," Ragoczy Franciscus whispered.

"For how long?"

Forcing himself to speak as loudly as he could, Ragoczy Franciscus said, "Since we left the slavers' cabin."

"Are you sure?" Rojeh looked about in alarm.

Yes. Very. He pointed off toward the hut. *Trap.*

Although Rojeh did not share Ragoczy Franciscus' apprehension, he pulled his horse back a few steps. "Then let us go on. Night or no night, it is better to *stay* out of a trap than to have to *get* out of one."

Ragoczy Franciscus gave the sign of agreement and managed to say, "It is dangerous here."

"Then we'll press on," said Rojeh, and held his horse back so Ragoczy Franciscus could take the lead.

Ragoczy Franciscus got his horse and mule moving again. For the next two leagues the night continued to be unnaturally quiet; once an owl had flown over them, hooting softly, and once they heard the yipping cry of a fox, but other than that the night might as well have been deserted, a constant reminder that the two travelers were not alone on the trail. Finally Ragoczy Franciscus signaled a halt, saying, "The road divides ahead."

"Are both branches well-used?" Rojeh asked.

"They appear so." His voice was no louder than a purr, and he had to repeat himself twice before Rojeh heard everything he said.

"South could lead to Pityus and the Caucasus Mountains. Continuing west should bring us to the Sea of Azov," said Rojeh.

Yes. Which way? The movements were exaggerated to allow Rojeh to see them plainly.

"The mountains near Pityus are said to be full of robbers and brigands," Rojeh said slowly, following his own thoughts. "But if the weather improves, we might be able to take a ship—" He stopped as Ragoczy Franciscus held up his hand and pointed to his chest of native earth. "Oh. Yes, that is a problem if we travel by water." He nodded to the right-hand branch. "Then I suppose we should go on to the Don and overland from there," he said as they moved on.

About midnight, Ragoczy Franciscus drew rein and gestured in the direction of a wood-stockaded compound; in the pale wash of moonlight, Rojeh could hardly distinguish it from the trees surrounding it; only the dome of the central church was identifiable as a structure apart from the trees. "Is it occupied?"

"By monks," Ragoczy Franciscus said quietly. "There is incense on the air, and someone is chanting one of Saint Ambrose's."

"Do you think it is safe to go there?" Rojeh glanced back over his shoulder as if expecting to see hordes of outlaws descending on them with drawn weapons at the ready. "If they are chanting, I reckon they must be cenobites."

A chain with a pull on the end of it hung down next to the small gateway into the stockade; Ragoczy Franciscus tugged on it and was rewarded with an unmusical clunk from a pot-metal bell. There was no immediate response, so he rang a second time and heard the chanting falter, and a short while later, a wizened face appeared in a crude slide-back window, and the monk stared out.

Rojeh decided to speak up; choosing Byzantine Greek as the most likely language for mutual understanding, he reverenced the monk and began, "I am Rojeh of Gades, and I and my companion, Ragoczy Franciscus, merchant, are traveling west. We have need of a place to stop for the night, to rest our horses and mules, and to see they are given water, and feed, if that is possible."

"I am Brother Dorus," he answered. "And this is the Monastery of the Ascendant Christ."

"Undoubtedly a protected place, and one where travelers may rest without fear," said Rojeh.

Brother Dorus hesitated. "I must warn you that we have Lice Fever here. May God spare us from His Wrath."

"Amen," said Rojeh.

When Ragoczy Franciscus remained quiet, Brother Dorus stared at him. "He does not say 'amen'?"

By now, Rojeh had an answer. "We have had a most difficult journey, and because of the many losses we have had, he will not speak until he is safely at the home of his fathers."

"A pious act," said Brother Dorus, "if he has remained faithful to it."

"It is as if his throat had been cut," said Rojeh with a quick glance at Ragoczy Franciscus, his face revealing nothing, as Ragoczy Franciscus reverenced the monk.

"Do you have weapons?" Brother Dorus asked.

"Only those any prudent travelers would carry," said Rojeh.

"You must surrender them as you enter, or we may not receive you," said Brother Dorus.

"We will not serve you ill," Rojeh said.

"We will give you a place to sleep and provide food and drink for your creatures, in the Name of Christ," said Brother Dorus, at last opening the gate. "You may give your weapons to Brother Acacius as you enter." He nodded toward another monk, whose face was obscured by the massive cloud of his beard. "You will be given them back when you leave."

Rojeh began to unbuckle his shimtare's scabbard from the saddle, and to reach for the dagger in the back of his belt. "You are kind to receive strangers."

"Thus do we serve God," said Brother Acacius. "In the hope that we may extend our hospitality to angels, unaware."

Text of a letter from the Apostle Gideon of Kuldja-and-Almalyk to the Apostle Jude at Cambaluc, carried by a clan of Turks and delivered two months after the Apostle Jude's death from Wet Lungs.

To the pious and worthy Apostle Jude at Cambaluc, the Apostle Gideon of Kuldja-and-Almalyk sends his greetings and blessings, with the assurances that our work goes on here in spite of the many difficulties that continue to confront us, for which perseverance God be thanked, for it brings us nearer to our Crowns in Heaven. In this time as we remember the trials of Christ, so may we accept our burdens in His Name, for the glory that is to come.

It is fortunate that the Turks bearing this message are bound to the East, for they are the first clan to travel that direction in over a year, and there has been so little trade in this region that bound either east or west, merchants have not been seen for a very long time. I have not been able to spare any couriers of late, either, and so I have almost no news beyond what has transpired here to offer you, as I hope you will send me word of your apostlary and congregation when you can rely upon the good offices of travelers bound to the West.

The winter is still holding on here, although not with the ferocity it had shown last year at this time, when Yellow Snow still fell, and the cold continued for most of the summer. This year there is yellow in the snow, but not as last year, and the cold may break a little sooner, all of which is most welcome to us, and for which we offer many prayers of thanksgiving to God, and His Son. The people of Almalyk have also been preyed upon by many robbers and other desperate men who are not redeemed through Christ, and many good Christians have lost their remaining goods and their lives to these desperate companies of unsettled people.

I have ordered our apostlary here expanded to provide shelter and protection to our increasing numbers, for it was not adequate to the needs of the many who have joined our faith, accepting Christ as their Savior, and Confessing, in the hope of Heaven. We have had fewer trains of traders with lumber and skins, as well as a shortage of brick makers. This has meant that our expansion has been slow, and what we had wanted to have ready by this Season of Resurrection will not be completed until late in the summer, and that is assuming our region suffers no more calamities, and that fevers do not reduce the number of our workers still more.

For myself, I am always tired, although I am ashamed to say it, for God has not taxed me with the afflictions He has imposed upon others. My thoughts are sometimes muddled as I try to maintain all that must be kept up for the Christians here. I pray and pray for God to help me keep my mind clear, and I ask for the patience to find my way in this perilous time to the haven Christ has made for us. I ask for your prayers and your strength to sustain me, and those who have come to me for the succor of faith, that they will be preserved from my sins, and if I err, it shall not endanger them.

Food continues to be in short supply, and many of the poorer people have starved this last winter, some of them unto death, others only into illness and lethargy, which may in time prove fatal. For this we have provided burial for any who seek it, conversion not being required. There are some who oppose this and say it is lax in us to do this, but I am minded to recall that God is the Judge, not Man, and because of that, I believe it is incumbent upon us, as a sign of Grace, to do all that we may to ease the suffering of those around us, in Christ's Name, and for the triumph of our faith.

If you know of any traders in wood who might be seeking buyers for their logs, tell them that we here in Almalyk have need of logs and boards for our apostlary. In Kuldja, I have appointed Esaias to act as Apostle there until my return; he has proved himself capable and worthy of such a post, and the people of Kuldja hold him in high

*regard. As soon as the compound here is complete, I will return to
Kuldja and take up my position there again. When I am about to leave
Almalyk, I will inform you of my plans again, so that if there is any
task that may be done to our common benefit while traveling, it will
be done.*

*May God raise you up, may He sustain you in this time of tribu-
lation, may He give your wife many healthy sons, and may He welcome you in Paradise when your life here is done. In this the 537th
year of Man's Salvation, in the Fortnight of the Old Mountain
Winds. Amen.*

*Jude
Apostle of Kuldja-and-Almalyk*

5

As the junction port of the Sea of Azov and the Don River, Sarkel was
far from prepossessing, being a partially walled settlement with a
hodgepodge of wharves and warehouses on the southeastern bank
where the Don emptied into the sea, and a cluster of brick-sided,
wood-topped buildings collected behind them, with three market-
squares, just now every one of them empty but for a few local hunters
and farmers displaying their offerings to wary townspeople. Under a
gray sky, the promise of spring seemed to have vanished, leaving behind a dejected air over the whole region.

At the Fair Winds, the most appealing of the travelers' inns available, Ragoczy Franciscus and Rojeh were ending their three-day stay,
preparing to take the ferry over the Don. It was a long crossing, and
the river was running high and fast, making the innkeeper, a Donman
using a Greek name for the sake of Byzantine business, caution the
two foreigners, "Make sure you lash everything down, and put two
leads on your animals."

"We will," muttered Ragoczy Franciscus, handing over two gold
coins, a most generous settlement of their account.

"Well, you are the sort of travelers I want to see back again," said Leandros, winkling the coins out of sight. "Assuming anyone travels again."

"We must hope that they will," said Rojeh.

"They say there has been fighting far to the west. The Byzantine Emperor is striving to increase his empire," said the innkeeper.

"We have no argument with the Byzantine Emperor," said Ragoczy Franciscus, who had overheard Leandros' remark. "I hope it will not adversely affect your business."

"What business? If men like you are not carrying merchandise from the East, what is left for me? Just monks and other religious," scoffed Leandros. "They expect to be housed for nothing, as a recognition of their holy work."

"That is unfortunate for you," Rojeh sympathized, and looked over at Ragoczy Franciscus, who nodded once and glanced out into the courtyard. "The mules are loaded and the horses saddled. We have only to take them and depart. I have copper coins for the grooms."

"Good," Ragoczy Franciscus said; his voice was husky but improving from what it had been. He made a point of using it with Rojeh. "And feed?"

"They've sold us a sack of grain, and they say that in Donrog, they have more grain for sale—or they have had. A sack on this side and another on the far side of the crossing, and we should reach the Dnieper without running out of grain." Rojeh pointed to the sack on Ragoczy Franciscus' mule's saddle. "They've shifted your chest of earth to my mule, and the clothes case to yours, as well. It makes a more equitable distribution of loads."

"So long as the weight is even," said Ragoczy Franciscus, and went to mount his blue roan.

"The ferry is at the foot of the Red Wharf," said Rojeh as he took his stallion to the mounting block and swung into the saddle. "They said they only have three other passengers—local fur traders."

"I imagine they have delivered their hides and are returning to their hunting grounds," said Ragoczy Franciscus.

They rode out of the courtyard and along the end of the market-square, their horses walking briskly, and the mules, for once, willingly keeping pace with them.

Turning toward the Red Wharf, Rojeh reminded Ragoczy Franciscus, "We've paid our passage already. If they ask for more, I will remind them."

"Yes. Good." He was already hoarse and so welcomed the chance to remain silent until asked to identify himself at the loading end of the slip.

The ferrymen were thick-bodied, their shoulders made massive by their work, and their hands hard as planking from constant exposure to salt spray; they were dressed in wide-cut paragaudions belted in broad bands of leather, with fur leggings and northern-fashion boots; they all had short thwarts to sit upon to ply their oars, and poles to use in shallow water. They got the two men and four animals aboard their ferry with minimal fuss and helped to tie the double leads so that the horses and mules would not be moving about the deck of the wide-beamed boat.

"Is there somewhere we can sit during the passage?" Rojeh asked, seeing Ragoczy Franciscus turn pale. "Donrog is a distance away."

"Of course," said one of the men. "At the edge of the hold. There's a wide lip on the hatch."

"Very good," said Rojeh. "Is there much cargo in the hold?"

"Enough for ballast," said the man, and laughed.

"What about their cargo is amusing?" Ragoczy Franciscus asked as he sat down, taking hold of the rim of the hold with both hands.

"Probably nothing," said Rojeh. "You know how men of this stripe are."

Ragoczy Franciscus rubbed his newly trimmed, very short beard and remarked, "The fur traders are not aboard yet."

"No. But they will be shortly. I heard one of the ferrymen mention it," said Rojeh, who could sense Ragoczy Franciscus' discomfort more than he could see it. "Unless something has changed from last night, we should then be off for the northern shore."

"Doubtless the fur traders have business to attend to, and that delays them," said Ragoczy Franciscus a bit distantly; he stared out across the swirling water to the far shore, and he calculated how long their crossing would be. "This may be difficult."

"So I thought," said Rojeh. "I have your seat-cushion for you. It is filled with your native earth."

"That will help," said Ragoczy Franciscus, and waited where he was while Rojeh went to take it from their clothes case. "Thank you, old friend. I apologize for being surly, but—"

"You are hungry. I know. You need not explain." Rojeh sat down beside Ragoczy Franciscus and handed him the cushion. "Anyone fasting as long as you have may be expected to be querulous from time to time."

"Yes. Lamentably, I am that. It is wearing upon me, these months of no nourishment." He took a deep breath and went on, "In a few days, when you get your meal, let me try the blood before you kill it, if you would."

"Do you think you're ready?" Rojeh asked.

"I will know soon enough," said Ragoczy Franciscus a bit grimly.

"All right. Tell me when you want—" He stopped as the ferry lurched; three fur-clad men were coming aboard. All three carried a considerable array of weapons associated with fur traders—knives, bludgeons, scrapers, hatchets, awls, and pikes—and all three looked eager for a fight, for they swaggered up to the tillerman and confronted him with crossed arms, their stances promising bellicosity.

"I'll fight you for passage," a fur trader grumbled, his head lowered as if to charge the tillerman.

"No, you will not," said the tillerman, unaffected by this demonstration of pugnacity. "You will pay as all must pay."

"Are you afraid to fight me?" the fur trader challenged.

"No. I am afraid to damage my hands," said the tillerman. "That should make you careful about fighting me, since you want to reach Donrog."

"We can hold it on course," said the fur trader pugnaciously. "You, Tszandi. You're strong enough."

"I may be," said the third fur trader. "But I know nothing of these waters."

"You see, fur traders, if you know the course, you can steer it, just as he observed," said the tillerman in a very rational tone: clearly he had had such encounters in the past. "But the Don is treacherous, and the tide is turning."

Grumpily satisfied, Bahkei stepped back and slung his arms around his two companions' shoulders, saying, "If he is so worried about his precious fingers, then let's leave him to it."

The men strutted away as if they had bested the tillerman in a contest; they took up positions in the bow of the ferry, braced on the rise of the hull at the loading plank, elbows resting on the wale, facing the water they were bent on crossing.

"Powerful men, those three," said Rojeh.

"And ready to be away," said Ragoczy Franciscus, adjusting his cushion against the vertiginous pull of the river.

In a very tittle time, the ferry shoved away from the Red Wharf and started across the expanse of the Don's mouth, the ferrymen poling the boat out as far as they could before sitting down to row the rest of the way. Beneath the boat, the water churned and contended, tide against current, making eddies of froth along the way. The ferrymen knew their jobs well, and the boat made good progress toward the northwestern shore, passing groups of fishing boats and small open craft in which one or two men pulled up nets of fish and crabs. They were somewhat more than halfway across when the wind kicked up, bringing spitting rain and blustery gusts that rocked the ferry and made the crew strain to keep at their work. As the ferry continued to bounce toward the far bank, the horses and mules grew restive and struggled against their cross-ties. Rojeh and Ragoczy Franciscus went to tend to the animals, making every effort to calm them with reassuring words and gentle pats, but in spite of such attention, the horses sweated and pawed in dismay and the mules kept their heads up and eyes rolling.

"Knock them on the head," one of the fur traders recommended while Bahkei and Tszandi leaned over the prow as far as they could next to the hoisted landing plank, to mark their progress through the water.

"It would only make matters worse," said Ragoczy Franciscus as calmly as he could. "They have a long way to go yet today."

"A hide that color, it could be worth a lot," the fur trader said.

"She is worth more as a living horse," said Ragoczy Franciscus.

The fur trader laughed and went back to his place in the bow; he spoke with his companions and elicited laughter from them as well. The men made loud, derogatory remarks about foreigners, but gave it up when neither Ragoczy Franciscus nor Rojeh bothered to respond.

Gradually the far shore grew nearer, and as if to make the passage more memorable, the ferry was increasingly the plaything of the wind, skidding and wallowing on the capricious waves. The horses neighed in distress and strove not to fall; the mules became more refractory, striking out with their hooves and teeth when the boat pitched too vigorously.

Rojeh came up to Ragoczy Franciscus and raised his voice to be heard. "This is very hard. They're overexcited and that makes for problems."

"We will have to rest the animals on the other side," said Ragoczy Franciscus as loudly as he could.

"Is there anything you can give them?" Rojeh asked.

"I have no more syrup of poppies, or pansy infusion." He cocked his head toward the fur traders. "If there were beer aboard, they would have consumed all of it by now, I should think."

"They would like beer," Rojeh agreed.

"Keep with your horse and your mule. Between us, we should be able to quiet them." There was more hope than certainty in this remark, and as Ragoczy Franciscus spoke, an especially treacherous wave sent a cold spray over everyone on the ferry; the horses tried to bolt and the mules brayed their outrage. He, himself, was feeling the stress of the water, and as he moved about the deck, he had to hold on to lines and braces to keep from succumbing to the queasiness that had possessed him since the ferry had struck the confluence of tide and current.

The tillerman bellowed instructions to the men at the oars, and the ferry began to turn into the waves, riding up and down in a more regular rhythm, but making steadier progress. They kept on this angular course until the northern shore was looming ahead, and then they turned to starboard and made for the slip that was their port; three large docks flanked it, and four ships were tied up at them, sailors busy dropping fenders over the sides to keep these ships from being damaged by the rising storm. Maneuvering among these trading vessels, the ferry slid into the slip, the ferrymen pulling their oars just in time to avoid splintering them on the pilings that marked their berth.

A half dozen men on the dock had come running and were now shouting for lines to secure the boat in its slip, making way for the landing plank to be lowered. Amid a chorus of shouts, the plank came down, the guardrails were secured, and the tillerman swung the tiller up and lashed it in place. "You may disembark," he shouted, and directed his attention pointedly to the three fur traders.

Rojeh had taken a short, Roman crop from the chest of horse supplies, and he held it securely as he went to unfasten the leads of the mule, expecting resistance; he was not disappointed—the mule planted his feet and prepared to withstand any attempt to move him. Rojeh flicked the crop lightly on his rump and tugged lightly on the lead, then repeated the process: a tap followed by a pull. He did not yell or beat the animal, but kept up the steady routine, all the while aware of how Ragoczy Franciscus was getting his horse and mule off the ferry. Ragoczy Franciscus had untied all four leads, then mounted his horse and brought the mare next to the mule, using the nearness of the larger horse to force the mule to walk forward or risk being driven up against the hull of the boat. Once the mule started forward, the blue roan, used to being in the lead, walked up the landing plank, all but dancing on her forelegs in her relief to be returning to solid ground. The mule kept pace with her, and both strained as Ragoczy Franciscus stopped them at the end of the dock, where he waited for Rojeh to get the mule going.

"We can pull him for you," said Bahkei as he and his two companions sauntered toward the landing plank.

"He'll move soon enough," said Rojeh, administering another tap-and-pull combination.

"Ignorant foreigner!" the third fur trader shouted, and laughed angrily. "Doesn't want our help."

Suddenly the mule, tired of the constant repetition, took a step forward and seemed willing to continue. Rojeh loosened the leads holding his stallion and scrambled into the saddle, reaching for the mule's leads and bringing him up behind the spotted horse as they made their way off the ferry and into the streets of Donrog.

The town was smaller than Sarkel, more of a way station than a village, with only one market-square and a clutch of thatched-roof inns that were little better than the stables behind them. Most of the buildings were within the double stockade that provided a degree of protection to the inhabitants of Donrog; the few beyond the walls appeared to be part of a small compound constructed around a domed church with an Orthodox cross atop it. Even now, at midday, no official met the new arrivals, but a swarm of youngsters came running to

surround the newcomers, blocking Rojeh's and Ragoczy Franciscus'
progress as they begged for money and food.

Ragoczy Franciscus opened his wallet and took out a handful of
copper coins, which he tossed some distance away, opening a path
for him and Rojeh to approach the market-square. "We need more
grain."

"Yes, a sackful at least, if we can find a peasant selling any." Rojeh
did a quick scrutiny of the market-square and pointed to the far end.
"There. That stall."

"I see it," said Ragoczy Franciscus.

"The price is likely to be—"

"—high," Ragoczy Franciscus finished for him. "I assumed that
would be the case. And we are in no position to refuse to pay."

"Need I remind you that we are getting low on funds?" Rojeh
asked.

"I'm aware of that, too; at least we still have a handful of jewels. If
we can find a merchant who knows their value, we should have sufficient to cover our expenses between here and the Carpathians," said
Ragoczy Franciscus as he rode up to the stall in question. A short-
bearded peasant sat in one corner of the cloth-walled stall, a small knife
in one hand working away on a length of wood in which he was carving
leaves, flowers, and the faces of animals. He looked up as Ragoczy
Franciscus halted and dismounted, then gestured a greeting, adding in
dreadful Byzantine Greek, "Sacks of feed. Two sizes. Good for horses
and other draft animals." He reached over and patted the remaining
sacks as if approving of a pet dog.

"How much?" Ragoczy Franciscus asked. "For the larger."

"Six silver coins—Angels, if you have them." His eyes were sunk
in deep wrinkles that gave the impression of goodwill and amusement; only strict business was in his voice.

"That is almost as much as an ox," said Rojeh, who had stopped
behind Ragoczy Franciscus.

"I have grain. You have animals. You need feed, and I have a family." He went back to carving.

"Twenty coppers. Persian coppers" was Ragoczy Franciscus' counteroffer.

"Perhaps, for a smaller sack," said the peasant.

"For the larger sack," Ragoczy Franciscus insisted. "And the sack's contents emptied from those hempen ones into a linen sack, to be sure it contains only grain, and to keep the grain from leaking away."

"What do you take me for, a foist?" the peasant grumbled.

"Grain is scarce and money is also." Ragoczy Franciscus leaned forward in the saddle. "Twenty Persian coppers for a large sack." Something about his manner made an impression on the peasant, for he sat back, startled by his sudden willingness to consider the offer.

"Let me see the coppers," he said, looking away from the foreigner in the black paragaudion edged in dark-red silken cord. He stared down at the gloved hand that contained eight large coins. "Are they all the same?"

"Every one of the twenty is the same," said Ragoczy Franciscus. After a short silence, he said, "If you do not wish to sell, then we will look elsewhere."

The peasant stumbled to his feet. "No. No. I will take twenty Persian coppers for a large sack, and I will show you it has only grain in it." He was surprised to see Ragoczy Franciscus dismount and go to his mule to take a sack from the wad of cloth behind the pack saddle.

"You may use this sack," said Ragoczy Franciscus, handing it to the peasant.

Knowing better than to protest to a man of such bearing, the peasant took the sack and went to open the largest sack of grain; he used a scoop to bring out the contents, transferring them into the linen sack, saying as he did, "Three years ago, you could have got two large sacks of grain for three Persian coppers, for grain was plentiful and the travelers came through Donrog in droves. Now grain is costly, and there is little to buy. Not even the rats are thriving."

"It is thus all through the world," said Ragoczy Franciscus, watching the scoop carefully.

"I will not cheat you," said the peasant in disgust. "If the market were busy and the crops bountiful, I might slip a stone or two into the sack. But not now, when people sicken and starve, and sheep and goats wander untended in search of grass."

"Sheep and goats are not the only ones wandering," said Ragoczy Franciscus, thinking of the Desert Cats and many of the other clans that roamed the steppes.

"That does men like me no good—the eastern men come with their flocks and their herds, and before my neighbors and I can drive them off, half our crop is gone, and not one coin or a pair of goats to show for it." He spat again and got the last scoop of grain out of the hempen bag. "There. Is it satisfactory?"

"Yes," said Ragoczy Franciscus, and handed over the twenty coppers, counting each one aloud as he placed it in the peasant's cupped palms.

"If you are returning this way, remember me," said the peasant as Ragoczy Franciscus lifted the sack and went to secure it to his mule's pack saddle. "Be careful on the road. There are desperate men about." He stepped back from the foreigner on the handsome mare. "You and your companion should have guards."

"If they are safe," said Ragoczy Franciscus. "If not, the guards are more dangerous than outlaws."

The peasant laughed raucously, rubbing his knuckles into his eyes. "True. True. True," he repeated as Ragoczy Franciscus and Rojeh rode away, their mules following up behind them.

Beyond the market-square a dozen children thronged around them, most of them begging belligerently; Ragoczy Franciscus took out a few small brass coins and cast them some distance away. The children rushed after the money, shrieking as they strove to gather up the coins. Once again Ragoczy Franciscus and Rojeh slipped away, bound toward the southwestern gate and the road that led toward the Black Sea.

A pair of unkempt men served as guards at the gate; they demanded payment of Rojeh and Ragoczy Franciscus, accepted four copper coins, and shouted after them that the first inn on the road could not be reached by sundown.

Ragoczy Franciscus glanced toward the expanse of water visible through the trees. "At least the dizziness has stopped." His voice was raw.

"There are still the Dnieper and the Bug to cross," Rojeh reminded him.

"And the Dniester and perhaps even the Danube," he said as they entered the shelter of a copse of willow, taking care to keep on the poorly maintained track.

Rojeh nodded. "Will we reach your homeland by autumn, do you think?"

"I hope we may," said Ragoczy Franciscus. "I would prefer not to spend another winter on the road."

They continued on through the willows and out across a field of cold-dry grasses, then into another stand of trees; the road led almost due west and they marked their progress by the angle of the sun ahead of them. Occasionally they caught a flash of ever-more-distant water through the trunks and branches, but by midafternoon, this was lost to sight as they angled away from the Sea of Azov.

"What town do we reach next?" Rojeh asked as they noticed a distant barn at the far side of an empty field.

"Poranache, as I recall," said Ragoczy Franciscus. "If it is still there."

"I take your point." Rojeh said nothing more for almost a league, then spoke up again. "Do you think that we should ride until we reach that inn?"

"The one the guards shouted about? Who knows if they are to be believed," said Ragoczy Franciscus. He noticed a few head of cattle standing in the shade of the trees. They were skinny and messy enough to have been on their own for some time, and so he approached them with caution, only to have them bolt away, lowing in distress. "They are wise to run, I suspect."

"You mean that they would tempt more than animals?" said Rojeh.

"Either as stock or as meat," said Ragoczy Franciscus. "At least there is a little grass coming up now, and so they can forage for their food." He continued on away from the cattle. "Whoever had claim on them no longer does."

"But think of them, out there, where anything might befall them," said Rojeh.

"They are no worse off than we are," Ragoczy Franciscus reminded him.

"We have weapons and—" He got no further, for a sudden burst of whooping and shouting made the woods ring as a small band of heavily armed men on ponies rushed down upon them, swords and lances drawn, and murder in their impassive faces.

"Back against the largest trees!" Ragoczy Franciscus ordered, moving his blue roan with pressure from the side of his leg. "Use your shimtare."

Rojeh struggled to comply, holding the stallion and pulling on the mule's lead; he managed to get his shimtare out, but could not bring it into play without risking cutting the mule. He swung the curved blade around his head, hoping to deflect anything the attackers might hurl at him. "I can't get the mule around."

Ragoczy Franciscus did as much as he could to make more room for Rojeh's mule and nearly exposed himself to a number of furious blows. He drew his mace from its sheath and swung it, striking the nearest attacker on the clavicle so forcefully that the sound of the bone breaking and the man's immediate shriek of pain rose above the general clamor of the fight; the injured outlaw reeled in the saddle and almost fell.

"Kill him! Kill him!" one of the other attackers shouted, rushing directly at Ragoczy Franciscus, his wedge-shaped sword positioned to strike.

This time Ragoczy Franciscus changed hands and brought the head of the mace crashing in under the man's raised arm, pummeling his side and knocking him off his horse.

Rojeh had struck one of the assailants on his forearm, opening a long cut that bled freely; he lashed out at another man who rode as close as he could, a long-handled ax in his fist. The shimtare parried the chop, but the raider was able to get hold of the mule's lead and, in an abrupt jerk, broke Rojeh's hold, riding off with the mule before Rojeh could attempt to recapture the animal. In his efforts to catch the mule, he hacked an attacker in the thigh, and another on the hand.

Although he had struck the most heavily armed man in the group, Ragoczy Franciscus could not stop the assaults completely; he maintained his position and used his mace to keep most of the raiders at a distance; his mule had backed up against the trees and stayed there, letting the blue roan provide protection from the battle.

The man who had fallen clambered to his feet and was picked up by one of his comrades; riding double, they hurried away from the encounter; their departure acted as a signal to the rest, for they hurried after the two, the man with Rojeh's mule's lead in his hand shouting his victory at the capture of the mule.

"Are you all right?" Ragoczy Franciscus asked Rojeh as the raiders disappeared on faint trails among the trees.

"I am," said Rojeh, chagrined. "I should not have let the mule go."

"Had you tried to hold him, you might have been badly hurt," Ragoczy Franciscus said, wiping the stellated head of his mace before returning it to its sheath.

"Still, I shouldn't have let him go," said Rojeh.

"You could have done no differently and been safe," said Ragoczy Franciscus as he started away from his defensive position by the trees; his mule came with him reluctantly, the lead taut.

"But we've lost your chest of native earth," Rojeh exclaimed. "And you have need of it."

Ragoczy Franciscus nodded once with maddening composure. "But I can manage better without my native earth than I could manage without you." He made no indication that he saw Rojeh's astonished expression, adding only, "We will contrive something, and for now, old friend, we will travel by night."

Rojeh could think of nothing to say as he and Ragoczy Franciscus resumed their journey toward the Black Sea and the town of Olbshe at the mouth of the Dnieper River.

Text of a letter from Brother Theofeo in Antioch to the Holy See in Roma, through the office of the Papal Secretary Archbishop Julianus Fabinius of Ravenna, carried by merchant ship and delivered in July 537.

To the most reverend, devoted, and well-reputed Papal Secretary, his Grace the Archbishop Julianus Fabinius, the heartfelt salutations of Brother Theofeo at the Church of the Apostle Luke in Antioch, on this the beginning of the Paschal Season as the priests and monks here reckon the time, and not being wholly in accord with the True Church in such matters, nor endorsing the calculations of the Eastern Rite, but following what they believe is set forth in the teachings of Saint Peter, in the 537th Year of Salvation. Amen.

It is with a heavy heart that I take pen in hand to tell you of recent events in this place: Lice Fever has struck here in Antioch, and many of the faithful Christians have succumbed to the disease, so many that Father Augustulus has not been able to keep pace with the dying and has had to have bodies interred before all the liturgy they need has been offered for the salvation of their souls. I, myself, have assisted him as much as I am able and have joined with other monks in helping to care for the dying and the dead. So far, this congregation has lost twenty-nine members, all of whom were sincere in their faith to the end, and whose deaths have left great holes in the fabric of our community. Amen.

One cannot walk abroad without finding dead animals, many of them from starvation, but others from all manner of ills that beset their kind, from heated bowels to colic, to the Madness, to bloat from bad water. As there are many who cannot bury the Christian dead, so there are few to tend to the animals, and so there are many vultures, and rats, and even jackals, all coming to feast on what cannot be interred before the sun has hatched the maggots in the dead flesh, for although the sun remains weak, it is strong enough to engender maggots. Both the Bishop here and the preachers of the Eastern Rite have let it be known that those persisting in eating the flesh of dead animals risk not only sickness but excommunication if they are obdurate. Thus far, only one man has suffered that fate, and he is a butcher who claims not to be able to make a living for his family if he does not take flesh from dead animals. Now, he cannot sell anything to Christians and his family has lost the right to their home for his apostasy; we must ask what profit was so great as to make such losses worthwhile. Amen.

Because of this and similar developments, it may be a blessing that trade remains poor, for the Lice Fever is everywhere and it could easily expand its miasma as more strangers enter Antioch. Some of the officials in the city had declared that the city must be closed for holy days, so that all may pray for the alleviation of this terrible fever, and for the general protection of all Christian souls, here and throughout the world. The churches here—Eastern Rite and Roman—have endorsed this plan and have appealed to the city's officials to do their utmost in preparing the populace for the observance of all fast days and holy days, during which time no one is to enter or leave the city, and even the port is to be closed; any ships arriving on such days will be required to anchor in the harbor and keep all the sailors, *passengers, and others on board until the fast day or holy day is past. I and many other monks have been asked to aid in enforcing these civic regulations, and so we shall do. Amen.*

There are constant rumors here in Antioch that the Emperor Justinian is determined to summon all churchmen to Constantinople for the purpose of establishing leadership and suzerainty in the Church once and for all, ending the schism that currently exists between East and West. This has already been established by Christ Himself, Who declared that Saint Peter was His Rock upon whom His Church was to be built, so the successors to Saint Peter must be leaders and sovereigns of the Christian Church, no matter where the Empire is seated. Roma is where Saint Peter made his Church, and it is in Roma that the center of the Church must remain or lose its right to minister to the peoples of the earth in the Name of Christ, to ensure the salvation of all, and to proclaim the Kingdom of God when the Last Judgment is at hand. If the Emperor persists in promulgating this council, he must be aware that he flies in the face of Christ Himself, and that questioning the authority of the Pope is concomitant to denying the Will of God. If the Pope accepts the summons to Constantinople, it must be assumed that the Emperor has abandoned his faith for the exercise of worldly power, surely as much a sin as any ever committed in the long history of sinful Man. Amen.

Most highly esteemed Archbishop, I ask you to inform the Pope that we in Antioch have need of the support of more clergy. Daily we see the increase among those of the Eastern Rite, and we know that without more of our own, the Roman Rite will fail, and all these souls be lost to the True Church, and the Glory of God. Once the danger of the Lice Fever is over, we will need every priest and monk who can be spared for the task to come to aid us in this difficult time. For the sake of the Church and the fulfillment of God's promise, I ask you to plead with the Pope on our behalf, and for which merciful act I send my blessing and the pledge of my prayers at Mass for as long as I am in this city. Amen.

Brother Theofeo

6

Both the eastern and northern walls of Poranache had been torn down, the thick double ranks of logs left strewn about the wild fields that spread out from the ruined walls like skirts; at the back of the village, a wide, shallow stream ran amid birches and sycamores. Beyond the stockade, pens and pastures were empty, and the grasses had been indiscriminately hacked down, emphasizing the hunger behind the ruin that had been visited upon Poranache no more than a week before; a lingering odor of decay soured the night air, and the last of the scavengers were at work among the corpses of the defenders of the village. As they approached Poranache shortly after midnight, Rojeh stared ahead into the night, his skin cold with anticipation of trouble.

"The town isn't deserted," said Ragoczy Franciscus. "There are many people in the far part of it."

"You hear them," said Rojeh, knowing how keenly Ragoczy Franciscus' senses were attuned.

"I also see the lights they have left from burning lamps," Ragoczy Franciscus said, pointing to the jumbled center of the town. A dozen little sparks of brightness wavered deep within the part of the village that was still standing; a clumsy barricade of hewn logs had been set up across the exposed streets, and some of the buildings now served as guard posts. "Not everyone was killed, or taken."

Rojeh sighed. "Do you think they will admit travelers?"

"They must realize we are here, so we may as well discover if they will let us in," said Ragoczy Franciscus, and rode his horse nearer to the improvised wall. "Hello to Poranache," he called out in Byzantine Greek; his voice was still somewhat rough; he repeated the cry, then waited while a light in the nearest window flickered more brightly, casting sharp, irregular shadows on the face that peered out.

"Who are you?" The question came in a deep bass, resonant and meant to impress.

"I am Ragoczy Franciscus, merchant, returning to my homeland with my companion, Rojeh, and our animals," he answered patiently.

"Where is your homeland?" The demand boomed across the night.

"At the far side of the Black Sea, beyond the Dniester—you may know that river by another name." Ragoczy Franciscus listened to hurried whispers.

"Where is your caravan, if you are a merchant?" the big voice challenged.

"Most of our goods have been lost on our journey, along with the animals that carried them."

"Through misfortune or bad business?" The voice made this question seem more a test than a simple inquiry.

"By the look of your village, you know something of our losses." It was a risk to mention the destruction around them, but Ragoczy Franciscus dared it.

"The band of marauders came from far away," said the voice. "We have done what we could, and we will continue our fight."

"You present a fine example to others," said Ragoczy Franciscus.

"And may you have an opportunity to help in that good fight, as you are bound in that direction." This was clearly intended to determine his loyalty to his homeland. "You must do all you can to preserve your people."

"If I reach my homeland, I will: like you, I am pledged to defend my native earth." He did not add that his people had been gone from their mountains for twenty-five centuries, and that he was the only one of them left.

"A worthy sentiment," the voice approved, and was caught up in another round of eerie whispering. "You say there are only two men, and three horses?"

"Two horses and a mule," Ragoczy Franciscus corrected gently.

"Two horses and a mule," the voice confirmed. "You are not scouting for a band of warriors, and you do not bring a miasma with you, to overwhelm us with sickness?"

Ragoczy Franciscus coughed, then went on, "If I were planning to do you ill, I would not tell you. We have been traveling for more than two years, and we have no sickness."

"You are either very clever or you are very correct. If you are honest, you do your people honor."

"*Dulce et decorum est,*" said Ragoczy Franciscus: *It is sweet and fitting;* he did not add the last of the Latin aphorism—*to die for one's country.*

"The language of Roma," the voice announced. "You are conversant with that tongue?"

"Yes," said Ragoczy Franciscus, continuing in slightly old-fashioned Latin. "I have spent some time in Roma, in my travels." He had not been in the city for more than two centuries—then he had stopped Diocletianus' agents from seizing his estates, creating a Deed of Succession to protect his property. How important that had seemed then, and how insignificant he thought it now.

Another buzz of whispers, and one or two hushed outbursts, then there was a long silence. Then the voice spoke again. "You must dismount and lead your horses and mules. We will draw back the logs next to the church, and you may enter. Be aware that six armed men will be waiting for you, and they will not hesitate to use their weapons if you do anything untoward. They are instructed to aim for the chests of your animals and then for your guts."

"I understand. We will comply," said Ragoczy Franciscus, and signaled to Rojeh, *Do it.*

Rojeh dismounted at once and took the leads of his stallion and the mule and came up behind Ragoczy Franciscus just as he stepped out of the saddle. "Is this wise?" Rojeh asked in Chinese.

"They should have information of what lies ahead, and we need that," Ragoczy Franciscus said in the same language. "Also, if we do not stop after asking for entry, we risk a spear or an arrow in the back, or in our horses, for they would then be convinced that their worst suspicions are true."

"It would be best for us both to sleep indoors," said Rojeh purposefully.

"You have the right of it: I will have to be out of the sunlight come dawn." Ragoczy Franciscus motioned Rojeh to silence as the first of the logs was pulled back, the sound deafening.

"There is some grass left, too; the horses and mule can graze."

Ragoczy Franciscus swore testily. Almost at once, he added, "I'm sorry, old friend. I have become irascible again."

"You're famished. No wonder you're short-tempered," said Rojeh, who had dined on a goose the night before.

When the fourth log had been moved, another voice—also male, but clearly much younger than the impressive bass—shouted, "You may come in. Single file. At a walk. Unarmed."

"That we will," Ragoczy Franciscus replied. "I have a dagger in my boot, and another next to the mace buckled to my saddle." He did not mention the slim-bladed knife lying under his belt along his back.

"Any traveler must have something to protect himself," said the young voice; an oil-lamp was held up to help show the entrance more clearly. "Come ahead."

Ragoczy Franciscus made a quick signal, *Careful,* to Rojeh, then led his mare through the opening in the logs. Immediately three young men surrounded him, spears in hand, warily inspecting him. All three were thin, and they had the skittish demeanor of those who had recently endured a deadly attack.

A big man in filthy priest's vestments approached on crutches; his thick profuse hair stood out around his face like a lion's mane, and his beard lay on his chest like a wolf 's ruff. His pectoral crucifix was silver and gold, hanging from a silver chain, and he wore a ring with a simple cross cut into its stone. The priest came closer and Ragoczy Franciscus could see he had only one leg. "So," the voice resounded, "a pair of travelers returning from the distant East with little to show for it, and arriving late at night."

"Yes. Sometimes night travel is safer than day," Ragoczy Franciscus said steadily.

"You have the right of that," the priest said, and called out, "Admit the other, and the animals."

Another trio of young men took up their positions and lifted their spears. "Ready," one of them said.

Rojeh came in at a deliberate walk, his horse and mule behind him. "So you will not be troubled when you find them, I have a shimtare fastened to the saddle, a dagger in my belt, and another in a sheath along my arm." He, also, did not include the dagger he carried in a sheath down his back, wanting to be sure he had reserved some extra measure of protection for himself.

The priest pegged forward and stood contemplating the two newcomers. Finally he said, "Two men and three animals, as you said. I am Irkovoyto, the priest here in Poranache, and by default, I am the leader of what villagers are left. I am the one who will determine if you must be guarded or kept apart from these good Christians." His

Byzantine Greek was very good, and his manner suggested a superior education and a comfortable life in childhood.

"I am Ragoczy Franciscus of Transylvania, and this is Rojeh of Gades," he said, regarding the armed youths with the semblance of aplomb. "We have come a very long way."

"So I surmise," said Irkovoyto, shifting his stance for better balance. He summoned the young men to him with an imperious single syllable, then stood with them, conversing in whispers. Finally he moved toward Ragoczy Franciscus. "Our church—the Church of the Armenian Martyrs—was looted by the raiders and it has not yet been reconsecrated. We will put you into it, with your animals, for the night. In the morning, we will make a final decision regarding you."

Ragoczy Franciscus did not know which title to use when addressing Irkovoyto, so he simply said, "Good Priest, we thank you for a place to spend the night, and we ask that you permit us to sleep well into the day; it is very late at night now, and we still have many leagues to go before we reach our destination, and neither of us is young."

"This may be acceptable. We have to observe the Lord's Day tomorrow, and most of us will remain within doors until sunset. Only the guards and the watch will be about the village until after our Mass at midday." Irkovoyto took a firmer hold on his crutches. "My wives will prepare a meal at noon tomorrow, if you would make a donation to our work of rebuilding, you would be welcome to join us."

"We thank you, but we will look to our own nourishment," said Ragoczy Franciscus, "although we will contribute to your work."

This announcement startled Irkovoyto, who regarded Ragoczy Franciscus narrowly. "Why would any merchant part with money for no gain?"

"Ah, but there is gain in having a town to return to on our next journey, particularly where good-will has been established," said Ragoczy Franciscus, reverencing the priest. "Only a very short-sighted merchant would fail to see the advantage."

After a moment's reflection, Irkovoyto touched his pectoral crucifix. "You have a clever tongue and you seek advantage in time to come, as good Christians must. Tomorrow we will talk further, and with God's Grace, we will learn much that will benefit us."

"May it be so," said Ragoczy Franciscus. "If your young men will show us where your church is, we will settle in for the night."

"To sleep the sleep of the just," said Irkovoyto, and pointed to three of the young men. "Mopuoli, Heovo, Otsija, accompany these men and their beasts to the church and see them into it. You may light up to three of the oil-lamps for their use." Without waiting to be obeyed, he swung away from the opening in the wall, calling out, "Eloka, you see to putting the logs back."

"Yes; we will," one of the youngsters answered for all.

None of the young men had an accomplished command of Byzantine Greek, but they did their best. The tallest of the three given the task of escorting Ragoczy Franciscus and Rojeh with their animals to the church identified himself. "Heovo. I will walk ahead; Otsija will walk between you; and Mopuoli will bring up the rear. Anything you do, one of us will see." He pointed down a narrow street. "That way."

"If you lead, we will follow," Ragoczy Franciscus assured him, and prepared to accompany him down the street.

"Then we go now," said Heovo, striking out through the darkness. The church was not any great distance, and as they reached the square in front of it, Heovo ordered a halt. "I will go open the door and strike oil-lamps alight until there is enough brightness for you to see. Then you may come behind."

Ragoczy Franciscus stood quite still, his full attention on the church; it was three times as long as it was wide, with stubby cross-arms two-thirds down its length; the walls were made of heavy planking with a squat dome on top surmounted by a simple Roman crucifix. There were twelve windows set high in the side walls, hardly large enough to admit any more light than a beam the size of a plate. "We can rest here," he said to Rojeh in Byzantine Greek so that they would not be suspected of subterfuge.

"And rest is much needed," said Rojeh. "We have been riding too long, and our horses are in need of a day's rest before they can journey farther."

"So they are tired, and so are we," Ragoczy Franciscus said, and made a point of stretching. Then he asked Otsija, "How can we get water to our animals?"

"I will have buckets carried to you," said Otsija.

"Thank you." He continued to wait patiently until Heovo appeared in the door of the church and waved them forward. "There are pallets on that side. You may sleep on them," he said as Ragoczy Franciscus came up the stairs to the narthex of the church.

Ragoczy Franciscus took note of the dark corner Heovo had indicated and nodded. "You are most kind to travelers."

"If Irkovoyto did not command it, it would be otherwise," Heovo said grimly.

"Then I thank him through you," said Ragoczy Franciscus, pushing his blue roan aside so that Rojeh could come in through the tall, narrow door.

Scowling at Ragoczy Franciscus' mare, Heovo declared, "The Devil rides a black horse."

"This is not a black horse, as you will see in the sunlight," said Ragoczy Franciscus, unperturbed.

"You ride in the dark," said Heovo sharply. "Then it is black."

"She is a blue roan, a fairly rare coat, but handsome." He moved the mare a little nearer the oil-lamp. "Look for yourself."

"She seems as black as night to me," said Heovo,

Rather than give a brusque answer or argue the point, Ragoczy Franciscus said amiably, "I fear I must have done something to offend you, and if I have, I offer my apology, although such affront was not intended."

Only slightly mollified, Heovo glared at him. "We are not well-disposed to strangers; had Irkovoyto listened to me, you would have been left outside our walls—such as they are."

"I can understand your distrust of strangers in these hard times; it would be irresponsible of you not to question any traveler." Ragoczy Franciscus wondered how old the young man was—sixteen? seventeen? certainly no more than that—and that his life was probably half over. "You have done a courageous thing in remaining here."

Heovo shot an angry look at him. "The brave ones are dead," he muttered.

Ragoczy Franciscus shook his head. "No. For their bravery is over and was brief; yours is just beginning and it must last you all your life long."

"However long that may be." The stare Heovo gave him showed he was at least considering what Ragoczy Franciscus said. Turning abruptly on his heel, Heovo ordered Mopuoli and Otsija out of the church, announcing, "We will keep a guard on the door. If you have to leave the church, call to the guard first, or he will spear you."

"We will," said Ragoczy Franciscus as the three young men left them alone with two oil-lamps burning.

"Not an easy situation," said Rojeh when they were alone.

"No, but being in the open at dawn would not be . . . pleasant." He watched Rojeh take their bucket and measure out into it the grain for the night. "A pity we cannot tie them out to graze tonight, but to-morrow afternoon, perhaps the villagers will allow it."

"I'll take them outside the walls. There is some grass there that the raiders didn't cut." Rojeh began unloading the mule's pack saddle. "Who do you think the raiders were?"

"Probably a clan driven by hunger and bad weather, as we've seen before," said Ragoczy Franciscus. "They are not the first, and they are not the last."

"Then you are concerned." Rojeh set down their case of clothing. "At least you know—" He stopped. "I didn't intend to—"

"To imply that I am not at my best? I know I am not, and I know you have been looking out for me, and have held your tongue," Ragoczy Franciscus said. "It is not the first time you and I have had to deal with people like these: isolated, attacked, abandoned. What mat-ters if Huns or other tribesmen are responsible for the damage? the people are bereft of possessions and family, surely as much an injury as a blow on the head."

"There is no Nicoris here, I think," said Rojeh with calm sympa-thy.

"No; there is not, nor would I want her in such a place. I gather most of the women were carried off; not the priest's wives, but many of the others, and the men know they are gone for good," said Ragoczy Franciscus. "Of those who are left, they are probably sequestered somewhere under lock and key." He pursed his lips in distaste. "That may be worse. Whatever the case, you and I will not be permitted to see any of those who remain, not even the priest's wives."

"You will still need sustenance." Rojeh tapped his hand.

"It will not be found here," Ragoczy Franciscus said in a tone that ended their discussion.

Rojeh said nothing more; he looked about, taking stock of the little church. "Windows for the Apostles? What do you think?"

"The Apostles or the Armenian Martyrs, whoever they might be," said Ragoczy Franciscus. "Twelve is a useful number, in any case."

"How many martyrs do you think there were?" Rojeh asked.

"I have noticed that twelve is the number of Magi who attended Christ's birth, or so some of the churches preach. One Magi for each Apostle, it would appear, and it may be the same with the martyrs. The Romans are now tending to three Magi, for the Trinity." Ragoczy Franciscus rubbed his chin. "I will need another trim in a few days."

Rojeh nodded. "Soon, then."

"Very good; I'll be glad to be a bit neater," said Ragoczy Franciscus as he lifted off the saddle and reached for a brush; a short while later he paused in his work. "I am disturbed by the raid here. It means that there are more bands of men about, and as the spring advances, their numbers will increase."

"And they will prey upon travelers as readily as they attack villages like this one," Rojeh concurred. "Desperate men do desperate things. Some travel thousands of leagues westward," he added deliberately.

"To the Egyptian abode of death," Ragoczy Franciscus said in a distant tone. He finished the on-side of his horse and went around to the off-side, starting to brush her neck, working down and back with the grain of the hair. "I wonder if she'll ever come into season again?"

Rojeh said nothing; he continued to groom the mule and then his stallion. The horse lowered his head into Rojeh's hand, nuzzling; Rojeh scratched his withers and saw the spotted horse crane his neck and flop his ears in pleasure. As he continued his care with a stiff-bristled brush, he said to Ragoczy Franciscus, "You know they put us in here to make sure we are not demons or other fell beings."

"No doubt, and if Priest Irkovoyto did not bless it as soon as the raiders were gone, he must have been unconscious; he is hardly the sort of man to allow his village to be contaminated by malign influences if he could do anything about them," said Ragoczy Franciscus, a sardonic note in his utterances. "I have no illusions about this village, or this church—this is a good jail, but it also provides other protection." He looked about the little church.

"Do you sense something?" Rojeh looked alarmed now.

"The church is set away from other buildings. It has been looted. They will want to cleanse it." There was a hard edge to his remark. "Come. Get the saddle-pad and hand me the pack-saddle."

Perplexed, Rojeh obeyed. "Is this really necessary?"

"Yes." Ragoczy Franciscus took the girth and saddle-pad. "He's well-groomed, thank goodness. We do not have to start with brushing."

Their efforts were interrupted by Heovo and Otsija, who carried two wooden buckets apiece, all filled with water. "Is everything well?" Heovo asked as he put the buckets down. Neither youth would look directly at either Rojeh or Ragoczy Franciscus. "Are you going to sleep shortly?"

"Yes," said Ragoczy Franciscus.

"Then we will bid you a good night; may God protect you and all good Christian souls," said Otsija; he and Heovo retreated, banging the door in their haste to be gone.

"Do you think they believed us?" Rojeh asked, trying not to sound worried.

"I do not know," said Ragoczy Franciscus, buckling the girth into place; he felt the mule stiffen in anticipation of more travel; he patted the mule's neck. "This is a poor way to thank you for all you have done, but we will need to get away tonight."

"What is it that you perceive?" Rojeh persisted even as he helped saddle the mule.

"I think I've smelled something, or heard something," Ragoczy Franciscus replied.

"Are you certain? Or are you reminded of being with the Desert Cats, who kept apart from you when they intended to sacrifice you?" This direct question was meant to be blunt; Rojeh stood still, waiting for Ragoczy Franciscus to provide an answer.

"This is not the same thing," Ragoczy Franciscus said at last, his voice so quiet that Rojeh almost wondered if his throat were hurting him. "We were no strangers to the Desert Cats, although we were foreigners. I may not have been so willing to visit their camp had not the clan been familiar to me and had we not been accepted as companions to the clan. I do not know these villagers, but I know something has gone wrong."

"As when Dukkai read the smoke?" Rojeh pressed on.

"No." Ragoczy Franciscus picked up the case containing their clothes. "If you want something else to wear, take it out now."

Rojeh said, "I will change my garments after we have rested."

"Then hand me the chest of medicaments. I know we have use of what it contains." He set it in place on the pack-saddle and lashed it there. "The sack of grain, to give a soft container for the chest of treasure to rest upon, and my roll of farrier's tools."

"Can you not tell me what has made you uneasy?" Rojeh asked.

"If I could identify it, I would." He handed Rojeh his saddle-pad. "I'll finish up here. You get your horse ready to go."

"And yours?"

"I will attend to her directly, just as soon as the net is in place." He sighed as he checked the mule's halter and leads. "I will make new buckles and repair the billets." He was almost finished when the mule brought up his head and brayed loudly; an instant later, the tang of burning wood was on the air. "They have set fire to the church!"

Rojeh hurried to tighten the saddle-girth and free the stallion's reins from the stout pillar to which they were secured. "You were right," he said as he vaulted aboard his horse and reached for the mule's lead.

Ragoczy Franciscus went to open the door and was not entirely surprised to find it braced from the outside. "Come. Back your horse up to the door and set him kicking."

Rojeh complied at once, using the mule's lead to tickle his stallion just above the stifle; almost at once, the horse lashed out with his back legs. Three more kicks and the wood splintered, and Rojeh kneed the horse around, dragging the mule with him. "How do we get out of the village?" he shouted back to Ragoczy Franciscus, who had bridled his blue roan and, taking a fistful of mane, swung onto her back, leaving his saddle behind as he rode her out of the church.

In the dark, the first brilliant flames were glaring at the far end of the church, and they were spreading fast. Four shadowy figures could just be made out near the fire, one of them carrying a pair of torches; they wheeled about as they heard the sound of breaking wood and the clatter of insistent hooves.

"Go toward the stream! There will be a door to the stream!" Ragoczy Franciscus shouted. Clinging to the mare with his calves, he urged her forward, passing near enough to the fire to feel the rush of its own wind. Then they were into a passageway that had a break in the wall at the end of it, where a waist-high gate stood; they made for it at the gallop. Even the mule cleared the low gate in a scrambling leap, Ragoczy Franciscus' blue roan immediately behind him. Almost at once they were in the stream, bound for the far bank, while behind them the flames from the church stretched hectically toward the sky. Water splashed up and foamed ahead of them. Shouts rising behind them faded quickly; they were not being pursued. At the far bank as the two horses and the mule climbed up the pebbly shore, Ragoczy Franciscus had to lean forward and wrap his arm around the mare's neck to keep from falling off. In the narrow meadow beyond the bank of the stream, they pulled in and took stock of their present situation.

"At least we have all our goods on the mule," Ragoczy Franciscus said, his voice hushed from the strain of yelling.

"You've lost your saddle," Rojeh pointed out.

"Yes."

"It was padded with your native earth."

"I know." Ragoczy Franciscus looked up at the sky and noticed a plume of smoke sliding along the night breeze. "That fire is going to burn more than the church, I fear."

"Serves them right for trying to burn *us*," Rojeh declared indignantly.

"It is—"

"If you say *sad* or *unfortunate* or *a pity*," Rojeh warned tranquilly, "I will . . . I don't know what I'll do."

"It is all those things, as well as mad and murderous. Relentless trouble is everywhere." Ragoczy Franciscus wiped his face, leaving a smear on his cheek above his beard. "We should have found a thicket in the forest, after all."

"We had better do that now," said Rojeh. "We don't want to be in the open when the sun rises."

"No; that would suit neither of us," said Ragoczy Franciscus, turning his blue roan and heading toward the west and a vast expanse of trees that vanished into the darkness.

⋄   ⋄   ⋄

Text of a letter from Thetis Krisanthemenis at Pityus to her uncle, Porphyry Cantheos, at Sinope, written on a thin plank of wood with a stylus, then rubbed with paint to make it legible; carried by trading vessel and delivered twenty-six days after it was entrusted to the Captain of the *Harvest Moon.*

To my most excellent uncle, Porphyry Cantheos, the heartfelt greetings of your niece, Thetis Krisanthemenis, from the port of Pityus, where I and my children have come. I fear I must ask that you and my brother reach an agreement in regard to my living situation. I have some monies provided to me by the foreigner Ragoczy Franciscus, which has allowed us to hire a small house here in Pityus, but it will not support us forever, and before it is exhausted, I must beseech you to determine where I and my children are to go.

Sarai has been evacuated due to an earthquake that broke the walls in three places and destroyed one of the docks. The town has been losing people steadily since the sun turned cold, and that has meant that there are not sufficient numbers of laborers to do the work that is required by the damage done to the town, for many of the houses were shaken so much that their walls caved in, and before Sarai can be occupied again, it must be cleared of all dangerous rubble, which, I am saddened to tell you, includes my husband's house and the house of Ragoczy Franciscus. His cook, a Persian named Dasur, was killed in the collapse of the kitchen, and my old servant Herakles broke his arm badly, which festered and killed him. It has been suggested that the town be moved, but I am not able to wait for a year and more for such advantages to be declared, and so I have come away. Ragoczy Franciscus has lost the house he hired and all he put into it, but he may well have died by now, so the losses might not matter after all.

It is a hard thing to have to leave a home, even one as distant as Sarai, for my husband took me there some years ago, and the town has become familiar to me. I have worshiped in the church there and been advised by Patriarch Stavros, who, even now, is returning to his family. Thus I am without spiritual guidance at a time I yearn for it, and I must implore you to provide an introduction to a Patriarch who is willing to take up the task of instructing me. In these dreadful times, I feel the lack of comfort of Patriarch Stavros' counsel, and the geniality of the Foreigners' Quarter. If you decide that I am to come to you, I ask that you send an appropriate escort for us, so that we will not be completely at the mercy of the sailors and others who might seek to enrich themselves at your expense.

My brother has told me in several letters that he cannot easily add my family to his, and if that is the case, I am loath to make such an attempt, which is the reason I have approached you before I try to reach him. May you show yourself to be made of finer stuff than my brother has proven himself to be. Whatever you resolve to do, I will always pray for you and for the well-being of all our family.

Thetis Krisathemenis
(her mark)
widow of Eleutherios Panayiotos

Faithfully copied by Brother Hyakinthos
on the twenty-first day after the Vernal Equinox

7

With the lengthening days curtailing their hours of travel, it took eleven nights for Ragoczy Franciscus and Rojeh to go from Poranache to Olbshe at the mouth of the Dnieper. There, at sunset at the end of their first day in the town, Ragoczy Franciscus, in a heavy black silk kandys with a hood to protect his face, took the last of their gold to a money changer who kept a shop a few steps from the largest market-square in the town.

The money changer was a small, thin man made up of ferocious angles, with the permanent squint of the shortsighted. A Persian by lineage and a Byzantine by inclination, he was suitably impressed with Ragoczy Franciscus' finery, but said, "Elegant plumage does not mean the meat is wholesome."

"No, it does not," said Ragoczy Franciscus, setting down a long bar of gold. "However, this may improve the savor."

"Oho!" the money changer exclaimed, lifting the bar reverently.

"This is from Cathay. Those scratchings are their way of writing, or so I am told."

"It is the name of the goldsmith—Chou Zhan-Wah—and the seal of his guild-master, and a statement of weight," Ragoczy Franciscus said.

"Chou Zhan-Wah! Dreadful names they give these foreigners," said the money changer, who was called Kurush Sadimatsrau. He weighed the gold carefully. "We don't see much metal from Cathay of late."

"Travel has slowed," Ragoczy Franciscus agreed.

Sadimatsrau waggled a finger at the black-clad foreigner. "You must know that I have to be careful. With so much hardship about, many have resorted to all manner of counterfeiting of gold and silver. I have to be sure—you understand."

"I understand that you do not want to accept lead for gold," said Ragoczy Franciscus.

"No, I do not," said Sadimatsrau. "You say you want to be given the worth of this in coins, mostly silver, a few gold, some copper, some brass?" The money changer was already reaching for his strong-box. "I charge twenty-five percent of the worth of this bar of gold."

"You will charge twenty, as is done in Constantinople, and you will not try to convince me that the value of gold has recently declined, making it impossible for you to assess this at a high rate," said Ragoczy Franciscus with a polite manner and steely purpose.

"How you merchants like to bargain," Sadimatsrau muttered, sighing. "This will be the ruin of me, charging so little and agreeing to higher prices than I can recoup."

"You will do very handsomely," Ragoczy Franciscus corrected him cheerfully.

"I am not a rich man," he began, fully prepared to launch into a lengthy self-justification.

Ragoczy Franciscus cut him short. "Possibly not rich, but you will be better off for making this exchange."

Sadimatsrau flung up his hands. "If you insist, then what can I do but comply?" He opened his strongbox furtively and stood so that Ragoczy Franciscus got no more than a glimpse of it. "Forty silver Emperors, five gold Angels, twenty copper Apostles, and thirty brass Empresses." He did his best to sound as if this were his highest offer.

"Fifty silver Emperors, ten gold Angels, thirty copper Apostles, and fifty brass Empresses," Ragoczy Franciscus countered promptly.

"You wish to beggar me," Sadimatsrau complained, then suggested, "Forty-five silver Emperors, eight gold Angels, twenty-five copper Apostles, and forty brass Empresses."

"Done," said Ragoczy Franciscus, disappointing Sadimatsrau, who had looked forward to a good haggle.

"All right," he grumbled, and began to count out the coins. "The gold bar had better be as pure as you claim, or I will have to ask the Master of Trade to demand recompense."

"Then satisfy yourself as to the quality quickly, for I am bound to the West in two days." Ragoczy Franciscus tried not to laugh at the money changer's dismay.

"If you are not here tomorrow, I will know you have cheated me."

"I will be here, and I will be pleased to accept your apology for the suspicions you harbor about me," said Ragoczy Franciscus, and left Sadimatsrau's shop to seek out a saddlery on the market-square where leather goods, hides, and furs were sold. There he purchased a Persian saddle, with a breast-collar and girth, and carried this back to the Inn of Many Lanterns, remarking to Rojeh as he entered their shared room, "I think the mare will be pleased."

"Not to have you riding bareback?" Rojeh suggested. "Perhaps. I know you will much prefer having a saddle. It would be better to have your native earth to add to the padding so we could ride in the day." He regarded Ragoczy Franciscus with determined optimism. "Well, we should reach your mountains more handily with you in a saddle: that's to the good."

Ragoczy Franciscus sat down, taking the saddle into his lap and looking it over carefully. "Unfortunately, there is no place to attach the straps for the Jou'an-Jou'an metal foot-loops. The frame has nothing to support them."

"You are not planning to fire a bow while riding, are you?" Rojeh laughed briefly. "Neither of us has such weapons, and so the foot-loops, metal or not, are hardly essential."

"Still, it eases the back, having those metal foot-loops." He put the saddle down, resting it on its pommel and the front of the short flaps. "Later tonight, I am going to see if there are any women I can reach who long for sweet dreams. It will not be much, but certainly preferable to taking more from the horses and the mule."

"A fine idea," Rojeh approved, and went on to provide an inventory of their remaining supplies.

It was after midnight when Ragoczy Franciscus left the inn, making his way along the narrow lanes that framed the four market-squares of Olbshe, listening intently to more than sounds; when he returned to the inn shortly before dawn, he was able to tell Rojeh that he had visited a youthful widow in her dreams and was feeling much stronger than he had been.

Rojeh took a handful of coins, announcing, "I will find more grain today, and dried fruit, if there is any to be had."

"A fine idea," said Ragoczy Franciscus. "If you find good saddle-pads, buy them, as well."

"I will," Rojeh promised. "Sleep well, my master." He let himself out of the room.

Two nights later, they were under way again, taking the road that followed the shore of the Black Sea. They kept on through three nights of high winds and one of spectacular thunderstorms. After eight nights they arrived on the outskirts of Odessus and found a barn in which to sleep for the day, wakening near sundown and preparing to enter the town. It was the first market-day of summer in Odessus and the first major market of the year, for the spring had come wet and late, making roads all but impassable for carts; peasants and travelers alike were reluctant to venture out. Now, with the first spate of clear weather holding for more than three days, the gates of the town had been thrown open at dawn, and men trooped through them with such wares and stock as they thought might be traded or sold. As the day waned, those among the marketers who could afford to dispersed into the inns and taverns for hectic revelry, so that as Ragoczy Franciscus and Rojeh entered the gates, they found a band of men celebrating their day's dealing by dancing to a tabor and bladder-pipe.

"Where are you bound?" the guard challenged as the dancers and musicians roistered by.

"We are looking for an inn," said Ragoczy Franciscus. "We want a place where we do not have to share beds and the stable has box stalls for our animals. We do not mind paying a bit more for such amenities."

The guard looked the two strangers over, taking visual stock of them. "There are four inns down that street that should suit your needs; one is much like another, and all are reckoned to be good, if you're willing to part with silver." He pointed past the celebrants. "Don't be put off by them; they may be a bit noisy now, but it won't last long. They will soon go to the brothels or the taverns or be too drunk to move." He rested his hand on the hilt of his short-sword. "If they get too frisky, we have ways to calm them."

"Is there a tax to enter the town?" Ragoczy Franciscus asked.

"Are you selling any goods or planning to buy them?"

"We need feed for our animals and a cask for water," said Ragoczy Franciscus.

"Those are not taxed. So long as you pay full price at your inn, there is no tax." He stepped aside to permit them to pass.

They settled on the inn set farthest back from the street, a fifteen-room establishment catering to Byzantine and Roman patrons, the Pelican's Nest. The landlord was a fellow of practiced joviality, a big-shouldered, square-bearded, once-hefty sort who took the coins Ragoczy Franciscus offered and explained, "We back up to a convent, and sometimes the women chant. If it bothers you, let me know and we'll move you to a front room."

Ragoczy Franciscus counted out the sum the landlord required. "Is there any way I might arrange to use your forge? I need to shape toe cleats for our horses."

"Going into the mountains, are you?" the landlord asked.

"That is our intention," Ragoczy Franciscus answered.

"The use of the forge for half a day will cost a silver Emperor, and that is if the smith is not working it," said the landlord, chuckling out of habit.

"Would your smith object to permitting me to fire the forge at night?" asked Ragoczy Franciscus with a genial half-smile to show he was prepared for a negative response.

"I'll find out," said the landlord.

The landlord snapped his fingers for a slave to come to escort the new arrivals to their rooms, which proved to be small and neat, each with a Byzantine bed and a stand for cases and chests. An Eastern Rite crucifix hung on the wall in each chamber, the only decoration.

Rojeh looked from his room to Ragoczy Franciscus' and back again. "Facing northwest—there should not be too much direct sunlight."

"My thought exactly," said Ragoczy Franciscus. He moved so another household slave could set down their clothes-chest on the stand in his room. "I think I will go out shortly."

Rojeh glanced at him. "Should I expect you back shortly?"

"I would hope not," said Ragoczy Franciscus. "It would mean I have not found sustenance."

"I will see if there are any chickens left in the market at this hour." Rojeh paused. "I suppose, if I bring one to the cook, he will dress one for me. I doubt the landlord would like me to fletch and gut a chicken in this room."

"I would imagine you are right." Ragoczy Franciscus opened the clothes-chest and took out a black-silk abolla and a fibula with which to fix it to his shoulder.

"Any finer and you would become the target of thieves," said Rojeh, his faded-blue eyes keen.

"I will endeavor to keep that in mind," said Ragoczy Franciscus as he left the room, closing the door behind him, and went down the stairs. Outside the revelry continued, and an ill-assorted group of sailors and peasants were playing an impromptu game involving groups of runners with linked arms: what few rules there were seemed to be casually enforced; Ragoczy Franciscus gave them a wide berth, making for one of the broader streets that led away from the square. He went at a steady pace, not too rapidly so that he could be attentive to things around him, but not too slowly. Two blocks along he came to a pair of churches, one with an impressive door with brass hinges and an extensive display of crucifixes on the facade, the other, opposite it, small and unadorned, all but the front enclosed in a wall. He stopped and studied the two buildings and concluded the more humble of the two had to be the convent the landlord had mentioned. Standing between the two churches, he was struck by the contrast—one elaborate and impressive, the other self-effacing; he wished he could see them by daylight, but knew that would be unwise. A bit reluctantly he moved on, following the wall of the convent, then crossing a street paved with ancient, cracked stones, going toward a well that stood on the far side, with a bucket for humans and a small trough for animals. As he approached, a small number of rats scattered into the night shadows; the strength of the water that tugged at him told him the well was deep and the water plentiful. He moved into the angle of one of the houses that faced the well and took stock of his situation, doing his best to work out some plan to find a sleeping woman whose dreams he could shape and share. He was so preoccupied that at first he hardly noticed the young woman in the faded, shapeless talaris who came from the side door of the convent carrying a yoke and two brass pails.

Setting down her yoke on the stone rim of the well, she began to draw up the bucket, tugging on the rope with surprising strength for so slight a woman. When finally she had the bucket in hand, she filled one of the pails, then dropped the bucket back into the well, preparing to repeat the process. Her face was set in unresponsive lines, and she stared listlessly about, her hands working as if of their own volition. When she had the bucket in hand again, she filled the second pail and once again let the bucket fall back into the well. Then, instead of shouldering her yoke and bearing the water back to the convent, she sat on the edge of the well and began silently to weep.

From his place in the protection of the housefront, Ragoczy Franciscus watched her, trying to decide if he should approach her; he could not remain indifferent to her distress. "Young woman," he said as gently as his throat would allow.

She gave a little shriek and jumped to her feet, almost stumbling over her pails as she did. "Go away! *Go away!*"

Ragoczy Franciscus did not approach her; he remained near the house, doing his utmost to reassure her. "I mean you no harm. You need not be worried."

"Go away," she repeated, but less emphatically than before.

Ignoring her dismissal, he said mildly, "I would not like to leave you here in so much despondency."

"I'm not despondent," she said in the accent of Troas, her stance a little too defiant to be persuasive; she wiped the tears from her face with a quick swipe of her hand. "You have startled me."

"I might say the same," he responded, remaining where he stood. "Whether or not you are despondent, something is troubling you."

"How can it be," she asked, acerbity coloring her question, "when it is my duties as an apprentice nun that aggrieve me?" Having said such an outrageous thing, she put her hands to her face in shock. "I didn't mean to say that."

"Your vocation is a burden?" he suggested, trying to discern the reason for her dissatisfaction.

"Vocation!" Tears filled her eyes but she did not sob. "My vocation." She came back to the well, wanting to talk to this kindly stranger. "If being given a choice of a brothel or a convent is a vocation, then that is mine."

"When did this happen?" He took a step closer to her.

"Almost a year ago, after my mother died." She shook her head and began to speak rapidly and softly, as if repeating something she had said many times before. "The crops failed twice, and there were only three pigs left. My father had to consider the farm and my brother, and so that left nothing for me. It wasn't his fault the crops failed—everyone's crops failed. And Mother died because she got the Bending Sickness; no one could do anything about that, either." Her hands tightened in her lap. "I must not decry my destiny," she said as if reciting a lesson. She dropped her head. "Who would offer for a dowerless girl in such a time as this?" Standing abruptly, she stared at him. "Why should I tell you this? You are a stranger."

"But you need to tell someone, and—"

"Only my Confessor and the nuns should hear these things," she said in mounting dismay.

"Do they hear them? Or do you keep them to yourself?" He saw he had guessed correctly. "Such unhappiness can fester if you do not speak of it, just as a boil must be lanced in order to heal."

She laughed mirthlessly. "Lancing boils. That is part of my work. Scrubbing floors where there is urine and vomit. Removing the bedding when someone has died. It is for humility and Christian example that I should do this, and do it gratefully." This last came quickly as if to cover over her disgust. "Apprentice nuns are given such tasks, and similar ones, in the hospital we keep for the sick and injured. It's so hard, with so much death."

"It offends you, doing those things?"

His question struck her and she thought about her answer. "I have worked on the farm since I was able to carry a hoe. I have tended birthings of calves and lambs and piglets. I have killed and dressed ducks and chickens and geese. I have milked cows and swabbed the floor afterward. I have dug for turnips in the mud and climbed trees to pick the fruit. I have pressed grapes with my feet for wine and turned barrels of mash for beer. I have sheared lambs and combed goats. I have treated cuts and fevers and cankers. But it was only a part of what I did. Here, it is expected that I will do the lowliest work every day and then pray to God to thank Him for permitting me to be the meanest of His servants. Some of the postulants do feel gratified, but I . . ." Her voice dropped. "Better this than a brothel, I am told. At least I am not spat at in the streets."

"Is there no one who would be glad of your help on a farm? An uncle or a cousin, perhaps?" His dark eyes lingered on her face, at fine skin that had never known fine oils or unguents, at soft brown eyes, at well-arched brows, at a straight nose, at pretty lips marred only by a thin scar that ran to her cheek.

"I have only one uncle alive and he has four living children," she said slowly. "No farmer where I lived could afford to take on another person—worker or slave—until a good crop is brought in again." She blinked slowly, as if trying to understand why she had volunteered so much. "I should not speak with you. Why am I talking to you?"

"You want to talk to someone, and I have the advantage of being a stranger," he said, for he had had such experiences many times before. "I do not matter."

"But I have said such things to you—" She put her hands to her face.

"I am honored to listen," he said, still keeping his distance; his esurience was awakening but he felt only ill-defined interest coming from her.

"I am Ilea, but here at the convent I am called Joaquim to show my renunciation of the world and the acceptance of the life of the convent. I didn't want to give up my name."

"It is a good name, Ilea," said Ragoczy Franciscus, and told her his. "Franciscus is my gens name, and Ragoczy is my patronymic."

She considered this. "You have lands, then?"

"To the west of here," he answered incompletely. "In the mountains."

"Our farm is to the south, across the straits and in the hills." The nostalgia in her words was poignant. "At the end of a valley, hills rising behind it. We have two fields and a vegetable plot. There are trees on the hills, and only some of them have fallen. If I have to die, I want to die there, at home. Not here." She looked up at him. "Do you understand?"

"Yes, Ilea. I understand."

"My father said that if there is a good harvest this year, he may send for me. I know he won't." Her hands shook as she folded them together. "I have tried to resign myself. But I dream about making cheese and carding wool."

"Surely those skills would be useful in the convent. The nuns must keep a cow for milk and need someone to look after the chickens and the garden."

"There are three goats and a sheep," Ilea said, sniffing. "Sometimes I go and watch them when I should be at prayers. Sometimes I go there to sleep. I like the smell of the animals, and the way they go on together, not at all like the nuns, or those who come here for help or nursing. I'm told it is a sign of pride, staying with them instead of keeping to my prayers and my assigned work, and I must give up such things."

He moved nearer, aware of her sense of isolation. "Faith is supposed to end loneliness, not cause it."

She drooped where she sat. "If that were so, I would feel better about how I must live." Then she got up quickly. "I must get this water to the convent. They'll whip me if I take too long."

He picked up the yoke and helped her set it in place on her shoulders. "I am glad to have met you, Ilea."

Her smile was quick and genuine. "And I to meet you, Ragoczy Franciscus. You see, I remembered it: your name." She prepared to leave. "I'll pray for you."

"If you like." Ragoczy Franciscus stood beside the well for a short while, his mind on Ilea and how she had lost so much through mischance and circumstance. He looked toward the convent wall, trying to discern where the barn was.

Three men came stumbling along the street, a wineskin sloshing among them; one of them—a laborer by the look of him—gave Ragoczy Franciscus a truculent stare, but was dragged on by his companions. The street fell silent and empty for a little time, then a pair of jugglers trudged past Ragoczy Franciscus, both worn-out from performing and celebrating; they carried short oars painted bright colors, the tools of their trade. When they had gone, a small monk in a drab habit went by carrying a covered box. The street remained empty for a time, and at last a pair of guards came along, one of them holding an oil-lamp, the other carrying a pike; they scrutinized Ragoczy Franciscus in silence, and then went on about their rounds. The town was growing quiet, and the shine of lamp-light in the windows diminished. In the two churches hymns were being sung, the chanting creating an unexpected harmony in the deepening night. Then that, too, ceased, and the street sank into a hush broken only by the wind. At midnight the convent bell rang, and there were a few lamps lit in the chapel, and a few other parts of the compound; Ragoczy Franciscus waited until the place was still, then he made for the side gate and the barn, where goats could sustain him. As he went, he wondered if Ilea would be there, asleep, and if she would welcome a dream.

Text of a letter from Hormuzd Bashri, merchant from Ecbatana presently at Edessa, to Phemios the Byzantine at Palmyra, written in Persian, carried by merchant courier and delivered three months after it was dispatched.

To my dear colleague Phemios the Byzantine, Hormuzd Bashri sends greetings on this the longest day of the year and asks him to consider what he has to impart as well-intended advice and an alert to what likely lies ahead.

This autumn I will send to you two casks of seeds, which I urge you to arrange to be planted in the fields around Palmyra; these are grains from cooler regions, and with the cooler sun, they should flourish where you are, making it possible for all of us to have a bountiful crop at the next harvest. I no longer believe that the sun will be as warm as it was in a year or so: I am convinced that these cooler conditions will prevail for some time to come, and only by shifting our planting can we provide enough grain to prevent more hunger than we have already seen. I, myself, have contacted Goxach from the banks of the Vistula, to ask him to provide grain from his region that I might sell it from here at Edessa to the wide valleys north of the Caucasus Mountains. I will provide it for nothing if the peasants will agree to set aside twenty percent of their harvest for me as payment. You may find a similar agreement would be advantageous to you, as well.

In order to do this, I have taken on some riders as my representatives. I have doubts about them, but they have sworn a blood-oath to me and have declared they will do all that I ask so long as they are not abandoned to starve and wander. They are led by a young man who is known as the Kaigan of their clan. He is called Neitis Ksoka and his people are named the Desert Cats. There are about forty of them, thirteen able-bodied men, the rest women and children and two ancients, and they have come a very long way to escape the cold years and what they have described as yellow snow. I have provided the women and children and old men a plot of land to farm and graze, with the stipulation that they also care for my horses. These Desert Cats have ponies and they ride as if they were born in the saddle. Even the women are fine riders. They have flocks of goats as well as their pony herds, and these they have agreed to cull and then to provide me and my family with meat from their flock, and with cheese. From what they have said, I would expect more bands like theirs to move in from the East as time goes by, for if their accounts are accurate, many clans have been displaced by the cold and will be seeking lands more to their liking.

We have been having thunderstorms quite frequently, and I fear we may have a summer of them. Many of the merchants have complained that the roads are as muddy now as they are in spring, and that has slowed our already slow trade some more, making it likely that this will be another year of poor business. I have been told that three forest fires have been caused by the lightning, and that the devastation the fires have wrought will make foresters as unhappy as farmers by the time the year winds down. I, myself, have seen huge expanses of burned trees and blackened scrub, and I know that the rains will wash away much of the damaged land before spring comes. I can understand why the Christians are claiming that the world is nearing its end, and that soon all of earth will be gone, but I do not agree with their views. It seems to me that if the world were

going to end, it would have done so two years ago, at the start of the
cold sun, not now, when we see the first signs of improvement. In all
my years as a merchant, I have not encountered such neatness, and
in such times as we have now, I see less neatness, not more. But al-
though they may be right, I will plan for the future and do what I
can to ensure it will be less harrowing than these past years have
been.

Extend my greetings to your brother and father, and tell any you
think would want to participate in it of my proposal in regard to the
grains and planting. The more who will join our venture, the greater
our chance of success.

Hormuzd Bashri
(his mark)

By the hand of Josepheus the scribe from Ecbatana

8

With a gesture to protect herself from evil forces, the old peasant
woman stepped back from the two men standing in the narrow door
of her one-room house. "The crest? You should not go near the crest.
No one should go there!" she exclaimed. Night had just fallen and
the forest felt as if it were coming across the meadows and fields to
besiege her.

"But why not?" asked the dark-haired man, who spoke her language well, but in an old-fashioned way. "The innkeeper down the
mountain said that you would explain it to us if we asked you, that you
know the story."

"Old Noccu! Well, did he, now?" The old woman grinned, revealing few teeth; she was thin, wiry, and spry; the language she spoke
was not descended from the one Ragoczy Franciscus had learned as a
child, but was that of much later settlers in the region. "Did he send
you here?"

"He told us that you knew the secrets of the crest and the

stories of its past," said the second man. His command of the language was less elegant than his companion's, but it was enough to impress the old woman, who was becoming nervous in such august company.

"It is haunted," she said with such total seriousness that neither Ragoczy Franciscus nor Rojeh could laugh at her. "Everyone knows it."

"Why do you say so?" Ragoczy Franciscus asked her. "We have come a long way, and we intended to journey to the crest of this part of the mountains." They had begun the long climb two nights before and had made steady progress up the neglected roads that led to the high passes and the Transylvanian plateau beyond.

"Because it is true," she declared.

"How can you know?" Rojeh lowered his head to show he meant no disrespect.

"It is an old story," the woman said, and waited to be coaxed. "Noccu was right about that. He does not care about such things."

"Will you tell us? For the safety of our journey?" Rojeh reverenced her as if she were a great lady in the court of the Emperor at Constantinople.

"You must not think me foolish," she said, holding up her gnarled hand as if to demand an oath from them. "I will not be laughed at or thought a fool, jesting for your amusement."

"No, we will not think that," said Ragoczy Franciscus.

"I do not tell stories to be held in contempt," she persisted.

"We offer none," said Ragoczy Franciscus. "We seek only to know what you can tell us."

She gave this her consideration, then ducked her head. "If you want to come in, you may. It is warmer by my fire." She stepped back, as if suddenly aware of the grandeur of her two visitors. "I have just the one chair."

"And it is yours by right," said Ragoczy Franciscus. "We can sit on the floor."

"It is just packed earth with rushes on it," she said apologetically.

"Never mind," Ragoczy Franciscus said, sinking down and sitting cross-legged at an angle to the hearth and her chair.

She started to laugh, but stopped as quickly. "I meant nothing against you."

"Nor did I think otherwise," said Ragoczy Franciscus.

Rojeh also sat on the floor, his abolla gathered closely around him. "This is a cozy house," he said, thinking that the smell of smoke, old cooking, and old woman made it so close that he felt the air itself was a presence in the single room. Yet it had a completeness that made it a pleasant place.

"I had the story from my grandmother, who lived to be forty-eight summers old; I love to tell it in her honor." The old woman nodded three times to confirm this figure. "I, myself, have seen forty-seven summers," she added with pride.

"A considerable age," said Ragoczy Franciscus, knowing that among the living, it was.

"I have passed this to my granddaughters, and they, one day, will tell it to their grandchildren." She managed a deeply wrinkled smile. "It is to our credit that our family is long-lived."

"That it is," said Rojeh.

As if satisfied that she had given her credentials, she sat down in her chair and gazed into the flames of the fire, a distant expression in her small, dark eyes. "It is a story that goes back to the ancient times, when the world was a different place than it is now. There is a great citadel up there at the crest, from long, long ago. It was built before the walls of Byzantium were put in place, even before the great heroes of the Athenians and the Spartans were roaming the world. The lord of the citadel was a powerful warrior who had allies among the angels and devils and old gods of the land, and they all stood against those who would attack the lord and all he held as his." She looked from Rojeh to Ragoczy Franciscus. "This lord was one of a great line, and he had sons to follow him, twenty fine sons and twenty lovely daughters, each more worthy than the last." Pausing, she took a sip from her wooden cup. "This is plum wine, if you would like any?"

"No, but thank you," said Ragoczy Franciscus. "I do not drink wine."

"Nor do I," said Rojeh.

"I will drink more, then," she said, satisfied, and reached for a stoneware bottle to refill the cup; she managed a tense little chuckle as she poured for herself. "As I was saying, there was this great lord, from a great line, with fine sons to follow him, and a band of loyal warriors to fight with him. All the land held in the long curve of the mountains was his to command, and all the plains behind the mountains bowed to him as well. He built his citadel on the highest crag over a river gorge so that no enemy would dare approach it—remote as any eagle's nest—and guarded by a splendid line of fifty fortresses leading from far below us to the crest. These fortresses were as grand as any palace in Constantine's City, and they were so large that they held a thousand warriors and two thousand horses."

"Was it difficult to build, the citadel?" Rojeh asked. "In such a remote place, it must have been."

"It took many years and the efforts of powerful old gods to build it, and the toil of ten thousand men, all of whom labored for the glory of it," she said with relish. "The citadel was as large as a great camp of famous generals, and it boasted buildings three stories high."

"A formidable place," said Ragoczy Franciscus with an ironic half-smile.

"A very great place. Warriors flocked there in their thousands, and the thunder of their horses' hooves made the mountains echo." She slapped one hand on her knee. "The enemy might have thought there were storms on the peaks, or congregations of demons."

"Wise, to guard himself so well," said Ragoczy Franciscus with a fleeting recollection of his father's face. "He must have been a very provident man."

"So you would think," said the old woman.

"Then the lord had protected his citadel as well as any man might," said Rojeh.

"You could hope it, but it turned out not to be as wise a plan as one would think, for an enormous army from the East heard of this citadel and came at the behest of the lords and the King of the lands in the southeast and across the water to claim it, and all it contained, for themselves. They came in waves, these warriors, and they drove the lord of the citadel back from his fortresses." She had another drink, this time a large gulp. "One by one the fortresses fell until all the warriors and their lord retreated to the citadel, where it is said all of his soldiers, and their wives and children, pledged to fight to their last breath and asked their gods and devils and angels to stand with them. The old gods rode with his horsemen and his sons against the marauders from the southeast." She took another sip, a longer one this time. "It is said that the old gods of the lord and the land were killed—but how can anyone kill a god?—and the oldest son of the lord, who had led the fight, was captured by the enemy to be given to the King of the southeast, who had commanded the war, as tribute." More plum wine went down her throat and she smiled muzzily. "It is a very sad story."

"Why is it sad, if the warriors and their lord heroically defended the citadel?" Rojeh asked.

"Because all their efforts failed," she said.

"By might or by treachery?" Ragoczy Franciscus asked.

"It is said that the lord was betrayed by his adviser, who told the opposing leaders many things about the fortress and the citadel, and the enemy was able to attack the citadel," she said.

"Treachery," Ragoczy Franciscus mused.

The old woman nodded. "Then the gods and angels and devils deserted the lord and the citadel was besieged and finally it fell. The lord and most of his sons were executed, but some were made slaves of the conquerors, and the oldest was sent far away, to show that the lord of the citadel was wholly vanquished, and to demonstrate to all the world that the citadel on the mountain peaks had fallen. Among the defenders, those who were not captured and enslaved were burned when the citadel was put to the torch. Anyone venturing near the crest may hear their cries today, and they may be led astray by the spirits of the dead, for the ghosts yearn for vengeance. If you go there, you may find yourself surrounded by specters and driven mad by their screams." She drank down the rest of the plum wine. "I don't have much left. There were almost no plums these last years. This year there have been only a few."

"You deserve a cask of plum wine, good woman," said Ragoczy Franciscus. "That was a most instructive story."

"Then you will not go to the crag," she said apprehensively. "You must tell me you will not go to the crag." In her agitation she almost overturned her jar of wine; she caught it in the nick of time and set it upright. "Tell me you will not go."

"We will keep to safe roads," said Ragoczy Franciscus.

"We will be careful if we have to cross the crest," said Rojeh, trying to soothe her.

"Good, good," she said. "Yes. Good."

Rojeh reached for her jar of wine and refilled her cup. "Drink to our safe journey, good woman, and I am sure we will have nothing to fear."

She gave him a startled stare. "Is that what you want?" Ducking her head, the old woman wrapped her hands around the cup and held it up as if to receive the divine chrism, saying, "Go safely, come safely, and never have cause to fear." Then she drank down half the contents of the cup quickly and totally, to insure the magic was not wasted.

"A most gracious wish," said Ragoczy Franciscus as he rose from the floor. "You have told us much of worth, and I am grateful to you." He knew that leaving her money would insult her, so he took a small jade ornament he had removed from their clothes case and laid it on the ground next to her chair. "To remember us by."

Her eyes glittered. "Noccu did right in sending you to me," she said, slurring the last of her words. "I do not often have visitors but my grandchildren, so I am honored to have such fine guests, if only for a short while. You may be sure I will remember you until I am long in my grave."

"Thank you." Ragoczy Franciscus reverenced her once more, this time with a flourish.

Rojeh also stood up. "You have been good to receive us."

She was trying to rise from her chair, without much success. "I have never had two such grand gentlemen as you come into my house before."

Ragoczy Franciscus extended his hand to her. "Let me help you."

She took his hand and struggled to her feet. "Too much plum wine," she muttered.

"Drunk in a good cause," said Rojeh, helping to steady her.

"The summer is ending," she said, and put a hand to her eyes. "Soon the winter will return, and the cold will be everywhere again. Terrible cold."

"Winter comes every year," said Ragoczy Franciscus. "As does summer."

"But not as winter has come the last two years," she said in a tone that would countenance no dispute. "The last two years have been different. Longer. Harsher." She rubbed her forehead as if trying to stimulate thought. "Wolves have come down from the high mountains and taken hens from their roosts and lambs from the fold. Fields have lain barren from ice. The dead lie unburied."

"Certainly the years have been colder," said Ragoczy Franciscus, starting to make his way to the door.

"And the sun darker," she persisted.

"Yes, that as well," said Ragoczy Franciscus as he and Rojeh reached the door. "We will speak well of you to others." He started toward his horse, relieved to hear Rojeh behind him.

They mounted up as the old woman watched them from the door of her house; Rojeh had the mule's lead and he fell in behind Ragoczy Franciscus as he resumed their long journey up the mountain trails to the rocky crest. The small house was soon lost in the dark and the trees behind them, and they made their way by starlight at first, and moonlight later. When they stopped at the base of a waterfall to permit the horses and mule to drink, Rojeh finally asked, "That story of hers: how much of it was yours?"

"Too much: the people here have not forgotten. But it is not accurate, either. There were no twenty sons and twenty daughters, nor thousands of warriors; our best fortress was never grand, and there were no more than three fortresses below the citadel, not a line of fifty of them. The battles would have turned out differently if there had been even a third of that number of men, or fortresses. My father's lands were extensive, but he did not rule all of the Carpathians and the Dacian plain," he answered. "My father did build the citadel—that much was true—and it was burned with most of the defenders in it. I had already been taken in battle and was the prisoner of the troops sent to attack us. It is most unlucky that so much of the story remains intact." He stared off into the night. "My father was betrayed, but not as she said: one of his brothers-in-law was promised the leadership of the Erastna—"

"Your people," said Rojeh.

"Yes. And the foes were the Cimmerians," he said slowly, the recollections gathering in him and holding his full attention. "They were the ones who killed me, the Cimmerians, since I would not oblige them and die in battle. Over time, they killed all of us Ragosh-ski, including

my uncle who helped them." Birds were beginning their morning car-
ols, and Ragoczy Franciscus stopped to listen to them. "How good to
hear so many songs again. I had feared the birds were gone."

"How many escaped the flames?" As soon as he said it, Rojeh
wished he had not spoken.

"I do not know. I had been taken away from these mountains by
the time the Erastna left. But I know all the men of the family were
executed one way or another, and most of the women. And all of our
gods." He fell silent again. "As many as could fled westward, away
from the enemy."

"The gods were the ones who made you what you are," said Rojeh; he wanted to encourage Ragoczy Franciscus to talk, since he so
rarely said much about his early years. "Your gods were vampires.
Does anyone remember that?"

"If they do, they keep their memories in whispers."

"Would she know the stories told of you if there are only whispers?"

"I would think she would: she would probably know that I was
born at the dark of the year, and that one of them—the gods of my
people—met me in the sacred grove at the main fortress, many
leagues from here, at the Winter Solstice on the night I turned fourteen, and I drank his blood from his palms, which meant I would become like them when I died. If she knows about the citadel, she
surely knows of this, as well." He lapsed into a brief reverie. "I could
not see which one it was, but I always hoped it was God Menisho."
His expression changed, shifting his attention. "I have not spoken his
name for centuries."

"But you have not forgot him," Rojeh said carefully. "Or any of
your forgotten gods." He waited a moment. "Does it bother you to return here?"

"No," he said, his dark eyes enigmatic as he looked past the
mountains into the past. "It did the first time, for it was all still too
fresh, too raw, and I was too engrossed in exacting full suffering from
the descendants of those who conquered this place." He sighed. "I
made the memory of my family abhorrent, and deservedly so."

When he did not continue, Rojeh said, "It was long ago and you
are not that man now."

"Ah, but I still have the capacity, and I forget that at my peril." Ragoczy Franciscus glanced up at the sky, marking the positions of the stars. "Dawn is coming, and we should move on."

"Does it pain you to hear the stories about your kind?" Rojeh could not help asking; Ragoczy Franciscus rarely said so much about himself and Rojeh was curious.

Ragoczy Franciscus considered the question. "It did at one time, far less now. This is my native earth, and it has a strength for me that nothing can change, no matter what the legends say."

Rojeh looked down at the ground. "This place where we stand: is this your native earth?"

"No, not yet," Ragoczy Franciscus said. "But I can sense its nearness; if we keep going, by morning we will not have to stop for the day and seek shelter from sunlight." He patted his mare on the neck and prepared to remount. "It is not much farther now."

They continued up the mountain as the sky in the east began to lighten, finally showing the rubicund promise of dawn, which had been their signal to stop, but now Ragoczy Franciscus kept on, his posture in the saddle straight, showing no trace of fatigue. As they topped the ridge of the mountain's flank, Rojeh called out, "It is getting light. Should we find shelter?"

"No," said Ragoczy Franciscus. "We will soon be where we are going."

"We have not come this way before," said Rojeh as they continued along the crest.

"No, nor to this place. This is the hardest to reach of all the fortresses. When we have come to this land in times past, we have arrived from the west, not the east, and gone to the main fortress, in the center of my father's lands, not here at the edge. But this is where it ended, and it is fitting that we are here."

"If you mean to let this be your ending." As kindly as Rojeh spoke, he was challenging Ragoczy Franciscus. "You must do it alone."

For a long moment, Ragoczy Franciscus said nothing. Then he looked up the face of the crags. "If the land still knows me, I will do whatever it requires."

"I will not help you to die the True Death," Rojeh warned.

"I did not think you would, old friend." Ragoczy Franciscus tapped his blue roan with his heel, moving her to the side of a narrow pathway. "The ground is not steady here; keep to the verge."

"I will." Rojeh wanted to know how Ragoczy Franciscus could be so certain about the road, but he held his question for the time being. "How far is the citadel?"

"Less than half a league. You should be able to see it, at the point of that crag." He held out his arm to show Rojeh where to look, but nothing had the appearance of a fortress; there was only the forbidding face of rock. "So much to remember."

"I still cannot see it; it must be the angle of the light," Rojeh said, feeling he had to justify his lack of recognition.

"No doubt," said Ragoczy Franciscus. "The citadel is a ruin. It has been a ruin for more than nine hundred years." He shaded his eyes in the slanting sunlight. "I know where to look, and what was there."

"Then I must follow you and trust you will lead us aright, as you always have," Rojeh said lightly, giving the mule's lead a decisive wrench to keep him moving.

Ragoczy Franciscus' crack of laughter was colored with chagrin. "You know that is not so, as well as I do. I apologize for all the times I have taken you into danger; this should not be such a time," he said as he rode on into the morning toward the ruin of the citadel. A short while later he pulled in his horse at the edge of a low, crumbling wall of rough-hewn stones. Growing trees had forced their roots through the ancient stones, leaving cracks and reclaiming the wall as a part of the mountain. Ragoczy Franciscus dismounted and stood still, looking at the space the line of rocks enclosed, and he said to Rojeh, who had ridden up behind him, "Welcome to my father's citadel." He laid his hand on the nearest section of broken wall. "When I was a living man, this was three times my height and had an archers' walkway." He started along the perimeter of the wall. "The gate is just ahead. We should go in there."

"Because it is the gate?" Rojeh was puzzled.

"Because it is easier on the horses and the mule," Ragoczy Franciscus answered, moving more vigorously as he turned past what might have been the base of a tower long ago.

Rojeh got off his horse and took the leads for the stallion and the mule in hand. "I'm surprised he hasn't balked," he admitted, meaning the stallion, for the mule had balked often.

"He trusts you; you have given him good care and you do not fight with him," said Ragoczy Franciscus. "But he could still decide not to do as you tell him."

"I am aware of that," said Rojeh, and said what was troubling him. "If anything should happen to the horses, how would we manage to bring your native earth down from here, if no one will come to this place?"

"We may not leave for a while; we will work something out if we must," said Ragoczy Franciscus, pointing ahead. "There. You see: the gate." A wide break in the wall framed by two broad bases. He stepped through the opening, saying, "You are welcome to my father's citadel."

Following him into the wide, ill-defined interior of the walls' outline, Rojeh said, "I am gladdened to be here."

"And I, and I," said Ragoczy Franciscus, touching his throat. "It has a power for me, though it is nothing." He opened the collar of his kandys: where there had been a mulberry-colored weal marking the path of Dukkai's knife there was now a pale line that was almost visibly fading away.

Rojeh had seen Ragoczy Franciscus' remarkable restorative powers, but this astonished him. "So quickly."

"The cut was ready to heal," said Ragoczy Franciscus, turning slowly in a circle. "I know you cannot tell very much from what is left, but there, in that part of the courtyard, was the stable. It held up to eighty horses, as I recall. There were some paddocks set up outside the stable." He swung around toward the northwest. "Over there they had the soldiers' quarters—they were crowded little cells, but the men expected nothing better, and complained no more than most soldiers do." He stared at a long mound with the suggestion of a roof-line at the far end. "That must have been the soldiers' dining room." His next turn left him facing north and the gate. "There were two guard-towers, both three storeys tall. The marshaling yard was where we are standing. And that jumble behind me was my father's keep." He faced the south. "Family quarters were there, on the second floor. The main hall was where those two trees are growing. The kitchen was immediately behind the main hall, and the spring that fed all the citadel, and there was a garden behind the keep, and pens for animals."

"Much like many others," said Rojeh.

"Truly." He lowered his head. "In another three or four hundred years, it will be gone. The rocks will be only rocks, and the trees will claim the courtyard, the marshaling yard and the garden as their own. In better years, when there is more grass, we would not see so much."

Rojeh took stock of the citadel. "We have certainly stayed in worse places."

"But you are right—winter is coming," said Ragoczy Francsicus.

"And it will be a harsh one," Rojeh added. "Perhaps not as bad as last year, but bad enough."

"If this seems too remote, then perhaps we can go to the main fortress. We could reach it in a day, assuming the roads are passable."

"This is a very isolated place." Rojeh gave a sweep of his hand. "Once the snows come, how could we find nourishment here, for any of us?"

There was a long, twisting quiet, then Ragoczy Franciscus laughed. "You are right, of course: these walls are useless, and this crag is too removed from everything to provide anything more than a source of my native earth, which all of my father's lands can provide." He strode toward the crumbled keep, saying as he went, "This place has power for me, but nothing else—after twenty-five centuries, why should it have?"

"Then we will move on?"

"I suppose it would be best," he said thoughtfully. "Tomorrow, then, yes; we can go to the central fortress. There is a settlement near it, or there was ninety years ago. We should be able to pass the winter there. It is not as high, and it is, or was, a crossroad." Ragoczy Franciscus swung around and took in the whole of the citadel. "It did what it was intended to do long ago. It is time for it to be over at last, so the living may forget." His vigor was more apparent now, and he moved with the graceful ease that Rojeh had not seen in more than a year. "As I recall, there was a goatherd's cottage back against the rear wall. Some of that building might still be intact enough to provide us a place for the night."

Rojeh watched him stride along the stone heap that marked the keep. "In a settlement, there would be opportunities for more nourishment than your native earth provides."

"No." Ragoczy Franciscus stopped. "No, that would not be wise. The people in those settlements have heard tales of those of my blood, and they fear us, and hate us." He faltered, then went on. "It is not only because of the tales that keep such beliefs alive, it is because of the vengeance I took, so long ago. They told stories of it, and repeated them, adding to the horror as they did, and so now, most of the people of Dacia, Transylvania, whichever you wish to call it, are terrified of all vampires—not without reason."

"You mean there are more of your blood here?" Rojeh asked, truly surprised by the prospect.

"Not any longer," said Ragoczy Franciscus and did not elaborate. He resumed walking toward the rear wall, not as energetically as he had at first.

Rojeh followed after him. "What do you mean?"

"It was many centuries ago," said Ragoczy Franciscus, his dark eyes turning flinty.

"Why should something from so far in the past bring trouble now?" Rojeh persisted, knowing his questions distressed Ragoczy Franciscus. "Does being here remind you of—?"

"It was not a worthy undertaking." His frown deepened.

"Because it was against your own kind?"

Ragoczy Franciscus stared into the distance. "They and I . . . There was a campaign, I suppose you would call it; slaughter would be a more accurate word." He stepped into what had been the kitchen garden; it had long since become a riot of weeds and thickets. "It seemed necessary at the time, but I would not want to have to take such action again."

"Because of the Blood Bond," said Rojeh, moving in the same direction Ragoczy Franciscus was walking, drawing the horses and the mules after him.

"Of course," said Ragoczy Franciscus, stopping once again to peer around an outcropping of rock. He stood for a while, seeing the fallen cottage and noticing the three old wild apple trees that grew through the wreckage of the cottage; the trees held his concentration for a short while, their ordinariness in this place of hoary bloodshed engrossing him. His expression changed slowly and he spoke to Rojeh in a more tranquil tone. "You are right. This is a place of the past. It and I are no longer coalesced as we once were. You and I should go on." As Rojeh blinked at this unexpected change Ragoczy Franciscus came back toward him. "We will let the horses and the mules graze a bit—there is grass enough to provide them a good meal—and give them water from the well; then we will start toward Castru Rastna." It was the name given to the settlement near the remains of Ragoczy Franciscus' father's central fortress.

"I remember that place," said Rojeh, "But why did you change your mind?"

"Because the land has decided," said Ragoczy Franciscus with a fleeting smile. "There is new growth on the oldest apple trees."

Text of a letter from Tsa Tsa-Si in Yang-Chau to Hu Bi-Da at Eclipse Trading Company in the same city, with copies provided for the Magistrate and the Prefecture.

On this, the second day of the Fortnight of the White Dew, I take pen in hand to inform you of the disposition of the property held by Zangi-Ragozh in this city, specifically, in regard to his compound, now that his steward Jho Chieh-Jen has died. As foreigners go, Zangi-Ragozh conducted his affairs in an exemplary manner, and that makes this duty all the more compelling, for I am not constrained by any barbaric customs he might have imposed, or a disregard for our ways and our laws.

As you must know, Jho died of Wet Lungs two fortnights ago, leaving the household in disarray, and the responsibility for the compound in my hands for as long as the Magistrate accepts my serving in that capacity. In response to the orders of the Magistrate, I have ordered the preparation of a complete inventory of household goods, all moveables, such items as may belong to the individuals of the household, and all other items which are recognized as possessing some level of value. Once the inventory is registered, the various bequests and grants may be performed, in preparation for the closing of the compound itself.

All the household workers are to receive one silver bar for each year of service, and those who have occupied senior positions are to receive one additional bar each for the higher demands of their offices. These sums are to be drawn from the money left on deposit with the Prefecture, for which duty the Prefecture is to receive five bars of silver. For any widows or orphans of former household workers, the sum of two silver bars is authorized. Proof of the payment of these sums is to be recorded by the Magistrate.

In terms of furniture, Zangi-Ragozh has left specific donations of major items to the persons whose names are appended to this letter, with my chop upon it. Five of the individuals named by Zangi-Ragozh as recipients of furniture have died, and so the names of their heirs have been substituted for the names of the originally intended recipients. The furniture not specifically granted in Zangi-Ragozh's instructions is to be offered first to household workers for a reasonable price, and, if a piece is unclaimed, it may be sold in the market and the proceeds given half to the Magistrate and half to the Eclipse Trading Company.

All common household items from cooking-pots to bedding to garden-tools are to be given to the workers who used them, and to be theirs without condition or qualification whether or not Zangi-Ragozh returns to the compound. This provision is binding on any heir of Zangi-Ragozh who may arrive in this city to claim the property of his senior relative, for Zangi-Ragozh has also stipulated that aside from these bequests, he would leave his property and business only to a blood relative, and that such a relative would produce such items of identification as are described in his official Will at the Prefecture.

The gardens within the compound are offered to the physicians and herbalists of Yang-Chau, any one of whom may request a time to select such plants as would suit him for the next three fortnights. After that time, the garden is left to the gardeners, to help them in their work and to ensure that they will have the fruits of their trade.

In light of the hard years we have endured, I recommend that the compound be turned over to the Magistrate for whatever civic use he may designate until Zangi-Ragozh or his heir should come to Yang-Chau. There are a number of good uses to which the compound could be put that do not in any way conflict with the instructions Zangi-

Ragozh left. I am aware that his business-dealings were as meticulous as his private ones, and therefore I ask that you agree to meet with me for the purpose of coordinating our duties and activities. It would honor a most Worthy Foreigner, and would enable many to show their appreciation for his generosity and estimable acumen.

Tsa Tsa-Si
(his chop)

Epilogue

Text of a letter from Atta Olivia Clemens at Roma to Ragoczy Sanct' Germain Franciscus at Naissus, carried by Brother Irenaeus and delivered nine weeks after it was written.

To my oldest, dearest, most aggravating friend, Ragoczy Sanct' Germain Franciscus, the heartfelt greetings of Atta Olivia Clemens on this, the Feast of the Epiphany, in the 1291st Year of the City, and the Pope's 538th Year, from my Roman estate, which, I am sorry to say, is much in need of restoration and repair, and not simply because of the hard years we have had to endure of late, but due to the various barbarians who have come to Roma for the purpose of raiding and plundering.

Just at present, we have few attackers, for the bad weather that has been so ruinous to many of those living in and around the city has also kept most of those who would pillage Roma and the country around it at a distance. That is one of the reasons I view the slight improvement in the weather with mixed emotions, for now it is likely that Justinian will renew his assault on all of Italia, with the purpose of bending us to the Byzantine yoke. Even with so well-reputed a General as Belisarius in charge, I cannot believe that the soldiers under him will conduct themselves as penitent pilgrims, showing humility and deference to all who live here. I am going to be at pains to repair as much of my walls and buildings as I can before the Byzantines arrive—as they surely will do—so that I will not have to surrender any more than necessary when Witiges makes another attempt at conquest; his siege took a heavy toll on the surrounding countryside, and I intend to be prepared for more ructions, for assuming Belisarius is determined to keep his hold on the city, the clash of Ostrogoth and Byzantine will not be good for Roma. Because of that, and because you entrusted the place to me, I am also giving orders to have Villa Ragoczy repaired and fortified, as I suppose you would want; Niklos Aulirios is in charge of the project, and he has found reliable workers to do the reconstruction. Your estate has not fared as well as you

*would want, and I am determined to reestablish it in a manner you
would find satisfactory.*

*You cannot imagine how relieved I was to receive your letter of
the Ides of September. I had not thought you were so near, for I have
been dispatching my letters to Yang-Chau, which you tell me is three
thousand leagues from here, a distance that, if accurate, staggers my
mind. To think you have been returning to the West for so long, and
that you are closer than I dared to hope. Back in my breathing days,
messages moved much more rapidly, but the world has changed, and
the times impose upon us all. I will inform Brother Irenaeus, who carries this, to put it into your hands, if he has to pursue you from that
town to whatever place you have gone.*

*At least you have warned me that you intend to move frequently
for a time. Is this a habit you acquired, coming back from China, or is
it an example of your self-proclaimed inclination not to become too
caught up in a place, as a means of escaping scrutiny? Have you come
to enjoy the rigors of travel, or do you wish to present yourself as a
foreigner in all places and at all times? I hope you will explain this to
me, for I admit I am baffled by what would seem a reversal of your
previous views. I would also like you to take the time to inform me
when you plan to move, and whither you are bound. I do not want to
have to spend two decades sending letters into the void in the hope
that eventually one may reach you. Yes, the Blood Bond has made me
aware that you had not died the True Death, but that is hardly sufficient information to satisfy me.*

*As you are staying in the Eastern Empire, I hope you will inform
me if you hear rumors in regard to Pope Vigilius, who has shown
himself to be most accommodating to Justinian, making arrangements to attempt to find ways to reunite the Eastern and Western
Rites even before Pope Silverinus had officially resigned his office.
This Vigilius is willing to remain in Constantinople, debating with the
Patriarchs and Metropolitans on the state of the liturgy rather than
remain in Roma and actually have to defend the faith he claims to
lead. I have little use for the Church in general, but I must say, some
of the Popes have been estimable men who had the courage of their
positions, which cannot be said of Vigilius. He has actually accepted
the title of Elect instead of Holiness, which has caused the Bishops
and Archbishops consternation, and typically, they are upset about*

the form of the thing instead of the substance. We do not often receive timely news on these matters, and that adds to the difficulties these dealings create, which is why I ask you to inform me of any and all developments you may learn of, and that may be significant to us in Roma.

In your letter, you warned me that many eastern clans are on the move, driven by the same catastrophic weather as that which has plagued the Empire. Do you think that these clans will prove to be as dangerous as the Goths and the Huns? If they are of such ferocious character, tell me what you would recommend in regard to facing them, if we must, in battle. The skill and sprit of the Legions has been gone for three centuries, and the discipline was lost before then. I welcome your observations on the danger we may face, and your advice on what might prove to be wise strategies, although I cannot promise to follow your recommendations.

In the midst of all these disruptive events, there has been an odd development in Roma, in the old Forum, where a fellow professing to be a world traveler has set up a display of wonders he has found during his journeys, most of which seem to be nothing more than the efforts of inventive children, not actual marvels that are only encountered in distant lands. He is charging handsomely for a look at his collection, and for the most part I counted it a waste of money, but for one item he had on display, which I cannot explain beyond it being what he says it is—an enormous bone made of stone. I looked at it carefully and it did not have the characteristics of carved stone, and the color of it made me think that it must be authentic. But you cannot imagine the size of it—it is probably an upper leg-bone, and if that is what it is, the creature from which it came had to be much larger than an elephant, and I find such a creature would be more incredible than the idea that the red-feathered bird he has is actually a phoenix and in a century will burst into flames. If you have any knowledge of such animals as might possess such gigantic thigh-bones, I ask you to tell me of it, and where it is to be found.

Looking over this, I see I have given you much to do on my behalf, and I would apologize, but whomelse am I going to trust as I trust you? I hope you will accept my requests in the manner in which I intended them, as the proof of my half a millennium of devotion to you, and as a demonstration of the high value in which I hold your opinions. You saved me when everyone else deserted me, and you have never failed me in the centuries since, so it must be that my reliance upon you is the result of the love we have shared, and the blood that binds us still and will until the True Death.

Olivia

By my own hand at Roma